Born in Lancashire and educated in Yorkshire, Alexandra Connor has had a rich variety of careers, including photographic model, cinema manager and PA to a world famous heart surgeon, but it is as a novelist that she has found her real forte. As well as writing over twenty bestselling sagas she has also written thrillers and non-fiction art books. When she isn't busy writing, Alexandra is a highly accomplished painter and presents programmes on television and BBC radio. She is also a Fellow of the Royal Society of Arts.

The
Tailor's Wife

ALEXANDRA CONNOR

headline

First published in 2005
by HEADLINE BOOK PUBLISHING

First published in paperback in 2006
by HEADLINE BOOK PUBLISHING

1

ISBN 978 1 4722 1942 8

Typeset in Sabon by Avon DataSet Ltd,
Bidford-on-Avon, Warwickshire

Printed and bound in the UK by
CPI Group (UK) Ltd, Croydon, CR0 4YY

Headline's policy is to use papers that are natural, renewable and
recyclable products and made from wood grown in sustainable
forests. The logging and manufacturing processes are expected to
conform to the environmental regulations of the country of origin.

HEADLINE BOOK PUBLISHING
A division of Hodder Headline
338 Euston Road
London NW1 3BH

www.headline.co.uk
www.hodderheadline.com

Acknowledgements must go to Susan Lee, Visitor Services Officer, Salford Tourist Information Centre, who was very patient and helpful – even when I kept changing my mind!

Teach me to feel another's woe
To mind that hurt I see.
That mercy I to others show
That mercy show to me.

Alexander Pope

PROLOGUE

I'll tell you about the tailor's wife. How I remember her.

It was dark: a late summer night on a grim Salford street. We all stood there, in silence, waiting for her. At any moment she would walk around the corner into Hankerton Street. She would not have heard us, because we were silent; she would not expect us, because for all she knew the news hadn't got out yet. She would just walk around the corner and see us.

Waiting for her.

It was drizzling, hardly noticeable, apart from the fact that it made the street look greasy under the lamplight. A man next to me coughed, then spat into his handkerchief, a child solemn in another man's arms.

Finally we heard what we had all been waiting for: her footsteps. People exchanged glances. Alerted, venal looks traded between neighbours. It was so easy to hate. The steps came closer, growing in volume, Hankerton Street echoing with the sound of one woman's feet.

Then she saw us. Her face flickered with fear for only one instant – and then, incredibly, she walked towards us.

That was the tailor's wife.

PART ONE

Please let my parting move you
And my ending grieve;
But only sometimes: only sometimes,
And let the pain be brief, and in the dark.

Anon

ONE

1910

Mention Hanky Park to anyone and they would cringe. The worst slums in Salford, named by some joker with a nice line in irony. There were no trees in Hanky Park. Only terraces, sordid pubs and industrial businesses: abattoirs, glueworks or the myriad other sweatshops which lined the narrow, airless streets.

In summer you could smell Hanky Park before you saw it. A line of mean shops plied a poor trade, whilst behind them houses crouched, steaming, under the sun. It wasn't the district for summer. Let the rich enjoy the heat up on Eccles Old Road, but not Hanky Park. Not when the flies walked all over the meat offcuts in the butcher's window, and the back toilets flooded every July.

There were no young women. They might have entered Hanky Park young and hopeful, but within a few years, work and childbearing meant their looks had coarsened. Washing filthy work clothes in cold water, giving birth with the local nag in attendance – because no one could afford the shilling for the doctor – aged a woman fast. If she had a man – and many didn't – she often ended up supporting him. Sometimes even going on the game to put food on the table.

And the most terrifying thing about the place wasn't the poverty, the cramped, dirty conditions or the danger. Or even the frequent outbreaks of sickness. It was just one, irrefutable fact. If you were born in Hanky Park, you didn't get out.

Jacob Clark knew that only too well. He was the only child of Sara and Elijah Clark, his father a local carter. Not that anyone needed to be told that fact: one look at Elijah was enough to mark out his trade. Years of humping coal had left his hands blackened, the back of his neck pitted, coal dust in his very pores. Out in all weathers, Elijah wore a leather-shouldered coat, but if it rained he got wet. And stayed wet. In summer, the clothes dried on him. In winter, they never got the chance. They would dry partially – from the heat his exertions were throwing off – but never completely. And then it would rain again, water dripping off the rim of his cap, the sacks hard to lift, slimy to the touch. Gradually, over the years, Elijah got used to feeling his skin chilled, his hands so numb that driving the coal horses was done by rote, not feeling. That was when a carter needed a good horse.

'If I didn't have Sam,' he'd tell Jacob at the stables on Hardy Street, 'I'd have my work cut out. Understands every word I say, that horse does. And a soft mouth, hardly have to twitch on the rein and he knows.' He reached up lovingly to pet the great shire. 'When your turn comes, lad, you make sure to get a good horse and treat it well. It'll repay you for your kindness.'

Jacob watched his father but felt that he would rather throw himself under Sam's hoofs than be a carter. His whole world had echoed to the sound of horses whinnying, and the monotonous, dead rumble of the coal carts going up and down the street, from seven in the morning until six at night. Another pungent memory was of the coal dust. Even on the hottest days in summer the doors and windows of the house were closed to keep out the filth from the siding. If you opened them – even briefly – the dust covered every surface.

Rain and coal dust. Cold and poverty. Those were the memories of Jacob's childhood, and when he was sent to school, nothing really changed. The building faced another siding, the coal dust sneaking in through the windows and marking the few grimy school books. And outside – always, day after day, week after week – the sound of the wagons chugging and shunting. No place to make learning easy.

But then people didn't expect kids from Hanky Park to do much with their lives. They were to be the future coal workers, dockers, mill hands: slum fodder to keep the great city of Manchester afloat. No one had ambition in Hanky Park. No one had *anything* much in Hanky Park. Other kids – wealthy kids up on Eccles Old Road – had presents bought for them. But the slum kids made their own. The streets were their toys, half a brick a make-believe gun, a ruined wall the hull of an ocean liner. And there were other diversions: the sight of the rent man coming for his money making them run home over the backs, in time to tip off their mothers.

'Gerry Fitt's coming, Mam!'

Sara Clark spun round, closed the back door and pulled her son behind the battered curtain of the lobby. Jacob could smell the bleach on her hands as they both peered through the hole in the door curtain.

Gerry Fitt was knocking loudly on the door. Once, twice, three times. Each time louder. Then he moved to the window and looked in. Both of them automatically held their breath.

'Mrs Clark? Are you in there, Mrs Clark?'

Silence. Jacob could hear the tap dripping and noticed a fly hovering round the slop bucket under the sink.

'Mrs Clark, I need the rent money. I'll be back tomorrow; make sure you have it then. I'll treat you fair because you've not been late before. But only this once.'

He paused, took off his bowler hat and wiped the coal soot off his forehead. Gerry Fitt had one leg and used a crutch; no money for an artificial limb. It slowed him down and people could always hear him coming, clack-clacking on the cobbles. Mothers used him as a warning to their kids: *If yer cheeky, yer leg'll drop off. Just like Gerry Fitt's . . .*

7

Suddenly Fitt pushed his face up to the window, his nose squashed to one side. Without thinking, Jacob sniggered, Sara pinching his ear to make him stop. Finally the disgruntled man moved away. For another minute they waited in the back lobby, both peering through the curtain. Often the rent man doubled back. You could get caught that way unless you were careful.

When she was sure the coast was clear, Sara moved back into the kitchen, her expression anxious, her narrow face drawn, her gnarled fingers folding and refolding the laundry on the kitchen table.

'I should have had that money for him. But with your dad being ill last week . . .' She paused, moved to the table and began to spread some bread with dripping. 'Here now, get your tea. Your father will want a bath when he gets home and he won't want you under his feet.'

She hadn't the time to be kind. Not when the squalid kitchen walls were peeling with damp, water from a burst pipe trickling through a break in the windowledge. One armchair, rescued from a skip, Sara had covered with some cotton from the Flat Iron Market, but the curtain at the narrow window was already soiled at the bottom from the water leak, and everywhere smelt of mould. Thank God they had had no other children, she thought with relief. She had taken good care not to get pregnant again. One child was enough to support. God only knew how the big families managed.

'Things will be easier when you're working, Jacob,' she said brusquely. 'When we've got two wages coming in, we'll be able to have a bit of luxury.' Her son wasn't sure what luxury was, but he was certain there wasn't much of it in Hanky Park. 'We might get you a proper bed.'

Jacob wasn't too bothered about the cast-off cot he was using, even though the end had been removed and a chair put there to accommodate his growth. He was grateful that he didn't have to share his bed – however hotchpotch – with brothers and sisters.

His closest friend, Bert Gallager, had five sisters and two brothers, and not enough clothes to go round. It was common knowledge that in the winter a couple of the children would be kept off school in bed to keep warm. The next day, they would go out and another pair would stay home.

'You finished now?'

Nodding at his mother, Jacob gulped down his watery tea and made for the door with half a piece of bread in his fist.

'Go and play,' Sara said absent-mindedly. 'Your father needs some space when he gets in. And be back before dark. You hear me?'

Jacob had just finished his bread and dripping when Bert Gallager came up to him on the corner. With a knowing look he leaned against the wall, his thin legs weedy in shorts.

'That Gerry Fitt . . .' He left the name hanging in the air. 'That Gerry Fitt . . .'

'We couldn't pay him this week,' Jacob confided, digging his hands into his pockets and leaning against the wall next to his friend. 'Old Fitt wasn't best pleased.'

Bert clicked his tongue disapprovingly.

'It's no one's fault! My dad were ill last week,' Jacob replied, jumping to his father's defence. Besides, he wanted to add, at least he's honest. Not like your father, who'd thieve the eyes out of a potato to sell to a blind man.

'Hey, yer'll not guess what I'eard?'

Jacob's curiosity was immediately aroused. The Gallagers knew all the scandal.

'What?

'Yer an only child—'

Some news. 'I know that!'

'Yeah, but did yer know that yer'll *always* be the only one?'

'How d'*you* know?'

'M'mam told me. Said yer mam told 'er that she couldn't have any more babies.'

Jacob screwed up his face. 'Why?'

'Something wrong down there,' Bert replied dramatically, pointing to his crotch. 'All closed up, like that vault at the bank.'

'You what?'

'Yer mam, she's shut up tight.'

'She never!'

Bert nodded, sagely, rapidly thinking up another lurid embellishment to the story. 'In fact, she told m'mam – and no one else knows – that she had 'erself sewed up.'

Jacob's eyes were glassy. 'Sewed up?'

'Like a dress hem,' Bert replied, adding darkly, 'Even if she had a baby in 'er, it couldn't get out.'

'If it couldn't get *out*,' Jacob asked, not unreasonably, 'how could it get *in*?'

Shrugging, Bert jumped off the wall. 'M' mam says that it's a right shame about yer mam. Her having only one kid. But then she said yer'll be having kids of yer own one day.'

This was an unwelcome thought. 'I don't want kids!'

'Sure yer do! Lots of 'em, like us.'

'I hate kids!'

'Yer'll have dozens,' Bert went on, provoking him mercilessly. 'Daddy Clark,' he snorted. '*Daddy Clark . . .*'

Which was when Jacob belted him.

TWO

At the time Jacob Clark was growing up in Hanky Park, Gloria Siddons was living half a mile away, in Rivaldi Street. A notorious area, Rivaldi Street was a stamping ground for prostitutes, drunkards and thieves. It was also full of cheap doss houses, a pub on each corner. Pubs that opened one month and closed the next. Pubs that any respectable woman would skirt.

And Gloria's mother *was* respectable. No part-time whore, just a stupid girl who had married young and been widowed a year later. An accident down at the docks, she would tell everyone, never mentioning that Derek had been almost gutted by a grappling hook. Instead she made a martyr out of him; a saint out of a brutish backward who had left her with a child to support.

No one would have raised an eyebrow if she *had* gone on the game. She was in the right area, after all. But that wasn't going to be the way for Betty Siddons. She had no family, apart from Gloria, no money, no education and no prospects. But she was blessed with optimism. Optimism which came at a halfpenny a pint. *Stout* optimism.

In her cups, Betty believed the far-fetched stories in the penny dreadful romances and saved up to go and see the singers and dancers at the music hall. Afterwards she walked through Salford imagining a prince on every corner. Her late husband had been a great lifter: taught Betty how to drink. And quickly she'd developed a hard head. Better than a hard heart, she'd have said. So, with a bottle or two of beer inside her, Betty Siddons could be insane with

11

optimism, crazy with hope; the sordid sleaze of her surroundings temporarily transformed into something bearable, even cosy.

Dreamy Betty they called her. Drunken cow, they added, whores calling out from the ginnels where they were being humped up against a wall for the price of a pint. Even drunk, couldn't she see how bloody awful the place was? How it stank? How there were drunks sicking up outside the Black Horse on a Friday night? And what about the prossies with crusted sores around their mouths? The prison lags? The petty crooks? The pub landlords who gave the 'long pull' – five gills for the price of a pint? Didn't she see the slime around the blocked drains? The rats running down the ginnels after dark? And the abortionist on the corner of Gorland Street, plying his trade for the working girls?

Christ, didn't she see it?

Not when she was drunk. And that was how Betty Siddons kept going. She was never obviously drunk, never loud, never sick in public. The booze put a skin between her and life – but it never made a fool out of her. Betty could function *and* hold down a job as a cleaner at the timber works. She was a fair mother too. *Times will get better*, she told her daughter repeatedly. *Things will change.* And so Gloria grew up with the one advantage no amount of luck or money could buy. Hope.

Looking out of her front window, Betty's attention was suddenly caught by the sound of brawling in the street outside. Wincing, she turned up the radio. Quite a luxury, one she had indirectly worked for long and hard, scrubbing for the likes of Denny Cathcart up at the timber works. He had taken a shine to her, had Denny, but not in a sexual way. More protective. He might slide his hand up all the other women's skirts, but not Betty's. She was too plain.

Plain, but not slow.

'Mr Cathcart,' she'd said that morning, 'I wonder if

12

you'd mind me asking you if you're going to get rid of that radio?'

He'd bent down, all his six foot to her five foot two. 'How's that, Betty? You want it?'

'I'd like it for Gloria,' she'd replied, flushing. 'I mean, only if you're throwing it away . . .'

'Bad reception.'

'Pardon?' Betty had replied, her head on one side.

'It's not that clear. You can get music sometimes. But then again, Betty, you could get music down at the end of your street any night, in the Brewer's Arms.'

Flushing again, she had shifted her feet. 'I don't go in there. And not with Gloria.'

Denny Cathcart was feeling magnanimous, willing to give. Carefully he looked Betty Siddons up and down. He knew only too well that she finished off the beer slops he left behind – and why the hell not? She'd little enough, living on Rivaldi Street. He thought of her child suddenly. Raising a daughter decent in that rented hellhole would be almost impossible. Especially a pretty girl like Gloria. A pretty girl who was developing fast.

'You take the radio, Betty. And you can have this too.' He passed her a pack of cigarettes, Betty staring at him blankly.

'I don't smoke.'

'You can sell them! Force yourself into the Brewer's Arms or the Black Horse and you'll get plenty of takers, believe me. Good tobacco in those, Betty, you should get more than a bit of change for them.'

He paused, unexpectedly moved by her. Denny Cathcart, touched by some plain-faced little runt? Giving away radios and fags for nothing? Jesus, he was getting soft in the head, he must be.

'No mention of this to anyone, Betty, all right? We don't want people getting ideas, do we?'

Smiling, she lifted the radio and looked up at Denny Cathcart. 'You're very kind to me. And Gloria,' she said sincerely. 'I don't know what we've done to deserve such consideration from an important man like you.'

Flattered, Denny smiled back at her. 'We're friends, you and me, Betty. Friends don't measure favours. Anyway, one day you might be able to help me.'

'Anything!' she said eagerly. 'Just ask.'

Denny tapped her paternally on the shoulder, moved by his own kindness.

And people called him a bastard. There was no justice.

THREE

Jacob didn't understand what was happening; only that everything was getting furred round the edges. He thought at first that it might be due to the fight he had had with several of his classmates. After all, his head *had* hit the wall of Hope Street a few times and for an hour afterwards his ears had been ringing. But as the weeks passed and the blurriness didn't get any better, he began to worry.

If he was honest, Jacob hadn't been seeing too clearly for a while. Playing ball was getting hopeless, he missed every catch, and when he'd been trying to catapult tin cans off the wall with Bert, he'd missed the whole row of them and caught Mrs Arnold next door on the back of the head.

She – moving impressively fast for a fat woman – had grabbed him by the collar and marched him home.

'What the hell d'you call this!' she barked as Sara opened the back door.

'Jacob?'

'Damn near took my bleeding ear off, yer little bugger did. There I were, making for the privy, and he shoots me in the head.' She felt through her thin hair. 'If there's blood—'

'Jacob, is this true?'

He stared up at his mother, the collar digging deeper into his throat as Mrs Arnold twisted it.

'It were a mistake—'

Sara winced. 'It *was* a mistake—'

'It were *that* all right!' Mrs Arnold bellowed, letting go of Jacob's collar and allowing him to fall heavily on to the stone floor. 'Yer want to mind this lad, Mrs Clark. This is how it starts. A bloody hooligan today and up Strangeways tomorrow.'

'Well, you would know all about that,' Sara replied coolly. Three of the Arnold boys either had been or were at present in jail.

Mrs Arnold was red-faced with fury. 'He hit me!'

'Not on purpose.'

'How would yer know? Mothers can never see the badness in their own brats. He took aim and fired at me—'

'I never did! I never did! I never even saw you!' Jacob said suddenly, his voice raised.

Surprised, both women looked at him, Sara's voice questioning. 'What d'you mean, Jacob, you never even saw her?'

'I can't see *anything* clear. Things are all blurred,' he explained. 'Close to, I can see fine, but things a bit away are all furry, like.'

A memory of her father came back to Sara in that instant. Hadn't he been short-sighted? Worn glasses all his life? Broken several pairs too, when he was the worse for wear. Damn it! she thought. Why did Jacob have to take after him? And glasses were so expensive. Another cost to find, and not even the rent paid.

Foolishly, Mrs Arnold chose that moment to push her luck. 'If yer lad can't see, how come he managed to hit me?'

'I don't want to be cruel, Mrs Arnold,' Sara replied caustically, 'but let's face it, he had a big enough target.'

The following Saturday, Jacob was walking along Rossall Street, rattling a stick against the iron railings. Feeling a complete ass, he kept his head down. Bloody glasses! he thought angrily. Why did he have to wear them? Ugly, round things that made him look like a right idiot. Ruined his reputation as a scrapper, they had. Who the hell could be thought of as a hard man wearing glasses? You didn't see Pa Gallager wearing glasses. And you didn't see Douglas Fairbanks playing a pirate in bloody glasses. Only the creepy, clever kids like Lionel Almond wore them. Bookworms who the teachers liked and the lads hated. Kicking a tin can viciously, Jacob stopped walking. Everyone had had a good laugh at his expense. Bert too. In fact, all the sodding Gallager bunch had been braying like jackasses when they'd seen him.

'Yer look like the bleeding rent man!' Bert had said, collapsing with mirth and pointing to Jacob's thick lenses. 'Hey, Speccy! Yer must have bloody good eyes to see out of those.'

And even though Jacob knew how expensive they were, even though he knew they had cost a *shilling*, he hated them. Because they made him look *soft*. Jesus, he thought despairingly, taking off the spectacles. The street was immediately blurred. A clammy memory came back to him. Hadn't the lad in the class above them refused to wear his glasses? And hadn't he fallen off the canal bridge? And hadn't the headmaster made a right spectacle out of him at assembly?

Grimacing, Jacob put his glasses back on.

She felt like Alice in Wonderland. Only this was no wonderland to get lost in. Pausing on the street corner, Gloria Siddons looked around her anxiously. The Hanky Park sky was becoming overcast, her beautiful white dress with its ivory ribbons standing out like a piece of lace on a midden. Don't panic, she told herself. She couldn't be *that* far away from Rivaldi Street. Perhaps if she just kept walking? Or asked someone the way?

At once, her mother's warning sounded in her head like a clock chiming. *Don't talk to strangers. Don't talk to strangers.* OK, Gloria thought, but if she didn't ask someone for help, she might never get home.

Straightening the ivory ribbon in her hair, Gloria crossed over the street, ignoring a couple of lads wolf-whistling at her. Not that she wasn't secretly delighted, of course. But she wouldn't tell her mother about it. Not even when Betty was mellow after her second evening pint. Better to let her mother think she was still her little girl, still her baby.

After all, it was no hardship to be the focus of Betty's world. Gloria liked being the only child, petted and adored by her mother. Their closeness suited them both – or had done, until lately. Now Gloria was growing up fast, developing and getting curious – if not a little apprehensive – of the world beyond the Rivaldi Street flat. So although she was patently lost, she was also a little excited. It was nice to be off the leash for once. After all, no one could stay a baby for ever, could they?

Head down, Jacob hurried on, the stick making a satisfying clanking on the railings. Then suddenly he found himself face to face with a young girl. He could see – very well, actually, with his glasses on – that she was unusually pretty. And clean, not like the usual kids in the neighbourhood. Even standing within fifty feet of the coal sidings, she was unmarked. Which, in Jacob's eyes, made her an angel.

'Hey, watch where you're going!' Gloria said imperiously.

Flushing, Jacob stood up to her. She was only a girl, after all. And a rude one, at that. 'It's not your street.'

'It's not yours either,' she replied, the ivory bow in her hair fluttering like a summer kite. 'Anyway, I want to pass.'

'Lady Muck, hey?' Jacob replied, glad to have someone to mock himself. 'Where you come from?'

'Nearby,' Gloria replied, not letting on that she was hopelessly lost and desperate to get back to Rivaldi Street.

'Where nearby?'

'Rivaldi Street.'

Jacob blew out his cheeks. He was glad that she came from the slums. No better than him, for all her washing and ribbons.

'That's a bit of a way away.'

'I know!' she snapped.

'So what you doing here?'

'Walking.'

'You'll be black from head to toe in another few minutes if you don't move,' Jacob told her, jerking his head towards a passing coal cart. 'Wind's coming up.'

Looking round her, Gloria could see a line of horses approaching, driven by the carters. Overhead the sky was darkening, the thick smog of coal smoke bringing in the rain.

'Are you lost?'

Embarrassed, Gloria turned on him. 'No, I'm not! I know *exactly* where I am.'

He laughed, infuriating her further. 'Yeah, right. Well, you look lost to me.'

'I'm not lost!'

'There's no shame in it.'

'I'm not lost!' she snapped again, as rain began to fall. 'Anyway, what would you know, you four-eyed runt?'

Rocked by the insult, Jacob flushed scarlet and then, without thinking, picked up a handful of soot from the gutter. He had had enough. Enough of people laughing at him because he had to wear the bloody idiot glasses. As Gloria walked away from him, he threw the dirt at her. His aim was good, the dirt hitting her full on, marking her dress and smearing the ribbon in her hair.

She turned round, stunned, staring at him.

And because she seemed so staggered, Jacob was mortified by what he'd done.

'God—'

'You pig!' she snapped. 'You rotten pig!' And then she began crying, her hands uselessly trying to rub off the soot.

'I didn't mean . . .' Jacob began, running up to her and staring, shamefaced, at the shambles of her outfit.

'You've spoilt it! Mum will be so angry with me . . .'

'I can fix it . . .'

'I don't want you to fix it! I don't want you to touch me!' Her face was red with fury and outrage. 'You've ruined my dress! Look at me!'

Jacob was almost pleading now. 'Oh please, let me help. Come home with me and m' mother'll sort it out. She'll sort it out good and proper.'

The rain was falling heavily on the two of them, Jacob's glasses smeared with rain, Gloria's hair ribbon wet and dangling down over her forehead. Behind them the grim terrace emptied of people, a woman scurrying indoors with a bucket, a man standing motionless in the sheltered doorway of the corner pub.

'Come on!' Jacob urged her, taking her hand and pulling her along. '*Come on!* We'll clean you up and then take you home. Your mam'll be none the wiser.'

The rain came down in sheets as Jacob almost dragged Gloria through the ginnel to the back door of his home on Ellor Street. Once there, he pushed her in first. Sara was in the middle of peeling a bag of potatoes.

'Who's this?' she asked her son, startled by the sight of a dishevelled, bedraggled girl trying hopelessly to wipe the soot stains off her dress.

'This is . . .' Jacob paused, turning to his companion. 'What's your name?'

'Gloria. Gloria Siddons,' she said, glancing over to Sara and adding vehemently, 'And I hate your son!'

FOUR

By the time Jacob was fifteen, his future was set. He would – short-sighted or not – work as a coal carter with his father. The firm needed some new blood, and it was a job, Elijah told him. Yes, but what a God-awful job, thought Jacob gloomily. But then what could he expect? Weren't all his peers going into carting, or working at the various mills or other, less salubrious places? Jacob thought of Bert. His friend had left school early and was now ensconced at the slaughterhouses off Unwin Street, where his brothers worked.

The Gallager brothers, in their bloodied aprons and caps, would swagger home with a pig's head and hold it up at their mother's window to scare her. Which it never did. Dora Gallager had seen it all before: the pig's trotters peeping out from under the door curtain, the pig's ears in the sink. It was, she told her daughters, the sort of bloody daft stuff men thought funny.

Some men. But not Jacob. He'd changed. Having previously enjoyed a good fight, he had been quickly weaned off aggression by breaking his first pair of glasses. The look on Sara's face had been enough. As for his father, Elijah didn't have to tell his son how hard it was to buy one pair of glasses, let alone two. So Jacob had gone back to school with only one lens in his spectacles, reading the blackboard with his hand over the blank side.

By the time he got his new pair, his old pals had moved on and no one wanted some four-eyed cretin hanging around them. What good was Jacob in a fight any more?

21

He'd tried taking off his glasses before a scrap, but then he couldn't see who he was trying to hit, and so, gradually, his friends shunned him. Ironically, the studious look was all a sham. Jacob Clark might have street sense, but he wasn't academically bright. He wasn't anything much at all. Not especially tough, talented or driven. He was just Jacob – just one more Hanky Park brat.

Only one of his peers admired Jacob, and that was Gloria Siddons. It had taken her almost a month to forgive him for throwing the soot at her, and another month before she had let him walk her home. A week after that, Jacob had told her he thought she was pretty, and the following night he'd kissed her on the cheek.

In return, she had slapped him. Hard. But he had been smitten – and could tell she liked him more than a little. After all, didn't she always laugh at his jokes? When he took off his glasses and put them on the back of his head so he could see who was coming up behind them? He worried about her too: like the time she fell off the gasworks wall and scraped her knee. He'd laughed at first – he was a boy, after all – but then he'd taken her back to Sara and got her knee bandaged up nicely, reassuring Gloria that the cut wouldn't leave a scar. Nothing to spoil her pert perfection.

And so gradually Jacob had begun to spend more and more time occupied with Gloria. And grew more and more adrift when she wasn't around. Regarded as a bespectacled runt by most, he felt oddly grown-up with her, and had even begun to daydream of a future with Gloria Siddons. He knew that his choice of wife would be limited to Hanky Park, but if he could land Gloria – the prettiest and pertest of the bunch – he would be triumphant. So much for wearing glasses; it hadn't held him back where it really mattered.

'I've got to go to the washhouse, lad,' Sara said suddenly, breaking into Jacob's thoughts. 'Can you give me a lift down with the laundry?'

Picking up a loaded basket, he followed her out on to the street. It was mortifying, trailing behind his mother with a load of dirty washing and passing the end of Earl Street just as Bert Gallager was crossing over. Bert saw Jacob. Then his mother. Then the washing. Then he sniggered and moved off.

This was too much for Jacob. 'I've had enough!'

Sara looked at her son in amazement. 'What *are* you talking about?'

'All this!' he snapped, dropping the washing on to the cobbles. 'Trailing round after you like a flaming kid—'

'You *are* a kid.'

'I'm not! I'm grown-up – nearly.'

'That Gloria Siddons is turning your head,' Sara replied, looking down at the washing. 'Pick it up!'

'Why should I?'

Her voice rose. 'Because I say so!'

'You're always telling me what to do. *Do this, do that.* You treat me like a bloody girl. I shouldn't be hanging around with my mam – all the lads think I'm soft.' He snatched off his glasses, waving them at her. 'These ruined everything! They make me look a right berk.'

Without saying another word, Sara bent down and picked up the washing herself. She was well aware that Jacob had been shunned by his old mates and was sorry for it, but there was nothing she could do. Maybe, if he was lucky, he would marry Gloria; they were obviously fond of each other. But then again, maybe not. After all, what did her son have to offer the pretty, lively Gloria Siddons?

Wearily, Sara tightened her grip on the washing and walked away, leaving Jacob standing. Amazed, he put his glasses back on, watching his mother. For the first time he realised how much she'd aged, slope-shouldered with work and disappointment, her skin dull as chammy leather. Struggling to carry the load of laundry, Sara moved forward relentlessly, her regretful son running after her. But before he had time to apologise, a small, dark-complexioned man accosted his mother on the corner.

'Mrs Clark,' he said, fussing around her, 'let me help you with that.'

At once Jacob was at his mother's side. He had never really taken to the tailor. As everyone in Hanky Park knew only too well, Stanley Tobarski was a foreigner.

'Thank you,' Jacob said sniffily, 'but *I'm* helping my mother.'

Tobarski looked him up and down, then turned back to Sara. 'It would be no trouble to help. No trouble at all.'

For over two years Sara had worked as a cleaner for the tailor; usually when Elijah was laid off, or sick. And for all of Stanley Tobarski's eccentric ways, she had found him a fair employer. You did right by him, she told everyone, and he did right by you.

'You look exhausted, Mr Tobarski.'

'I have a problem, Mrs Clark.' He paused, moving a fraction closer. She could smell his cologne; a luxury for Hanky Park. But then Mr Tobarski was a foreigner, and they did things differently. 'My apprentice . . . I had to let him go.'

'Where?' Jacob chimed in suddenly, his eyes fixed beadily on the tailor.

Surprised, the two adults glanced at him, Stanley Tobarski taking a moment to recover. 'I had to let him . . . leave.'

'Why?'

Sara turned on her son. 'Stop asking questions!'

'I was just being curious.'

'And you know what curiosity did,' Sara replied darkly, turning back to Stanley Tobarski. 'You mean you had to let him go because . . .'

Jacob was feeling guilty for the way he had spoken to his mother earlier and was now being ultra-protective.

'Because of *what*?'

24

In one smooth gesture, Sara clipped her son on the left ear, Jacob yelping and falling back behind the two adults.

'He was stealing,' Stanley admitted finally, Jacob listening avidly although his ear was on fire. 'Took half my takings last week, that young villain did. Half my takings.' The tailor's voice fell. 'I gave him a good apprenticeship. He could have had a trade. But no, that wasn't enough. Not when he could steal money from me and get rich that way.'

'How much?'

Sara's expression should have melted Jacob into a pile of ash.

But Stanley Tobarski was in full flow and not stopping for anyone. 'Stole from me! Me, who put a roof over his head. Me, who fed him, paid him. Not much of a salary – but what's an apprentice worth, Mrs Clark?'

'I'm sure you gave him a fair wage,' Sara replied, turning to Jacob. 'And if you ask how much, I'll kick you all the way home!'

'And me,' the tailor went on, 'all alone in this world. Without a family, my wife dead. All alone, and not even an apprentice to carry on the trade when I'm gone and buried.' He paused, taking out a spotted handkerchief and blowing his nose loudly, his voice wavering. 'Betrayed by one of my own—'

'You said you had no family,' Jacob said, without thinking.

'I must apologise for my son, Mr Tobarski!' Sara said furiously. 'I can't think what's got into him lately. Why, only just now I was having an argument with him! My own son, arguing with me in the street . . .'

But Mr Tobarski wasn't listening; he was thinking instead. Thinking that Sara Clark was short of money. After all, hadn't the appalling Gerry Fitt told him she couldn't make the rent? And as for Elijah, his health was bad again . . . Stanley Tobarski's gaze moved to Jacob.

The lad was an odd one, all right. With those glasses and that small, jockey-like build. Too small to be of much good working at the abattoir. Too small to make a carter. Or a miner. In fact, too small to do anything particularly strenuous. Stanley's gaze moved to Jacob's hands; neat, delicate hands. Maybe *clever* hands?

'Jacob, my boy, come here,' he said suddenly, beckoning for the lad to approach. 'Let me see your hands.'

'What for?'

Another clip from Sara had Jacob put out his hands. The palms were mostly soft, smooth.

'A girl's hands—'

'I'm no bloody girl!'

'Jacob!' Sara snapped, aghast. 'How *could* you show me up like this!'

'Hush now, Mrs Clark, I offended the boy. Not meant, lad, not meant.' Tobarski smiled, putting his large head on one side. 'Mrs Clark, I would like to offer your son a chance.'

Suspicious, Sara looked hard at the tailor. 'A chance? What kind of chance?'

'I've a mind to try and make a tailor out of him.'

She flushed, embarrassed, looking down. 'We can't afford an apprenticeship, Mr Tobarski.'

He waved away her objection. 'Oh, I want no fee. We'll sort something out a different way. I'll teach your son for free, Mrs Clark, if you'll keep house for me. For a small wage, of course,' he paused, sugaring the offer. 'If Jacob is half good, in time I can give him a skill, a proper profession. He would be a tailor. Think of that. A better job than all the other lads, hey? And for what? You looking after me and my house.'

'Sewing is girls' work!' Jacob said suddenly.

'Do *I* look like a girl?' Stanley Tobarski asked, his eyebrows raised. 'Or do,' he jingled the change in his pockets, 'I sound like I have money?' He sniffed his wrist. 'Enough money to buy cologne from Germany. Enough money to never get my hands dirty stacking coal. You are a *very* stupid boy.'

It was Jacob's turn to be stunned. 'You what!'

'You heard me,' the tailor repeated, turning to go. 'I give you one hour to make up your mind.'

'He'll do it,' Sara said urgently.

The chance was too good to miss. Her son would have a respectable, clean job, a profession. Some standing. And a way to keep hold of Gloria Siddons – or any Hanky Park woman he might chose.

'But Mam—'

She silenced him with a look. Later she would explain, spell it out for him – now she just had to secure the offer.

'I'll be frank, Mr Tobarski. I don't want to see my son flogging himself to death, working for next to nothing. I've seen too many good men ground down that way.' She put out her hand; Stanley Tobarski took it and shook it warmly. 'I'll agree to your offer.'

'Your lad will have to work hard.'

'Oh, he'll work, all right. But you're taking a chance. What if he's no talent for tailoring?'

Tobarski put his head on one side again, his expression quizzical. 'Talent, hah! A good teacher *makes* talent.'

'If you're sure, Mr Tobarski. It's a fair offer.'

'The best you'll get in Hanky Park.'

She nodded. 'If you can give Jacob a life with hope, I'll clean for you till I drop.' She glanced at her son. 'You make this work out, you hear me?'

Jacob could tell that his mother wasn't going to take any more cheek. She had that look she only wore occasionally. That *cross me and I'll kill you* look.

So, wisely, he agreed.

FIVE

'Go on, you can kiss me,' Gloria said, putting back her head and waiting patiently. A second later she opened her eyes, staring at Jacob in astonishment. 'I said you could kiss me!'

'Oh yeah—'

'Oh yeah!' she repeated, sitting upright and staring at him furiously. 'There's many a boy round these parts who'd just *die* to kiss me.'

'Oh, I can believe it. Only the other day I was tripping over a pile of bodies on Hull Street.' He nudged her affectionately, sliding his arm around her shoulder. 'I've got my mind on something else.'

'Better than kissing me?' she asked pertly, resting her head on his shoulder. He smelt of soap, not cheap cigarettes, and definitely not beer. Jacob didn't like drinking much, only now and then. And she admired that. After all, didn't she see enough drinking with her mother? In fact, it was just one more thing she liked about Jacob Clark – in amongst all the other traits she had grown to love.

It had been very easy to love Jacob. It was true that he might not be the tallest of lads, or the best-looking. He might wear glasses too, but he was special. He was kind, protective, loving. And she felt safe with him. Something about Jacob told Gloria – not in words, but instinctively – that he would die for her.

'So what were you thinking about?'

Jacob took a deep breath. 'I've news for you.'

'That why you brought me to the park?'

'I didn't want anyone overhearing.'

'Like Mam, you mean?'

He nodded. 'It's like this, Gloria – I've got a job.'

'I know, love, carting,' she said, sitting up on the park bench.

'Nah, I'm going to be apprenticed to Mr Tobarski. The tailor.'

'But you don't like him!'

Jacob shifted his feet. 'Well, it's true I didn't like him much before – but I do now. He's a bit weird – he's foreign, after all – but he's given me a real chance to make something of myself. A leg up in life.' Jacob remembered what Sara had said and hurried on. 'Stanley Tobarski's given me an opening. Offered me an apprenticeship. I'm going to be a tailor! Think of it, Gloria. *Me*, Jacob Clark, a tailor. Why, I might even inherit the shop in time.'

Her eyes were fixed on him in open astonishment. And people thought he'd amount to nothing – what did they know?

'Jacob, you'll be a real somebody.'

He was luminous with pleasure. She was proud of him! Now he would be able to keep her. Not have to watch some other lad come and steal her away. Because Jacob Clark was going to be a tailor. A somebody. A man worthy of the glorious Gloria.

'Oh, Jacob,' she said simply, kissing him. 'You're so clever.'

He was dizzy with triumph. No point worrying about whether he could sew, or even cut out a pattern. No point lying awake thinking about all the weird things he had heard about Stanley Tobarski. So what if he kept a stuffed reptile in his kitchen? So what if you had to listen very hard to understand half of what he said? Stanley Tobarski was going to make him into a tailor. A tailor who would naturally have a tailor's wife. And in Jacob's eyes, that made him little short of a god.

'Gloria?'

She stared at him adoringly. 'What is it, love?'

'You and me – we're going to get on. We are, you know. I'll make you right proud of me. Work hard and give you a nice home. Good clothes.' He grabbed her hand and squeezed it. 'I'll be Jacob Clark, the tailor. And you . . .'

She held her breath.

'You'll be *Mrs* Jacob Clark. The tailor's wife.'

Flushing, Gloria flung her arms around his neck. 'Oh, Jacob, I love you so much. So much.'

She smothered him in kisses, hardly caring if anyone saw them. So what if they did? They were in love, and they were going to be married. The future was theirs for the taking.

'But we can't marry yet,' Jacob said seriously.

'*What!*'

'We have to wait. Until I'm qualified, earning money. Until we're both eighteen.' He paused, suddenly anxious again. 'You'll wait for me, Gloria, won't you?'

She thought her heart was going to burst. Would she wait? Of course she would! She could imagine people's faces when they heard about this. Her fella was going up in the world. She wouldn't be stuck working at Tyson's milliner's shop all her life. Oh no, she was going to be a wife and mother. Gloria sighed to herself. It was all she had ever wanted, and now *this* bonus. Now not only did she get Jacob; she got a lad who was on the up. A lad with a clean job, a bit of standing in life. Dear God, Gloria thought, light-headed, their life would be charmed.

'Gloria, you will wait for me?' Jacob repeated anxiously. 'You *will*, won't you?'

Pulling off his glasses, she kissed every inch of Jacob's face. 'Oh yes, yes, yes! Of course I'll wait for you!'

Laughing, he drew back. 'It might take a while. But it'll be worth it in the end.'

She nodded, thinking of the tailor's shop on Hankerton Street. Cramped between a tobacconist's and a pub, the

Golden Fleece, Stanley Tobarski's shop stood out like a lamb amongst pigs. His windows were always clean; his blinds – yellow-tinted to stop the sun harming the suiting – pulled down in summer. And his dummies – *mannequins*, as Stanley insisted on calling them – were the talk of the town.

They were old, but still regal, their faces painted a quaint flesh colour. A colour more suited to Devon than Salford. And all three of them were different. One was bearded, the mature dummy; another was often seen sporting a boater, the juvenile lead; and the smallest was a boy mannequin with a rakish grin. Once, before Stanley Tobarski bought his guard dog, Ralph, someone had broken into the shop. Not only had they taken a quantity of good cloth, but all the dummies' wigs. Which was bad enough, but they had also rearranged the window dressing.

The following morning a small crowd had gathered outside the tailor's shop, laughing. In the window the mature dummy was standing with his bald head tucked under his arm, red paint smeared over his neck and chest. The juvenile lead's arms had been raised above his head, a bloody hatchet in his hands. And as for the boy dummy – he too was bald, slumped on the floor with an empty glass in his hand and several beer bottles scattered around him.

'Do tailors make a *lot* of money?' Gloria asked, dragging her thoughts back to the present.

'A tailor can make a very respectable wage,' Jacob assured her. 'If he's a good tailor.'

'And you'll be the best,' Gloria said firmly, 'the best tailor in Salford. You might even end up with a string of shops across the north-west. People will point you out in your flash car as you pass by and say, "That's Mr Jacob Clark, the tycoon." '

He laughed, hugging her to him. 'All I want is you.'

'Well, I want more!' she teased him. 'I want you, at least six children, and maybe two or even three tailor's shops.'

He was flushed with pleasure. 'I can do anything –

anything – if you love me. If you're by my side I can take on the whole world.'

'And we'll win!' Gloria said, laughing. 'We'll win, hands down.'

SIX

His short arms folded across his chest, Stanley Tobarski regarded his apprentice. His nose itched and he scratched it absent-mindedly, staring at the seam Jacob was stitching. Then a small harrumphing sound echoed in his throat. A sound Jacob knew only too well.

'What is it?'

'You're going off the chalk mark. Sorry, I'm too critical. Not meant, not meant.'

Surprised, Jacob looked at his handiwork. 'I thought I was straight—'

'You need new glasses?'

'I got stronger glasses six months ago.'

'Maybe they're not so good,' Stanley replied, moving over to the fireplace and taking down an elaborate carved pipe. 'Maybe we get stronger. So you see the seams.'

'I'm just tired, that's all,' Jacob admitted, leaning back.

He had been with the tailor for a year. Twelve months in which Stanley Tobarski had coughed, sighed, nudged and cajoled Jacob through the first stages of his apprenticeship. He hadn't been a good teacher; he had been a *great* one. And in the misfit Jacob Clark he had found a lad desperate to excel at something. So desperate that he thought of nothing but being a tailor. Oh, and Gloria, of course, though even she came temporarily second when Jacob was working. And work he did. Because he was overwhelmingly grateful to Stanley Tobarski; the man who had given him *purpose*. And purpose in Hanky Park was more valuable than platinum.

The routine at the tailor's shop seldom varied. Around six every morning Jacob would hear his mother come in and set the breakfast on. Lighting a winter fire in the gloomy back kitchen, Sara would clean any dirty dishes, empty the ash can and then go shopping. Spending every penny of Stanley Tobarski's money as wisely as she did her own, she would then make something for the evening meal: a potato pie, a bit of stew. Then she would come into the shop.

If Stanley was there, Sara would leave. If not, she would have a quick word with Jacob. Always encouraging, her bony hands touching his work reverentially. But she never said much, only told Jacob how his father was, or reassured him that she was coping well. And if the week had been a good one, Jacob gave her what little cash he could spare. Because by now Jacob's father was a semi-invalid. In summer Elijah could work a little, but when the first chills and fogs came in, he was crippled with chest infections. He puked up blood that was black specked with soot, and sat huddled up by the kitchen fire, racked with coughing bouts until he was exhausted, spittle flecking his lips.

'You take a little rest now,' Stanley said, breaking into Jacob's thoughts. 'Then we sew more. You rest. Then we sew again.'

And sew and sew . . . The second year came and passed. Gloria was still working at Tyson's and patiently putting aside a little money in her bottom drawer. And Betty – in her cups – repeatedly told everyone in Hanky Park about how Jacob was going to be a tailor. Even though they had all heard the story a hundred times before . . .

Tailoring hadn't come easily to Jacob. His short-sightedness was useful for close work, but his eyes became strained at times and he would fall asleep at the work table, his head resting on his pattern. But still Stanley continued to push him, both of them often working late into the night. It took a lot of effort, but as the second summer passed and the second winter came in, Jacob finally got the hang of tailoring. In fact, he turned out to be a real find, with a feel for cloth. He was a canny haggler too. Send him over to Davies Street, Manchester, or Shude Hill, and he'd get a fine length for less than most men could. And no one ever cheated him. Jacob knew cloth like other men knew beer.

And as he got the hang of tailoring, he got the hang of his employer too. Stanley Tobarski might be a foreigner and an oddball, but his heart was as big as a tram. So big that by the end of the second year's apprenticeship, Stanley was like a father to Jacob. And to Gloria.

'You come in now, come in,' he fussed her, opening the kitchen door and hustling Gloria towards the fire. 'You cold? You look cold, little dove.' He held her hands between his own, warming them. Odd behaviour, but that was Stanley. 'Here, sit by the fire, sit closer. I build it up for you. More coal.'

She smiled at him. 'How's Jacob doing?'

'Made his first suit,' Stanley said, winking. 'I say it's no good, but it's very good. Very good.' He looked back to his visitor. Prettier by the day, Stanley thought, and bright. Make a good wife. 'What's matter?'

'Nothing.'

'You tell me, you tell Uncle Stanley,' he encouraged her, pulling a chair up to hers.

'I just wondered . . .'

'What?'

'Time seems to go so slowly,' Gloria admitted, taking the shawl from around her head and draping it over her shoulders. 'I mean, I don't want to complain, you've been so good to Jacob . . .'

'He unhappy? I make him unhappy? Not meant, not meant,' Stanley said, mortified.

'No, Jacob's very happy here!' Gloria reassured him quickly. 'It's just that I hardly see him any more and he's got another year to go before he'll finish his apprenticeship.' She smiled, trying to sound light-hearted. 'I miss him.'

'I keep him too busy?'

'Forget what I said!' Gloria replied hurriedly. 'I had no right . . .'

'It will be worthwhile, in the end,' Stanley said, then leaned towards her. 'I had a wife once. She was very sweet. But she died. Long time ago now, and maybe I'm too old to remember what it feels like to be in love.' He got to his feet and moved to the door. There he paused, studying Jacob working in the room beyond.

Stanley had no doubts that Jacob would make a fine tailor, so fine that he would be a credit to the little shop in Hankerton Street. So fine that someone from Manchester might well come along and offer him a good wage to go elsewhere . . . Stanley shuddered at the thought of losing his protégé. He had grown fond of the lad; and of Gloria. Life without their comings and goings would be dull for an old man.

Taking a deep breath, he walked into the workshop. 'Jacob, I want a word with you.'

Jacob looked up at his employer. 'Is everything OK?'

'No, not at all.'

Paling, Jacob stammered, 'I thought you were pleased with my work—'

'No, you've disappointed me, Jacob,' Stanley went on, his tone serious. 'You've neglected your duties.'

'What!'

'I think you need more help.'

'I can do it!' Jacob replied, outraged. 'I'm just a bit tired, that's all. You can't criticise me for being tired.'

'You don't laugh.'

'*What!*'

'Or smile. No smiles,' Stanley went on. 'I need a happy shop. A shop where people come to feel good and get good clothes.'

Jacob was incredulous.

'But—'

'It has to stop.'

'But—'

'You have to get married.'

Jacob's mouth fell open. 'What *are* you talking about, Stanley?'

Stanley was laughing, pointing to the back room. 'Next door is your woman. She misses you. She would make a good home for you, Jacob – for all of us.' He leaned towards his apprentice. 'You eighteen in a month, right?'

Jacob nodded.

'We have wedding!'

'But I can't afford to keep a wife!'

'And I can't afford to lose the best tailor in Salford. Or my stand-in son.' Stanley paused. 'I give you little rise, OK? Not much, but enough. You live here with Gloria. Too much room for just one old man. I like company.'

Shaking, Jacob sat down, dropping the suiting in his hands. 'We could live *here*?'

'On one condition.'

'Name it.'

'That you stay here, work here always.' Stanley paused. 'Not so much to ask, I think. This shop will be yours one day, Jacob. I've no son of my own, and you're like family to me. The only family I *want* to know.'

Surprised by the hardness in his tone, Jacob's natural curiosity got the better of him. 'You've got family?'

As though hit by lightning, Stanley flinched. Involuntarily, he grasped some striped suiting in his hands and twisted it. 'My brother. A pawnbroker,' he said coldly. 'Lionel Taylor. Changed his name, ashamed of his family. Lives over in Moss Side, Manchester.'

Surprised, Jacob stood with the cutting scissors in his hands, staring at his employer. Over their heads a pigeon was pecking half-heartedly at the glass skylight; the outside tap dripping slowly, hypnotically.

'He's immoral,' Stanley went on. 'Bad. He's thieved and made a living out of thieving. A face like a bulldog, and a heart like black marble.' He paused. 'I made a promise to our parents. I promised them I would look out for Lionel. And I've kept my word. But he's not having any of *this*.' Stanley looked around him at the workroom. It was cramped: two trestle tables; patterns; chalked-out cloth on a headless dummy; the walls stacked with rolls of material. 'This is *my* place!'

'Stanley, calm down!' Jacob said soothingly.

But Stanley was beside himself. His hated brother, Lionel, Moss Side Lionel, had suddenly materialised in the safe haven of the tailor's shop: as welcome as a demon at a children's tea party.

'He's not to know about this place,' he said, dropping his voice as though his brother might somehow be able to overhear him from miles away. 'He never must. He always thought *he* was the clever one. Never gave me credit for anything. *Too stupid to come in out of the rain*, he used to say.' Stanley smiled craftily. 'I've never told Lionel about my shop. He thinks I'm penniless, a council clerk. Lets me alone because of it. Worried I might ask him for money, for help.'

'But surely he must have heard about you?'

'Why? He runs with thieves and cheats. I've kept myself clean. All my life, clean. There's not one person knows me, knows him. And we have different name, remember?' Stanley stared into Jacob's face anxiously. 'What connection could there be between the comical little tailor in Hanky Park and a thug pawnbroker in Manchester?' He caught hold of Jacob's hand. 'You never tell Lionel about this place, you hear? You tell no one. You never even *think* about Lionel Taylor again. You've never heard of him . . . I'm going to get this place tied up tight. Like a knot.' Stanley waved his clenched fist in front of Jacob's face. 'Get a will made. Put with the legal lads. Nothing overlooked, no keyhole for greedy Lionel to slide through. You do right by me now, Jacob, and you've a shop when I've gone. No conditions – only that you keep it a respectable business. And away from the likes of my brother.'

SEVEN

'I don't bloody believe it!' Bert Gallager said, coming in and throwing off his coat. 'Jacob Clark's married!'

'Yer what?' his mother said, putting down a plate of corned beef.

'How the hell did he land a girl like Gloria Siddons?' Bert went on, incredulous. 'I'm much better-looking.'

'Well, you've got a bigger head and that's a fact,' Dora Gallager said, slapping Bert round the back of the neck. 'Where yer been till now?'

'I were—'

'Messing about. Like always.' She glanced over to four of her other children, all squashed in around the kitchen table. '*They* got in for dinner . . .'

'Aw, Mam, give it a rest. I'm not a kid.'

'Don't cheek me! Or I'll tell yer father.'

The threat was enough. Not even Bert stood up to Pa Gallager. They all knew only too well that their father had been jailed for theft repeatedly. Just as they knew he'd once beaten a man half to death round Tatter's Corner. What for, no one asked. Everyone was just grateful it wasn't them.

Sullenly Bert sat down next to his sisters, budging them along the bench to make room for him. At once a plateful of grey boiled potatoes was slammed down in front of him.

'Nah, Mam, not tatas again—'

'When we've money for kippers, yer'll 'ave 'em. But until then, it's spuds.'

The front door slamming closed made everyone flinch. At once the atmosphere was strained, Dora watching as her husband walked in. Silently, Pa Gallager glanced at his family, then sat down, his newspaper opened to the racing pages. His wide, almost Asian face was turned away, his sleeves rolled up, the tattoo of a snake on his left forearm glowing sinister in the firelight.

Dora had thought about saying grace, but now thought better of it and turned to Bert.

'So, *what* about Jacob Clark?'

Pushing a potato grudgingly around his plate, Bert answered her. ' 'E's married Gloria Siddons.'

'That's no surprise; they've been courting for years,' Dora replied. 'Yer just jealous—'

'Of Jacob Clark? Do me a favour!'

'Yer've always been right put out that Gloria didn't go for yer.'

'I've got m' own girl!'

'Oh aye, Minnie Goodland,' his sister said, laughing. 'What a catch!'

'She's a looker,' Bert replied, shooting her a mean glance. 'There's loads of blokes would like to be with Minnie—'

'There's loads that have been,' his sister replied drily.

Irritated, Bert fell into silence, his mother watching him. He'd made up a good-looking lad, and for all his tough talk, soft-hearted. Not that Bert would let anyone see that. Especially his father. Best not to let Pa Gallager suss out any weak spots. You got picked on that way.

'Jacob and Gloria'll make a good couple,' Dora said finally.

'Hah!' Bert replied, his tone curt. 'Who in their right mind marries at eighteen?'

'The kind of lad who's got his head screwed on, that's who,' his mother retorted. 'The kind of lad others used to poke fun at. But Jacob Clark's not so pathetic now, is he? Wed and tailoring for a living.' Dora sighed, then ruffled her handsome son's hair. 'Aye, come on, cheer up! Yer not ready to settle, lad. The right girl's not come along yet.'

He shook off her touch.

'Who wants to be married anyway! I'm free and footloose, I'll not marry. Not me,' Bert replied, glancing over to his father and puffing out his chest. 'Oh no, I'm not making an ass of myself. There's not a lass in Hanky Park could get *me* up the aisle.'

For the fourth time in an hour, Gloria buffed the wedding ring on her left hand and then admired it. Smiling, Jacob watched her.

'It won't make your finger go green.'

'Oh you!' she said, laughing and falling back on the bed. Below them they could hear Stanley moving around. 'He did us proud, didn't he? Laying on that little feast. We should offer to clear up.'

They had decided not to go on honeymoon, even a weekend in Blackpool. The money – both Jacob and Gloria agreed – could be put to better use, like bedlinen, a few bits of china from the market and a new clothes horse Gloria had been saving up for. Who needed a honeymoon, when they had work, a roof over their heads and each other?

Resting his head on her chest, Jacob listened to his wife's heart beating. 'Mam's downstairs, she said she wanted to clear up for us.'

'She *insisted*,' Gloria said, grinning. 'And no one argues with your mother. I'm sorry your dad didn't live to see us married, though. What'll your mam do now?'

'She's talking about moving to Hull to live with her sister.'

'*Hull!*'

'She'd have company there,' Jacob replied. 'She never liked Hanky Park.'

Thoughtful, Gloria stared up at the ceiling, the lettering

from the old lamp outside reflected above their heads –
GENTLEMAN'S OUTFITTERS.

'You know something?'

'I know everything.'

She laughed. 'One day we'll be lying here and we'll read "Jacob Clark, Tailor—" '

' "And Sons".'

'Hey?'

' "Jacob Clark and Sons, Tailors".'

'What if we only have girls?'

'Then we'll keep trying until we get a boy.' Laughing, Jacob rolled over, wrapping his arms around his wife. 'I love you, Mrs Jacob Clark.'

'Mrs Jacob Clark,' Gloria repeated dreamily. 'Fancy that, I'm a married woman. With my own man and my own home.'

'And your own job.'

'How's that?'

'Because now,' he said, kissing her gently on the lips, 'you're somebody special. You're the tailor's wife, Gloria. That's who you are. And who you'll always be.'

EIGHT

'Dear God,' Stanley said, wincing, 'I love your wife. I love dear Gloria, but her *voice*! It's cruel. Tell her, please, stop singing.'

Nodding, Jacob glanced upwards. Apart from his wife being tone deaf, he had no complaints, and was, in fact, indecently happy. Gloria had continued to be as loving, sweet and amusing as she had always been. She was tolerant of Stanley's pernickety eating habits and stuffed reptiles, and always welcoming to the customers. By the time she had been the tailor's wife for a year, she knew everyone and everything involved in Hankerton Street.

She had made it her business. People came to Gloria to talk, and even though she was little more than a child, her good nature made her irresistible. Gloria didn't need beer to be elated; she was giddy with life. What she had wanted, she had achieved, and when their first child was born a year later, she was ecstatic.

The pregnancy had been relatively easy, the delivery uncomplicated.

'Like shelling peas,' she told Jacob.

'Some pea,' he said, gazing proudly at the newborn.

Eighteen months later, Jacob was made a partner. A partner at twenty! people said, astonished and not a little jealous. And another kid on the way. And then another. *It's always the quiet ones you want to watch ... Always the dark horse ...* Up and up went the Clark bubble. Bert became reconciled with Jacob now that he was no longer

43

jealous. Of a bloke landed with a wife and three kids before twenty-three?

'No way! *I'm* not getting stitched up like that.'

Gloria was holding the new baby, Helen, and smiled up at her visitor. 'Big talk, Bert Gallager, but the toughest fall the hardest in the end.'

He stared at the baby, blank-faced. 'They don't look like anything, do they? Just blobs.'

'Some grow up like blobs too,' Gloria replied, winking.

Rumour had it that Bert was a womaniser; couldn't be faithful to any one girl. Gloria didn't doubt it. After all, now he had filled out, he was a good-looking man, his blue eyes wicked, inviting. Irresistible – but not to her. No, Gloria had only ever wanted her Jacob. Let the other girls go for the flash types; she knew where her happiness lay.

'How yer coping with the shop work as well as all these kids?'

'Stanley's helping out,' Gloria said, smiling. 'He encourages us to have more and more children so he can work in the shop more.'

'He's getting on.'

'Seventy-nine next.'

Bert blew out his cheeks, looking round. His own father had been involved in another vicious attack, splitting open a man's head with a crowbar. As for his brothers, they were already set to follow Pa Gallager's route. Worn to the bone, Dora had died the previous winter. The Hanky Park cough, people said, as if it was amusing when a person puked their guts up and died from pneumonia, or got sectioned off up at the TB sanatorium on the moors.

'Yer'll be set for life when Stanley pops his clogs.'

'*Bert!*' Gloria snapped, genuinely shocked. 'Don't talk about him like that. Anyway, no one should count their chickens before they're hatched.'

'Unless yer happen to be in the nest already, with yer arse on them,' Bert replied drily.

Later that night, Gloria recounted the conversation to Jacob as he undressed. In the cot beside their bed lay Helen, and in the room beyond were Suzannah, and Girton, their middle child. Their only son.

'I don't want to talk about who's inheriting the shop!' Jacob said, for once impatient with his wife. 'Stanley gave me his word and that's good enough for me.'

'But d'you know if he's made a will or not?' she pressed him. It was all right to trust Stanley's word, but you had to make sure. Look out for your own family. Life was always on a knife-edge in Hanky Park. You could be steady one day, the next destitute. 'We have the children to think of—'

Irritated, Jacob took off his trousers. 'Let it rest!'

'You can't tell me off standing there in your socks,' Gloria mocked him, trying to take the sting out of the conversation. 'And anyway, you know how much I love Stanley. Of course I don't want anything to happen to him for years. But we have to think of the future. Of our future—'

'It's bad luck,' Jacob said, getting into bed and turning his back towards her.

'What's bad luck?'

'Talking about the shop and Stanley dying.'

'You've never been superstitious before,' Gloria replied, sliding down the bed and nestling against his back. 'Don't be cross, sweetheart.'

'I just don't like talking about the shop and who's going to get it.'

Neither did she, but she wasn't going to let the matter drop. 'I was just—'

'Being morbid.'

'*Jacob!*'

'And greedy—'

'For God's sake, Jacob!'

'Go to sleep, Gloria.'

Annoyed, she rolled on to her back. It was fine being careful of Stanley's feelings, but who would worry about *theirs* if they were thrown out on to the street? A trickle of anxiety slithered down her spine. Families had to stick together in Hanky Park. If you didn't, you were as good as done for. You had to pool your money, chores, problems – and fight to keep what you had. *Anything* you had. In their teens, Hanky Parkers brought in what wages they could and lived at home until they married. The grindingly poor never left home and lived in cramped, unsanitary conditions. There were – everyone knew – more than a few incidences of incest.

Many a couple that couldn't afford to marry had furtive sex and only tied the knot when the woman got pregnant. Abortion was a way of life, a solution for many overworked mothers or single girls. Gloria sighed. In Hanky Park a person knew their route from the womb to the tomb. You left school early, barely educated, went into the ironworks, the foundry, the mills, the abattoirs. If they didn't marry, single women stayed home and looked after their siblings, and later their parents. They gossiped in doorways, prayed on Sundays and stayed respectable. But some of the men took another route: became criminals, thieving what they could. Some got caught, or took to drink. And a few, usually the lonely, died mad.

If a family was to last, it stuck together. Hanky Park was populated by an enduring tribe who had learned the hard way how to survive. Fiercely protective of their streets and their people, they were suspicious of outsiders and wary of life. The reason was simple: everyone knew how short the step was from security to oblivion.

And Gloria knew only too well how lucky she had been. And how lucky she wanted to stay. Gently she kissed Jacob's shoulder. He was angry; she would have to bring up the subject of Stanley's will another time. But not now; now she wanted to break the quarrel between them. So, softly and mischievously, she began to sing.

Smiling despite himself, Jacob turned and put his hand

over her mouth. 'If you don't stop singing, I'll have to kill you.'

'Death by music hall,' she mumbled, pushing his hand away.

'Let's not fight, Gloria.'

'I don't want to fight,' she replied quietly. 'I just want to do the best for us. *All* of us.'

'Then for Christ's sake, don't sing,' Jacob said, laughing. 'Please God, don't sing!'

NINE

'Hey, Mrs Hall! Mrs Hall!'

Unceremoniously woken, the old woman put her head out of the upstairs window. She was hardly able to make out the little girl below.

'What's the hollering about!' she bellowed.

'It's Mum, she's having the baby.'

Moments later, Mrs Hall was hurrying down Chapel Street, towards the tailor's shop. Beside her, running to keep up, was Suzannah, the seven-year-old daughter of Jacob and Gloria Clark, who had taken it upon herself to call out the old crone up on Chapel Street. After all, the girl thought to herself, her mother was dying. Or must be, for all the crying.

When they arrived at the shop, Suzannah ran up the stairs two at a time. Jacob was standing at the top, waiting for her.

'Where have you been?'

Out of breath, Mrs Hall heaved herself on to the landing, her hat ribbon coming untied. 'I 'ear yer wife's having her fourth—'

'Suzannah!' Jacob said incredulously, looking from the crone to his daughter. '*You* fetched Mrs Hall?'

'Well, is she or isn't she?' the old woman snapped. ' 'Cos if she's not, I can get back to my bloody bed. Although I'll want paying for my trouble—'

A sudden sharp cry from the bedroom behind made her turn, and hurry off as Jacob caught his daughter's arm. In the doorway of the sitting room, a solemn little boy stood watching them both.

'See now, you've woken your brother,' Jacob said kindly, picking Girton up and sitting down with Suzannah beside him. Tenderly he touched his daughter's hair. Only a kid, and she'd had the gumption to get the Widow Hall . . .

'Your mum will be all right.'

'She was screaming.'

'She's having a baby,' Jacob reassured Suzannah. 'A little brother or sister for you.'

He glanced at the bedroom door again. It was quiet suddenly, the screaming temporarily stilled. Neither he nor the children moved, just stayed cramped together on the horsehair sofa on the landing. In the back bedroom, Helen slept on oblivious, too young to wake for anything.

Then, unexpectedly, Jacob tensed, a sensation of dread creeping up on him as the silence continued. Jesus, was there something wrong? After all their good fortune, their healthy children, their happy marriage, was it all finally going wrong? He could feel Girton holding on to his hand tightly. Did he sense something too? God, why wasn't there any noise? Was the baby dead? Was Gloria dead?

Getting abruptly to his feet, Jacob rushed into the bedroom. The bedside lamp was lit, its beam casting a waning light on Gloria's face and throwing the shadow of Mrs Hall – huge and menacing – on to the side wall. She was bent over the bed, her black shape humped. In panic, Jacob pushed her aside.

'Hey! Mind yer kid!' she snapped.

He turned, looked down at the bundle in her arms. 'A baby?'

'No, it's a bleeding carrot!' she snorted. 'It's a baby all right. Another boy.'

Still anxious, Jacob turned to stare at his motionless wife. 'Is she all right?'

'Worn out. But then so would you be,' Mrs Hall replied, bundling together the bloodied pile of towels and sheets. 'I've changed yer bed and I can get these washed fer sixpence extra.'

Jacob nodded gratefully. 'Yes, thank you . . .' He looked at his new son, taking him carefully from Mrs Hall. 'He's handsome.'

She shrugged. 'Looks like the undertaker Bert Foreward to me. Got a hump like a bloody camel when he were old, but lucky with money.' She pulled her shawl round her shoulders and picked up the bundle of laundry. 'Yer've a nice family, Mr Clark. In fact, yer a lucky man.'

He nodded, his voice wavering. 'Oh, I know that, Mrs Hall . . . Believe me, I know that.'

Turning, he beckoned for Suzannah and Girton to come in, his daughter clambering carefully on to the bed beside her mother. 'Wow . . .' she said simply, touching the baby's head.

Wow indeed, Jacob thought. Four healthy children and a beautiful wife. How lucky could any man get? It was a lot to look after, clothe and feed, but he knew what he was doing. Jacob smiled to himself. Who would have thought it? Who would have put money on Jacob Clark turning out so well? Only in his twenties and respected, with a family.

'Fine baby.' Stanley had arrived, and was moving from foot to foot nervously at the end of the bed. 'A boy too. That's good. Two girls, two boys. You've taken on a lot, Jacob.'

'Some burden,' he replied, smiling.

Dropping his voice, Stanley moved over to him. 'We must talk, Jacob. About the shop. About the future. Children need providing for. When I'm gone, you'll be sorted.'

'Stanley, you don't have to do anything else for me, or my family.'

'I don't *have* to do anything – except what I want. So we sort out the business, OK? We sort it out good.' His voice dropped lower. 'Make sure no greedy hands from Manchester way get what's yours by right.'

I remember climbing on to the bed beside my mother and touching the crown of the baby's head. Looking back, it seemed that life was charmed then; that nothing could ever shake the secure world of the Clark family. We were living amongst and yet immune from the reality of Hanky Park; the poverty which daily drove families into the poorhouse or men into thieving didn't touch us. Illness, loss and deprivation passed the tailor's shop by.

We were marooned, safe, becalmed. Maybe even bewitched.

On the night my brother was born I remember going to bed, too excited to sleep. Below, I could hear muted voices talking, and the rhythmic breathing of my sister in the bed beside me. But there was another noise I heard that night; a sound I will never forget. It came unexpected and terrible: like an omen, an intimation of evil. And it was so clear, so loud, the noise travelling on the night air from Unwin Street. From the stalls behind the abattoir, where the cattle were held for slaughter the following day. I never remembered hearing it before, but that night – long into the darkness – the cattle cried out, the noise eerie, desperate. Waiting for the slaughter. As if they knew what was coming.

I heard their cries, but was too young to understand. Only felt – for the first time in my life – afraid. Suddenly aware that beyond the tailor's shop was a world that was black, dangerous, fathomless.

And very close.

TEN

For once her milk wouldn't come. It had always been easy to feed the other children, but not the new baby. Anxious, Gloria spent long hours with her son, nursing him, and then finally gave in to common wisdom and supplemented his feed when he was a month old. She felt – she told Jacob – a failure.

'Don't be daft,' he cajoled her. 'No one's a better mother.'

She looked round, harassed. 'Maybe . . . I'm not too happy about Suzannah either.'

'What's wrong with her?'

'She's got a bad chest again!' Gloria replied impatiently, as if he should have known. 'Just like she had last winter.'

'She's just coughing a bit. All the kids cough round here. It's the Hanky Park fogs, you know that, love.' Jacob leant down towards his wife, kissing the top of her head. 'You're just tired, that's all. You're worrying too much. Relax, Gloria, this isn't like you. You normally take everything in your stride.'

But suddenly her stride didn't seem quite long enough. And it was no good turning to her mother for guidance. Betty thought that four children was more than enough. Almost embarrassing, in fact. Gloria and Jacob were so young to have such a big family. Young and obviously very hot-blooded.

'I suppose you'll not have another now,' she said hopefully that afternoon. 'I mean, four's plenty for anyone. You don't want to end up like those big Catholic families – can't pay their rent or even put clothes on their kids' backs.

And the Church encouraging them. The Pope should feed the kids, I say, then he'd see how easy it is.'

Gloria sighed. 'Jacob says we can afford it, Mum. And Suzannah's helping me out with the baby.'

'She's got a bad cough.'

'Doctor's seen her and says she's all right,' Gloria replied defensively, her usually easy-going manner rattled. What was her mother implying? That she didn't know how to look after her own children? It was true she was tired, but she could cope. With help. 'Girton's always taking the baby out for walks. Get him some air—'

'Girton's only a child.'

'He's very capable,' Gloria retorted. Admittedly, Girton was only five, but he was a boy who liked to take responsibility. A serious child, old for his years. A child everyone expected to be reliable, because he had a wise look.

'You lean on him too much.' Betty said disapprovingly, watching Girton push his little brother down the street to the corner shop. 'He should be out playing with lads of his own age, not baby-sitting.'

The pram was old, pressed into use by the four Clark children, and God knew how many before that. Amazing how people changed, Betty mused. Not that many years ago Gloria would have played hell if anyone had suggested she have anything second-hand. Only the best had been good enough then. But not now; now Gloria reckoned that she already had the best of what mattered. The best husband, the best children. As for the incidentals of life, who cared about those?

It was the same with their living quarters. For years they had all lived together, Stanley happily moving up the house as the Clark family increased, until he ended up in the attic room at the top of the tailor's shop. But it wasn't the cramped quarters or the long haul up the stairs that finally made him decide to leave; it was the nappies, teething rings, bouts of colic, and eternal bottles of milk warming on the stove. They were all right if you were young. But the years of broken nights were beginning to take their toll on Stanley Tobarski. He adored the brood of Clark children, but had decided that it was time to adore them from a distance.

'You can't leave the shop!' Jacob had admonished him when he had brought the matter up. 'This is your home.'

'Too crowded now—'

'We have room. We'll always have room for you,' Jacob had reassured him.

'No, no,' Stanley had insisted. 'You need it more. Enjoy, enjoy.'

So a relieved Stanley relinquished the responsibility of the shop, moving to a rented flat in Vera Street. But he left his dog, Ralph, with the Clarks. *Keep you all safe*, he had insisted. And who would have argued with that? Because Ralph had a reputation that every thief from Salford to Bury knew about. No one tangled with Ralph. He was – if you listened to some – part wolf. Others insisted that he'd been imported from abroad, some exotic species of man-killer which only a foreigner like Stanley Tobarski would know about. In truth, Ralph was a mix of mastiff and Great Dane, with the temperament of a cobra and a weakness for children.

Anyone under thirteen was safe with Ralph. They could ride on his back, pull his ears, even tie ribbons in his spiked collar for the Whit Walks. But – as though by magic – the dog knew when a child reached its teens. It had then entered the adult world, and was fair game. But whilst they were kids, Ralph was a priceless companion. For one thing, no one bullied a child when he was around, and when the Clark kids took him to the Flat Iron Market, it was amazing how many treats the barkers and stall owners handed out as bribery.

'Git 'im away from m' bloody stall, will yer? I'm losing trade 'ere.'

And now Betty was watching Ralph walking down the

street next to Girton as he pushed his baby brother, Arthur, out in his pram.

'How far's that lad of yours going?'

'Oh, Mam, stop fussing!' Gloria replied, getting up and taking some laundry off the rack.

Folding the bed sheets, she glanced over to the old sofa where Helen was sleeping, then studied Suzannah, back home from school and doing her homework on the kitchen table. She did seem better, her colour a little restored, but when she coughed suddenly, Gloria winced and moved over to her.

'How are you feeling? How's my favourite darling?'

'I'm OK,' Suzannah replied, looking up at her mother.

'Maybe you went back to school too soon . . . You're still coughing.'

'Not that much, Mum.'

Noticing with relief that her own mother had fallen asleep, Gloria sat down next to Suzannah at the kitchen table. As ever, Gloria was surprised at her daughter's strong features, so different from her own.

'How's school, sweetheart?'

'All right.'

'Did you miss your friends when you were off last week?'

'Nah,' Suzannah replied, smiling. 'I like being home with you.'

Nudging her with her elbow, Gloria asked: 'Have you nearly finished your homework?'

'Only got Scripture to do. Can you test me?'

'Test you, love? What for?'

'It's about Moses . . .'

Smiling, Gloria closed the notebook. 'Do it later. Come and sit with me for a while, Suzie. Come on.'

Her daughter didn't need asking twice. Delighted, she sat down on the old settee, Gloria's arm around her. They had always been close, a special bond between them.

'Did I ever tell you about when your father and I met? How he threw soot at me and ruined my dress?'

Suzannah had heard the story a hundred times, but loved it. 'He wrecked your hair ribbon too.'

Gloria nodded. 'I was covered in dirt from head to toe.' She glanced over at the sleeping Betty. 'I could imagine what Mum would have said if she'd seen me like that. She'd worked a whole extra shift for Denny Cathcart to pay for that ribbon.'

'Was he handsome?'

'Denny Cathcart?' Gloria teased her daughter, knowing full well who she meant.

'No, *Dad*!'

'He was very . . . fine,' Gloria replied proudly. 'Mind you, not a tailor then. Not a professional man. But I always knew he'd do well. Your father's worked hard all his life. Never betted on the horses, never been drunk, never so much as looked at another woman. A bit short-tempered at times, true. But that's his way. He's always loved me, though. Always.' She looked down at Suzannah. 'That's what you have to find when you're older. A good, hard-working man who'll do right by you.'

'A tailor.'

'Maybe. Aye, you could marry a tailor.'

'I could *be* a tailor.'

Laughing, Gloria hugged her daughter. It was true that Suzannah loved to spend time in the workshop with Jacob. After all, she had grown up watching Stanley and her father tailoring; it wasn't surprising that she should have an interest. Gloria thought back to the present her daughter had made her last Christmas. An exquisite little waistcoat created from silk offcuts from the Flat Iron Market. Almost perfect, hand-stitched. Incredible for a child – even a tailor's child.

But tailoring wasn't a life for a woman.

'You can't be a tailor, sweetheart. That's men's work.'

'Why?'

A sudden stirring from Betty stopped the conversation in mid-flow. Waking up, she sat upright, rubbed her eyes

56

and looked round. She was beginning to itch for a drink. Visiting her grandchildren was all well and good, but Gloria didn't need her help and – if the truth be known – resented any interference. And the idea of a nice glass of stout listening to Denny Cathcart's old radio was rapidly becoming irresistible.

'I should be off.'

'In a minute, Mam. You heard about the Halls?'

'What about them?' Betty asked, curious.

'Did a midnight flit. Packed up and off, Tuesday last. God, it makes you think.'

It did more than make you think, Gloria realised. It was just one more example of the frailty of Hanky Park lives. And now there were rumours, rumblings about a war. There *couldn't* be, could there? Not so many lives lost, so much hardship, when life was hard enough. Thank God she had a good husband with a profession and money coming in. Not much, but enough. Absent-mindedly, Gloria tightened her grip on Suzannah. If only she could make sure that nothing ever happened to *her* family. If only Stanley would get that will drawn up, so that it was set in writing that the shop would come to them. She knew he *meant* to do it, but something always got in the way – and however much it preyed on Gloria's mind, she didn't dare mention it to Jacob again.

But the Halls' flitting had unsettled Gloria more than a little. People stealing away in the early hours of the morning, with what they could pile on to a cart, quitting their home and their bills. Sometimes they fetched up in another part of Hanky Park, sometimes in the poorhouse, where you only went if you were desperate – or too afraid to throw yourself into the canal. No one knew when his or her luck would run out. One minute on the up, the next in the midden. Even some of the most unlikely people had ended up without money to pay Gerry Fitt.

Gloria winced. The rent man was even nastier after his stump had become infected. Nowadays he was in no mood to do anyone a favour, and the stomping of his peculiar gait echoed eerily down the Hanky Park ginnels. The news that Denny Cathcart was now employing Fitt was also causing many sleepless nights; people owing money to Cathcart for betting debts dreading the knock on the door.

Unsettled, Gloria stood up and glanced out of the window. Down the street a couple of carters' horses were bringing in the third load of the day, their breath blowing vapour into the cold afternoon. Leaning forward, she peered into the rapidly darkening day. A fog was starting up. Damn it, Gloria thought, she hated fogs. And there were so many accidents when the weather turned. Only last winter Amy Davies got hit by a tram on Broad Street. The driver swore blind he hadn't seen her until she was only inches away. And everyone believed him. Like they said, Amy Davies might be a vicious old gossip, but not worth running over.

Gloria kept staring out of the window. If the fog *really* set in, her mother would be staying for the night. And no beer in the house . . .

'Girton should be back any time now.'

Noticing the anxiety in her mother's voice, Suzannah glanced up. 'Shall I go down the end of the street and look for them, Mum?'

'No, stay indoors, love.'

'This smog's no good for a baby's lungs,' Betty said.

At once, Gloria overreacted. 'Oh, stop panicking, Mam! Ralph's with them, and you'll wake Helen up if you keep going on.'

'But what if the fog sets in?' Betty went on annoyingly. 'Honestly, Gloria, I think I should go and look for the lad—'

As if on cue, Girton walked in. He was smiling, his nose glowing with cold as he pushed the old pram into the kitchen, the dog immediately moving over to the fire. Wrapped up in its nest of blankets, the baby was fast asleep.

Relieved, Gloria looked at her mother.

'You see, both of them safe and sound.' She turned to Girton, kissing him on the cheek. 'You're a good lad to come home before the fog got bad. Baby good, was he?' She peered into the pram, her unease evaporating. 'Honestly, I don't know why I ask. Sleep through anything, this one would. You could set off a firecracker next to Arthur and he'd not even wince.'

But then suddenly Suzannah began to cough: deep, racking coughs which left her gasping. Snatching a breath, she tried to control the spasm, but began coughing again, this time more deeply. Alarmed, Gloria hurried over to her. She could see that her daughter was struggling to breathe and turned to Betty.

'Get the doctor! Now!'

As her mother hurried out, Gloria held on to her daughter, Suzannah leaning against her shoulder, exhausted. She was white-faced, drained of colour, her lips bloodless. And as she breathed, she wheezed, her chest rising and falling with effort. Laying her down on the sofa, Gloria banked up the fire and turned to Girton.

'Get the blankets off her bed, and hurry!' Tenderly she stroked Suzannah's forehead. It was clammy with sweat. 'You'll be all right, love, you'll be all right,' she soothed her. 'Your mum's here. I won't let anything happen to you.'

Anxiously, Gloria glanced over to the clock. How long would the doctor be? And hadn't he said only the other day that Suzannah was OK? Taking the blankets from Girton when he came back downstairs, Gloria tucked them around her daughter, holding Suzannah's hand tightly as she began to cough again. Jesus, Gloria thought desperately, she was getting worse. Coughing as though her lungs would burst.

'Is she going to be OK?' Girton asked, terrified.

Gloria nodded, holding Suzannah to her as the coughing subsided. 'She'll be fine, Girton. The doctor will give her something to make her better . . . Go to the door and look for him, will you?'

It *would* happen when Jacob was away, Gloria thought helplessly. He'd gone over to Liverpool for some new material. Why today, of all days? And hadn't she told him that she was worried about Suzannah? Why hadn't she listened to her? Laying her hand on her daughter's forehead again, Gloria felt the cold clamminess and her heart speeded up. *God, don't let anything happen to this child, please God, not Suzannah . . .*

'He's coming! Doctor's coming!' Girton called out suddenly, watching as Dr Grover hurried into the kitchen and opened his bag. Taking out a stethoscope, he listened to Suzannah's chest, tapped her back and then looked over to Gloria. 'Bronchitis.'

'I thought you said she was better. I'd have kept her off school longer if I'd known.'

He shrugged. 'She *was* better the other day. It's just been so cold, and what with all the fogs. And it's not the first time your daughter's had bronchitis, is it?'

'I look after her as best I can . . .'

'Of course you do, Mrs Clark. Some kids just have a weakness, that's all.' He wrote out a prescription and passed it to Gloria. 'Keep Suzannah home and warm, at a constant temperature. She should start to pick up.'

'But she's coughing so much.'

'Give her the linctus, that'll help,' Dr Grover replied reassuringly. 'She's a strong girl, she'll get over it. But she must be kept very warm and quiet, or it could get worse.'

Gloria looked up at him. 'Worse? How?'

'It could develop into pneumonia,' he replied, putting his stethoscope back into his bag. 'But try not to dwell on that. We'll just take a day at a time, all right? Just one day at a time.'

ELEVEN

In the days that followed, Suzannah lay on the sofa in the kitchen by the fire. The fogs came curling around Hanky Park, a thousand Peeping Toms at as many windows. Despite Dr Grover's best hopes, her bronchitis worsened, and within forty-eight hours she had developed pneumonia. Too ill to move, or hospitalise, she was kept on the sofa. Exhausted, she was no longer coughing, but silent, sweating and sleeping fitfully. As the third day passed, her temperature rose, suddenly and dangerously. And then she fell into a deep, unresponsive sleep.

'You have to rest,' Jacob told his wife.

But Gloria wasn't moving. 'I'll stay with her.'

'You have to get some sleep.'

She turned, took his hand and squeezed it. 'I have to stay here. I *have* to stay with her.'

Unable to concentrate on his tailoring, Jacob would pause, standing at the door of the workshop, watching his wife and child. The optimistic, cheerful Gloria had altered; she was now quiet, calm and very removed from him. Her attention was on their child . . . Repeatedly people came to the tailor's shop to give advice. Mrs Broadbent left a note about some old wives' remedy, and all the other neighbours and shopkeepers to whom Gloria had shown kindness tried to help out. Food was made and left by the back door. Even a half-bottle of whisky from Bert Gallager. And fruit – always an expensive luxury – was brought to tempt the sick child. Every thoughtful deed that Gloria had ever undertaken was suddenly being repaid, with interest.

61

People knew only too well how many children died from pneumonia. In a bad winter families lost sons, daughters and newborns – who were always most at risk. No one benefited from the fogs like the undertakers, Carshaw's on Broad Street doing a brisk trade from November to March. And the Clark family – having been considered so lucky for so long – were suddenly under threat. Because of that, they belonged more than they had ever done before. Their distress had made them accessible; *real* Hanky Parkers. They were struggling and everyone understood that. People who had considered Jacob to have led a somewhat charmed life saw that fate could be as vicious with him as it was with everyone else. And they sympathised.

Not one day passed without a letter being left, or someone offering help. Not one hour was empty of good wishes and thoughts; even the men on Unwin Street talking about Jacob's sick little girl. And whilst Gloria and Jacob kept watch, so did everyone else in the surrounding streets.

After all, the Clarks were one of them.

She was falling, Suzannah thought. No, not falling. In her delirium she could hear her mother talking and then sense her father leaning over her. But she couldn't talk and didn't want to. Everything seemed so limp, so odd, her chest bleeding inside as though it had been scraped with a hundred razor blades. In her fever she heard the sounds of Ralph's breathing and the far-off noise of the baby crying.

What baby? Oh yes, Suzannah thought, Arthur, her brother. The new baby . . . She wanted to see Girton then, but couldn't open her eyes. Couldn't move, just hear the quiet sound of the fire crackling close by and feel the weight of blankets pushing her deeper and deeper into the old sofa. But inside her head everything was *very* loud. The clock banged the hours and in the distance the sound of the carters' horses tracked noisily through her dreams. She imagined she could even hear her father chalking up the suiting, and then – far off – the screaming of the cattle from the abattoir yard.

Day slipped into night, into day again. She burned, then shivered, every part of her body either overheated or feeling that it had been rubbed with snow. One time she was convinced she had been pushed into the outside water butt, the ice closing over her head as the lid slammed down.

Fever and delirium took her up into the clouds where the abattoir cattle stampeded and the carters' horses fell off the end of the world.

A child doesn't know about dying, but Suzannah knew enough to be afraid. Knew enough to recognise the helplessness in her mother's voice and the pleading prayers of her father in the small hours.

Waiting until he was sure his mother was asleep, Girton crept on to the sofa and lay beside his sister. He could feel the burning heat of Suzannah's skin through the blankets and counted her laboured breaths. One, two, three ... Closing his eyes, Girton willed her to wake up, then opened them again and looked at her. She hadn't moved.

He had a child's belief that wishing made things so; and Girton wished and *kept* wishing throughout those early-morning hours. Dr Grover had said that Suzannah might die – oh, they didn't know that he had overheard the conversation, but he had. And Girton wasn't going to let his sister die. He would lie next to her and *make* her live, give her his breaths in return for the scratching ones in her own lungs. His eyes closed again, his breathing regular; willing Suzannah to breathe with him. Hadn't Dr Grover said that this was the worst time? This was the *crisis*? Girton didn't understand what a crisis was, but he knew that if Suzannah didn't wake up that day, she never would.

One, two, three ... Girton opened his eyes. Suzannah hadn't moved, her eyelids bluish, closed, her lips bloodless.

One, two, three . . . Girton counted again. Come on, come on, breathe . . . His gaze moved to his mother, for once asleep in the chair, her head leaning awkwardly over to one side, her hand closed tight over her daughter's. This was the crisis, Girton thought helplessly, *this was the crisis* . . .

For another twenty minutes Girton kept watch. And counted. The dawn began its slow stumble into morning, the knocker-up man tapping on the pub windows. On the kitchen table Girton saw the fruit piled up and longed to eat some of the full-bellied grapes, but resisted. They were Suzannah's. If he stole from her, she would never get well. And if she didn't recover there would be no more games with her, no more teasing, no more big sister who always – *always* – stood up for him. Again Girton began to count, his eyelids drooping, tiredness almost overwhelming him.

Then, as he fell asleep against his sister's shoulder, Suzannah stirred. Her lips parting, she gasped, her lungs suddenly contracting violently, her hands opening and closing frantically in the silent air.

TWELVE

Not all prayers are answered. At least that was what Jacob told himself the following month. But against all the odds, Suzannah had recovered. That terrifying crisis had come and passed; she had held on, come through it. She was alive. He smiled to himself, aching with relief. So what else really mattered? He would keep his own problem a secret; work it out for himself, somehow. No one needed to know for a while, if he was lucky.

Like he said, not all prayers are answered.

But when the time *did* come, what the hell was he going to do? It would be hard for anyone to lose their sight, but for a tailor, it was a disaster. Jacob stared into the distance. He had found out only that morning. After telling Stanley and Gloria that he was off to buy some worsted, he had gone to Hope Hospital instead. Waited amongst the coughing kids and a couple of old women bundled into shawls. They had never spoken, had just stared ahead, lean-faced, their hands knotted at the knuckles with long hard work.

When Jacob's turn finally came, the eye specialist – whose name he hadn't caught – examined him. Put a patch over one eye and asked Jacob to read the letters on the board. Then he'd put the patch over the other eye and repeated the command. Jacob had done as he was told, hardly able to make out a letter without his glasses. So what? he'd told himself. He'd always been short-sighted.

'I'll just have a look at the back of your eyes now, Mr Cork—'

'Clark,' Jacob had corrected him. 'It's Clark.'

It had made no difference; the specialist had just carried on. Probably some well-off doctor from out Eccles way, someone who had been drafted in to do his duty for the rabble of Hanky Park.

'You said you thought your eyes were getting worse?'

'Suddenly, like.'

Again the doctor had looked at the back of Jacob's eyes. Very carefully. Then he had turned up the lights. In silence, he had written some notes down in a file and then he had paused, tapping his front teeth with the top of his pen.

'It's not good news, I'm afraid.'

Automatically Jacob had put his glasses back on. Outside the window he could see the high roof of the timber mill, and a little further away the chimney of the cotton mill, exhaling smoke into the chilled air.

'Mr Clark? Did you hear what I said?'

Jacob hadn't wanted to hear the next words. In fact, he had wanted to get up and leave – but that would have been disrespectful.

So instead he had nodded. 'I heard you. How bad is it?'

'In the end, you'll go blind.'

The smoke had stopped coming out of the cotton mill chimney. Jacob prayed that it would start again. If it did, it was an omen to tell him that the doctor was wrong.

But the chimney had stayed unsmoking.

'Blind?'

'I'm afraid so.'

Jacob hadn't been able to take it in. 'Why?'

'Your sight's deteriorating—'

'But why *now*?' Jacob had pressed him. 'I've always been short-sighted; why would it suddenly get worse?'

'There's been some infection at the back of your eyes. Something which has damaged them permanently. We can't correct it.'

'What about drops? Tablets?' Jacob had said, desperation coming thick and fast. 'Cream – what about some cream, ointment?'

'I'm so sorry, but we can't save your sight.'

He had shaken his head. 'You said "in the end". I'll go blind in the end . . . How long have I got?'

'It might take a year, or twenty, if you're lucky . . .'

'Lucky,' Jacob had repeated dully.

'No one can predict exactly.'

'I'm only in my twenties! I've got a wife and family . . .'

The doctor had been trying his best. 'As I say, you may keep your sight for another twenty years—'

'I'll only be in my forties then!' Jacob had snapped. 'I've kids to feed and raise. A wife who needs the best. I've got prospects . . .' He'd paused then, trying to fight panic, his voice wavering. 'I married the best-looking girl in Hanky Park and I'm going to inherit a business one day. I'm going to be the best tailor in Salford . . .' To his shame, he found his hands shaking. 'How can I be a tailor if I can't see?'

'Mr Clark, there are other occupations—'

Jacob had got to his feet in that instant. Anger had temporarily replaced hopelessness.

'Making baskets? Like the other blind men? What kind of a wage will that bring in, hey? How many bloody baskets do people want in Hanky Park?'

'Mr Clark—'

'I see you got my bloody name right this time!' Jacob had replied. 'Yes, I'm Jacob Clark, tailor. That's who I am. That's *all* I am . . . We nearly lost our little girl. Did I tell you that?' He shook his head. 'No, of course not. I prayed so hard for her to live, said I'd do anything, give anything—'

'This isn't due to some bargain you made with God.'

'I didn't say it was!' Jacob replied, his tone brusque. 'But we'd been so lucky for so long, it couldn't have lasted. Something happened. I don't know what, but something. Our lives altered, we changed, and now suddenly nothing will ever be the same again.'

It had been a strange afternoon, the light halfway between daylight and the brewing fog. And as Jacob had made his way home he had tried – with every step – to adjust to the news. *It might take a year* – he'd stopped, gasping – *but it might take twenty years* . . . His heart rate slowed. Twenty years would be bad, but not too bad. His son would be twenty-five; he could easily have taught Girton the rudiments of tailoring by then. Perhaps bring in another pair of hands to help the lad whilst he learnt.

Who was he kidding? Jacob thought, distracted. There wasn't enough money to bring in anyone else. Not now, and if things continued the way they were going, certainly not in five, ten or twenty years. In twenty years' time he would be lucky if he still had the tailor's shop. Oh Christ, Jacob had thought despairingly, as he leaned against a wall, why hadn't he listened to Gloria? Why hadn't he encouraged Stanley to make his will in their favour? He had a family, a wife and four kids to feed – and he was going blind.

The reality of his situation made Jacob tremble. Even if he *had* made a will, Stanley could easily change it when he knew Jacob's situation. After all, even Stanley could hardly leave his shop to a blind man. Jesus, Jacob thought suddenly. Would Gloria stay with a cripple? And his kids – how could he give them an education, feed them, clothe them, keep them out of the coal carting and the mills?

It was hard enough for a *normal* man to keep himself and his family out of the Hanky Park gutter. Hard enough to make a decent life. To stay ahead of Gerry Fitt and the poorhouse. It was hard for a strong man with all his wits about him.

So what bloody chance did a blind man stand?

THIRTEEN

Gloria was sitting in front of the kitchen fire, rocking Helen. The anxiety over Suzannah had passed; she was back to herself, a neighbour just leaving after a long chat. One thing her daughter's illness had taught Gloria was how to value what you had. And know how quickly it could be taken from you. God knows she had plenty to be grateful for. Catching Stanley's eye in the door of the workshop, Gloria smiled. The old man had been so concerned; everyone had. Strange how it took a crisis to show how much you mattered to people.

In a little while she would get up and make tea, but not just yet. Gloria sighed with relief. They had survived, they were all together; life was good. Whatever happened now, they could cope. She would tell Jacob that later. Curl up with him and fuss him. After all, she hadn't been herself for a while, worrying so much, maybe even neglecting him a little . . . But no more, Gloria thought. Tonight she would hold her husband in bed and make him laugh. Make love to him; celebrate their victory over fate.

The sky overhead was caught suddenly in sunshine. Odd winter sunshine, without warmth, bleaching the colours out of the terraces. Almost in monochrome, the coal carters began their dinner run up the street, the carts three in a row, on the last jobs of the day. When they'd finished this delivery they would take the horses back to

Hardy Street, clean them and then bed them down for the night.

Slowly the horses lumbered on, the unexpected sunshine dipping back behind the winter clouds, a gust of wind bringing in a violent shower. Shielding his eyes, Girton looked down the road. He was already wet; about to make his way home, the big dog walking beside the pram as he retraced his steps. He was due for a telling-off, and he knew it. Hadn't he sneaked off, determined to do what he wanted, and ignored Suzannah?

He could see his sister now, head down over the work table in the back of the shop, her shoes kicked off, as they always were when she was concentrating. Back to full health, full colour, full life.

'It's not your turn today. *I'm* taking Arthur out,' she'd said, pulling a face at him. 'Leave him alone, Girton. It's my go.'

'But—'

'It's my turn!' she'd repeated. 'Aw, come on, you can't hog him all the time. I've hardly had a minute with him today.' She had laid down her scissors and winked at Girton. 'Tell you what, just give me another ten minutes and we'll both go. How's that?'

It was perfectly reasonable, but Girton had become very possessive of the baby. So he'd waited until Suzannah was preoccupied again and then sneaked out with Arthur in the pram and Ralph lumbering beside them.

What Girton hadn't counted on was the sudden rain storm. He looked anxiously into the pram. The baby would be soaked, he thought uneasily, quickening his steps for home. His dad would have a thing or two to say about it too. Maybe, if he rushed, Girton thought hopefully, he could get back before they'd even noticed he'd gone.

But someone had already noticed. Calling out for Girton, Suzannah realised at once that he'd left alone and snatched up her coat, heading for the end of Hankerton Street. The rain storm caught her unexpectedly, and she wiped the water from her face and peered down the misty street.

Finally she saw them: Girton hurrying home, the huge, water-soaked carters' horses coming up quick behind him. Cupping her hands around her mouth, Suzannah called out to warn him, but Girton couldn't hear, just kept walking with his head down against the driving rain.

And then suddenly one of the horses shied, the animal strapped beside it in their shared harness losing its footing and slipping on the greasy street. Turning, Girton ducked as the first horse reared up, overturning the cart, the coal man flung under the oncoming hoofs of the second cart's horses.

Only yards away, Suzannah began to run. She was so intent on the noise, the whinnying, the screaming of the horses and the men, that she didn't notice the pram at first. *The pram which was buckled under the overturned cart.*

Still running, she began to scream, watching Ralph crushed under the fallen horse as one of the carters tried to beat the animal to its feet. But no one had noticed the children . . . God, she screamed inwardly, didn't they see the pram? *Didn't anyone see the pram?*

Hysterically, she began shouting, passers-by staring at her as she pointed desperately ahead. And then suddenly Suzannah saw the fallen horse struggle back to its feet, taking the cart up with it. As it rose she could see underneath. See the pram. And her brothers.

On the floor lay Girton, his arms wrapped protectively around the baby, blood running over the cobbles and under the horses' hoofs.

My mother was told the news and collapsed.

The doctor was sent for, but all I remember is someone carrying Girton into the kitchen and putting him down on the old settee. The dead baby I'd wrapped up and carried home in my school coat. Watermarked with rain.

Someone took him from me, but I don't remember who.

But I do remember – will never forget – how the injured horse screamed so eerily. For minutes it screamed in the street outside whilst my mother screamed indoors, the sound reverberating around the house. Outside I saw people running past on the street, and a little while later heard the loud crack of a gunshot. Then silence. The horse was quiet.

Only my mother was still screaming.

FOURTEEN

Dead-eyed, Gloria stared up at the ceiling. She had been sedated by Dr Grover over forty-eight hours earlier, but still she couldn't sleep. Below, she could hear the muffled sounds of voices – but louder voices in her head. *You shouldn't let that lad of yours take the baby out . . . he's too young . . . You expect too much from Girton and Suzannah . . . They're only children.*

It was all her fault, Gloria realised. She had been a bad mother. After all her loving and caring for Suzannah, she had failed in the end. Not fit to have children. Not fit to raise a family. Indirectly, she had killed her own child . . . Her eyes closed, her temples pounding, nausea burning in her stomach.

All she had ever wanted was to be a wife and mother. She had had it all. A good husband, wonderful children, a place in life. *The tailor's wife* . . . And she'd thrown it away, been careless with the very things that mattered to her most. An image of Suzannah came back to her, carrying the dead baby wrapped in her school coat. And Girton, brought home unconscious.

Lucky he wasn't killed too, they'd said. But if he hadn't taken the baby out, if he'd waited for Suzannah to go with him . . . Gloria opened her eyes, dry from weeping. It wasn't their fault, it was hers. Jacob had said as much. In the first shock of Arthur's death, when he had struck out blindly.

Why didn't you stop him? Why didn't you stop Girton going out with Arthur? But she'd been rocking Helen in the back room and hadn't seen Girton leave. She had four children; you couldn't keep your eye on them all. Not all the time. And who would have believed such a tragedy would happen? After Suzannah nearly dying? *Who would have believed it?* Jesus, Christ in Heaven, Gloria raged, wasn't there a God? Wasn't there any justice?

She hadn't been a bad person, she hadn't done anyone a wrong turn. She had just loved her children, all of her four children . . . *Her four children.* But now she had only three. One injured, one traumatised. Gloria turned over, pressing her face into the pillow. She couldn't bear to look at Suzannah. Her beloved daughter. And worst of all, she couldn't, *wouldn't*, attend to Girton.

Unable to accept her own guilt, Gloria's shattered mind had found a scapegoat in her son. Her own crime of carelessness was too much for her to accept, and coming on top of Suzannah's illness she couldn't take it. The blame had to be shifted elsewhere. And so it fell on Girton. *He* had taken the baby out; *he* had been careless; *he* had caused Arthur's death.

It was all his fault.

Carefully Suzannah made tea for her father. He was in the workshop, staring at the cloth on the table, Stanley sitting silently beside him. When Jacob saw his daughter he smiled distantly, putting his glasses back on.

He had to get control of himself, take over. His little girl was nursing them all. His little Suzannah . . . Taking the offered tea, Jacob watched his daughter tidy the workroom table. Her eyes were red from crying, but she wouldn't stop working. It was Suzannah who had helped her father make food for the family; Suzannah who had fed Helen and changed her clothes; Suzannah who had repeatedly taken drinks up to her mother. And brought them down, untouched. And it was Suzannah who had sat with Girton, changing the bandage on his cut leg, following the instructions the doctor had given her.

'Let me help,' Stanley said suddenly. 'You do too much, little one.'

'I can manage,' Suzannah replied, moving towards the stairwell.

She knew that later her grandmother would call round again; knew Betty would sit with Gloria and try to elicit some response. But she would fail. Gloria wasn't talking to anyone. And besides, Nan Siddons was no help, too shocked to be of any practical good. There had been talk of someone calling Sara back from Hull, but she was a semi-invalid now with arthritis, in too much pain to travel.

Carefully Suzannah carried the tea upstairs and moved to the side of Gloria's bed. Her mother was in her day clothes, hadn't changed since Arthur's death, and she was motionless.

'Mum,' Suzannah whispered, 'have a drink, Mum. It'll do you good.'

There was no response. No smile, no reaching out, no embrace. The mother Suzannah had adored had been turned off, some remote stranger in her place. Afraid, Suzannah slid on to the bed beside Gloria, laying her head against her mother's cheek. It was her fault, Suzannah realised; if only she had left the workroom, gone with Girton when he'd asked her ... But she hadn't, she had made her little brother wait, too busy with cutting up some stupid cloth. And so Girton had left without her. And now Arthur was dead.

But worse for Suzannah was the fact that she realised Girton was being blamed. Their mother would never have ignored her son before, and certainly not when he was injured and needed her. And then Suzannah remembered the look on her mother's face when she had finally stopped screaming.

Gloria had turned round, staring at her family, at her husband and then at Girton, and something – Suzannah didn't know what – stirred inside her mother. She realised it, and Girton did too. Gloria looked at her son – and it was in her expression, her eyes, it shimmered on the very air only for an instant – but it was enough.

Trying to dispel the memory, Suzannah touched her mother's face. 'Mum? Can you hear me?'

Desperate, she longed for Gloria to rally, to hold her, to soothe her as she had done all her life. But she didn't move, didn't show any sign of life. This Gloria wasn't talking to her daughter, her son, or anyone. This Gloria was terrifying.

'Mum, I'm sorry, I'm so sorry. It wasn't Girton's fault, it was mine. I should have taken Arthur out ...' She reached for Gloria's hand and squeezed it, but it was cool and unresponsive. 'Please, Mum, please, don't blame him ... Don't blame Girton.' She was begging and crying. 'Mum! Talk to me. Talk to me ... *please.*'

But Gloria stayed silent.

The funeral of Arthur Clark took place four days later, most of the Hanky Park residents turning out and lining the streets to watch the tiny coffin being carried from the tailor's shop and laid in the hearse. Bad luck, the neighbours said, was like a pit fall; once it started, nothing could stop it. And the Clarks had had more than their fair share now.

Holding his wife upright, Jacob supported Gloria, Suzannah following with Girton. Helen had been left with Nan Siddons, taken to Rivaldi Street so that she wouldn't see the dismal, haunting spectacle of her brother's funeral.

But Girton and Suzannah saw it. They went with their parents to the church and then the graveside. They saw the little coffin laid in the cool northern earth and watched their mother, blank-faced, with Jacob crying silently beside her.

Suzannah held tightly to her brother's hand as though she was scared to let go of him. The family, which had been so happy, so unified, was now inexorably divided. Mother and father. Daughter and son. Together, yet apart. Helplessly, Suzannah squeezed Girton's hand. He squeezed back as though his life depended on it. But he never took his eyes off his mother's face.

By contrast Gloria focused on nothing. And after the burial she even shook off Jacob's helping hand and walked on alone. She turned only once. And no one who saw it would ever forget the long, hostile stare she fixed on Girton before, finally, moving on.

Still holding her brother's hand, Suzannah could feel Girton's grasp tighten and his body begin to shake. All the enormity of Arthur's death had been laid to rest. On him.

FIFTEEN

Stanley couldn't sleep. Finally, exasperated, he got up in his flat on Vera Street and decided to walk over to the tailor's shop. There must be something he could do there. Help Jacob, even make breakfast for the kids. After all, Gloria still wasn't functioning properly.

Like everyone else, Stanley had hoped that she would rally, but Gloria's depression had deepened as the year passed. She spoke occasionally, but it was always about Arthur, and to everyone's amazement, she ignored her surviving children.

It wasn't really Gloria, Stanley told Jacob, it wasn't *their* Gloria. She was ill. She was still in shock. She was— Stanley turned the corner of Hankerton Street and stopped dead. The door of the tailor's shop was wide open. Surprised, he hurried in and looked round. No sign of an intruder, thank God. But who would have left the door open like this? And on such a cold morning?

He moved in further. No fire lit in the kitchen, no kettle on to boil. Well, Stanley reassured himself, it *was* very early. But then the shop door had been opened, so someone was up and about. Still anxious, he moved into the back room and stopped. All over the floor were torn-up photographs, of the children, the shop, and Gloria and Jacob's wedding.

Startled, Stanley jumped as the door into the kitchen opened, Jacob staring at him incredulously.

'Stanley!'

'I didn't do it! Not me, not me,' he said immediately. 'I

just walked in. The shop door was open, Jacob, wide open.'

'Where's Gloria?' Jacob asked, looking round anxiously.

'I don't know . . .'

'But she came down a while ago. I heard her.' Frowning, Jacob glanced back at the ripped photographs, then hurriedly ran upstairs. A moment later he returned to the kitchen, his face waxen. 'Her coat's gone, and some money we had hidden away.'

'Jacob, calm yourself—'

'She's gone!' Jacob said desperately. 'I thought she might do something like this.'

'She might just have gone for a walk.'

'You know that's not likely!' Jacob snapped. 'She's not in her right mind. She could kill herself.'

'Maybe I should call the police? A doctor?'

'Just stay with the children,' Jacob replied urgently. 'I have to go. I *have* to find her!'

The news was all over Hanky Park: the tailor's wife had done a runner. Upped and gone, with not a word to anyone. Poor Gloria. Poor soul, it had all been too much for her. No woman could cope with all that grief. With all that bloody awful luck. Poor Gloria, poor kids . . .

'What are yer talking about!' Mrs Bradshaw snorted to the small knot of gossips. 'I only saw Gloria yesterday. And I'm the Clarks' neighbour, I should know.'

'Oh, she's gone all right. Yer don't want to sleep in so long. Yer miss things that way,' another woman said. 'Left in the middle of the night. Mind you, poor Gloria were never the same since that little lad of hers were killed.'

Mrs Bradshaw pulled a face. 'That were over a year ago.'

'A year ago or not,' another, kinder woman countered, 'Gloria Clark's been going downhill steady.'

'Maybe she ran off with another man?' someone said excitedly.

'Don't be ridiculous! The poor girl's been heading for a breakdown for months. It was bad enough thinking she were going to lose Suzannah – but then the accident happening afterwards . . . Anyone with eyes in their head could see she were nearly driven mad with grief. Shame, nice young mother like her. It's sad, but she just went' – the woman tapped her own forehead – 'a bit odd up there.'

'They'll go and look for her?'

'Course they will!'

'And they'll find her, surely?'

The woman shrugged. 'I hope so, for Gloria's sake.'

'Well, it's her husband I feel sorry for,' an older woman intoned. 'Left high and dry with three kiddies. He'll not get over his wife running off, those two are devoted.'

'*Were* devoted,' Mrs Bradshaw corrected her. 'But now it looks like Hankerton Street's lost its tailor's wife.'

SIXTEEN

Enlisting the help of the police, Jacob Clark searched for his missing wife. They checked the hospitals and the morgues, they put up posters and asked for public assistance, and Jacob offered a substantial reward for any news of Gloria Clark, the tailor's wife. It was a tragedy, but war had just broken out and there were so many other tragedies, so many other disrupted lives, and before long Gloria Clark's disappearance was old news. People might be sympathetic, but they had more pressing worries. Day by day the young men began to volunteer for active service, the women facing the unpalatable truth – life without their husbands, lovers, brothers, sons. Struggling even more to make ends meet, waiting for news, dreading the sight of the telegraph boy coming towards their door. And the shortages: of food, clothing, coal. Wives and mothers knew only too well that they would have to take on work: the factories, munitions, iron foundries all needing manpower when the young men were gone. It was true that people had cared about Gloria Clark, but only so far. She might be dead – but then again, before long, they might be too.

But the rumours kept coming. Sightings of the tailor's wife on the canal side, late at night. Or up by the Tin Whistle pub, where the whores went . . . She was everywhere. Nowhere. And every time Jacob followed a lead, it wasn't her. No, no one had seen the *real* Gloria Clark. Or heard anything of her. Every lead was a dead end, every hope fizzled out to nothing, and by the end of six months

Jacob told his children that their mother was missing. Not dead, just missing.

Girton looked at him solemnly. ' 'Cos of me? What I did?'

'No, lad,' Jacob said kindly, 'not because of you.'

'She'll come back!' Suzannah said, her voice firm. 'She'll come back. Maybe she just wanted a holiday. She was always talking about us having a holiday. Going to Southport – maybe she went there for a bit. You know, until she got better.'

His voice faltering, Jacob looked at his daughter. 'Your mother's not been well for a long time, love. You know that. You know how I told you she wasn't herself? Well, she might—'

'She's not dead!' Suzannah snapped unexpectedly, taking Girton by the hand and looking him full in the face. '*Mum's not dead*.'

'It's 'cos of me.'

'It's *not* because of you, and she's *not* dead,' Suzannah replied, her face flushed.

'I didn't say she was dead,' Jacob interrupted her. 'We don't know where she is.'

'Well, I know she'll come back. We just have to find her . . .'

'Suzie, we've been looking everywhere.'

'So we *keep* looking,' she replied, close to tears.

'You have to know something,' Jacob said quietly. Maybe it was time to suggest another terrible possibility. 'I'm not saying anything for sure, sweetheart, but it's possible your mother might not come home—'

'I know Mum's alive! I *know* it,' Suzannah replied heatedly. 'She'll come back. You'll see, she'll come back and it'll all be like it was.' Hurriedly she moved over to the kettle, filled it, then placed it on the grate. 'We have to keep everything the same, Dad. Look after each other and then when she's well Mum can come back and it'll all be as it was. You just have to keep looking for her, Dad. *Please*, just keep looking.'

He would have done anyway, without his daughter's pleading. But time still passed without any trace of Gloria, and after another six months, Jacob was desperate. The police were losing interest; there was a war on – what was one missing woman in all the growing anxiety?

So he enlisted more unconventional help.

'I'll do anything to give you a hand,' Bert Gallager said. He had been a good friend to Jacob since Arthur's death. 'Just name it.'

'Your father—'

'The bastard.'

'Yeah, him,' Jacob said, smiling for the first time in months. 'I need his help. Pa Gallager knows everything that goes on around these parts, Bert. More than the police do. Your dad has contacts.'

'He's already been asking round for yer,' Bert replied, shaking his head. 'Nothing doing. He's had no leads on Gloria.'

'I just wondered . . .'

'I know,' Bert replied, 'but Pa won't give up. Yer know him. A right sod, but stubborn. If anyone gets to hear anything about Gloria, it'll be Dad. Unless he's back in jail, of course.'

Listening on the stairs, Suzannah was suddenly jabbed in the back by an elbow. Turning, she shushed Girton and jerked her head towards the kitchen.

'They're talking about Mum again.'

'Any news?' Girton asked anxiously.

'Nah, not today.'

He sighed, then dragged his sister to her feet and moved out into the street with her. Girton had grown fast, with a prodigious appetite and a quick brain. At eight, he was one of the top three in his class, Suzannah encouraging him repeatedly.

'Just think how smart you are. And how proud Mum will be of you,' she'd say. 'When she sees how well we're all doing, she'll *have* to come home.'

It was the mantra of their childhood, Suzannah keeping the dream alive. The dram that the old Gloria, the mother who had loved them so completely, would one day return. Yet if the truth were known, Girton didn't long for the return of his mother. What if the *hard* Gloria came back? The woman with the cold stare who blamed him for Arthur's death?

He didn't want *her* back. Didn't ever want to see *that* mother again.

'We could go to the park.'

'Nah,' Girton replied, glancing over to his sister. 'I don't feel like it.'

He had to hand it to Suzannah – she was amazing. Never complained about looking after him and Helen, and everyone knew that Helen could be downright cheeky. *He* wasn't cheeky, though. Didn't think there was anything to be cheeky about. Not since Arthur died.

In fact Girton didn't really think *anything* was important after his brother's death. For many months nightmares had broken his sleep, the scar on his leg reminding him of that terrible day. And when he heard the sound of the carters' horses coming down the street, he would clap his hands over his ears and shake.

He should have died too. How much easier that would have been. He would never have seen the results of his carelessness, never have had to watch the family fall apart. But he didn't die. He lived, and knew that he *had* been responsible, whatever Suzannah said. Or however much his father reassured him. His mother had told him the real truth – not in words, but in her eyes. She had embedded in her son the thought, which never left him, *You let me down. You failed.*

'I've been thinking,' Suzannah said suddenly, 'you could be a doctor, Girton.'

'I don't want to be a doctor!'

'You would look very handsome in a white coat.'

'Aw, go on!' he laughed, secretly delighted.

'What about a chemist then? You'd still get the coat.'

'I'd get a white coat working in the abattoir on Unwin Street.'

She pulled a face. 'Like Bert Gallager?'

'Why not? He's a nice enough bloke.'

'I know . . . But you're smarter than that, Girton. Don't sell yourself short.' She linked arms with him, walking along. '*I'd* love to be a tailor.'

He laughed. 'A tailor!'

'Why not? I could do it – if Dad taught me.'

'It's men's work.'

Suzannah pulled a face. 'Why should men get all the best jobs?'

' 'Cos we're men,' Girton replied grandly, then added, more quietly, 'I'm going to leave this place one day, Suzie. Get out for good.'

Surprised, Suzannah stopped walking and turned to him. 'You're just a kid—'

'I said *one day*,' he replied. 'Not now, but one day, I'll leave Hanky Park.'

For a moment she felt a wrenching sense of loss. 'You *can't* leave, Girton. What about when Mum comes back?'

He turned, old for his years, his expression solemn. 'If she *ever* comes back, Suzie, it won't be to see me.'

Before Suzannah could answer, Helen ran up behind them, swinging a bag Mrs Bradshaw had given her. Their neighbour, who hated everyone else in Hanky Park, loved Helen.

'What are you two talking about?'

'Going to the park,' Suzannah replied, looking at her sister. 'You've pulled your hem down again, Helen. Honestly, can't you keep anything nice?'

Helen wasn't listening. 'I got a magazine from Mrs Bradshaw today. All about the movie stars in Honeywood.'

'Hollywood,' Suzannah corrected her. 'It's called Hollywood.'

'Not in this book,' Helen replied smartly. She always

had to have the last word. 'Mrs Bradshaw thinks I'm pretty enough to be in pictures.'

'Yeah,' Girton said drily, 'you could play Frankenstein.'

Miffed, Helen fell into step beside her sister. 'That horrible man's at home.'

'Which man?'

'Pa Gallager.'

'Is he?' Suzannah countered, 'He wasn't there a couple of minutes ago.'

'Pa Gallager said that I'm like a ray of sunshine—'

Suzannah cut her short. 'Are you *sure* it was Pa Gallager and not Bert?'

'You could hardly mix them up,' Girton said sullenly, looking ahead and spotting a couple of his friends making for the waste ground. He waved to them hurriedly. 'I'm off for a game of footie, Suzannah. See you later.'

Enviously, she watched her brother run off, longing to join him. It was all right being a stand-in mother – in fact, Suzannah rather enjoyed it – but she was only a child herself and sometimes longed to act her age. Like now.

'Helen,' she said sweetly, 'will you do me a favour?'

'Depends. What is it?'

'Go and see Mrs Bradshaw, will you, and ask her to keep an eye on you for an hour. Until I come and pick you up.'

'Aw, but I wanted to go to the park.'

'I'll give you a thru'penny bit,' Suzannah said, holding out the coin.

It did the trick, Helen pocketing the money and turning to retrace her steps.

'And stay there until I come and get you, you hear me, Helen?' Suzannah called after her sister. 'I'll be back in an hour.'

It took Suzannah only moments to catch up with her brother. Girton was in a huddle with a group of his schoolfriends. Looking around her to check that no one was watching, Suzannah tucked the hem of her skirt into the legs of her knickers to turn them into makeshift shorts, and tied back her hair.

Then she called out: 'Could you use another player?'

The lads waved her over at once. Girton's sister was popular with the local boys. Not only could she cook, and mend the tears in their clothes before their mothers found out, but she was a right tomboy at times and could kick a mean ball.

'OK, lads, watch this,' she said, taking aim.

She felt good, the air cool on her cheeks and legs, and nothing to worry about for an hour. No cooking, no cleaning, no responsibility. Aware that she was being watched by a bevy of her admirers, Suzannah took aim again and then kicked the ball hard. Six pairs of eyes watched it rise up in the air, Suzannah whooping, Girton grinning as it soared upwards. And then dropped suddenly. They all froze as the ball disappeared into the street below. Then seven pairs of ears heard the sound of the bakery window being broken.

Everyone scattered, the boys running in all directions – but Suzannah made it home first.

SEVENTEEN

The following summer Girton was sent home from school. He was, the teacher said, getting unruly, his work suffering. An ever-protective father, Jacob went to the school, the female teachers all buzzing around him. He was single, wasn't he? And a tailor. Not a bad catch. Besides, although his eyesight had prevented Jacob from fighting, he was still a man. And men were thin on the ground in wartime.

'Not *really* single,' one of the teachers said. 'His wife left him three years ago.'

'And no sign of her since. I call that single,' another replied. 'If his wife had wanted to come home, she would have got back by now.'

Jacob didn't even notice the small flurry he was causing; his mind was on his son.

'You see,' Miss Butterworth explained, 'Girton is very easily led, and it would seem that he's fallen in with some rough boys.'

'I know all his schoolfriends,' Jacob replied. 'They're a good lot.'

'These boys aren't from the school. If I can speak plainly, they're the worst kind of Hanky Park ruffian. Girton was caught smoking—'

'Smoking! He's only a kid.'

'I know, Mr Clark, that's why we're concerned. And he's been playing truant.'

'Truant!'

She paused, looking at Girton's report. 'It's a shame; he

was doing very well, a bright lad. Everyone knows that the war's unsettling the children, but I wouldn't like to see Girton waste his life.'

Jacob shook his head. 'I don't understand. I know Arthur's death hit him hard, and his mother leaving . . .' He trailed off, embarrassed. 'But that was a few years ago. I thought he would have got over it by now. I hoped he had.'

Then he thought of Suzannah, always believing that Gloria would come home. And he remembered the advert he kept putting in the paper, every year on the anniversary of his wife's disappearance. How *could* Girton forget the past when it was so much in the present?

'I'll talk to him,' Jacob said firmly. 'Leave it with me, Miss Butterworth, I'll sort my son out.'

Biting the side of her fingernail anxiously, Suzannah waited at the tram stop at the end of Hankerton Street. When she finally saw her father approach, she could see that the news from the school hadn't been good.

'What's up?'

'Your brother's fooling around,' Jacob said simply, helping Suzannah on to the tram which had pulled in to the stop. Sighing, he sat down beside her. 'He's been smoking, and skiving off school.'

'He never!'

'He has,' Jacob replied, looking out of the tram window.

No young men on the street, and no end to the war in sight. He would have liked to enlist, like Bert, but no one would have him with his bad eyesight. And besides, he was needed at home by his children. Not that it appeared he was making too good a job of that.

'The teacher said that Arthur's death and your mum going off was still affecting Girton . . .' Jacob paused, taking a deep breath. 'Look, it's been three years now, Suzie. Maybe we *do* talk about your mum too much—'

'But we *have* to talk about her!' Suzannah replied, alarmed. 'When she comes back—'

'What if she doesn't?' Jacob asked, turning to his daughter. Only ten, and yet so capable. 'Perhaps it would be better if we *didn't* talk about it—'

'Dad!'

'Look, Suzie, I know you want your mother home. So do I, but we've heard nothing all these years. We've had no news, from anyone. If your mother had wanted to contact us, don't you think she would have got in touch?'

Suzannah's eyes were filling. 'She might be sick. Too ill to come home.'

'We've been to all the hospitals, we've checked them out, over and over again. We put the advert in the paper every year. I do what I can to find her—'

'You don't want Mum home!'

'Suzannah!' Jacob said disapprovingly. 'That's not true. I just have to think about the whole family. We can't have a proper future unless we let go of the past.'

Sullenly, his daughter turned away. She was crying, he knew that, but maybe it was kinder to curb her hopes now before she built her whole life around the dream of Gloria's return.

'I'm not giving up on your mother, sweetheart,' he said gently. 'I'm just asking you not to talk about her so much. We have to think about Girton now. Get him back on track. He listens to you, looks up to you. What you say counts.'

'As long as I don't talk about Mum,' Suzannah replied, her voice low.

'You can talk about her, of course . . . but not so much.'

Turning back to her father, Suzannah held his gaze. 'Do you think she'll *ever* come home?'

He paused, and in that pause she realised that even if Jacob hadn't given up on his wife, his hope was fading.

'Suzannah . . .'

She nodded, looking away. 'I know, Dad. I won't talk about Mum so much . . . And not to Girton at all.'

They made the rest of the journey to Manchester in silence, getting off at Davies Street, in the heart of the rag trade. Jacob could tell that Suzannah was upset, but he wouldn't back down. It *had* been a long time; maybe it was time he forced them all to move on. Maybe it was time *he* thought less about his wife . . . The idea pained Jacob, and so did Suzannah refusing to take his hand as they entered the warehouse of Governs Bros.

The place was full of tailors, mostly old, the few young ones either unfit, or wide boys who had skirted the call-up. Pushing through the press of bodies, Jacob held tightly on to Suzannah's sleeve. He had promised that he would bring her here for years, but now she was finally here she was remote, preoccupied.

'Well, hello there, Jacob,' an elderly man said, looking down at Suzannah. 'So this is your daughter, hey? Pretty girl, and a good help at home, I hear.' He leaned down towards her. 'You like to see the cloth? See how we sell?'

Suzannah's curiosity momentarily outweighed her reserve as the old man took her hand. 'I take good care of her, Jacob. Just show her the ropes. A tailor's girl should know about the business.'

Surprised, Suzannah looked up at the old man, his bushy sideburns white dust. 'I want to be a tailor some day.'

He smiled. 'Why not, why not?'

Suzannah's spirits lifted. 'You don't think it's crazy?'

'We're fighting, killing each other, at war. The *world* is crazy, little one,' he replied, pushing her ahead of him towards the front of the auction.

Fascinated, Suzannah watched the men lift up rolls of cloth, the bidding intense in the cramped, smoky room. Only a few feet away she could see her father keeping an eye on her – and then bidding for some worsted, shaking his head when he was outbid. The old man seemed to know everyone, nodding to the men around, pointing

Suzannah out and telling them she was going to be a tailor some day.

And Suzannah found herself suddenly elated. No one here thought her wanting to be a tailor was a crazy idea . . . She stood up on her tiptoes to get a better view, the smell of tobacco mixing with the scent of new wool. All around her men waved money in their hands, bidding frantically for the limited supply of stock, the auctioneer banging his gavel to settle a sale, the prices marked up on a vast piece of green slate.

Then suddenly Suzannah heard a name and turned. *Someone had mentioned Gloria Clark. Someone was talking about her mother* . . . Pushing her way through the bidders, Suzannah moved towards the voice and then paused nearby, listening again.

'Oh aye, I've just seen Jacob. With his lass . . .' The man's voice dropped a little. 'Like I say, I 'eard something the other day about Gloria Clark being seen in the Crompton Arms . . .' Her heart thumping, Suzannah strained to listen. She couldn't make out the next words, but then heard: 'Aye, in Oldham . . . Well, it might be. It might be her, at that.'

A touch on her shoulder made Suzannah jump. Jacob was looking down at her. For a moment she was about to tell him the news, and then remembered their earlier conversation on the tram and stayed silent.

Whatever her father said, her mother *was* going to come home one day. And if he couldn't find her, then Suzannah would.

EIGHTEEN

Scratching his beer belly, Lionel Taylor emptied his glass and looked around the pub. A scowling man by the snug door met his gaze and then looked away. Lionel smirked to himself. Bloody weakling, he thought; the world was made for the strong, not the bleeding feeble. He was glad he was too old to fight. Dodging the war would have been a pain, but in this case his age had worked for him.

Not that he was as old as his brother, Stanley . . . Beckoning to the publican for a fill-up, Lionel watched the door. He was bored already at the thought of seeing Stanley. Right little twerp, still with his comic-book accent and his foreign ways. Never had the gumption to change his name like Lionel had. Now Taylor – that was a name that gave nothing away. But then again, Lionel thought, his brother had never amounted to anything, so what did it matter if he kept his bloody daft name and accent?

Another thought occurred to Lionel in that moment. Maybe Stanley wanted money off him. He could bleeding whistle! he thought meanly. He wasn't giving any of his hard-earned cash to his poverty-stricken brother. Oh no: if Stanley was going to try and touch him for a loan, he had another think coming. For Lionel, *cash* was thicker than water any day.

'Did we have to meet here?' Stanley asked, suddenly emerging by Lionel's table. He was more plainly dressed than usual, almost poor-looking. 'I could have come to the shop.'

'Nah, I fancied it here. Like a pint after work. So what's up?'

'I just wanted to see how you were,' Stanley answered, already uncomfortable. He didn't really want to have anything to do with Lionel, but he'd made a promise once and he intended to keep it. Besides, it was good to play the poor council clerk brother – if just to keep Lionel in the dark.

'It's your birthday,' he said, pushing a pack of cigarettes across the table.

'You could have baked a cake,' Lionel replied sarcastically, pocketing the smokes.

'You well?' Stanley asked.

'I'm fine.'

No return enquiry. Lionel didn't want to know how his brother was; that might lead to a sob story. He looked around. Thank God no one knew he was related to this little twit. That wouldn't have done anything for his reputation as the hardest man in Moss Side. A reputation built on his pawnbroking business – and the loans set up on the side.

'I just wanted to say happy birthday,' Stanley said, looking at his brother with well-disguised loathing. Their meetings were always short and uncomfortable, but now and then Stanley needed to check that Lionel was secure in his Moss Side mire. In the dark; contemptuous of what he believed was his unsuccessful brother. That way Stanley – and Stanley's shop – was safe.

He needn't have worried. Lionel was only too eager to end the meeting.

'Well, thanks for the ciggies,' he said, heaving himself to his feet. 'See you around, Stanley.' He turned back, dropping his voice. 'Next time maybe you *should* come to the shop, hey? Don't want people to see us together. You know how it is?'

Fuming, Stanley watched his brother leave the pub, then made his own way back to Salford. As the miles passed he relaxed, finally getting off the tram at Hankerton Street.

Away from Moss Side and Lionel he felt suddenly light-headed with relief, and stood outside the tailor's shop, proudly scrutinising his window-dressing.

It was sad, but maybe the boy mannequin would have to go, he decided. Most of the paint had flaked off his face, and far from looking boyish, his grin was borderline seedy. Others had noticed it too. In fact, some bright spark had actually asked Stanley if he would donate the dummy for Guy Fawkes Night. Goodness, he thought, irritated. And that mannequin had cost him a bob or two once . . . To his amazement, Stanley suddenly realised that *once* had been over thirty years earlier.

'How do, Mr Tobarski,' a woman said suddenly, pausing beside the tailor.

'Oh, hello, Mrs Gibson.'

She stared at the decrepit dummy in the window. 'Hard times, hey? What with this war and everything. Not much trade coming yer way, I guess. Mind you, yer saving money on yer window display. I reckon that dummy's older than m'grandfather.'

'It's an antique!' Stanley replied defensively.

'It's creepy. People call it the Dummy of Dread.'

Astonished, Stanley stared at her. 'What?'

'The Dummy of Dread,' she repeated grimly. 'Mothers frighten their kids with it down our way.' Her voice became spooky. 'Yer eat yer crusts or the Dummy of Dread'll get yer. Oh aye, it's a right talking point. I 'eard people are coming from miles to have a look at it – 'specially now that its eyes have gone all hazy. It looks like that publican that used to be down Grace Street. Eyes like underdone eggs.'

Unable to think of a response, Stanley turned back to the window, the boy dummy gawking back like a cadaver.

'I'll move it.'

'Oh, I wouldn't do that,' the woman interrupted him. 'I mean, it's a right feature. Makes yer stand out from the other tailors, I reckon. Everyone in Salford knows the Dummy of Dread.'

NINETEEN

To her amazement, Suzannah wasn't feeling in the least nervous. There might be a war on, and fewer trams than usual, but she was used to looking after herself. Waiting until she could read the number on the approaching tram, she boarded it and paid her fare to Oldham. She was clammy with hope, following the clue she had overheard at Governs Bros. Gloria had been seen at the Crompton Arms. Her mother had been *seen*. She was alive . . .

Looking for a seat on the tram, Suzannah passed a couple of soldiers on leave. They were in high spirits, joking, making the most of their time off. Taking a seat at the back, she turned the name over and over in her mind – the Crompton Arms, Oldham. She knew of the place, in Mumps. Had heard its reputation. Not sordid, just rough. No worse than any pub in Hanky Park.

Beside her, an old man dozed. Suzannah wiped the condensation off the tram window and looked out. It was cold, but soon it would be spring. Maybe spring with her mother home. The tailor's wife back . . . Suzannah smiled to herself. Her father would be so pleased. And she was sure that when Gloria was home she would make it up with Girton. Suzannah imagined sitting with her mother again in the kitchen, Helen, pert as ever, making them both laugh, Gloria kissing Suzannah on the top of her head as she passed. *You're my favourite, my sweetheart.*

So preoccupied was she that she nearly missed her stop. Hurriedly climbing off the tram, Suzannah paused and straightened her coat, tidying her hair. Her mother had to see how well she looked, how everything had been running smoothly whilst she'd been away. Then, purposefully, she walked over the bridge to Mumps, in the centre of Oldham. There were only a few people about, and in the distance she could just catch the sound of a muffled radio playing and a factory hooter going off.

Finally she stopped outside the Crompton Arms. Her heart was banging with excitement. What would she say? Would her mother recognise her? She had grown so much. And then another, unexpected thought followed on. What if Gloria was angry? What if she didn't *want* to be found? What if – dear God – she told her daughter to go away? For an instant Suzannah was too fearful to move, and then gingerly she pushed open the pub door. A thick fug of smoke greeted her, a solemn group of older men sitting around a sombre fire, a couple of crones stooped over their pints of stout.

No one paid her the slightest attention. In many of the poorer areas kids hung around pub doors waiting for their parents, solitary children often sent in to drag their fathers home. But there were few men in the pub this evening. News of the continuing war had dampened everyone's spirits, conversation muted as Suzannah moved further inside.

Stretching up, she looked over the bar and into the snug. No women on their own, no one she recognised, just a drunken pedlar resting his feet on the fender, his dog at his side. And then suddenly Suzannah noticed a woman right at the rear of the snug. A woman with her back turned to her.

Her mother . . .

Gasping, Suzannah moved forward, making her way towards the snug doors – only to be stopped by the landlord.

'Oi! Yer can't go in there.'

'I have to!' Suzannah replied urgently. 'I have—'

'No kids allowed. Yer should wait outside.'

'But I *have* to go in,' she pleaded, trying to shake off the man's grip on her arm. 'My mother's in there.'

He paused, looking over the bar into the snug.

'Yer mam?' he asked, releasing his grip, obviously surprised. 'Well, hurry up then – and tell 'er we don't want kids in here again.'

Hastily Suzannah made her way towards the woman, never taking her eyes off her. She took in every detail of her mother's appearance – the woollen coat, the dark red hat – and then, reaching her side, she grabbed her arm.

The figure turned, shocked. ' 'Ere! What's going on!'

Stunned, Suzannah backed away. 'I thought ... I thought . . .'

'She said yer were her mother,' the landlord explained, laughing.

'It's not one of mine!' the woman replied, rolling her eyes. 'I'd have remembered. Get off with yer!' she told Suzannah impatiently. 'Let a woman have a drink in peace.'

But Suzannah couldn't move. Just stood there, staring at the woman, her hopes shattered. She had been so sure it was Gloria. So certain that, finally, she was going to find her mother. Bring her home to the tailor's shop. To her father, to Hankerton Street. All the years of hoping and waiting were to have been over. The Clarks were to have been a family again . . .

Distraught, Suzannah stood motionless, her mouth dry, her head ringing to the echo of her own heartbeats and the landlord's laughter. And then – without uttering a sound – her legs gave way under her and she passed out.

TWENTY

The only fortunate part of that terrible evening was that Bert Gallager had been home on leave and visiting the Crompton Arms. He had arrived to find a group of people collected around a young girl lying on the floor. A young girl he knew only too well. Leaving his date behind to wait for his return, Bert took Suzannah home.

She didn't say a word to him. She didn't have to when the landlord explained what had happened, Bert passing on the information to Jacob later.

'It's my fault,' Jacob said simply, when he had settled Suzannah in bed. 'I'd asked her not to talk about Gloria so much. She probably thought I didn't give a damn about her mother any more.' He leaned his head against the back of his chair, staring upwards. 'Thanks for bringing her home. I was imagining all sorts when I found out she'd gone.'

'You've got to hand it to her – she had some guts going out there on her own,' Bert replied, unfastening his army tunic and taking off his cap. 'I didn't like the woman I was with anyway.'

Jacob laughed. 'She'll wait for you.'

'Yeah, until someone else buys her a drink.'

Pouring Bert a beer, Jacob regained his seat in front of the fire. He was – he was ashamed to admit – unexpectedly envious of his old friend. People admired soldiers, looked up to them. Thought of them as heroes. You couldn't be a hero if you were stuck at home with bad eyesight and a brood of kids. Kids that were getting to be a handful.

'You don't have to stick around here, Bert. You want to get some fun whilst you can.'

To his surprise, Bert slumped further in his seat and stared at the fire. 'Yer know, Jacob, I'm right glad to be here. I mean, not with Suzannah being upset like that, but just being quiet. I never wanted a family before the war, but now . . . Now I'm not so sure.'

The irony wasn't lost on Jacob. 'I never thought I'd hear you say that.'

'I never thought I'd hear myself say it,' Bert agreed, smiling wistfully, 'but all I need now is to find the right woman and settle down.' He took a long drink of his beer, then paused, staring ahead. 'If I can just get through the war, then I can come back, buy a little house, even get a bleeding dog.'

'And a wife.'

'Oh aye, and a wife.'

'That'll be no problem for you, Bert, women like you, always have.'

He nodded. 'But there's been no one special. Yer know what I mean?'

'There will be one day,' Jacob replied. 'And when you find her, you'll know she's the one. Whoever she is, whatever she's like. You'll know. And after you've met her, there'll never be anyone else. Whatever happens, there'll *never* be anyone else.'

Chastened by her experience, Suzannah stopped talking about her mother. But she never stopped thinking about Gloria. She knew that the advert was still going into the paper every year, but she and her father didn't discuss it. Sometimes she imagined she had spotted Gloria on the street, but she learnt to control her longing, concentrating on everyday life instead. She did make herself a promise, though. One day, Suzannah told herself, she would find her mother. *One day . . .*

In the meantime she went to school, looked after the precocious Helen and watched Girton change. A good talking-to from Jacob had seemed to bring her brother back into line – for a while. The war ended and life settled down, Bert Gallager coming home and going back to work at the slaughterhouse, a constant visitor to the tailor's shop.

When Girton turned eleven he fell in with another rough crowd of lads, impressed by their way of life and easy money jobbing for the Hanky Park roughnecks. His schoolwork deteriorated and again Jacob intervened. For the next two years Girton was pushed, cajoled and bullied along. And as ever, Suzannah was supportive and encouraging. Jacob determined that his only son would not ruin his own life. He was thirteen, for God's sake, not a child any more. Kids in Hanky Park started work in the mills and mines at thirteen . . .

But Suzannah wasn't having any brother of hers down a mine.

'Don't push it out so far,' she said, watching Girton launch the cheap toy boat across the Peel Park lake. 'Be careful.'

Helen was watching them both, sitting on the side in a pretty dress, letting people admire her.

'You'll ruin your trousers if you have to go in the water and get the boat back, Girton,' she said, a parasol over her blonde hair. A miniature dowager at nine. 'Dad will be *soooooo* cross.'

But Girton was in a strop and pushed the boat out further with a stick.

Irritated, Suzannah watched it lurch towards the little island in the middle of the lake. 'Now look what you've done!'

'It's only a stupid boat. And cheap,' Girton replied, his tone sullen. 'I don't see why I have to be with you and Helen anyway, when I could be with my own friends.'

'Because,' Suzannah said coolly, 'Dad doesn't trust you. And it's your own fault. Honestly, Girton, smoking *again*.

And if he hears about you and your friend taking the lead off the church roof . . .'

Girton paled. 'How d'you know about that?'

'Because I know everything,' she replied, nudging him, her tone softening. 'I won't tell Dad, but you have to stop mucking about, Girton. Settle down, study – and do something with your life. You're always saying you want to get out of Hanky Park one day; well, you could. You've got the brains, use them.'

'There are more ways of getting out of Hanky Park than by studying.'

'What's *that* supposed to mean?' Suzannah countered, facing her brother. Now fourteen, Suzannah was tall and looked older than her years. 'You mean you could be like Denny Cathcart? Cheat, lie, steal your way out? Or what about Pa Gallager?'

'*Bert's* straight.'

'No thanks to his father,' Suzannah countered. 'Girton, don't be thick. You don't want to end up like all the other rubbish in Hanky Park.'

'They've got money.'

'Yeah, and prison sentences,' Suzannah replied shortly. 'You're better than that.'

'Why?' Girton asked her, his tone belligerent. 'Why am I so special? I'm not, I'm just Girton Clark, just another Hanky Parker.'

'With a chip on his shoulder.'

'If you say so.'

'*I* don't say so,' Suzannah countered. '*You* do. There's something always been eating away at you, Girton. You never think you're important. That you're worth anything. That you matter.' She paused, tapping him on the shoulder. 'But you do. You matter to me.'

He shrugged. 'Suzannah, there's something I should tell you—'

'The boat's stuck!' Helen cried out delightedly, pointing to where the little boat had beached itself on the island.

'You've gone and done it now, Girton! Dad will be *soooooo* cross.'

Ignoring the commotion, Suzannah kept her eyes fixed on her brother. 'What d'you want to tell me?'

'I've done something—'

'The boat's sinking!' Helen cried out again, even more shrilly.

Suzannah caught Girton's sleeve. She was suddenly anxious. 'What is it? Tell me, Girton. You know you can tell me anything.'

'It wasn't just the lead we took off the church roof . . .'

'Go on.'

'We took the altar candlesticks too,' Girton said, hanging his head. 'I didn't want to, but they dared me.'

'They dared you!' Suzannah repeated, incredulous. 'What if they had dared you to kill someone – would you have done that too?'

'No! Course not.' Girton kept his head down. 'I just couldn't lose face. They're older than I am.'

'But they're nobodies, Girton, they don't count. *They* aren't the people you have to impress.' She dropped her voice. 'Where did you put the candlesticks?'

'Under my bed.'

'Then we go home now and put them back.'

'I can't!' Girton said anxiously. 'What if I get caught?'

'You should have thought about that when you stole them.'

'But if I'm seen, everyone will know it was me.'

'Then *I'll* put them back!' Suzannah replied shortly, turning to Helen. 'Come on, love, we're going home.'

'But the boat—'

'Can wait.'

'But Dad will be—'

'I know, Helen,' Suzannah replied, trying to keep her patience. 'I know he'll be cross, but we'll come back for it later. We just have to go home now. It's important.'

Suzannah never got to return the candlesticks. When

the trio returned to the tailor's shop, Jacob was sitting in the kitchen, the candlesticks on the table in front of him. Shaking, Girton looked at his father, Suzannah moving protectively in front of her brother.

'I'll put them back, Dad.'

'You'll cover for him, will you!' Jacob replied, his tone terrifying. 'You'll cover for your brother, the thief?'

'Dad, please—'

'*Steal*, will you?' he asked, rounding on Girton. 'A son of mine, stealing. And from a church. Just how low are you prepared to go?'

'Dad, I was—'

Intervening, Suzannah tried to calm the situation down. 'He knows he's done wrong, Dad. He won't do anything like this again.'

'You're right there!' Jacob bellowed. 'Get upstairs and pack.'

'Pack! Where are you sending him?'

'Where I should have sent him a while back. He can go and work on my cousin's farm in Derbyshire. Some damn hard work should knock the thief out of him.' Jacob turned back to his son. 'You've got a chance to make things right, Girton. You get to that farm and work like a dog. Make yourself useful and keep away from these bloody streets for a while. And when you've got the urge to thieve out of your blood, you can come home. But not before.'

'Dad, I can change—'

He cut his son off. 'Good thing, because now you'll have to prove yourself to me, lad. You've some making-up to do.'

'Dad, *please* don't send him away,' Suzannah implored him. 'Girton can't—'

'My mind's made up!' Jacob replied, lifting the candlesticks. 'I've spoken to the vicar; he'll be round later and you can explain what you've done to him in person. Own up, Girton – and be damned grateful he's not going to the police.' White-faced with anger, Jacob then turned to

Suzannah. 'And don't you ever – EVER – cover up for your brother again. You hear me? *His* actions are *his* responsibility. Not yours. Girton's life is his, to lead how he chooses. You're not his mother. You're not his keeper. You've done enough. Stand back.'

PART TWO

He wasn't a regular lover,
Well, she wasn't a regular whore:
But the two of them danced with the clouds that
    night
On the shiny ballroom floor.

Anon

TWENTY-ONE

1926

The war had decimated Hanky Park. It seemed that every family had lost someone. Women who had been engaged to marry their sweethearts now mourned their dead lovers, a generation of young men lost. Women who had taken over the men's jobs when the fighting broke out now stayed on, making up the numbers, and widows took on extra jobs to meet the rent. In the viciously hard years which followed the end of the war, some of the poorest were forced to turn from respectable ways of earning a living to streetwalking and stealing. But in the end life settled back into a routine: tailors stayed tailors; whores stayed whores; and thieves stayed thieves.

At his desk in the timber works, an older, fatter Denny Cathcart was reading about Harry Houdini in the evening paper and wondering if his assailant was going to get charged with murder. But then again, wasn't it Houdini's own fault? Boasting that he could take any punch? Didn't that just *invite* a good slapping?

And Houdini had got one. Or rather, *two* punches. Just above the appendix . . .

'I 'eard about that,' Gerry Fitt said, walking in and seeing the newspaper headline. 'Houdini's dead then?'

'Well, if he isn't, it's the best bloody stunt he's ever pulled,' Denny replied drily.

Putting down the newspaper, he scrutinised his sordid employee. He had offered to get Fitt a proper false leg, but the offer had been summarily rebuffed.

'I've managed this long, why bother now?'

'You'd get around better, Gerry.'

The old man's expression turned wily. 'I get about all right for yer. What yer complaining about? Yer'd have to go a long way to find another who'd do yer dirty work as well as me.'

Denny leaned back in his office chair and lit a cigarette. Times had certainly changed since the war had ended. People were more uppity, the women at the timber works expecting to have their wages put up. And as for the iron works, some of the bloody females wanted to keep the jobs their men had done before the war.

Fat bleeding chance . . . Inhaling, Denny thought about his new factory. Be a nice little earner to have another timber yard. That, along with the row of houses he'd bought in Hanky Park, would fetch him a nice pile of money by the year's end. Especially with Gerry Fitt around to collect the rents. Dear old Fitt, with one leg and no conscience.

'So tell me what's going on.'

'What *should* be going on?' Fitt replied pugnaciously.

Denny pushed the box of cigarettes across the desk, Fitt pocketing a handful before replying.

'You heard about Pa Gallager?'

'What about him?'

'Got another twelve months in Strangeways. Spends more time inside than out.'

That was a shame. Denny had occasionally relied on Pa Gallager to get some not-so-forthcoming rents. Still, thugs were ten a penny in Hanky Park.

'What else?'

'If you stopped driving around in yer bloody car and walked the streets more, yer'd find out,' Fitt replied caustically, secretly delighted that he was the conduit of all the Hanky Park gossip. 'Tell yer who I did see the other day – that girl of Jacob Clark's.'

Curious, Denny leaned forward. 'Oh aye?'

'She's turned out good-looking.'

'Like her mother.'

'Oh, that crazy cow!' Fitt replied dismissively. 'I thought she'd have turned up again by now. But then again, maybe she couldn't face her old man. Not having buggered off like that when the kid were killed.'

'Sad day, that.'

'Yeah, sad. But what kind of woman would run off?'

'Maybe she was in shock?'

'Lasted a bloody long time if she were. And what about 'er family?'

Denny leaned back in his chair, thinking. He had asked the same question of Betty, who was still cleaning for him at the timber works. At first Betty had made excuses for her daughter – Gloria had just gone off to think. She would come back, in time. But when she didn't, Betty went into shock and increased her drinking. Until she wasn't much help to anyone any more.

'I reckon Gloria Clark's on the game somewhere,' Gerry Fitt said, breaking into Denny's thoughts. 'She'd have to earn a living somehow – and she was never that keen on shop work.'

'I hope she's not whoring,' Denny said genuinely. 'It'd be a waste . . .'

He'd always had a liking for Gloria. Her pert prettiness had appealed to him. In fact, if she hadn't gone off and married Jacob Clark, he'd have made a play for her himself: sod what her mother thought. He could have got round Betty Siddons easily enough.

'Amazing she's stayed hidden for so long. I reckon she's gone down south.'

Fitt narrowed his eyes. 'Why should yer worry? She doesn't owe yer money, does she?'

'Of course she doesn't owe me money! It's just that I don't like mysteries,' Denny replied, his thoughts shifting to Gloria's son. 'I heard Girton was back from Derbyshire. All quietened down now. A regular farm boy.'

'And respectable.'

'At the moment,' Denny replied, smiling wolfishly. 'Oh, come on, Gerry! You know his type. Young Girton's a handful, and no mistake. His father might kid himself that the lad's changed, might daydream about making a tailor out of him, but he's not got a chance. Girton doesn't want a quiet life, he wants something to stop his brain whirling round.'

'Oh aye,' Gerry Fitt replied, unconvinced. 'And how would yer know what goes on in 'is mind?'

'Because it's what used to go on in mine,' Denny replied, turning away from his employee and looking out of the window across the timber yard. 'Every kid with a guilty conscience thinks that way. Every kid that grows up with a sack of shit on his back thinks that way. You have a nagging in your gut that nothing helps – until you make it. Until you get so big that no one can touch you. Whatever that takes.'

'So yer'd make a bad lot out of Girton Clark, would yer?'

Denny swivelled his seat round to face Fitt. 'Young Mr Clark has all the makings of a wide boy. A likely lad, a very likely lad indeed. And if he's smart he could make a good living for himself.'

'Or end up in jail?'

'*I* didn't,' Denny replied smoothly. 'And by taking Girton Clark under my wing, there's some who'd say I was giving a fellow Hanky Parker a chance.'

Struggling to his feet, Stanley watched Jacob enter. The latter, drenched by a vicious winter shower, paused, took off his coat and shook it vigorously outside the door.

'Hurry, hurry! Don't let out all the heat!' Stanley urged him. Jacob closed the door and hung up his damp coat. 'So, how did it go?'

'What?'

'Your appointment.'

Jacob hesitated before answering; always awkward at having to lie. 'Fine. No problem.'

'Mr Lewis wants another pair of trousers?'

Jacob nodded, distracted. 'Yes, another pair.'

'That makes six. Six pairs of trousers for one suit. What is this man – a centipede?' Stanley leaned his large head over to one side, his hair now silvered. 'Come on, tell me the truth. We need to sort this out.'

Jacob sighed. It seemed ironic now. His sight *had* deteriorated, but he wasn't blind. And yet how much he'd worried about it at first. How important it had seemed. And how trivial now, when there had been so many other, bigger tragedies.

'I don't understand what you're talking about, Stanley.'

'You're looking for another job.'

'What!'

'I know, I know the signs. I don't mean to criticise you. Not meant, not meant.' Stanley paused, huddling back into his chair, his fob watch catching the winter light. 'I should be dead by now.'

To his amazement, Jacob laughed. 'What *are* you talking about?'

'If I was dead, you would have inherited the shop. You wouldn't be thinking of going off somewhere.'

'I'm not going anywhere!'

'I can see you are,' Stanley replied, looking away. 'Two appointments in the last three weeks. Two appointments – all so secret. Appointments, or interviews, Jacob? You're a good tailor now, I know you could go anywhere. Leave Hanky Park. Better yourself.'

'Stanley, you don't know what you're going on about.'

'You think I don't know!' he said, heartbroken. 'I see my protégé turn away from me. Go elsewhere. You would have stayed if I'd died and left you the shop. This is punishment for living so long. *I* should have died, not your son. That's the right way of things, dying in order.'

Taking off his glasses, Jacob slowly polished them. He

113

could hear Suzannah moving around in the back, Helen calling out to her sister from the scullery.

'Stanley, believe me, I'm not leaving you.'

'Hah!' he replied, folding his arms, his bottom lip thrust out like a child's. 'How much do you want?'

'This isn't about money,' Jacob replied patiently. 'Stanley, you're like a father to me. More than mine ever was. You've been involved with my life and what I've done for so long now. You were there when I married and when my children were born. You were there when Arthur died.' He paused, momentarily shaken by the memory. 'I've not been looking for another job. I've been to the hospital.'

'You're ill!'

'No,' Jacob answered, putting his glasses back on. 'It's just my sight.'

Stanley was so relieved he found himself blustering idiotically. 'Your sight! Then I'll buy you new glasses. Two pairs!'

'I don't need new glasses.'

'A bigger skylight in the workshop,' Stanley replied, running on. 'I could get someone in to do that. It would be expensive, but that's not a problem. It would make life easier for you. Give you more light to work.'

'Stanley, a bigger skylight won't do it. My sight's fading.'

Confused, his employer studied him. He had never known Jacob minus his glasses; they were so much a part of him that he couldn't imagine his colleague without them. Jacob Clark without glasses was like a house without windows. Jacob needed glasses. Everyone knew that . . .

'My sight's going downhill fast.'

'Fast?'

'Years ago I was told that I would lose it completely. It might take a year, the doctor said, or twenty.' Jacob paused; Stanley was staring at him, expressionless. 'I was so afraid I'd go blind. And lose my job, with a wife and family to support . . .'

'But you can see!'

'Lately not so well,' Jacob replied, attempting to keep his voice light, but failing. 'You were worried about me going somewhere else. Now I ask you, Stanley, who'd want a blind tailor?'

It was the last thing Stanley had expected to hear. He'd been prepared for Jacob to ask for an increase in wages. And he would have agreed to it, even though money was tight. Agreed to pretty much *anything* to keep Jacob. But this news was too much to bear. Jacob had had so much bad luck. And he was only in his thirties. It wasn't right. It wasn't fair.

By contrast, Jacob misread his employer's hesitation and felt suddenly under threat. The memories of his apprenticeship came back to him poignantly: the way Stanley had rapped his knuckles with the bone measure when he was careless; all the minutiae of cloth, of pinning and cutting; all the patterns Stanley would unfold in front of him like treasure maps, urging him onwards, always onwards. To be better. To be proud of his profession. It had been easy for Jacob to love the tailor's shop – and the tailor.

'This is not a problem.'

Shaken out of his reverie, Jacob glanced at his employer. 'What?'

'We get a second opinion.'

'I did.'

'A third.'

'I did that too.'

'Oh come on!' Stanley replied, suddenly galvanised. 'We fix this.'

'How?'

'We train Girton to be a tailor.'

Jacob shook his head. 'It's not going to happen.'

'Why not? He's back from Derbyshire now. Needs something to keep him busy, off the streets.'

'My son's not got the makings of a tailor.'

'I remember what *you* said once,' Stanley retorted. ' "Sewing is girls' work." '

115

'But Girton's no discipline. He's too headstrong.'

'That's the point,' Stanley replied deftly.

'I have to give him more time to settle down.'

'He didn't want to stay farming?'

'Had enough of it,' Jacob replied. 'Told me he'd changed, wanted to come home. I had to give him another chance.'

'I agree . . . but here is not the place for anyone to try and find their feet. You need to be strong. Hanky Park has too many distractions for an aimless man.'

Jacob's voice was unexpectedly hard: 'I can handle Girton.'

'He could get into trouble again.'

'Now look here!'

Immediately Stanley threw up his hands. 'I'm not trying to hurt you, Jacob. Not meant, not meant. But you know what happened to that boy when Arthur died. He blamed himself—'

'I never blamed him!'

'You didn't have to. His mother blamed him. That's a lot of guilt to put on anyone. Especially a child.' Stanley tapped the back of Jacob's hand. 'Don't worry about it, friend, we can sort this out. This is mendable.'

Jacob shrugged. 'Mendable? My son is not a pair of trousers.'

'Pity. Cloth mends faster than hearts.'

TWENTY-TWO

It was Saturday, and Suzannah was sitting on the back step, thinking, the evening paper beside her. She had no interest in Harry Houdini and was far more concerned about the photograph of Greta Garbo with bobbed hair. She picked up the paper again, then unfastened her own dark hair, shaking it loose over her shoulders. Her father would kill her, of course. Hadn't he said something about women with bobbed hair being fast? And then there had been that newsreel about the flappers in their short skirts, and all the lads whistling and cheering down in the cheap seats at the Gaumont . . .

Even if she could get her father to agree to it, it would cost too much to get a haircut like that. Hardly something Krink's on Broad Street could handle. She thought of their advertising slogan, pasted up on the alley wall:

Krink's 'Never Fail'
Makes hair grow
2/3 a bottle

But she didn't want her hair to grow, she wanted it like Greta Garbo's . . . Getting to her feet, Suzannah studied her reflection in the kitchen window. Dark eyes and hair, nice-shaped mouth. Good-looking – if she had a bob. If she had a short skirt and could dance like the girls in the Busby Berkeley musicals.

'What *are* you doing?'

Jumping, Suzannah turned to face her sister. Helen was

117

staring at the newspaper photograph, a smile spreading over her impudent features. 'You wouldn't *dare* cut your hair! Would you? Dad would be *soooo* mad!'

'I didn't say I was going to. I just wanted to make myself look different.' Suzannah struggled to find the right word. 'More sophisticated. Glamorous.'

'Mrs Bradshaw said that I was wasted working at Ellis Costumes. She said I should go to drama school. Said I could be a movie star. That I was getting prettier every day.' Helen paused; the story was an old one and elicited no response. 'D'you want to go to the pictures tonight? There's a film on at the Gaumont. Rudolph Valentino—'

'Rudolph Valentino?' Suzannah asked, her thoughts wandering. 'Imagine a man like that in Hanky Park. Just think of it . . .'

Sighing, she moved to the back door and looked out into the yard, complete with the old pram and the washing line with its wooden gypsy pegs. Today it was fine, but soon winter would be back and the fog and soot falls would drive the laundry indoors, clothes hanging on a rack over the kitchen fire. The Clark family clothes – and Stanley's. Rows of steaming laundry from October to April, or longer. If the weather was bad, until Whit.

They weren't that poor, like so many others, but old Mr Leonard next door was nasty with gout, and on the other side Mrs Bradshaw had been ill for weeks with her nerves. Hardly the place for Rudolph Valentino to come calling . . .

'Oh my God!' Helen shrieked suddenly, staring in the mirror over the kitchen range.

'What is it?'

'I've got another spot!' she wailed. 'No one will *ever* ask me out if I'm covered in spots.'

Suzannah rolled her eyes. 'It's just one—'

'One today, three tomorrow. By Monday my whole face could be covered. I'll *never* get a boyfriend like this!'

'Helen,' Suzannah said lightly, 'it's just one spot. You can hardly see it.'

118

'*Hardly see it!* It's the size of a cabbage.'

'Rub it with the edge of your handkerchief to take off the grease . . .'

But Helen was distraught. 'I *can't* go to the pictures! I just *can't* be seen like this.'

Turning away, Suzannah picked up the newspaper again. Greta Garbo's implacable face stared out at her, offering everything, or nothing. But at the moment the image seemed to be a clarion call. Whilst Helen was wailing about her spots, Suzannah snatched up her father's tailoring scissors, stood in front of the kitchen mirror and began, recklessly, to cut off her hair.

Surprised, Girton spotted his father waving to him from outside the tailor's shop and crossed over. The sun was still shining, flattering the street, Mr Leonard sitting on the pavement with his foot up as Girton approached.

'By 'ell, yer've grown some,' Mr Leonard said, his mouth sunken in. Never bothered with his dentures unless it was a wedding or a wake. 'That farming lark must have suited yer.'

'It was a change,' Girton replied, moving on into the tailor's shop. Hurriedly Jacob shut the door behind him and turned the sign to CLOSED.

Then and there, Girton felt under threat: believed himself in the wrong and was on the defensive immediately.

'What is it?'

'Why should it be anything bad?' Jacob asked, sitting down in one of the shop chairs and inviting Girton to do the same.

He did so, but without grace. If the truth be known, he had enjoyed his banishment in Derbyshire. Jacob's second cousin had been a strange, reserved man, but the outdoor life had been a change and Girton had eagerly lost his virginity after a local dance. In fact, if he was honest, he had grown up there. But that was the problem. Farming had been all right for a boy, but not a man – and after a while the lure of the Hanky Park streets had been too strong to resist. He might have buckled down and proved himself a good worker, but it had only been to pacify his father. And a way of getting back to Salford. Country was all right, but too quiet, Girton thought. And it gave you too much time to think.

'I'll find a job soon, Dad.'

Jacob smiled, trying to reassure his son. 'You've just come back, Girton. I'm not pushing you.'

One thing was certain: Girton didn't intend to be sent off on any more of his father's banishments.

'There are jobs going in Unwin Street—'

'At the *abattoir*?' Jacob asked incredulously. 'You're worth more than that.'

'It would only be temporary—'

'It wouldn't do!' his father replied, then tempered his voice. 'I want to have a serious talk with you. About your future. And not a future in Unwin Street. That's not for you, Girton. You can make more of your life.'

Girton shrugged. 'I'm not qualified for anything.'

Patiently, Jacob looked at his son. Amazing how the responsible little boy had turned into such a misfit. But hadn't he had good reports from his cousin during Girton's sojourn in Derbyshire? How responsible Girton had become? How caring with the animals? More like his old self. Would it last, though? Jacob wondered. Back in Hanky Park, with all the distractions Girton found so difficult to resist?

Jacob looked at his son's hands, scrutinising them carefully. 'You know that Stanley's retiring?'

'He's been saying that for years,' Girton replied. 'He'll never retire. I saw him sewing buttons on a jacket yesterday – his hands were shaking so much he had to hold his elbow to get the needle in straight.'

'Tailoring's his life. And it's been a good life for him,' Jacob said, sliding into the subject gently. 'You know that he's going to leave me the shop when he dies?'

'So he says.'

Jacob winced at the bitterness. 'He means it, Girton. Don't doubt everyone, or people will live down to your expectations.'

Was this the time to talk about his failing sight? Or would that put too much pressure on his son to accept the offer he was about to make him? Perhaps he should say nothing, Jacob thought anxiously. Just hope that Girton would come into the business from choice, not from duty.

'You're right about Stanley,' he continued. 'He isn't up to it any more. He'll dabble until he dies, but no more than that. Which is why I wanted a word with you. I need help in the shop now. Another pair of hands to train up. It's a life with prospects.' He paused. Girton was looking at him. But his face was expressionless. Unreadable. Was that a good or a bad sign?

'I'd like you to think about joining me. Nothing would please me more than to have my son working here.' Jacob paused again, then hurried on. 'I would teach you everything Stanley taught me – and some tricks of my own. We have a good business here, regular clients – and now that the war's over people are spending a bit of money again. There's a life here, Girton. Security. When I die you'll inherit—'

'You don't know that Stanley will leave you the shop,' Girton replied flatly. 'He says so, but has he *really* made a will in your favour?'

Piqued, Jacob waved the question aside. It was true, he hadn't been told that the will had been made. But then again, Stanley might have drawn up the documents without telling him. After all, it wasn't something he could ask him outright, was it?

'If Stanley has given his word, I believe him,' Jacob replied, changing the subject. 'But we're not talking about Stanley, we're talking about you. I want you to train to be a tailor, Girton, have a profession.'

'I can't.'

Jacob flinched. 'Think about it.'

'I can't.'

'It's a good offer . . .'

'It is,' Girton agreed, his voice low. 'But not for me, Dad.'

Jacob wasn't going to take no for an answer. It didn't take a genius to work out how quickly a man could hit the Hanky Park gutter. One of the Gallager sons was back in Wormwood Scrubs for GBH, leaving behind two kids. And – if the story was true – Jenny, Bert's sister-in-law, was streetwalking in Manchester Piccadilly to meet Gerry Fitt's rent demands.

Jacob wasn't about to see his son waste his life. 'Please, Girton, do this for me.'

'I can't.'

'You can't – or won't?' Jacob snapped. 'Stop thinking about yourself! Think about someone else. I *need* the help.'

His voice had risen sharply, carrying up the stairwell to where Suzannah was sitting in her room above. The room she shared with Helen. Surprised to hear the raised voices, they exchanged a glance. God, Suzannah thought warily, their father was in a bad mood – on this day of all days.

Putting a towel over her ruined hair, as though she had just washed it, she moved out on to the cramped landing, Helen following. Together they sat on the top stair and eavesdropped on the conversation below.

'Girton, you need to listen to advice!'

'Pa, I can't do it.'

'You can and you will!' Jacob shouted, losing his temper. 'I can't stand around and see you mess up your life! You have a chance here, take it. It was the making of me.'

Always hating arguments, Helen ran off into the bedroom and closed the door. But Suzannah continued to listen, her heart banging. There was something about her father's voice that struck a warning note. He seemed to be almost pleading with Girton. But why? Why would their father suddenly need his son so much?

And then she remembered seeing Jacob in the workshop the other day, bent down very low over his stitching.

She had approached him curiously. 'Dad?'

He'd jumped up, startled, then smiled. ' 'Lo there, sweetheart.'

'If you'd got any closer to that you'd have had your nose resting on it.'

He'd smiled awkwardly. 'These glasses aren't strong enough. I should get some better ones.' He had then turned away from her, for once not meeting her eye.

She remembered the scene now – and the time she'd overheard her father talking with Stanley. They had been huddled together around the old work dummy, Stanley, his mouth drawn down at the corners, looking at Jacob with concern. 'Remember, we can fix this. It's mendable, Jacob. Mendable.'

But just *what* was mendable? Suzannah wondered as the raised voices continued. And not just her father's now, but Girton's too.

'I don't want the bloody job!' he hissed. 'I don't want to spend day in, day out in this place. I don't want to dress dummies for the rest of my life!'

His voice was raised so loudly that it vibrated around the stairwell. Dear God, what was happening? Girton *never* shouted, Girton never showed much emotion at all.

'Keep your voice down!' Jacob roared. 'I won't have my own son shouting at me—'

'And I won't be pressed into a job I don't want!' Girton bellowed back. 'I'm not staying here. I want to get away from this shop for ever.'

Taking a breath, Suzannah crept further down the stairs. The argument was picking up speed. So many unexpressed words suddenly coming, sticky and bitter, to the surface.

'Leave here?' Jacob echoed. 'And go where, do what?' He paused, his voice hopeful. 'You want to farm? Go back to Derbyshire?'

To Suzannah's amazement she heard her brother laugh.

123

'Farm! God, Father, you don't understand anything, do you?'

There was a sudden sickening thud. Running down the remaining stairs, Suzannah hurried into the kitchen to find Girton's left ear bleeding, Jacob shaking with anger beside him.

Astounded, Suzannah rounded on their father. 'You hit him!'

'I will not have my son talk to me like that! He'll show me respect, if nothing else.' Shaking his head, Jacob slumped into one of the shop's chairs. He was clenching and unclenching his hands, his head bowed. 'I just want the best for you, Girton. I want you here, I want to make you into a tailor – whether you want it or not.'

He paused, defeated. Let the matter end here, he thought, resigned. He wasn't the kind of man to emotionally blackmail anyone – least of all his own son.

'Girton,' Suzannah said calmly, 'why don't you want to be a tailor?'

'I just can't do it.'

'Why not?' she asked. 'It's a good life, and you'd be at home again. We'd all be together, like we used to be.' She stared into her brother's face. 'Why are you so against it?'

'I want to get away from here.'

'Why?'

He looked at her, willing her to understand, his eyes pleading. 'I don't belong here.'

'You *do* belong here. You always have,' Jacob replied, bewildered. 'You belong in this family, in this house. With us. You're my son.'

Wearily, Jacob took off his glasses and rubbed his eyes. His world had collapsed like a circus tent, fallen in on him, and he didn't understand why. He hadn't understood anything much for a long time, he realised, only how to sew. If he could make a jacket or a good pair of trousers he had focus. If he could walk downstairs and turn the door

124

sign to OPEN at eight thirty, he was in control. He knew about material: worsted, silk, cotton. He knew about patterns and the sweet smell of woollen suiting warm under the skylight in summertime. He knew about how to fit out a customer: how to make a monster into the prince of a Salford street. Not much, but it was his talent, his role in life. His security.

And soon it would also be gone.

'I'm going blind.'

Suzannah frowned; Girton shaken to his core. His father, who had always been so strong, was going blind?

'*What?*'

'I need help in the shop because soon I'm going to lose my sight,' Jacob explained slowly. 'I've kept it longer than the doctors thought at first, but it's going now. Quickly. I can't tailor for much longer and that's why I want you to help out. To run the business after me. Before long, you're going to have a cripple in your midst.'

Hurriedly, Suzannah moved over to him. 'Dad, surely we can do something?'

'No, we can't.'

Stunned, Girton stared at his father. 'Why didn't you say something sooner? If you've known for so long, why did you keep it to yourself?'

'Why do *you* keep so much to yourself?' Jacob replied. 'Maybe you and I are more alike than we thought.'

He was tired suddenly. Girton didn't want to be a tailor. So be it, Jacob thought. He would talk to Stanley and hopefully they could get a new apprentice to train up. But would he have time? And after that, then what? Jacob knew that Stanley loved him like a son, but it was too much to ask for an old man to carry him. And for how long? He wasn't yet forty; how long could *anyone* carry him? Not for a day, if Jacob had his way.

And meanwhile Girton was staring at his father incredulously, at the clever tailor's hands, the thick glasses. He remembered their fights, their differences, remembered how much he had been in awe of his father. But he had never once seen Jacob vulnerable before – and he was horrified, compelled to help.

'Look, Dad,' he said quickly, 'I could give it a go.'

Jacob shook his head. 'No, you don't want it. And you don't have to do it. Do what you want, Girton. But don't waste yourself.'

'Dad, honestly, I can help you out—'

'I DON'T WANT CHARITY!' Jacob bellowed, his frustration and humiliation overwhelming him. 'I'm not washed up yet! You're right, Girton, to want to get out of this shop. Maybe it's not lucky. Maybe I clung on to it for the wrong reasons. Maybe we should all get out. Emigrate.' He laughed bitterly, Suzannah's heart shifting.

'Come on, Dad, you love this place.'

'I *loved* this place,' Jacob corrected her 'But what is it really? I'll tell you – a tuppeny-halfpenny tailor's shop, with its comical dummies in the window and its old-fashioned fittings.' He waved his arms around. 'I see it now as you do, Girton. I should thank you for that. I finally see it for what it is – nothing much.'

Taking a deep breath, Suzannah caught her father's arm. 'Let me do it. Train *me*, Dad. I've always wanted to be a tailor, you know I have.'

'But you're a girl.'

'And didn't you once say it was girls' work?' she countered deftly. 'I can't understand why everyone has always been against me wanting it.'

'Because it's not decent,' Jacob replied. 'A tailor has to take measurements, *intimate* measurements, from his clients. He has to get very close to all kinds of customers. *Male* customers.' He paused, embarrassed. 'Girls can't tailor . . . it's not proper.'

'I don't think that's fair! After all, nurses have to *wash* men—'

'We're not talking about nurses! That's different,' Jacob retorted hotly. 'Male patients are ill. Not able-bodied . . .

Customers might get ideas, Suzannah. Having a good-looking young woman so close to them.'

But she wasn't about to be put off.

'Dad, I love this shop, you know I do. You brought us up here, you raised us in these rooms. I remember everything that happened here. I used to sit on the back stairs and listen to you and Stanley talking, and hear the scissors cutting the cloth and the sound of the rain on the skylight. Sometimes I used to move your chalk around, hide it, just so I could listen to you grumble. "Where's that flaming chalk? Stanley, have you had my chalk again?" ' She paused. 'I could close my eyes and recognise – anywhere – the sound of the gas light popping in the workshop or the smell of the brown paper the new material comes wrapped in.'

'It matters *that* much to you?' Jacob asked, surprised.

'More than you could imagine. Did you think it was just a phase? Something I would grow out of?' She shrugged. ' 'Fraid not. I don't *ever* want to leave this shop. Oh, train me up, Dad, please, train *me*.'

Cautiously, Girton looked from his sister to his father. He could see how eager Suzannah was and realised that if he helped her she would get what she most wanted. He owed her that much at least, for all she had done for him over the years.

'You *could* teach her,' he told his father.

'But there *are* no female tailors,' Jacob replied, turning back to Suzannah. 'You could be a seamstress instead.'

'I don't want to be a seamstress!' she retorted heatedly. 'So what if there are no other women tailors? I could be the first.'

'People would talk . . .'

'People *always* talk,' Girton replied, taking Suzannah's side. 'Let her have a go. She *could* pull it off. She could, I know it.'

'She'd be an oddity.'

'Oh, Dad, please,' Suzannah said, her tone desperate.

'Give me the chance to be someone. To do something different.'

'I'll have to sleep on it.'

'No, that's not fair!' she said defiantly. 'You tell me now – yes or no?'

Jacob stared at his daughter for a long, silent moment before answering. 'All right. The answer's yes.'

And then she took the towel off her head.

TWENTY-THREE

'Of course she's only doing it to be noticed. Like cutting her hair off. Dad was *sooooo* mad,' Helen said, her arms folded as she queued outside the Gaumont with her schoolfriend Moira. 'Suzannah's never going to make a tailor. I mean, it's so . . . you know . . .'

'What?'

'Unfeminine.'

Moira let the word bounce round her head for a moment before replying. 'She'll get to meet lots of men, though.'

That was the point. It was galling that Suzannah would indeed get to meet so many men, literally on her doorstep.

'Your sister can't take *measurements*, surely?' Moira asked, laughing. 'I mean, she'd have to take a tape measure to the inside of a man's leg . . .'

'Are you going to snigger all the way through the film too?' Helen replied nastily.

'Well, think about it,' Moira went on, running her tongue over her big teeth. 'It's not respectable, is it? I mean, my mother wouldn't allow it—' Embarrassed, she stopped short and glanced over to her friend. Helen was biting her lip hard. 'I didn't mean to . . . I mean, sorry . . . Sorry . . .'

'You're so stupid!' Helen responded sharply. 'Don't you *ever* think before you open that bakehouse oven of a mouth of yours?'

Moira reeled. 'But I—'

'Bring my mother into it, would you? Well, let me tell you something, Moira Reid, my mother was better-looking and smarter than your mother could ever dream of being.'

'Your mother's a tart!'

Helen had heard the rumour one too many times. Striking Moira on the back of her head, she then pushed her into the cut-out poster of Jean Harlow. Both went down hard.

'You bitch!'

'Now, ladies,' the manager said, hurrying forward in his shiny black evening suit. 'We can't have fighting in the queue.'

'And you!' Helen snapped back at him. 'Your Auntie Beryl runs a knocking shop up in Deyton.' Grabbing her arm, the manager marched her hurriedly down the fascinated cinema queue. Everyone was looking at them but Helen wasn't finished yet. 'Oi, you!' she called out to a freckled redhead. 'Your husband's leaving his shoes under Amy Thornton's bed . . . And *you* – she pointed to a stringy lad smoking a roll-up – 'you've been working for Denny Cathcart on the sly.'

The lad flushed, his girlfriend punching him in the chest as Helen was ignominiously hustled past the remainder of the queue.

'Now get yerself home!' the manager barked. 'Yer dad would be ashamed of yer.'

'Not half as ashamed as your Uncle Don, I'll bet,' Helen replied, walking off into the night.

Furious, she swung her bag over her shoulder, her temper dropping with every step she took. No one was going to call her mother names. She might not remember Gloria, but she'd seen the photographs and sometimes got her father to tell her stories. Bloody cheek! Helen thought, remembering Moira's accusation. Then she started smiling to herself, thinking of the cinema manager's expression when she mentioned his aunt's brothel.

An unexpected warm snap had entered with the start of December; winter held back over the hills. It was like walking on a soft September night, rather than the weeks

130

coming up to Christmas, and Helen was mellowing with the temperature.

What a dull girl Moira was, she thought, making her own teeth stick out as she thought of her. And her mother was no flaming oil painting. Rumour had it that Mrs Reid had been left at the altar once. Jilted, in front of all of Salford ... Helen stopped walking and sat down on a nearby wall. Opposite her was a grocer's shop; where a young lad saw her and winked.

Now that was more like it! Helen thought, smiling back flirtatiously.

' 'Lo there, gorgeous,' the lad called over to her.

'Hello yourself,' Helen replied.

'You waiting for someone?'

'Might be.'

He grinned, sure of himself. 'I'm just finishing work. You might like to wait for me.'

Helen smiled slowly. Boys were all the same – and they all liked her. So why had she felt jealous of Suzannah for even an instant?

'I *might* wait for you, and that's a fact,' Helen replied, moving off. 'But then again, I might not.'

Her good mood was restored, the future suddenly brighter. After all, with those nice male customers coming to the shop, she could always help Suzannah out when she got busy. Well, couldn't she?

TWENTY-FOUR

Walking into Lionel Taylor's pawnshop in Manchester, Stanley waited for a moment to let his eyes adjust to the dim light. Although it was an overcast winter afternoon, there was only one lamp lit on the counter, its ghostly illumination striking the stacked objects on the wall behind. Beside a German helmet was a baby's christening gown, next to that a row of battered medical books supporting a mouldy deer head, the lamp underlighting the antlers and throwing long, twisting shadows on the ceiling above.

'Hello!' a voice boomed from the back room. Lionel Taylor lumbered out and turned the lamp round so that the beam hit Stanley full in the face. 'Oh, it's you. You should have come round the back. Besides, you never said you were coming today.'

Putting up his hands to shield his eyes from the light, Stanley moved towards the counter and turned the lamp away.

'Whatever is the matter with you?' he asked sharply. 'The war's over.'

'For you, maybe,' Lionel replied. 'I've still got to watch who comes in here.'

'You shouldn't make so many enemies,' Stanley told him, looking round at the crowded shop critically.

It was full of old garments, even some stained corsets hanging off a rusting steel rail. In amongst the flags and broken clocks, people's clothes were waiting to be retrieved, though Stanley knew only too well that some never would be. Coats and jackets which had been pawned to pay the rent man or bookie hung like suicides on Lionel's walls, the eerie light underlining the foulness of the place.

To a man as fastidious as Stanley, the shop was vile, but worse was the fact that he suspected his brother *liked* it that way. Liked the smell of old sweat and dust and onions – a sure sign of bugs.

'See something you fancy?' Lionel asked mockingly, leaning forward so that his face was fully lit. His nose was bulbous, his lips fleshy and his eyes bright with cunning. Reaching under the counter he pulled out two cigars.

'Here, you can celebrate with me,' he said, pushing one over to his brother with a mittened hand.

'What?'

'*Vot?*' Lionel parroted back, mimicking his brother's accent. 'You've lived here for years, why can't you speak right? You'll always stand out as a bloody foreigner. That's why you've never got on.' He bit the end off his cigar and spat it into the corner. 'If you'd been more ambitious, you could have had your own shop.'

Stanley blanched. Was Lionel trying to tell him that he knew? Yet another look confirmed that he was still in ignorance. Of course. He thought of his brother as a trifling, silly man. A council clerk, now retired, nothing more. Having little or no interest, Lionel never thought to question the story Stanley fed him. And Stanley liked to keep it that way. Let Lionel think he was doing badly. Poor, even. Let him think he was the plodder, the respectable brother with nothing to show for all his years of hard work. After all, any humiliation which kept Lionel at bay was bearable.

'You haven't asked me what I'm celebrating.'

Stanley smiled wanly. 'You made a good deal?'

'I make good deals all the time. See that?' Lionel said, jerking his thumb across the shop. 'That walking stick's got a silver top. I've someone coming to see it later.'

'To buy it?'

'What else?'

'What if the owner wants it back?'

Lionel inhaled, then blew out the smoke slowly. 'What if the owner doesn't know it's gone?'

'No more!' Stanley said sharply. 'I don't want to know about your dealings. You're dishonest.'

'And you're honest and poor. I know which I'd rather be.' Lionel paused, looking Stanley up and down. 'Why did you never marry again?'

The personal question caught Stanley completely unawares. 'I never met a girl I liked enough . . . Why didn't you?'

Slapping the counter with his mittened hand, Lionel laughed. 'That's what we're celebrating. I'm a married man now, brother.'

Nothing could have been so unexpected. *Lionel married* . . . Warily, Stanley stole another look around the pawnshop, at the sad reminders of so many desperate people.

I need money for the rent, for the coal, for a drink . . .

Please, Mr Taylor, you know I'm good for it . . .

Just a bit more . . . please . . .

Popping the weasel, pawning whatever they had. And telling themselves they would get it back. In a day or so. Or a week. But never reclaiming it. Just returning to pawn something else.

Dear God, he thought incredulously, what kind of woman would want to marry into *this*?

'Congratulations,' he said half-heartedly.

'You want to meet her?'

'She's here?'

'She's my wife!' Lionel replied sharply. 'Of course she's here! Rina!' he shouted into the back room. 'Someone to meet you. Come on, girl, get yourself out here.'

The first sight Stanley had of his sister-in-law was her outline silhouetted against the lighted room beyond. She was fairly tall, her hair pinned up on her head, her figure curvaceous, young-looking. For a moment Stanley thought that this must be a daughter, not a wife. And then she walked out into the shop, Lionel turning the lamplight fully on her face. Her eyes regarded Stanley levelly, with a heady mixture of sensuality and amusement. Slowly her gaze travelled over his features – and then her expression changed, at once melting into an innocent softness.

Stanley took in a breath; his brother laughed coarsely. 'You see, *that's* the kind of woman I can afford!'

Smiling, Rina met Stanley's eyes. He found to his astonishment that he was dizzied by the brightness of her: the unlined oval face, the pale blond hair, the dark blue eyes. Against the mouldering tat of the pawnshop she was luminous, unnervingly so.

'This is Stanley,' Lionel said, still smirking. 'My poor brother – in every sense of the word.'

She smiled again. 'Pleasure to meet you. You don't look a bit poor to me.'

'So,' Lionel asked proprietorially, 'what d'you think of her?'

'Very lovely,' Stanley replied honestly. But he was suspicious.

Why in God's name had a beautiful young woman married his brother? Lionel was repellent. Unattractive and crooked. Had she done it for money? And if so, what kind of woman did that make her?

'You're surprised! My poor old brother's had the wind knocked out of him!' Lionel laughed meanly. 'Bet you wish you could get a wife like this, hey?'

'I doubt I could ever be so lucky,' Stanley replied gallantly, turning back to his new sister-in-law.

'Would you like to stay and eat with us?' Rina asked, pushing the lamp away so that it was not fully on her. Even half lit she was potently sensual. 'I could easily make you something—'

'He's busy!' Lionel snapped, and at once Stanley realised that this ghastly marriage might prove to be beneficial. If he was so jealous of his new wife, Lionel would be even less interested in his brother.

'No, no, thank you for the offer, my dear, but I should get along now,' Stanley replied hurriedly, putting on his hat and buttoning up his Crombie coat. 'I hope you'll both be very happy. Honestly, I really hope you will.'

He was several streets away when he heard the quick footsteps approaching. The winter afternoon had turned into evening, the lamps coming on and lighting the cobbled street ahead. Nervously, Stanley began to quicken his step. It was a bad neighbourhood, and Lionel had many enemies.

'Stanley!' a voice called out. 'Stanley!'

At once, he turned. Rina was hurrying towards him, a black shawl over her blond hair, her expression anxious. 'Can I speak with you?'

He realised then that she wasn't from the north, her accent some mix of southern vowels and an intonation he couldn't place.

'Miss . . . *Mrs* Taylor. Of course you can speak to me. Can I help you in some way?'

She sighed, looked down, avoiding his gaze. Her sharp brain had sized up the little man quickly. Lionel might think his brother was an idiot, but Rina wasn't so sure. There were many hints to give Stanley away – if you looked closely enough. The soft, well-kept hands, the quality shirt almost, but not completely, hidden under the old coat. And the cologne. It had been very faint, but Rina had noticed it. Poor men didn't wear cologne. Especially poor council clerks.

Following her habit of a lifetime, she had decided at once on her course of action. That was Rina's way: devise a method of attack and strike immediately. Beguile, before the victim had time to rationalise. And this little victim looked like he might be worth cultivating.

'Mr Tobarski,' she began gently, 'I think you might have the wrong idea of me.'

'Mrs Taylor—'

'*Rina*. Call me Rina, please. Look, I don't blame you, I imagine you think I married your brother for his money.'

136

She rushed on, as though impulsive, anxious to please. 'Well, I did! But only because I needed security in my life so badly. The past hasn't been easy for me.' She caught Stanley's eye; sensed the lurch inside him. Be honest with this one, she told herself. He wouldn't appreciate slyness. 'I hope I can trust you—'

'Of course, of course. You can trust me,' Stanley reassured her sympathetically.

'I have no friends here, and I do so need a friend.' She paused, manipulating the old tailor to perfection. 'I come from London. No family, since I was very young. I've had to support myself however I could. There was a kind gentleman who looked after me until he died ...' She waited, watching the flush on Stanley's face. Had she played him right? Yes, of course she had. Shocked him, but impressed him with her frankness. 'Don't be so taken aback, please! You've no idea what a woman has to do to keep herself going.'

Stanley was caught somewhere between embarrassment and pity. 'My dear, you don't have to excuse yourself. I didn't judge you. I wouldn't. Not meant, not meant.'

'But I want to tell you what I am, I want to explain. So that you'll know I'm being honest with you from the start.' She touched his arm, drawing him in, fascinating him. 'You see, you're Lionel's brother, his only family – and now you're *my* only family, I want us to be friends. Good friends. I've had no one to talk to since I came here. I've been so lonely, and Lionel can be difficult. But he cares for me, in his own fashion. I know what you're thinking,' she said, looking down. 'You want to know if I love him.'

Stanley paled. 'I never—'

'Well, I don't,' she said, increasing the pressure on his arm gently. A whiff of cologne emanated from the old tailor again. Good scent, Rina noted, expensive. There might be rich pickings with Stanley Tobarski. 'But I'll make your brother a good wife, I promise you that. I really will.'

Confused, Stanley stared at her. What could he say? She

was already married to his brother, so how could he warn her that he was a toad of a man. An immoral, thieving, lying lout. A man no respectable woman would be seen with. How *could* he?

'I don't judge you. Honestly.'

'I can't tell you how much that means to me,' Rina replied, taking her hand off his sleeve and smiling distantly. 'People have been so cruel.'

Stanley was instinctively protective. Of course people would be cruel. And jealous. He was suddenly worried for Rina. How would she cope with his brother? With his lifestyle? His cronies? Stanley could imagine how they would leer at her, paw her. Or worse. In that sordid pawnshop, how long could she remain perfect? How long before she changed, became coarsened?

It was too much for him; he was suddenly beguiled, *compelled* to help her. And for once he forgot his ordinary caution. 'My dear, rest easy. If you need help, you can rely on me. I will be visiting the pawnbroker's more often. You're not alone. You have a friend now.'

Her eyes filled suddenly. Then she turned away and, without looking round, hurried back into the dark stew of streets.

Yet once she rounded the corner of Gordon Row, Rina paused and leaned back against the wall, smiling. It was so easy. Greedily she breathed in the night air, missing London. But she had *had* to get out. Her gentleman friend hadn't died, there had been a scandal. A hurried, sordid running out of town.

She sighed, trying to dislodge the memory. Lucky for her Lionel had happened along whilst she had been struggling, working part-time as a barmaid. On a business trip, he had told her, although the only business he was involved in was a murky one. But luckily the fat pig had been desperate to bed her, *so* desperate that Rina had played her outraged virgin act and got a wedding ring out of him. Sighing, she kept breathing in the cool night air. Coming to

Moss Side had been a revelation, the pawnshop a real facer. But Rina was nothing if not a born manipulator. Lionel had money, and if she was clever she could sift a little off for herself. Get together a nest egg whilst she was looking for another man. A better catch.

Maybe even Stanley Tobarski. Retired council clerk? Like hell! Rina thought. Lionel might be taken in, but she wasn't. The old man was more than he appeared, a lot more – and she already had him hooked. After all, he was her new, very *best* friend.

TWENTY-FIVE

Standing in the doorway of the workshop, Bert Gallager stared at Jacob and his daughter. Christmas was coming and that meant celebrations; Jacob always insisted on getting a tree to put in the shop window. A novelty, he called it, insisting that it brought in trade, though in reality it was done for his children. Over time, however, people *did* wait to see the tailor's tree go up; and for many it became the first marker for Christmas.

Even during the war Jacob had erected the tree. But instead of baubles he had hung white papers with the names of the fallen written on them. Every Christmas throughout the war he would hang the papers, people coming into the shop and silently adding the names of their own dead. It was obvious that with his poor sight Jacob couldn't fight, but he could pay homage. And people respected him for it. After the war the names disappeared – Bert grateful that his had never been added to the flutter of paper.

'That's too close to the pattern, you're not allowing for the seam,' Jacob said suddenly, taking the scissors out of Suzannah's hands and demonstrating the proper way to do it. 'One and a half inches should always be allowed.'

'What happens if someone gets fat?' Bert asked, walking in and perching on the end of the work table.

Seeing his friend, Jacob smiled. 'We let it out. That's what the surplus is for.'

'What if he gets more than three inches fatter?'

'Then he buys another suit.'

Laughing, Bert opened his own jacket and took out a

bottle of port. With a mock bow, he presented it to Jacob, winking at Suzannah as he did so.

'Port! My God,' Jacob said, impressed. 'Have you come into money?'

'We've a new boss down at the abattoir. He gave us all a bottle – wants to keep in with the workers,' Bert explained. Suzannah handed him two glasses. He looked at her, surprised. 'Get one for yerself, Suzie, yer old enough now.'

Delighted, she did so, avoiding her father's admonishing glance.

'What new boss, Bert?'

'Mr Noel Lyle has just bought half of Unwin Street,' he replied, passing the port to Suzannah and then Jacob. 'Yer *do* know Mr Noel Lyle?'

'Not the Lyles from Old Eccles Road?'

Suzannah turned to her father. 'Who are they?'

'One of the richest families in Salford,' Jacob replied, 'and Noel Lyle knows all the right people.'

'*And* all the gossip about them,' Bert added, refilling his glass and topping up Suzannah's. 'Yer should have seen him, all smooth and sleek-haired, walking about like an emperor. Steered clear of the abattoir, though, didn't care for the blood and muck back there.'

Almost at once Suzannah could feel the port take effect. Having never drunk such strong wine before, she was soon light-headed, relieved to see her father throwing a cloth over the table. Work was done for the day. Not that she would admit it, but Suzannah was tired. Her father was a hard taskmaster, pushing her insistently.

Sitting on the old sofa, she sipped her port, a warm drowsiness overtaking her. If Bert had come for a chat, he would be there for hours. After the port the beer might well come out, Jacob letting his hair down with his old friend. And with the booze would come the reminiscences . . . Suzannah sighed, blissfully relaxed, her eyes closing, the murmur of their voices soothing. In a while she would get up and make the meal, but not now. Helen was out with her friends and Girton was . . . Suzannah wasn't sure, and for once she didn't care. Happily she drank the remainder of her port, the alcohol warming her stomach and making her brain fuzzy.

She woke with a start to find Jacob fast asleep and Bert sitting on the back doorstep in his overcoat. Wrapping a shawl around herself, Suzannah stood up, unexpectedly dizzy, and leaned against the kitchen range for support.

'Ooops,' Bert said, offering her his hand.

'I feel odd,' Suzannah replied, sitting beside him, the night air slapping into her and making her giggle. 'Lord, what *was* that?'

'Port,' Bert replied, smiling. 'Yer OK?'

She shook her head, the back yard spinning. 'I think so . . . Dad's out like a light.'

'Port, followed by three pints on an empty stomach,' Bert replied. 'Yer dad's not used to it. Never was much of a drinker.'

She squinted at him. 'You're sober, though.'

'I was brought up by a drunk,' he replied, nudging her. 'Pa Gallager could drink a brewery dry and not feel it.'

'I don't believe you!' Suzannah said impishly. 'You're always telling tall tales about your father. I don't velieve it.' She stopped; Bert was laughing.

'Yer slurring yer words, Miss Clark.'

'I am not!' she replied, rocking slightly and then leaning against Bert's shoulder. 'You know something?'

'What?'

'I feel very happy . . . Like I could do anything.'

'Like what?'

'Be a tailor, be famous. Open another shop, in Deansgate, Manchester. For all the nobs.'

'Oh aye,' Bert replied. 'And I want to get a car.'

'A big one?'

'Like Noel Lyle's.'

'With shiny wheels?'

142

'Like Noel Lyle's,' he repeated, then added, his tone more serious, 'What do yer *really* want, Suzie?'

'Mum to come home.'

He nodded. 'Yeah, I thought yer'd say that . . . Pa said yer'd asked him to keep looking, but there's never any news. Might be time to let go, Suzie, yer know. Time to live yer own life.'

'I *do* live my own life – but I won't give up on my mother. Not ever.' She sighed, looking upwards into the winter sky. The night was cool, but not cold.

'I admire yer for that,' Bert said suddenly. 'Mind yer, I admire yer for a lot. Bringing up Girton and Helen, and now tailoring. Seems to me like Suzie Clark could do pretty much what she wanted in life, if she put her mind to it.'

'Not when she's drunk!'

He laughed again, but suddenly felt ill at ease. The nearness of her was unsettling, as was the scent of her skin. This was *Suzannah*, Bert thought hurriedly, Jacob's little girl. But she wasn't little any more. She was soft and warm and . . . God, Bert thought anxiously, don't even let yourself *think* about her that way.

'I could count every star in the sky,' Suzannah went on. 'One, two, three, five—'

'What happened to four?'

'I said four!'

'No you didn't.'

'*I did . . .*' she insisted, laughing and punching his arm lightly. 'I'll have you know that I'm *not* drunk, Mr Albert Gallager. Just happy . . .' Pausing, she sat up and looked at him.

God, Suzannah thought, surprised, was it the port? Bert looked so different. She'd never noticed how blue his eyes were, how his hair curled at the back of his neck, how well muscled his forearms were . . . Uneasy, she thought about moving away, but then thought differently and stayed where she was. His skin smelt of soap, tobacco and fresh air, and for a moment Suzannah found herself longing to touch him, but resisted, flushing and looking away. Her intoxication, she thought wildly, almost giddily, wasn't just down to the booze.

For the next couple of minutes neither of them spoke. Bert sat rigid, longing for Suzannah to move and yet praying she wouldn't. And Suzannah, tipsy and excited, was feeling the first frisson of sexual tension – with her father's best friend.

'Good God,' Jacob said suddenly behind them. Both jumped up guiltily. 'I was fast asleep.' Yawning, he looked from Bert to Suzannah. 'Put the kettle on, love, will you? I think we could all do with a cup of tea.'

TWENTY-SIX

Drawing up at the kerb on Broad Street, Denny Cathcart called Girton over to him.

'Hey, lad! A word.'

Surprised, Girton moved over to the car. He knew all about Denny Cathcart's respectable businesses. And he'd heard about the other ones: the black market he'd run in the war, the phony passports some said he'd arranged for people eager to get out of England before being called up. And then there was his bookie's down the 'Oller, off Rossall Street. Apart from illegal horse betting, they played pitch and toss there, throwing three coins on to the backs of their hands and betting on the combination in which they'd land.

'What d'you want with me?' Girton asked cautiously.

'I heard you'd been farming,' Denny replied, his tone pleasant. 'Hey, lad, get into the warm.' He opened the passenger door. 'Get in! It's bloody perishing out there.'

'I'm OK.'

Slightly miffed, Denny closed the car door. Girton Clark had grown tall, filled out a bit with all that hay baling. And not a bad-looking lad either, Denny thought, studying the dark blond hair and good teeth. Bit of class for Hanky Park.

'You want to make some money?'

Shaking his head, Girton moved away. He might be uncertain about his future, but he knew trouble when he saw it.

At once, Denny got out of the car and went after him. 'Now that's no way to treat a friend—'

'You're not a friend.'

'I could be,' Denny replied, his round face deceptively benign. 'I heard about your father and his trouble—'

'My father's doing fine.'

'You not fancy tailoring then?' Denny asked, all understanding. 'Not that a bright lad like you would take well to being pent up for life sewing.'

'Being a tailor is a respectable profession,' Girton retorted, the insult obvious. 'My father's earned every penny the right way.'

'But how much could he have earned the *wrong* way?' Denny countered, then laughed. 'Only joking! Your father's a fine man who's had too many troubles in his life. But enough of him. I heard your sister's training to be a tailor.' He laughed again. 'That'll not work.'

'Why not?' Girton asked, his tone belligerent.

'Women don't become tailors. No one'll accept her round here,' Denny replied, rubbing his hands together to warm them. 'God, it's freezing! Come back to the car to talk.'

'I'm going home—'

'To do what?' Denny asked, his tone suddenly sharp. 'Sit around with your sisters in front of the fire? Some might say a grown lad could turn into a nancy boy that way.'

Flushing, Girton turned on him. 'You keep your opinions to yourself!'

'They might not be just *my* opinions,' Denny replied, unfazed. 'You should be out in the world a bit now. You're not a kid any more. And not bringing in much of a wage either, I'll be bound.'

He had hit a nerve and he knew it. Girton had gone aimlessly from job to job, never settling for long. He had tried shop work, coal carting and even the pit, but nothing had suited him. Desperate to reassure his father that he wasn't going to waste his life, he had even considered joining the army, but what good would that be? He'd not be around to help out, or able to send home much of a wage.

146

Denny pushed his luck. 'I can offer you a job, Girton. A respectable job that your father would approve of.'

'I don't need your help,' he replied, walking off, Denny falling into step with him.

'Everyone needs a bit of help now and then, lad. Don't be too proud to take it. I dare say you've heard some stories about me – people exaggerate; you know how they talk in Hanky Park. Believe me, I'm not as bad as I'm painted.' His voice softened, 'Look, lad, your father needs help. And frankly I doubt if he'll get it from your sister. I mean, she's a game girl, but people won't take to a woman tailor. Besides,' he added, almost embarrassed, 'it wouldn't be decent.'

'Who are you to talk about decency?' Girton retorted unexpectedly.

Smarting, Denny held his temper. 'There's no point taking it out on me, lad! Before long Jacob will lose his sight – that's common knowledge – and old Stanley can't do much to help. I mean, even if he leaves your father the shop, how long d'you think it'll go on with a girl running it?' He could see that Girton was listening and pressed his advantage. Guilt, Denny knew, could be used to manipulate a person nicely; especially a person who was floundering. '*You* could help your father. I know you want to. Just think, Girton, think of how it would feel to give him your wages. Not a lousy carter's wage, but something tasty. Something he could use to get that shop tarted up a bit – and get a proper apprentice in.'

'Suzannah can do that job!' Girton replied hastily. But he was wavering. Could she? Oh, she could learn the trade, but could she force people to accept her? If she failed, the shop would be lost. And indirectly it would be his fault. But if he got himself fixed up now, got a good job . . . For one glowing moment, Girton could see himself a hero. He could help his father. He could do something worthwhile. At last.

'What kind of job are you offering?'

Denny struggled to keep the eagerness out of his voice. 'I need a driver, and I know you can drive. Someone who can deliver things and collect people. Someone reliable who could look after a car like that.' He jerked his head to the vehicle parked behind them. 'You'd look good driving that, Girton. And after a while I could find other ways to keep you occupied.'

'Nothing illegal?'

Waving aside the thought, Denny scoffed. 'Look, lad, you ask your grandmother about me. Ask Betty Siddons if I wasn't fair with her all the time she worked for me. I might like to walk on the wild side a bit,' he nudged Girton with his elbow, 'but I don't force anyone to do anything they don't want to.'

'Why me?'

'Why you? Because I like the look of you and I can see you're struggling. I've money to burn and no family. I've got women, but not one that would stay with me if I were poor. I've plenty of hangers-on, but no friends. I might like to have a clean-cut, respectable lad around for a change, instead of the likes of that pegleg Fitt . . . What d'you say?'

Her head bent down over the work table, Suzannah focused on her stitching. Hand stitching where it shows, her father told her repeatedly. Machine stitching where no one can see it to care . . . The sound of rain on the skylight overhead was soothing to her, as was the noise of the kettle whistling from the kitchen. Her father was a kind man, but a tyrant of a teacher. After the first week, Stanley had taken to overseeing the tutelage, rebuking Jacob when he was too severe. Sometimes Suzannah would look up, exhausted, only to catch Stanley mouthing, 'Not meant, not meant.'

Stretching, Suzannah stared at the headless, limbless working dummy. The dummy she jabbed pins into when she was nagged, or when – to her irritation – she cut a pattern wrong. Of course, her father hadn't trusted her with making a suit. So far, Suzannah's tailoring had been restricted to cutting out dummy patterns, and sewing on buttons, though even that was apparently beyond her reach. She couldn't make the button shank the right length. It was too short, or too long. And every time Jacob would jerk it off, clicking his tongue.

Putting aside the stitching, Suzannah set about tidying up the workshop, an apprentice's job after work every day. Carefully, she lined the odd wooden cotton reels in rows, shaded by pigment, and beneath them the silk threads in their battered cigar boxes, their labels faded to the colour of treacle. Then she polished the tailor's scissors – Jacob's and Stanley's – and hung them on the hook by the window.

She would succeed if it killed her, she thought, trying to regain her confidence. She would be a tailor. Turning down the gas light and moving into the back corridor, Suzannah paused. The door to the kitchen was open, her father talking to Stanley.

'She's coming on,' he was saying, rubbing his eyes, his glasses on his lap.

'You're too hard on her, Jacob.'

'I am not!' he said firmly. 'She has to be the best to succeed. Otherwise people will think that she was just a fill-in, doing the job my son should have done. They'll want her to fail – but I won't let her.' He paused, his voice firm. 'I know she can do it, Stanley. And I can't be soft with her now. We only have limited time, her and me. But we'll do it. She'll be so good that people will forget she's a woman. And one day she'll put us both in the shade.'

In the corridor outside, Suzannah heard the words and flushed. He was proud of her . . . Another thought hit her at once. Would he be so proud if he knew about Bert Gallager? If he knew that Suzannah had met up with his friend several times now? Gone walking with him? But it was all innocent, Suzannah thought urgently.

Or was it? Her mind slid back to the previous evening. She had been walking with Bert in a deserted Peel Park, too excited to talk properly, her words tripping over each other as though she was losing her mind. Suzannah flushed, remembering it. Noticing her confusion, Bert had teased her, taking her arm as they moved towards the steps. His hand had felt warm through her sleeve, his grip firm – and suddenly Suzannah had felt her heart speeding up. *Don't let go of me*, she had willed him, *don't ever let go of me*.

When they had reached the bottom of the steps she had turned, Bert looking down at her. The moment had been static, her cheeks crimson, his eyes longing as he stared into her face. For an instant he had paused – then leaned down and kissed her. And hadn't she responded eagerly? Clinging to him, Bert's arms wrapped around her, pulling her body to his, his lips tracing the line of her throat. Never in her life had Suzannah ever felt anything so exciting, so exhilarating. So overwhelming.

For a moment the world was closed off; shut away. What interest could she have in Peel Park? Hankerton Street? The tailor's shop? She was above all of that; madly consumed by longing for this man, her eyes closed against the sunlight, her whole body craving.

Shaking her head, Suzannah fought the memory and turned, catching sight of herself in the long mirror. A good-looking young woman, poised – and barefoot. Leaning down, Suzannah pulled her shoes back on, her thoughts leap-frogging over one another. She was taking a terrible risk – and knew it – but couldn't resist. How was it possible that she had fallen for Bert Gallager? He was too old for her. He was like an uncle. Hadn't he been around since she was a kid? Hadn't he been there that terrible night in Oldham? Didn't he know all about her?

And wasn't that the point? Wasn't Bert the only person she could talk to about her mother, about her ambitions? Didn't he listen, even encourage her? And more than that – wasn't he attractive? His expression, his pale skin and blue eyes, and the way he looked over his shoulder and winked at her . . . Confused, Suzannah tried to reason with herself.

It would have to stop, *now*. Before it went any further; before she *couldn't* stop it. Because *he* wouldn't. She knew that much already.

Hurriedly, Suzannah walked out of the tailor's shop and down Hankerton Street. It was cold; her breath was coming as vapour from her lips as she cut down Half Moon Alley. She would walk some sense into herself, clear her head.

'Suzie!'

She turned at the sound of her name, Bert running up to her. 'I was just coming to see you.'

Bowing her head, she walked on, Bert falling into step with her. 'What's the matter?'

'What d'you think?' she asked, her voice muted. 'I shouldn't have met up with you again yesterday, Bert. It was wrong. If my father found out, there'd be hell to pay.'

Bert was torn between two emotions. He knew she was right, and yet he couldn't *think* of giving her up. Hadn't he looked for his perfect woman for years? And now he'd found her, he was damned if he was going to let her get away.

'There's nothing wrong with what we're doing—'

'There is!' she replied heatedly. 'You're my father's oldest friend.'

'Then I'll talk to him. Explain—'

'No!' Suzannah replied, startled. 'No, you can't. And I can't keep it a secret from him. I can't look him in the face and tell him lies.'

Neither could he, Bert realised, but then again, he couldn't give Suzannah up. They were both caught in a sexual tension which was crushing. 'I have to see yer again.'

He reached for her hand, his fingers lacing with hers. Again the thrill struck both of them, drawing them in. 'Suzie, I can't stop thinking about you.'

'I know, I know, I think about you too,' she replied, miserable and ecstatic at the same time. 'But it's so risky. What if we *did* continue seeing each other and my father heard the gossip?'

151

'People fall in love every day.' Bert blustered. 'It's natural. It's life.'

She looked up at him. 'Is that what we've done? Fallen in love?'

'Well, I'm in love with yer,' he said honestly. 'I can't think about anything else. Nothing matters but yer. Not what Jacob thinks, or the bloody world. I want nothing else.' He leaned down, kissing her on the mouth, Suzannah pulling away hurriedly.

'What if someone sees us!'

She turned round, looking down the pathway to the park entrance. Mrs Harding from Union Row was just turning the corner; Suzannah standing red-faced and awkward as she passed.

'Did she see us?'

'What if she did?' Bert replied, stroking her cheek, overcome with tenderness. She had reached some core of him no other woman had touched; he wanted her with the craving of a madman. But not just sexually, it was more than that. They had been friends first, with a shared history – which was infinitely more seductive than lust. 'Suzie, don't stop this, please. I beg yer, don't. We should be together.'

'Bert, I—'

He laid his hand gently over her mouth, only taking it away to kiss her, slowly, longingly. Suzannah was enveloped and absorbed by the first passion she had ever felt. And she knew then that she wouldn't send him away. After so long being responsible, she was more than ready to lose control. Take some life for herself, some excitement. And so, even though Bert was her father's closest friend; even though he was twice her age; even though he was from the notorious Gallager clan, she wanted him blindly and urgently.

It was wrong. They both knew it, but it wasn't going to stop either of them.

TWENTY-SEVEN

The Monkey's Paw pub, Moss Side, was busy. Friday night was always packed, every scuffed, wooden-topped table taken, the atmosphere behind the etched-glass windows of the snug dense with cigarette fug. As Moss Side pubs went it wasn't the roughest, and Lionel settled his wife at the table nearest the fire. The most prominent table, where everyone could see her. After all, he wanted to show off his trophy.

'What's the bloody matter with you?' he hissed under his breath, as Rina crossed her legs and showed off a length of calf. 'Pull your skirt down.'

She did so obediently, her glance moving across the crowded snug. Many people were studying her with open curiosity. How had Lionel Taylor landed a woman like that? What the hell did she see in him? Apart from the obvious.

'But still,' one stocky punter at the bar said, 'money doesn't count fer everything.'

'And no one knows a thing about her past,' the landlady added, polishing the scratched counter absent-mindedly.

'She's not old enough to have much of a past,' another man replied, 'Can't be much above twenty.'

'Oh, she's older than you think. And anyway, you can do a lot in twenty-odd years.'

He glanced back to the landlady. 'I dare say you can. I dare say *you* did.'

She flicked her cloth at him, laughing. Then she sneaked another glance at the new bride. 'Fancy living above that horrible shop. And him always working at something shifty. I heard he had someone beaten up for not paying their loan off. Damn near killed the poor bugger. God knows how Lionel Taylor's kept out of prison for so long.'

'Maybe his wife's hoping he won't be so lucky in the future,' another, younger customer offered, his eyes boring into Rina as she recrossed her legs. 'I bet she wouldn't be on her own for long if old Lionel had to go away for a while.'

Sipping her port, Rina was fully aware of the interest she was provoking. Lionel was too. Only his idea of showing her off was backfiring: and his latent jealousy was threatening to make a fool out of him.

'You shouldn't wear your jacket so tight!'

She looked down at her full breasts, outlined by the sombre navy. Deceptively severe. 'You bought it . . .'

'Well, it didn't look like that until you put it on,' Lionel retorted, glaring at anyone who was looking their way. His moment of triumph was souring, his hand shaking slightly as he finished his beer.

'I was thinking about having my hair cut—'

'No!'

Rina couldn't resist provoking him. 'But Lionel, I don't look fashionable any more. All the stylish women are cutting their hair, and raising their skirts.'

'You're not a whore!' he hissed, his voice lowered. 'So don't act like one.'

Irritated, he stomped to the bar and bought another brandy. He was watching Rina out of the corner of his eye, drawing everyone's attention. In amongst the smoke fug her hair glowed luminously, the soft sheen of her fine skin flattered by the dim lights. With every languorous movement she seemed to entice; with every slow breath she made men long for her, and women grow drowsy with envy.

'I'd say that young wife of yers is a right looker,' the stocky customer said to Lionel at the bar. 'Yer'll have to keep your eye on her. Give yer something else to guard, hey? I mean, yer wife as well as yer money.'

Lionel's frost-grey eyes turned on the man warningly. 'Don't mess with me. You don't know what you'd be taking on.'

Alarmed, the man threw up his hands: 'I were only joking, Mr Taylor. Only joking.'

'Well, I've no argument with a man joking – but you can have your little laugh facing the other way.'

Fuming, Lionel leaned against the bar as the man walked off hurriedly. Behind him, he could hear the landlady saying something, but ignored her. His attention was on the other women in the snug. A few wives, a couple of working girls, and some hag who had come to the pawnbroker's the previous week. She was dressed like something that had fallen off a float, her hair tied up with ribbons, and more fraying ribbons holding together her old-fashioned coat. Bloated with drink, her eyes flat, she smiled inanely at everyone. And everyone smiled back at the poor simpleton carrying her little pug dog decked out like a May horse.

Lionel studied the woman, wincing as she nodded in his direction. 'Mad as a rat.'

The landlady nodded. 'But harmless. Poor soul.'

Not *that* harmless, Lionel thought, as someone started to play the piano and she began to dance. All around people began clapping good-naturedly, the woman turning round and round, laughing, the little dog's ribbons flapping giddily.

'What the hell is she dancing for?'

Leaning forward on the bar, the landlady watched the impromptu floor show. 'Because it's Christmas, and because she's happy.'

'She's bloody mad! Looks and acts like a clown. What the hell has she got to be happy about?'

'Maybe she doesn't understand how to be miserable,' the landlady replied deftly. 'You could give her tips, Mr

Taylor. You've got everything she hasn't and you're as sour as bile.'

Ignoring her, Lionel glanced back to his wife. Was it true what Rina had told him about her past? That she'd been beaten by her father and run away from home? But just *how* had she survived for the years that followed? Oh, she said she'd been a shop girl, but Rina wasn't the type. Maybe a shop girl for a week, until some customer picked her up. And after that, what? The mistress of some man? And if one, had there been others?

God, Lionel thought, why was he driving himself mad with such thoughts? Rina wouldn't lie to him; she wouldn't dare.

'She's a great-looking girl, your wife,' the landlady said slyly, butting into his thoughts. 'There's many a man round here who'll try and make a play for her.'

'You can tell every one of them, from me,' Lionel said nastily, 'that Rina is my wife. She's not going anywhere, with anyone. And if any man tries to steal her away from me, I'll kill him.'

The landlady didn't doubt it for an instant.

TWENTY-EIGHT

'I can help Dad this way,' Girton told Helen, 'bring in some good money. I know I let him down when I refused to learn tailoring.'

His sister put her head on one side. 'Yeah, but *Denny Cathcart*. Dad hates him. What does Suzannah think?'

'I haven't talked to her about it. She was out when I got back.'

'She's been out a lot lately,' Helen replied, staring into the mirror and piling her hair up on her head. 'What d'you think? Does it suit me better up, or down?'

Girton ignored her. 'Cathcart's not an out-and-out crook. And I'd not be doing anything important. In fact he's asked me to do a job tonight. Driving.'

'A car?'

'No, a milk float.'

She pulled a face. 'My, you're sparky tonight. Quite the wag.'

Irritated, Girton glanced away. He was missing Suzannah's advice and, as ever, finding it difficult to make up his mind. And he only had a little while left. Jacob might hate Denny Cathcart, but a good wage would be more than useful. The shop wasn't bringing in much and it would be a way for Girton to make a real contribution. For once.

'What if Denny Cathcart's not as bad as he's painted?' he asked, talking himself into the job. 'I mean, I'd be *working* for him. I wouldn't go making friends with him.'

'If you take my advice, you'll just take his money,' Helen said, snatching up her coat, 'and keep your distance.'

157

Helen wasn't in the mood for any more talking with Girton; she had other things on her mind. The work might have broken most of her nails, but she'd done it! Got her diploma, her secretarial certificate. She was now proficient in shorthand and typing, and her filing was a dream. Shame her father had been busy with Stanley and Suzannah had been out. As for Girton, going on and on about Denny Cathcart – what a bore.

She would just have to celebrate on her own, Helen decided, waiting at the bus stop. Ten minutes passed, then another ten, before finally she hailed the number 236 bus.

'What was your last stop? Dublin?' she asked the conductor smartly, sliding into her seat and staring out of the window.

God, it was cold. A bitter early February. Helen might not like the cold, but she liked New Year; that made her feel fresh, like anything was possible. Suddenly her eyes alighted on an exhausted woman with a small child, climbing on to the bus. The child's nose was running, the mother harassed, struggling with a large bag of potatoes.

No kids for her, Helen thought firmly. No snotty-nosed brats to clean up after. Not yet. She thought suddenly of Moira Reid, her old schoolfriend, all set to go off to teacher-training college. And full of it – as though Helen couldn't have *walked* the exams.

Finally the exhausted mother sat down, the child settling in the seat next to Helen. Typical! she thought, moving away and staring even more fixedly out of the window. She had to admit that in other ways Moira had turned out to be a good friend. Like her advice on clothes. That had been constructive, making the most of Helen's elfin looks – but Moira couldn't hold a candle to her when it came to flirting.

A moment later the bus stopped at the lights on Broad Street, and Helen's attention was taken by the shiny car which drew up beside them. She glanced down, then leapt up in her seat. It was Girton! So he *had* taken the job.

Excitedly she banged on the window. Everyone in the bus looked – but not Girton. Unfazed, Helen knocked again, and Girton finally glanced up and waved at her. God, he looked like a toff, she thought admiringly. So much for all their father's gloomy predictions. Girton had it made.

Extravagantly, she mouthed at him: 'You look like a masher.'

He frowned.

She repeated it.

He laughed, driving off as the lights changed.

'That's my *brother*,' Helen said to everyone within earshot.

'So why didn't he give you a lift then?' the bus conductor asked.

'What? And miss the opportunity to meet you?' Helen replied slyly, her eyebrows raised. 'He works for Denny Cathcart.'

'So does Gerry Fitt.'

'My brother's no Gerry Fitt!'

'Got two legs, has he?'

Piqued, Helen rang the bell for the next stop, eyeing the conductor up and down. Smiling, she then stood on the platform, holding the pole and swinging on it.

'You'll fall,' he warned her.

She kept swinging.

'Hey, stop that! You'll fall and it'll be all my fault.'

Suddenly Helen disappeared. Terrified, the bus conductor stared white-faced out of the back window, expecting to see a body on the road. But instead Helen had jumped on to the pavement and was now standing, laughing and waving, watching him.

Holding her left hand to his chest, Bert kissed the side of Suzannah's neck. She moaned softly, whispering to him. They were sitting in Pa Gallager's van, parked well away from Hanky Park, the moon coming up slowly overhead.

'I can't stop thinking about you,' he said gently.

Suzannah turned to him, her lips parted. She was absorbed by him; consumed by the excitement of being with him, by the touch of his hand, the feel of his breath on her cheek. Bert hadn't tried to seduce her, only kiss her and hold her. He hadn't tried to force her into anything – and if he had, she would have submitted willingly.

'I dreamt about you last night.'

He smiled, leaning back in his seat, his arm around her. 'I dreamt about you too.' Then he paused, suddenly sombre. 'Suzie, I've got something to tell yer, luv. I've got news. 'Bout yer mam.'

She flinched at the word, memories crowding back. Gloria at the window of the tailor's shop; Gloria helping her with her homework; Gloria winking as she pegged out the washing. The mother she had loved so much, searched for, longed for. And never found. The mother she had begun to believe might, after all, be dead. But now, after so long, there was news about Gloria. . . . For an instant the shock was so great that Suzannah could almost feel the body of her brother in her arms, and hear the sound of her mother screaming all those years before.

When she spoke, her voice was a whisper. '*Mum?*'

Bert nodded. 'Pa said there was talk of her. She's been seen at The Monkey's Paw, in Moss Side.'

Her voice seemed to come from a long way off. 'Is he sure?'

'He's sure,' Bert said steadily. 'Yer know my father, he'd not have said anything unless he was certain it were her.'

'I have to go. I have to see her . . .'

'It's not that simple.'

'Why not?' Suzannah countered urgently. 'I *have* to see her.'

'She's not well . . .' Bert paused, wondering how to break the news. 'Yer mam's in Snowhill.'

Snowhill, the psychiatric hospital. Snowhill, the place

160

Hanky Park kids were threatened with when they misbehaved. Up on the moors outside Saddleworth: remote and forbidding as a grave.

'Snowhill?' Suzannah repeated dully. '*Snowhill?*'

'I'll take yer, Suzie, if yer want to go,' he said gently. 'I'll take you over there.'

Suzannah couldn't think clearly. Her mother wasn't dead, she was alive. But in Snowhill – and no one went there unless they were very sick indeed. 'I want to go, Bert . . .'

'OK, I'll take yer home.'

'No, no,' she said, shaking her head. 'I mean that I want to go and see Mum.'

'Fine.'

'Have you told Dad?'

'Nah. Yer father doesn't ask me about Gloria that often any more. I didn't think . . . well, I wanted to tell yer first.' Bert stared through the windscreen. 'It might not be too easy for yer, luv. I mean, perhaps yer shouldn't see yer mam. She might not be how yer'd expect. Changed. Different . . . I could go first. Have a look at her, tell yer how she is.'

Suzannah took his hand gratefully. 'I know you'd do anything for me – but not this. I have to see her myself. You understand, don't you?'

'Yeah,' he said simply, 'I understand.'

TWENTY-NINE

Waving his arm vigorously, the man was trying to get Girton's attention. 'Oi, you! You!' he called out. 'I want a word with you.'

Surprised, Girton turned as the man approached him. He was well dressed, with a heavy beard, his voice London-accented.

'You on for later?'

Girton paused, polishing cloth in hand. 'Later?'

'Nine o'clock.'

'What about later?'

The man shook his head and walked off, almost bumping into Helen as she entered the garage.

'Whoa!' she said dramatically, jerking her head after the departing figure. 'Looks like something out of the films. A right George Raft.'

Girton thought the same as he continued to slowly polish the Daimler's bonnet. As he'd promised, he had managed to stay out of trouble by keeping his distance. He drove for Denny Cathcart, nothing more. Occasionally he might collect packages – from as far afield as Moss Side or Liverpool – but that was it. Girton could honestly say that he had never seen anything illegal take place, or been involved in anything shady. In fact he was beginning to wonder if people were wrong about Denny Cathcart – until now.

'What was he saying to you?' Helen asked, sliding into the car and pretending to drive.

'Hey, watch it!'

'There's no key in the ignition, Girton,' she said, rolling

her eyes. 'It's not going anywhere. Relax. So, what *was* that bloke saying?'

Girton glanced round before replying. 'Something about nine o'clock tonight.'

'I knew it!' Helen replied happily. 'I knew if you stayed here you'd get involved in something crooked.'

'I'm not going—'

'I know that!' Helen grinned. 'But really rather exciting, in a way. I wonder what they're going to do? Rob a bank—'

'For God's sake, Helen!'

'Hold up the mail train maybe? It might be all over the Pathé News tomorrow.' She paused, looking her brother up and down curiously. 'That's a new suit!'

Girton flushed. 'Mr Cathcart said he wanted me to look the part.'

'What part? Little Caesar? Dad'll be *soooo* mad—'

'He doesn't have to know – if you keep your mouth shut,' Girton replied, leaning down towards his sister. 'Anyway, I reckon you've got a few secrets yourself.' He touched her cheek. 'Make-up? I don't suppose Dad would approve of that.'

'Nah, but he'll approve of me getting a job,' she replied triumphantly.

Neither of them said what they were both thinking. Thank God more money was going to be coming in. They had both watched with admiration as Suzannah had learnt her trade, but income was falling off badly. The old customers were still coming, but others went elsewhere.

'A girl tailor! Do me a favour,' people had said. 'I'm not having some lass measuring the inside of *my* leg . . . It's not right. It's not decent . . .'

Undeterred by the locals' reservations, Suzannah had spent half an hour the previous night measuring Girton. At least she had tried to, but every time she put the tape anywhere near his crotch, he leapt back.

'For God's sake, Girton!' she had said, losing patience. 'Keep still.'

'I'm embarrassed—'

'I'm your sister, you twerp! I used to change your nappies.' She held up the tape again. 'Now stand still.'

But it had all proved too much for Girton; and Jacob laughing hadn't helped matters. In fact their father had thought the whole episode was hilarious – until his daughter suggested that she measure him. Then all of a sudden both men had had work to do . . .

Unceremoniously butting into her brother's thoughts, Helen dragged his attention back to the present. 'I went for an interview this afternoon at Clegg, Cuthbert and Rathbone, in Paradise Row.'

'The solicitors?'

She laughed. 'Yeah, solicitors.'

Impressed, he pushed her for information. 'What are they like?'

'Well, Clegg's a vampire, Cuthbert's a werewolf and Rathbone's a mummy—'

'You know what I mean!'

'They're stuffy, all look alike, even though they're not related, and Rathbone spent most of the time I was there staring over the top of my head.' She dropped her voice. 'He has a mirror on the opposite wall to his desk so that he can still see what's going on outside even when his back's to the window.'

'Go on!'

'True.' She grinned mischievously. 'Mind you, Clegg's not that bad-looking. Or that old. Only about fifty—'

'Fifty!'

'Oh, age doesn't matter that much. He must be quite rich. After all, there are no poor solicitors, even round here. Oh yes,' she went on, teasing her brother, 'I could do a lot worse.'

He gave her a knowing look. 'Helen, you should be careful what you joke about. One day someone's going to take something you say seriously. And then where will you be?'

'Well, at least I'll have good representation in court,' she replied, laughing. 'I can tell already that Mr Clegg wouldn't like to see me hang.'

THIRTY

Trying valiantly to put his eye drops in, Jacob tipped his head back. And missed, the liquid running down his left cheek. It should have been funny, but it wasn't. It was just one more example of how clumsy and helpless he was becoming.

'Here, let me do that,' Suzannah said, taking the vial out of her father's hand and expertly placing two drops in both eyes. 'Now, keep your head back for a moment and let them work.'

He sat down, head back. 'They don't work. You could put those drops in every hour on the hour for the next fifty years and they *still* wouldn't work.'

'You're just having a bad day.'

'I've had a run of bad days, Suzannah. A run of bad bloody days.'

She was surprised to hear his bitterness. It wasn't like him. But then again, it didn't take a genius to see that Jacob's failing eyesight was wearing him down. Apart from the fear of near blindness, he was also worried about the business. Wondering if he would have enough time to train Suzannah.

But he didn't have to tell her that; she knew it well enough.

'Are they stinging?'

'Nah, not so bad now,' he replied, staring blearily up at the skylight.

Jacob had thought that people would come round to the idea of a woman tailor, but few had done so. And even though he was still managing to make the suits with Stanley, no one seemed ready to accept his successor, no matter how good Suzannah might turn out to be.

The clanging of the doorbell broke into his thoughts. Suzannah moved out into the shop to find the elderly Mr Foreshaw waiting to be served.

'Well, hello there, luv,' he said happily. 'How are you keeping?'

'I'm well, Mr Foreshaw. What can I do for you?'

'Your father not around?'

'Not at the moment,' she said, adding without thinking, 'He's not too well at the moment. I'm sure I can help.'

Mr Foreshaw wasn't. 'Never mind, luv, I can come back in a day or two.'

She was round the counter in an instant. 'Oh, please, let me help!' she implored him, her voice dropping so that Jacob wouldn't overhear. All her anxiety welled out – unstoppable – over the unfortunate Mr Foreshaw. 'Dad's not well and he's relying on me to help him out now. Lately we've had no new customers because everyone thinks a woman tailor's odd, and I can't make them think otherwise. And Stanley and Dad are depending on me, because Girton didn't want to come into the business, but we're not making enough money. And I promised I'd never let the shop close—'

'I'll have a shirt!' Mr Foreshaw said, eager to stop the flow.

She nodded, hurried back behind the counter. 'What size? Colour?'

'Fourteen-inch collar, white.'

She turned back to him eagerly. 'Anything else?'

There hadn't been, but Mr Foreshaw felt he couldn't refuse. Suzannah reminded him so much of his grand-daughter that he was putty in her hands. He would – at that moment – have put in a bid for the shop if it would have helped her.

'Socks, I want socks.'

'Yes,' Suzannah said eagerly, tipping out the sock shelf on to the counter. 'How many?'

He chose several, then nodded, about to pay up when Suzannah leaned towards him.

'I see from the customer file that you're due for a new suit.' She paused, her eyes fixed on him. 'I can arrange that.'

'But—'

'I'm quite capable of taking the measurements and then passing them over to the workshop,' she said, her confidence growing. 'We've got an offer on at the moment.'

'You have?'

We have now, Suzannah thought wryly.

'Yes, if you order a suit we give you an extra pair of trousers.'

Blowing out his cheeks, Mr Foreshaw considered this. He *did* need a new suit and Jacob Clark was the best tailor around. The girl was trying to help her father out, and besides, she wasn't *making* the suit, just assisting in the workshop. He tried to avoid Suzannah's desperate gaze, still wavering. He wanted to agree – but have a girl take his measurements? Surely that wasn't decent?

Suzannah saw his hesitation and knew exactly how to reassure him. 'Of course, Mr Tobarski would be glad to take your measurements.'

She could see him visibly relax. 'Well then, that's fine. I mean, if you've an offer on—'

'We have.'

'And Mr Tobarski wouldn't mind—'

'He wouldn't.'

'Then I think you've just made a sale.'

THIRTY-ONE

As Mrs Bradshaw would say to anyone who would listen, Suzannah Clark was an uppity little cow. She had come to this conclusion ever since Suzannah had caught her throwing breadcrumbs on to the pavement outside the tailor's shop. Not unreasonably, she had asked Mrs Bradshaw to stop. Pigeon shit did little for custom.

In response, Mrs Bradshaw told her that she didn't own the street.

'Just the bit outside the shop,' Suzannah had retorted politely.

'But yer don't own that – *yet*,' Mrs Bradshaw had hurled back, her voice poisonous with spite. 'Relying on poor old Mr Tobarski to die and leave it to yer father, are yer? Well, he might just change his mind. What if he got married? Then what?'

Suzannah had dismissed the idea out of hand. But then, Mrs Bradshaw had thought slyly, Suzannah didn't know what *she* did.

'I tell yer,' Mrs Bradshaw said to her visitor, Miss Hull, later that morning, 'Suzannah Clark has changed completely. Yer should hear what I do through these walls. Things a respectable woman should never hear.'

That *was* a bit strong, Mrs Bradshaw conceded, but Suzannah had got on her nerves once too often. The world was going to hell in a handcart. Women had changed: and not for the better. She blamed the war. Men came back to find their wives doing their jobs and earning their own wages. And wanting it to stay that way.

'Suzannah Clark's made my life a misery. Can't even feed the birds without her complaining,' Mrs Bradshaw wailed, delighted that her winged accomplices were relieving themselves so often, and so regularly, outside the tailor's shop. 'An old woman like me. With all the grief I've had to bear. Widowed twice. And she treats me like that.'

'Fancy,' Miss Hull replied, reaching for a piece of sponge cake.

'Yer should have seen her face when I mentioned Mr Tobarski getting married—'

'Mr Tobarski's getting married!'

'No, no!' Mrs Bradshaw snapped, her cane rapping sharply. 'I just implied that if he did, he might leave that shop to someone else.'

Her eyes wide, Miss Hull's lean face became unusually animated. 'But Mr Tobarski's too old—'

'That never stops a man proposing, or a woman accepting. There's many round these parts that'd go down on their backs for a gold band.'

'Mrs Bradshaw!'

'Oh, grow up! No one notices the fireplace when they're poking the fire.'

Reaching for another slice of sponge, Miss Hull stared at her elderly friend in fascinated horror. 'But who would Stanley Tobarski marry?'

'Now, mind, yer've to say nothing to no one,' Mrs Bradshaw began, leaning her considerable weight forward in her armchair. 'But I 'eard a little rumour. My son – the useless bugger – told me that Stanley Tobarski was seen walking with a pretty young blonde in Manchester. Young enough to be his daughter. Maybe even granddaughter . . .'

Miss Hull dropped her slice of sponge cake. 'Never!' she said firmly. 'I don't believe it. Mr Tobarski's too old for that kind of thing. And he's not the type.'

'Yer wouldn't know that type if it came down yer chimney and took all yer washing. Yer've never even been married.'

'I had my chance!'

'Yer chance upped and married Elise Broadbent.'

Outraged, Miss Hull stood up to go. 'I'm not staying another minute! You've a wicked tongue, Mrs Bradshaw, and nothing good'll come out of spreading false rumours.'

'Oh, be off with yer!' the old woman replied, irritated. 'Yer've eaten all my sponge cake anyway.'

But Mrs Bradshaw's son had got it right. Walking into St Anne's Square, Manchester, Stanley was overjoyed to see the admiring glances his companion attracted. And Rina, brightly blonde in a pale blue suit, was fussing over him so delightfully that he had become the envy of every man that passed.

'My dear, you are too kind. I must be boring you with my old stories—'

'Not at all, Stanley,' Rina replied, smiling. 'I love to hear about the war.' How was she managing to keep her face straight? Rina wondered. God, old men could be so dull. But at least Stanley was sweet and paternal, not pawing her like other men. In fact, he had kept his promise and offered her friendship. Perhaps it was time to see what else he had to offer.

'You're retired, Stanley?'

He winced, dreading the lies which had to follow. 'Yes, my dear.'

'But you were a clerk?'

'Boring, I know.'

What a naughty little lie, Rina thought, almost admiringly. She would have to work harder to get Stanley to spill the beans.

'But a clever man like you – I would have expected you to have your own business. I mean, if your brother can do it, surely you're more than able? Lionel doesn't have your charm, or your intelligence.'

Flattered, for the first time in decades Stanley wanted to

let his secret out of the bag. Say, yes, I have a respectable tailor's shop in Salford and a little mound of savings put away. And although you've only seen me in sombre clothes, in my day they used to call me the Emperor of Hanky Park ... But he resisted. Obviously this sweet child wouldn't abuse his confidence, but Stanley knew his brother and how he could prise information from a clam.

'I'm happy with my lot. I have a nice little flat and now I have a new companion.' He smiled at Rina cheerfully. 'Lionel is treating you right, isn't he?'

She tossed back her hair. For two pins she would smother the bastard in his sleep, but for the time being she had to endure Lionel. At least until she had worked out if there was anything to be got from Stanley Tobarski.

'He can be very . . .'

'Yes?' Stanley asked anxiously.

'*Cruel* at times.'

He paused, taking her hand. The action was merely paternal, but didn't look like that to the passers-by. Instead it seemed like an old man helplessly smitten by a young beauty.

'Not violent?'

'No, no . . . Just harsh. Hard words.'

Stanley shook his head disbelievingly. Only his pig of a brother could treat her this way.

'Is there anything I can do to help you?' he asked, genuinely anxious. 'Is there *anything* I can do for you, my dear?'

Rina smiled bravely. 'I'm fine, don't worry, Stanley. Just knowing I can call on you is help enough.'

THIRTY-TWO

'You ready?' Bert asked, leaning over to open the van door for Suzannah. Nodding, she climbed in, wrapped in a dark wool coat, her hair covered with a red scarf.

She had thought long and hard about telling her father what she was about to do. But in the end, she had decided to stay quiet. She would visit Gloria and see how bad her mother was. What the doctors thought of her condition; if she would recover. Then – and *only* then – would be the time to tell her father.

'Are yer sure yer want to do this?' Bert asked kindly. 'Yer don't have to, luv.'

She took his hand and squeezed it. Bert started the engine.

'What did yer tell yer dad?'

'That I was going to the dentist,' Suzannah replied, staring out of the van window. 'Stanley's helping him out, they can manage for the afternoon.'

Pausing at the traffic lights, Bert glanced over at her. His heart shifted. Hadn't Pa Gallager said that Gloria was in a bad way? How would Suzannah take that? It was true that she had finally tracked down her mother – but it would not be the Gloria she remembered. The happy, spirited homebody, relaxed, good-looking, sure of her place in the world: that Gloria had gone long ago. No one knew where she had been, how she had kept herself, what she had done to survive. Suzannah had kept her mother alive in her head and her heart – but what would the reality do to her?

In silence, they drove on, Bert glancing over at Suzannah repeatedly and occasionally squeezing her hand as if to reassure her. *Yer not alone, not this time. I'm with yer. And whatever happens, I'll always be with yer . . .*

Finally they came to the double gates leading up to Snowhill. Bert drove in and parked, Suzannah sitting rigidly in her seat. In silence, she got out of the van and walked towards the entrance, waiting for Bert to catch up with her. Snow was falling, marking her red scarf with flakes.

'Ready?'

'No, not really.'

She had made an appointment with Dr Samuels, both of them walking in and waiting for the doctor in a narrow corridor outside the consultation rooms. Out of place, Bert was uncomfortable, pacing up and down; Suzannah sat still as a mill pond. Finally, after twenty minutes had passed, Dr Samuels approached them.

'Sorry to keep you waiting, we had an emergency. I believe you've come to see your mother.' He paused. 'You *are* sure it's your mother, Gloria Clark?'

Suzannah hesitated. 'I can't be certain until I see her. But I think it is.'

The doctor nodded. 'Her condition's very poor. I would say that the patient has been sleeping rough for a while, and there's some evidence of alcohol abuse.' Shaken, Suzannah thought of Nan Siddons, but said nothing and let the doctor continue. 'If this *is* your mother, I must warn you that she's very disturbed. Her reality's distorted, her memory's patchy. She's had a nervous breakdown, you see.'

'We did *try* to find her, we didn't just forget her, stop thinking about her,' Suzannah said helplessly. 'We looked and looked for years, but it was no good. Just rumours, dead ends—'

'Before you get your hopes up, Miss Clark, come and see the patient,' Dr Samuels said kindly. 'See if it is your mother.'

174

Glancing round to check that Bert was following her, Suzannah moved down the corridor. The doctor walked fast, taking several turns, before pausing outside the entrance to a side ward.

'The patient is in the bed by the window, on the left,' he said, opening the door and letting Suzannah pass through. 'She's asleep.'

Come here, my sweetheart, my favourite, come and sit with me ... Put that homework away for now, Suzannah, sit with me ...

Slowly, Suzannah approached the bed, screened off by hospital curtains. For a moment she couldn't move, then she gripped the material and drew the curtain back.

The patient was lying supine, her arms by her sides, her breathing shallow. Once dark, glossy hair was now coarse and grey around the temples, her cheeks puffy and mottled with thread veins. Hands that had once been small and smooth were now wrinkled, the skin dry, and around her eyes the lines were deep and of long standing.

But it *was* Gloria.

'Mum?' Suzannah said, her voice breaking. 'Mum, it's me. It's Suzannah.'

Her eyes flickered, Suzannah leaning closer towards her. 'Oh Mum, I've found you,' she said, tears coming fast. 'You're OK now, everything's going to be fine. You can come home.'

Slowly Gloria opened her eyes, focusing on her daughter. And not recognising her.

Catching hold of her mother's hand, Suzannah smiled. 'Oh Mum, *Mum ...*'

'Who are you?' Gloria asked, her voice thin, reedy.

'It's me, Suzannah, your daughter. I've been looking for you for so long. And now I've found you and you can come home.'

Gloria flinched, understanding nothing. 'I'll not move on, I'll not! I'm staying here for the night.'

'Mum!'

'Get away from me!' Gloria shouted, locked somewhere in her own dark memories. 'I can stay here. You can't move me. I'm doing no one any harm. They said they'd set the dogs on me, but they didn't . . .'

'Mum, *please*,' Suzannah begged desperately. 'Please look at me. It's me, it's your daughter.'

Intervening, Dr Samuels tried to move Suzannah away, but she struggled with him, her eyes never leaving her mother's face.

'Mum, it's me! I've come to take you home! Mum, please . . .'

And then Gloria started screaming.

It was Bert who finally managed to get Suzannah to leave. She was sobbing uncontrollably, leaning against him, her distress so painful that he could feel his own throat tighten. Gently he led her back to the van and tucked a rug around her, Suzannah resting her head back and crying quietly. Her mother didn't know her. It had all been so pointless, a waste of time. Gloria wasn't coming home; she didn't even know her own child.

Shaken by her distress, Bert pulled into a lay-by and parked. Then he took Suzannah in his arms and rocked her, trying desperately to soothe her.

'Come on, luv, come on.'

'She didn't know me . . . She didn't know me . . .' Suzannah said, demented with distress. 'What had happened to her, Bert? What was she talking about? Being moved on. Dogs being set on her . . . God, where had she been for so long?' She banged her fists on her knees helplessly. 'We should have kept looking for her! We should *never* have given up.'

'Yer didn't. Yer never did give up,' Bert reminded her. 'But yer mother didn't want to be found. She changed her name, Suzie. It were a miracle she were *ever* found. Oh, luv, please, please don't cry. Yer did what yer could.'

'But it wasn't enough!' she replied, turning to him, her eyes blank with pain. 'All these years I've waited to see my mother again, all this time dreaming about her, about her coming home. I was going to rescue her, take her back to Hanky Park. Bring the tailor's wife home . . .' She shook her head. 'How much did she suffer? With no one to help her, no one to look out for her—'

'Suzie,' Bert said, holding her even more tightly, 'yer'll make yerself ill if yer go on this way. Come on, luv, be still. Be still.'

Desperately she clung to him, the heat from his body warming her own, his strength holding her together. And in that moment Suzannah's pain was so great that she found herself pulling Bert towards her, kissing him urgently, panicked, desperate for comfort.

'No, luv, no, not like this. Think about it . . .'

But she persisted, asking, and taking, comfort from the man she trusted. And so, without thinking of what they were doing, without thinking of the consequences, they made love. Bert could feel Suzannah's tears against his face, her cries against his lips, her body clinging to his – her sexuality mixed with a grief too *bitter* to bear alone.

THIRTY-THREE

It was a warm day in Peel Park. A few kids had sneaked out a boat and were trying, furiously, to get it off the bank before the boatman caught them. Further into the lake, a couple had stopped rowing and were talking, deep in conversation, their heads almost touching, their figures unmoving, mirrored in the water beneath. The park was crowded, factory workers sitting under trees, pink-faced babies being pushed in prams, and the shop girls, with their shingled hair and straight dresses, eyeing up the boys.

Her hand covering her left cheek, Rina kept her head down as she approached the park. *The bastard!* she thought, shaken. Things had been going well for a while, but suddenly Lionel had over-reacted. Her head thumping, Rina walked on, her blonde hair catching the light, her dress outlining her body against the sun. Even distracted, she drew attention, a carter whistling as he passed. But Rina didn't hear him; she was remembering what had triggered Lionel's outburst.

The cap. The soldier's cap . . . Someone had brought it in to pawn the previous day, Lionel laughing and telling them to get lost. It had been her intervention which had forced the issue.

'Oh, we'll take it,' she'd said, glancing at the old woman on the other side of the counter.

'What do I want with a soldier's cap? There's thousands of 'em.'

'It were m'son's,' the old woman had said imploringly. ' 'E died.'

Lionel had rolled his eyes. 'Even better!'

'Don't be so hard-hearted, Lionel,' Rina had replied, leaning against him, her breast squeezed against his left arm. 'Give her something for it.'

And so he'd relented and chucked the soldier's cap on to one of the deer's antlers, high above their heads. Then he had forgotten about it. Until later, when he'd closed for the day. They had eaten dinner and he had been dozing; when he woke, he'd gone back into the shop to find his wife staring at the cap. Her expression had inflamed him. She was transfixed, her lips slightly parted, her eyes moist. Locked in an old, sweet memory.

'What the bloody hell!' he'd roared. 'What you gawking at?'

Uncharacteristically flustered, she'd backed away. 'I was just thinking about someone.'

In an instant Lionel put two and two together and came up with seventeen. 'You bloody whore!' he'd snapped, grabbing her arm. 'You snivelling over some lost soldier boy?'

'I never—'

'You bitch!' he'd roared, knocking the cap off the deer's antlers and then rubbing it against Rina's cheek. 'Is that what you're remembering? Did he rub up to you like that? Did he smell like that when you were lying with him?'

'Lionel, don't!' she'd replied, trying an imploring tone. 'Please.'

'*Lionel, don't! Please*,' he had parroted. 'You think I'm just a meal ticket for you, don't you? You only let me touch you because you have to. Don't you think I know what you want?' His eyes had been narrow with fury, spittle at the corners of his mouth. 'You want some young body next to yours. Some young man—'

'I never said that!'

'YOU DIDN'T HAVE TO!' he had shouted, gripping her arm. 'I bet you laugh behind my back, don't you? Snigger about me. About my beer belly?'

'I never say a word. I don't think that—'

His grip tightened. 'I know you! I know your sort.'

Frantically, he had thrown the soldier's cap across the shop and then swung back his hand and struck Rina full across the face.

If she had had a knife in her hand she would have stuck it in him there and then, Rina thought, her face burning as she walked along. Think he could treat her like that, did he? Well, she'd see about that. Remembering that Stanley had mentioned he was visiting the park that afternoon, Rina hurried on. She would bump into him accidentally, let him know what his brother had done. Get some sympathy, at least.

At that precise moment Stanley was ambling along in blissful ignorance of the trauma he was about to confront. He was deep in conversation, chatting to an old acquaintance – then paused, spotting a blonde woman entering the side gates of Peel Park. Uncertain for an instant, Stanley realised that it was Rina – and that she seemed to be sobbing.

'. . . And then I said, you bet your life—'

'Would you excuse me, George?' Stanley said hurriedly. 'There's something I have to see to. I'll catch up with you later.'

Without another word, he hurried off, his companion watching his retreat with surprise. Just what had got into Stanley Tobarski? Always urbane and steady, he seemed suddenly like a startled racehorse. The man peered into the distance to see what had caught his attention. There were a couple of men arguing, a dog fight – and a young woman walking with her head bowed.

Curious, George watched Stanley hurry on. Really, he was too old to be running around, and on a warm day too. The man had no sense . . . His eyes followed his friend intently as he approached the bridge over the lake. He

180

could hear – faintly – Stanley calling out a name he didn't recognise. And then George saw the blonde woman look up.

'Rina!'

Her head lifted at the sound of her name, mock surprise on her face as she spotted Stanley, just stepping on to the bridge. As he hurried towards her, the sunlight caught the side of Rina's face and illuminated the bloodied cut lip.

Alarmed, Stanley hurried over the hump of the bridge. His thoughts were distracted, his anxiety so intense that he missed his footing and slipped. In slow motion Stanley Tobarski fell, his legs doubling under him, the side of his head hitting one of the stone balustrades that supported the railing.

The impact cracked Stanley Tobarski's skull, a jagged piece of his cranium bending inwards and ripping into the brain below. Letting out a cry of terror and surprise, Rina ran towards him – then stopped dead. But her scream kept travelling on the still, warm air; the ducks flew away from the lake; the couple glanced up from the boat.

George heard the scream too and began to run towards the sound. He reached the bridge within seconds to find a woman standing stock still, staring at a body on the ground. His friend, Stanley Tobarski. The man with whom he had just been in conversation.

Stunned, he looked at Stanley's bloodied head and then at the woman. The same blonde woman who had entered the side gates of Peel Park only a minute before.

THIRTY-FOUR

'Just wait there,' Sid told Girton, looking around him furtively. 'Yer just keep an eye out, tip me the wink if yer see a copper coming.'

Girton nodded. What the hell, it was only once. All he had to do was look down the alleyway and get paid a fiver for it. And a fiver that easy wasn't worth giving up on. It was stupid how the coppers came down on betting anyway. There were plenty of worse things going on. Besides, it would be over in a few minutes – and anyway, who'd know?

Looking down the alleyway, Girton could feel his heart thumping. The excitement and fear was making his mouth dry, his stomach churning. Behind him, he could hear the men throwing dice and then whooping when someone won. Then silence . . . He peered down the alley again. Nothing happening. No one there. A sudden, dull murmur of voices told him there were bets being laid, a straggly kid of about fourteen running the results over to Sid.

Come on, come on! he thought urgently. He hadn't wanted to act as a lookout, but couldn't refuse Denny Cathcart. After all, Denny had been good to him. Knew how hard things were at the tailor's shop and put a bit of business Girton's way. Driving, moving stock from a Manchester warehouse to one in Wigan. But nothing illegal. Until this.

Girton kept staring down the alleyway. He could hear footsteps, but they passed, his anxiety growing by the minute. If he got caught it meant trouble. A court appearance. A criminal record. Denny Cathcart had told him he'd be looked after, but what did that mean? Girton knew only too well that some of the lookouts pleaded guilty so that they were fined while the bookies like Cathcart got off.

He felt queasy suddenly. It wasn't a game. He had promised himself he would do nothing illegal. But here he was . . . But it was only once, Girton reassured himself again, his anxiety growing. After this time, no more. Besides, it would soon be over; in another minute or so it would be done. He just had to keep his eyes open. Unblinking, staring. Watching down the alleyway.

He never thought they would come from behind.

How many weeks was it now? Suzannah asked herself, counting them on the calendar for the fourth time. Six weeks. *Six weeks without her period* . . . Swallowing drily, she moved back to the work table, trying to concentrate on the waistcoat she was making. Dear God, what was she going to do? Pregnant, with Bert Gallager's child.

Standing up, Suzannah began to pace the workroom. She had decided not to tell her father about Gloria yet – not in the condition she was in. Best to wait a little. But she had called the hospital several times, asking after her mother's progress. Dr Samuels had been kind, but noncommittal. No, he didn't know if Gloria would recover. She might . . . When? He wasn't sure. These things took time. Suzannah should be patient; miracles could happen, but they took time.

Biting the side of her fingernail, Suzannah touched her stomach. Why had she been so reckless? It wasn't like her. It wasn't like her at all. Didn't she know that she'd ruined herself? No decent woman slept with a man before marriage. Another thought came to her immediately: if she told him, Bert would willingly marry her, take on the child.

The thought should have reassured her, but instead it left her clammy with unease. She had been madly, crazily in love – but suddenly reality had set in and the feeling had gone. This wasn't some schoolgirl crush; this wasn't even a first innocent romance. It was an affair and she was pregnant with her lover's child. But there was something even worse than that, Suzannah realised, sitting down heavily. She and Bert weren't a couple; weren't really meant for each other. He wasn't the love of her life. Her infatuation had been just that: infatuation.

Shaken, Suzannah hung her head. She didn't love Bert enough to marry him. She didn't want to settle down; be a wife and mother. Keep his house, have his children. She didn't want to be Mrs Bert Gallager, with her life all mapped out – with the wrong man. It was true that she was fond of him, deeply attracted to him. But she didn't love him. Didn't want him as her husband . . . Oh God, Suzannah thought blindly, what had she done? To herself? To Bert? And what if her father found out? Pregnant and unmarried – the shame would kill Jacob.

Who would have expected it of Suzannah Clark? Hadn't she always tried to keep Girton on the straight and narrow, teased Helen about her new boyfriend, Archie Culshaw?

Don't let him go too far . . . don't let him take advantage of you . . .

Aw, Suzie, I'm not like that . . .

Suzannah flushed: who was *she* to talk?

And all her big ideas about being a tailor had come to nothing. It was obvious no one would accept her in Hanky Park. Over the past weeks Suzannah had seen the takings drop even further and knew that she was letting the side down. Wasn't that bad enough? What would her family think of her if they knew the trouble she was in now?

A loud rapping on the front door shattered her thoughts. Suzannah stumbled to her feet. Frowning, she took off her apron and moved into the tailor's shop, closing the entrance to the living quarters behind her. Seeing policemen through the glass, her eyes widened, her hand shaking as she unlocked the door.

'Are you Miss Clark?'

She nodded.

'Is your father at home? We have to talk to him, miss.'

'Has someone been hurt?'

'It's about your brother.'

'What about my brother?'

She didn't get the chance to say more, as Jacob walked in behind her. It took him a moment to focus on the men – and on the uniforms.

'What is it?'

'Your son, Mr Clark. He's in custody.'

Suzannah could hear her father take a breath. 'What's he done?' he asked curtly. 'Something for that bastard Denny Cathcart?'

'Your son was acting as a lookout, Mr Clark.'

Suzannah frowned. 'A *what*?'

'Off Corporation Yard. The bookies hire men who act as lookouts so they can tip them off when the police arrive.'

'Girton?' Jacob said incredulously. 'No, not my son. Why would he do that?'

The elder of the police officers took off his helmet, turning it round in his hands. 'Look, Mr Clark, you're a respectable family, not like many round here. Because of that, I wanted to come and have a word with you. Tip you off myself, if you like.' He paused, embarrassed as he shifted his helmet nervously.

Suzannah walked over to her father. 'Will Girton have to go to court? I mean, it's his first offence—'

'His first offence!' Jacob said hoarsely, pausing. 'Or is it?'

'As far as I know.' The officer's sympathy was obvious. 'I'm going to try to get your son off with a warning. But he may still have to go to court.'

Stupefied, Jacob looked down at his hands. His son in court, his son a lookout, a runner-around for the dregs of Hanky Park. But why? Why had Girton done it? Why had he let himself fall so low?

'I don't understand . . .'

'He said it was for the money.'

'The money?' Jacob repeated, incredulous. Shaking his head, he looked back at the officer. 'Where is my son now?'

'Outside.'

'Too scared to tell me himself, hey? The bloody coward.'

'You're wrong, Mr Clark,' the policeman replied. 'He wanted to tell you, but I wanted to have a word with you first. I've seen many men go bad round here, but your son's not the type. He could do better with his life. Talk some sense into him, will you? Before it's too late.'

With that the policemen turned and left. A moment later Girton entered the shop. His face was putty-coloured, his collar undone, his smart suit crumpled. He looked ashamed, genuinely distressed.

'Dad, I didn't—'

'SHUT UP!' Jacob bellowed. 'DON'T EVEN TALK TO ME! How could you? How could you do this? How could you disgrace me? This family? Yourself?'

And then – unexpectedly – Mrs Bradshaw hurried in from next door, her bulk making her breathe heavily with exertion. As she entered the tailor's shop she paused, momentarily awed by the family group which faced her: Jacob incandescent with rage, Girton's head bowed as his father railed at him.

Suzannah spotted their neighbour first. 'Not now,' she said, moving towards her.

'I think yer father might be the best judge of what 'e wants to hear, missy,' Mrs Bradshaw replied sharply, pushing past Suzannah to get to Jacob. 'Mr Clark, I've got something to tell yer.'

'I know!'

Her eyebrows rose. 'Yer do?'

'Yes, I hate to spoil your moment of triumph, Mrs Bradshaw, but I already know about my son.'

'Yer what?'

'You'd do well not to interfere in my family,' Jacob said warningly. 'Just leave. Please.'

'But—'

'I'll deal with this my own way! He is my son.'

Mrs Bradshaw frowned, momentarily wrong-footed.

186

'Yer son? Nah, it's nothing about Girton. It's poor Mr Tobarski.'

Jacob turned to her, the colour draining from his face. 'Stanley? What about Stanley?'

'I'm ever so sorry I 'ave to tell yer, but 'es dead. Poor Mr Tobarski's dead.'

Jacob shook his head. Stanley dead? No, it couldn't be true. His mentor, his surrogate father, dead? He could remember in aching detail the way Stanley moved, laughed, the way he put his head on one side when he asked a question. He wasn't going to put his key in the door of the tailor's shop ever again. Wasn't going to say 'not meant, not meant'. Wouldn't hang his suit jacket on the back of the workshop door and whistle – out of tune – as he chalked up a pattern.

'How?'

' 'E were in the park this afternoon,' Mrs Bradshaw went on, relishing the details. ' 'E fell over on the bridge. Banged 'is 'ead on the stonework. Killed 'im outright.'

Jacob's voice was unsteady. 'Was he alone?'

'Aye, no!' Mrs Bradshaw replied. 'Some said there were a woman with 'im. She were screamin' fit to bust.'

When he spoke, Jacob's voice was barely more than a whisper. 'I'm sorry I was rude to you . . . I misunderstood.'

Nodding, Mrs Bradshaw hurried out, not wanting to waste another moment in the tailor's shop. She had news to pass on; gossip to spread round Hanky Park. Within minutes everyone would know about the death of Stanley Tobarski. And how Mrs Bradshaw had had to break the news to the family. A family – she would add darkly – right in the middle of a corking good row.

In the tailor's shop, Jacob was still slumped in his chair, staring ahead. Several minutes passed. Suzannah was close to tears. Finally Jacob looked over to his daughter.

'Stanley *can't* be dead.'

She moved over to him, putting her arm around his shoulder.

'He can't be dead . . .' he repeated numbly. 'Not Stanley.'

'Oh Dad,' she said brokenly. 'I'm so sorry.'

For several moments Jacob remained motionless. Grief had paralysed him. Stanley was dead – as was the old life, the old way. They had to move on, somehow. Taking in a deep breath, he turned to his son.

'I want you to listen to me carefully now, Girton. I was soft with you because I was always trying to make up for the way your mother treated you. No more. You're going to be a tailor, whether you like it or not.' He glanced over to Suzannah. 'I'm not pushing you out, love. I'll never forget what you've done – but now Stanley's dead, everything's clear to me. We need a male apprentice in this shop. You're going to be a fine tailor one day, Suzannah, but people won't accept you. So we'll have to give them what they *will* accept – a male tailor. And that's you, Girton.' He turned to his son. 'I've had enough grief. This is the last I'll take from you. You walk away from Denny Cathcart *now*. You walk away from his world and the types he mixes with. I don't give a damn how you feel any more; *I'm* telling you what your life is going to be from now on.'

'Dad—'

'No,' Jacob said, putting up his hands. 'Not a word. If you have to go to court, so be it. But whether you go or not, your arrest will be the talk of the town. We have to join forces now if we want to keep this family and this business running. If we don't, we'll end up on the scrapheap like so many others round here. You want that? You think poor Stanley worked all those years to see his business fail? He worked to keep out of the gutter – and to *stay* out.'

Shamefaced, Girton could hardly meet his father's eyes. 'I thought I was helping.'

'No, you were bringing in money! Any fool can do that. I don't want money if it's been got illegally. I don't want my son working as a lookout for a villain. What in God's name possessed you? Don't you know the kind of man that usually does that job, Girton? A no-hoper. A man on his way into – or just coming out of – Strangeways. It's the first step going *down*. And if you want to take it, then go now.'

'Dad—'

He cut Girton off at once. 'I won't have a criminal in this house! I don't want the police knocking on the door at all times of the day and night. Filth isn't hard to find, Girton. The hard part's keeping it off you.'

'Listen to me—'

'No, Girton, you listen to me! I will *not* have my name dishonoured. I've lost too much in life to lose more.' His voice made his son cower. 'I can't undo the past, Girton. I can't even understand it myself. Why so many bad things happen. I couldn't stop any of it happening. To me, to you, to any of us. But I *am* going to stop you ruining your life. You do as I say now, Girton, or you follow your own path. But you'll do it alone.' He pointed to the door. 'You're free to make your choice. But there's no coming back, no changing your mind. If you want to live that way, get out now.'

Suzannah glanced over to her brother. 'Girton, don't go. Please.'

'It's his choice!' Jacob said sharply. 'Let him make his own mind up.'

'I don't want to go!' Girton blustered. 'I swear I'll settle down, learn the trade – if you'll teach me.'

'Don't ask me,' Jacob said magnanimously. 'Ask your sister.'

Shamefaced, Girton glanced over to Suzannah. 'OK with you?'

'I love you, Girton,' she said quietly, 'but I don't know if I can trust you any more. You say you'll do it now – but *will* you keep your word? Stick with it? This time you *can't* break your promise. There's too much riding on it – for all of us.'

THIRTY-FIVE

As quietly as she could, Suzannah splashed cold water on her face. Only moments earlier she had been sick – unexpectedly, violently sick – and then huddled, cold, against the basin. She couldn't go on like this. Now she had the nausea, someone in the family was bound to notice. And before too much longer she would begin to show anyway.

Despite everything else that was happening around her, Suzannah knew she had to sort out her own life. The walls pressed down on her, suffocating, enclosed. Abortion was out of the question. She would have to face up to her situation; tell Bert. And her family ... Wiping her face with a flannel, Suzannah stared at the floor. She couldn't put it off any longer. This weekend she would tell Bert.

It didn't help that she had avoided being alone with him since the night they had made love. Confused, Bert had continued to call round to the tailor's shop to see Jacob, but every time he tried to get Suzannah alone, she would make excuses. Finally, the previous evening, he had cornered her by the back door.

'What's going on?' he had asked, obviously confused. 'Suzie, what's the matter? Surely yer not regretting what we did. Or are yer?'

She had turned to him, her voice low. 'Bert, we shouldn't have ... Look, we can't talk here. It's not right. Nothing's right. We can't go on—'

Then Helen had interrupted them, barging past to shoo

next door's cat off the outside privy. Seizing her chance to get away from Bert, Suzannah had moved back into the kitchen where Jacob was reading the paper.

But avoiding Bert – and the truth – wasn't fair. It was cruel, Suzannah knew only too well, and he didn't deserve such callous treatment. So that morning she had sent a message asking to meet up with him on Saturday in Peel Park, by the refreshments café, at two p.m.

Meanwhile Suzannah had other things to attend to. It was Thursday, her day off from the shop, the day when she always went shopping in Salford. There was to be nothing unusual, nothing different in her routine to make anyone suspect anything. Glancing at Girton and her father in the workshop, Suzannah moved to the door.

'I'm off now, see you later.'

They waved in unison, preoccupied.

After doing some of the lighter family shopping, Suzannah boarded the bus out to Saddleworth Moor. Bert would have got the note by now, she thought, and be waiting to see her on Saturday. Wondering what she was going to say . . . Sighing, she rested her head against the cool glass of the bus's window, her reflection looking back at her.

She was going to be a mother. And a wife. Because Bert would do the decent thing, and because Bert loved her. It wouldn't be so bad a life, after Jacob came to terms with the situation. After all, Suzannah had known she would marry one day and have a family. And besides, it wouldn't stop her tailoring.

Her reflection looked back at her. Mocking her. *You had ambitions once, big ideas. You wanted more than Bert Gallager. You could do better than him* . . . Irritated, Suzannah glanced away from the window. Life never turned out the way you wanted it to. Like finding her mother – who didn't even remember her.

The bus chugged on through the snow, climbing higher, then moving on into the grim landscape of Saddleworth

Moor. Finally, it stopped near Snowhill, Suzannah and a couple of other passengers getting off. The cold was getting intense, a chill wind slicing down from the high ground, as she moved up the drive towards the entrance.

The way was familiar to her now. After all, she had made a number of visits. And every time Dr Samuels said there was no change. But not to give up; miracles happened. What did anyone really know about the brain? he always went on. About whether a patient would, or wouldn't, claw their way back? Who knew what would trigger a reaction? What might be reason enough to make them *want* to come back?

Walking into the ward, Suzannah approached her mother. Gloria was sitting up, a bowl of untouched jelly in front of her, her hair newly washed.

'You look nice,' Suzannah said, sitting down next to the bed.

There was no response.

'I've been shopping,' she went on, reaching into one of her bags and bringing out a bed jacket. Gently, she laid it around Gloria's shoulders. 'That'll be warm for you, Mum.'

Still no response. Sighing, Suzannah glanced around the ward. Visitors were sitting around other beds, deep in conversation, some laughing. One man was even playing cards with his wife. Everyone was busy, responsive. Except Gloria.

'I can't stay too long today,' Suzannah went on, talking light-heartedly, as though she expected her mother to answer at any moment. 'I have to get back and make tea. My turn, although Helen's cooking is getting better. Not great, but better.' She glanced around her, then looked back to her mother. Gloria's eyes were blank, staring ahead. 'I was thinking about something this morning. About how you used to draw those little cartoons. You remember, Mum? You used to doodle them to make me laugh when I was a kid. Little ants, wearing dresses, and alligators. I think you got that idea from Stanley's stuffed alligator.' She paused. Stanley was gone now, although the alligator was still at his flat in Vera Street. The flat which had to be cleared out. Only no one had had the heart to do it yet. 'I was thinking about the shop too. You remember the shop, Mum? The tailor's shop, with the yellow blind and the old dummies in the window?' She stared at her mother's face, urging her to remember. 'You were the tailor's wife. Married to Jacob Clark—'

'Jacob.'

Suzannah caught her breath. 'Yes, that's right. Jacob. And you had children, Mum. A family. There was me, Girton and Helen . . .' There *was* some response, Suzannah could see it. It wasn't just her imagination. 'Me, Girton and Helen—'

'I had a baby,' Gloria said quietly. 'A baby boy . . . He died.' Transfixed, Suzannah stared at her mother, Gloria turning slowly to look at her. 'Who are you?'

'I'm your daughter, I'm Suzannah.'

'Suzannah . . . I had a baby boy, he died.'

'That was Arthur, Mum. He died in an accident,' Suzannah said tentatively. God, please don't let her shut down again. Please let her remember.

'Yes, he died . . . There were horses, horses' hoofs on the street.' Gloria paused, her eyes widening. 'My baby died. My baby died. And . . . and I couldn't work out what to do. I wasn't a good mother; you were all better without me. So I ran away . . .' Her gaze moved from Suzannah to the far wall; memory coming intermittent and painful. 'I ran away. I thought you'd come for me. I thought you'd find me . . . but no one did.'

'We looked for you everywhere, Mum!' Suzannah said urgently. 'But you changed your name, we couldn't find you.'

'I went away . . .' Gloria paused again, rubbed her forehead, her hands coarse and dry. 'Oh God . . .'

'What is it, Mum?'

She turned, recognition suddenly in her eyes. 'You're Suzannah? You're all grown up.'

'Yes,' she said, her voice catching. 'All grown up.'

'I should never have left you. Any of you. Your father. Girton . . .' She winced at the name, the memory. 'And my little girl. I left you all.'

'It doesn't matter, Mum!' Suzannah reassured her. 'You weren't well. It's OK, you can come home now.'

'I can't come home,' Gloria said, shaking her head, her voice helpless. 'I can't go back, after what I did. And look at me.' She touched her face, stared at her hands. 'Jacob wouldn't want me now. No one would want me now. You'd all be so ashamed of me. I can't go back.'

'Mum, don't fret, *please* don't fret,' Suzannah said, soothing her mother. She dreaded spooking Gloria into another withdrawal. 'No one's hurrying you into anything. You just get well, you hear? And when you're well, then we can do things the way *you* want.'

'You can't tell them!' Gloria said suddenly, her voice surprisingly firm. 'Don't tell the others that you've found me.'

'Mum—'

'Don't tell them!'

'All right, all right, I won't,' Suzannah agreed reluctantly. 'I'll wait until you're ready.'

'I never will be,' Gloria said, looking down at Suzannah's hand on the bed and reaching for it. But at the last moment she stopped, letting her own hand come to rest an inch away. Close, but not touching. 'You don't know what I am, Suzannah, or you wouldn't want me back. You don't know where I've been, what I've done.'

'I don't care. You're my mother. That's the *only* thing that matters.' Tentatively Suzannah moved her hand over Gloria's. 'My father, Girton, Helen, Hanky Park, the tailor shop – they can all wait, Mum. It doesn't matter how long it's going to take, because you're alive, and you're here. And I'm with you.' She rested her cheek against the back of Gloria's hand, tears coming fast. 'I've looked for you for years. *Missed* you for years . . .'

Confused and panicked, Gloria stared at her daughter. And then, unexpectedly, something shifted inside her. Memory, regret, mixing with bad dreams, booze and breakdowns. And then, through the maze of confusion, Gloria remembered a little girl sitting doing her homework. A child she had loved so much.

Come and sit with me, sweetheart. My little girl, my favourite . . .

And *then* Gloria reached out. To a child from the past, a memory child who had once been hers. And now was hers again.

THIRTY-SIX

The jangle of the doorbell alerted Girton that there was a customer. Walking into the shop, he paused, surprised to find an obese man pointing a finger at him.

'Where's Jacob Clark?' the man said sourly. 'I want a word with him.' His gaze moved to the doorway which separated the shop from the living quarters. 'You Clark?'

Squinting, Jacob tried to make out the bellicose figure silhouetted against the light. 'What can I do for you?'

'Get out of my bloody shop!' the man snapped, banging his hand on the counter. 'Your days on Easy Street are over, Clark. You and your family can bugger off.'

'Now watch it!' Girton said sharply. 'Just who the hell are you?'

'I'm Lionel Taylor, brother of Stanley Tobarski.' He watched them both pale. 'Oh, heard of me, have you? Well, I were kept in the dark for years by my sly bloody brother. Not a word about this little haven. Told me he were a council clerk. Came round my place looking like a pauper when all the time he had this shop!' Lionel was seething. So his flaming brother had thought he could cheat him, had he? No bloody way: *no one* cheated Lionel Taylor.

'You don't know he left the shop to you,' Jacob said urgently. 'Stanley said he'd made a will which stated that he'd left it to me. And I believe him.'

'More fool you. Because whatever Stanley said, he didn't *do* it. There's no will,' Lionel said gleefully, 'so it's mine, as the nearest living relative. You know the law. I give you a week to get out. Be grateful I'm a reasonable man.'

'How d'you know there's no will?' Jacob pressed him, panic just below the surface.

'I've been round to Stanley's flat on Vera Street,' Lionel replied smoothly. 'Amazing what you can learn from a newspaper. Now normally I don't get the Salford rag, but someone happened to have left it in my shop. And there it was – "Man Dies in Fatal Fall in Peel Park".' Lionel looked round the shop, then glanced back to his shaken audience. 'I don't know why I read it, but lucky for me I did. And lo and behold, it was my poor brother. Dead in the park. A dead tailor, with a shop I didn't know about, and a flat in Vera Street. So naturally I went round and told the landlady I was sorting out my dear brother's things.' Lionel paused, to get the full flavour of his triumph. 'I went through everything, looked everywhere. No will, Mr Clark. *Nothing*. My brother died intestate. Hard luck.'

'I don't believe it,' Jacob repeated dumbly. 'Stanley wouldn't have lied to me. If he said there was a will, there was a will.'

'No will,' Lionel said, his tone nasty. 'And no more shop for you.'

Stunned, Jacob sat down. So it had finally happened. He was going to lose the shop. The sword which had hung over his head for so long had finally fallen. Dear God, Jacob thought helplessly, surely Stanley had made a will? He must have done! He couldn't have wanted the shop to go to this pig of a man by default. He had hated his brother.

'You can't just throw us out!' Girton said belligerently, facing up to the interloper. 'We have rights—'

'Bugger your rights! You've none. I've taken advice, legal advice,' Lionel replied, laughing wheezily, then leaning towards Girton. 'Back off, kid, you don't know who you'd be taking on.'

'My father's not well,' Girton continued protectively. 'He can hardly see.'

'So buy him some better glasses,' Lionel retorted. 'I'm

not a bleeding optician. And I don't have to sort out your problems.'

'This is our home, we've lived here for years,' Jacob replied, looking incredulously at his tormentor. 'You can't just throw us out. Everything we have is here.'

'Lucky you had so long,' Lionel replied coldly. 'But now I want you and your family out in a week.' He pointed to Girton. 'He's a big lad, get him down the pit, make him work for you.'

'But what about Suzannah? Helen?' Jacob said helplessly. 'My daughters. What can I tell them? Where can we go?'

Lionel waved his fleshy hand impatiently. 'You've all been living off my brother's good nature for too long.'

'We were partners!' Jacob snapped, looking at his nemesis with loathing. 'I put as much into this shop as Stanley did.'

'Shame he didn't look out for you then, isn't it?' Lionel replied, walking around and studying the old cabinets filled with shirts, socks, ties. 'Passed its best, isn't it? As for those dummies. Jesus, they're older than Moses.'

It was too much for Jacob to bear. 'Mr Taylor, I beg you—'

'Oh, don't beg me, it never works. Never has, never will.' Lionel moved to the door and turned. 'There's only one thing you can do for me. Get out. In one week I don't want to see any blind men, big dumb lads or bloody women here. You got it? This place is mine now. And there's nothing you can do about it.'

The snow was coming down even more heavily, Suzannah thought, looking out of the bus window. And God, it was cold ... She stared up at the sky, heavy and overcast. Lucky she had left early and would be home before dark.

Her emotions were all over the place. She was exhilarated about Gloria's progress and yet sad to have to keep a secret she wanted to shout out to the world. But then again, it didn't really matter, Suzannah told herself. In time her mother would come back. The tailor's wife would come home ... And then the joy about her mother faded as Suzannah remembered Bert and touched her stomach.

She could imagine her father's face when she told him. *I've been having a romance – no, an affair – with your closest friend. And I'm pregnant* ... Wincing, Suzannah looked back out of the window. She could imagine the look of horror on Jacob's face, the amazement that Helen and Girton would feel. And then the rush to arrange the marriage.

At least Suzannah knew that Bert would stand by her. Hadn't he told her often enough that he loved her? Hadn't he suffered when she'd drawn back, avoided him? It wasn't fair, but she would make it up to him. And try to repair the relationship with her father. Because there *would* be a rift – she knew that only too well. He would believe that his daughter had behaved like a Hanky Park tart. And how could she disagree? Or defend herself? Suzannah could never explain why she had turned to Bert – because that would betray her mother.

Suddenly the bus stopped, jarring Suzannah's thoughts back to the present. The snow was coming down heavily, making visibility difficult. Across the aisle a woman was sucking mints, a young lad flicking paper pellets at the back of the conductor's head.

'Oi, watch it, or yer off the bus!'

'Aw, yer couldn't throw me off in the middle of no-where,' the lad replied, slumping back into his seat.

'Where are we?' Suzannah asked. 'And why have we stopped?'

'Engine's overheated,' the conductor replied, shrugging. 'As to where are we, luv, yer guess is as good as mine. We're not even off the moor yet.'

Suzannah glanced at her watch, frowning. 'It's going to be dark soon.'

'Driver's working on it, miss. We all want to get home tonight.'

Another hour passed, the driver still working on the engine, the passengers huddling into their coats. Bitterly cold, Suzannah tried to rub some warmth into her hands, longing to get back to the tailor's shop. They would all be wondering where she was. Why she hadn't got home yet from her shopping trip to Salford. How was she going to explain *this*? God, Suzannah thought, tired and over-wrought, nothing was going right.

The snow kept falling. Repeatedly, the driver tried the engine. It spluttered but didn't catch, and he decided to leave it for a while to cool down. It began to get dark . . . Suzannah gritted her teeth, trying to stop them chattering, her hands deep in her pockets. She felt chilled and unwell, almost nauseous.

Once more, the driver climbed out to try and start the engine. It spluttered. It coughed. He tried again. Spluttering. Coughing. Then, finally, it caught, and slowly and labori-ously the bus began its long crawl back to Hanky Park, arriving a little after seven. Nauseous and chilled, Suzannah hurried along the streets, heartened when she spotted the light on above the tailor's shop. In a moment she would be home. Soon she could relax, lie down, get warm again. The sickness would pass; she just had to get home. Only a little further to walk. A few more steps.

But just as she put the key in the lock, Suzannah felt herself falling forwards, and a warmth, unwelcome and frightening, pouring from between her legs.

THIRTY-SEVEN

Suzannah knew at once that she had lost the baby. Just as she knew she had to hide the fact from her family. Telling her father and Girton that she had got a severe chill shopping, she made her way upstairs. Concerned, Helen followed her.

'God, are you all right?'

'I've got a really heavy period. And bad cramps,' Suzannah lied. 'But I'm OK. I'll be down soon. Just give me a few minutes.'

After changing her clothes and rinsing out her underwear, Suzannah finally made her way back downstairs. Her body felt heavy, her skin marble cold. And her stomach felt oddly empty, her emotions blanked. Should she be relieved? Wasn't it the answer to her problem? She didn't have to tell anyone now that she had been pregnant with Bert Gallager's child. She didn't have to tell *him*. Or marry him. It was solved. So why didn't she feel relieved?

'Maybe you should go to bed,' Girton said, studying his sister's chalk-white face as she walked into the kitchen.

Shaking her head, Suzannah put her feet up on the old sofa. Her stomach contracted suddenly, a spasm of pain coming sharp, then relaxing. *She had lost her baby ...* Passing her sister a cup of tea, Helen perched on the end of the sofa, her expression gloomy.

And then Suzannah realised that *everyone's* expression was anxious, upset.

'What is it? What's happened?'

'You rest—'

201

'Stanley's brother was here!' Helen blurted out helplessly. 'He's told us to get out of the shop.'

Taken aback, Suzannah looked over to Girton 'What? He can't—'

'He can,' Helen replied. 'I rang Mr Clegg for advice, and he said that if there's no will the property always goes to the nearest living relative.' She caught hold of Suzannah's hand. 'Lionel Taylor wants us out in a week.'

'There must be a will!' Suzannah said urgently. 'Stanley always meant for you to have the shop, Dad, he *must* have made a will.'

'I thought that too, at first. But we've looked everywhere you could think of.' Jacob sighed. 'Obviously Stanley didn't get around to it. We *have* to leave here.'

Softly, Helen began to cry, Suzannah's mind running on frantically. They *couldn't* leave the shop. It was their home. Jacob was safe here, he knew his way around. As for Girton, he was finally finding his feet, his role in life. And then there was Gloria. . . . How could the tailor's wife return, if there was no tailor's shop to return *to*?

Oh no, Suzannah thought, no one was taking *their* home.

'There must be a solution. A way out.'

'You should have seen Stanley's brother,' Girton told her. 'A fat, sweating slob of a man. No wonder Stanley didn't ever want him around. He was a pig. And worse, he was enjoying telling us how we had to get out. He was loving every minute.'

'There must be a will *somewhere*—'

'He'd been over to Vera Street,' Girton went on. 'Searched Stanley's flat from top to bottom. No will there. No will here. Lionel Taylor's safe, and he knows it.'

In silence, Suzannah studied her family. The shade which had dogged their lives was now threatening to eclipse them. She could see that Jacob was bewildered, unable to do anything and angered by his helplessness. And Girton was just staring ahead, arms folded, his expression blank. As if to say, *You see, there's nothing certain in life. There's no justice*. Beside Suzannah, Helen was still crying quietly, her hand gripping her sister's.

'What are we going to do?' she said at last. 'What are we going to do?'

'We're going to bed,' Suzannah replied. 'We're all going to get some rest. Tomorrow we'll be able to think more clearly.'

'There's nothing to think *about*,' Girton said wearily. 'The situation's hopeless.'

Suzannah glanced over to him. 'You never know. Life can change very quickly – in the most unexpected ways. Come on, we can't give up. We're the Clark family, remember? We don't *ever* give up.'

That night Suzannah slept intermittently, waking at four and lying in bed, staring up at the ceiling. The stomach cramps had been intense, but were now fading, although she had lost a lot of blood. And a baby . . . She watched the reflection of the shop lamp on the ceiling – JACOB CLARK, TAILOR – and thought of her mother. Then of the threat to the shop. Then of Bert . . . She wanted to be comforted, and yet knew it wasn't possible. Her secrets would remain just that: secrets.

Better for everyone, Suzannah thought, dry-eyed. Across the room, Helen turned over in bed and sighed in her sleep. If Lionel Taylor did get the shop, what would happen to them? Where the hell would they live? *How* would they live without the income from the shop?

Thank God she'd lost the baby; thank God there was one less complication . . . But for all her bravado, Suzannah was bereft, and finally she threw back the bedcovers and got up. Padding to the window, she looked out in time to see the lamp man lighting the gas. Must be six o'clock, she thought, dressing herself hurriedly and going downstairs.

It was Saturday, and although Suzannah was due to meet Bert that afternoon she couldn't wait any longer.

Wrapping herself up, she left the tailor's shop and made for Unwin Street. The abattoir was already busy, the two huge front doors open, steam and light pouring out on to the pavement, and the animals' cries coming, desolate and lost, from a long way within. The sound which had haunted Suzannah as a child.

She glanced round. If anybody saw her she would say that Jacob was sending a message to his friend. Nothing strange in that. Her gaze scanned the men, working in their bloodied overalls, their sleeves rolled up – and then she spotted Bert.

He had also spotted her and was making his way hurriedly towards the doors.

'What is it?' he asked anxiously. 'Yer all right? Yer look washed out.'

'I got a chill,' Suzannah lied; head down as she moved down the street.

He walked beside her, donkey jacket thrown over his whites. 'I thought we were meeting up later, in the park.'

'Bert,' Suzannah said suddenly, stopping and looking up at him. Her heart moved in pity and regret. She was going to have to hurt a good man, a man who had loved her. A man whose child she had just lost. 'I had to see you now, I couldn't wait any longer. I've not been fair with you, Bert. I'm sorry, but we can't go on. It was never right, not us. Not with you being so close to Dad, and—'

'So much older.'

'It's not that,' she reassured him. 'I was wrong when I turned to you. I shouldn't have done what I did. It wasn't your fault, it was mine.'

He was getting panicky, running his hands through his hair. 'What are yer saying? Yer want to be rid of me?'

'I don't want to be *rid* of you!' she replied, shocked. 'But we were never a couple. We sneaked around, kept it a secret from everyone. We were . . . I don't know *what* we were. But it wasn't meant. It's not right. Not for you, or me.'

'I love yer,' he said blindly. 'Doesn't that count for more than what yer father thinks?'

'It's not just Dad,' Suzannah retorted. 'You want a woman to settle down with, Bert. You want a family, you said so once.'

'I can wait.'

'But I'm not ready for that. And I don't know when I will be.' She thought of the baby she had just lost and was suddenly tearful. 'Bert, I can't see you any more. We have to end it now, before it goes any further. Before we ruin everything. I don't want you to hate me and I want you to remain friends with Dad. To visit him, like you always do. He needs a friend. Now more than ever.'

'Why now?'

'Because Stanley's brother has given us one week to get out of the shop.'

He took a deep breath, reaching out to put his arm around her shoulder.

But Suzannah stepped back. 'No, I can't rely on you again. I can't lead you on. It's not fair.'

'But I've never loved anyone else!' he said, frantically. 'I want yer. No one else. We could make this work. *We could*. I don't care what people say, what yer family thinks. I want—'

'I can't,' Suzannah said brokenly, moving away. 'I'm so sorry, so sorry for hurting you. But I can't.'

And then she moved off, slipping back into the clatter of the waking streets.

Three days passed. No one heard from Lionel and no one found anything to help their case. Clegg, Cuthbert and Rathbone were kind and offered good advice, via Helen. But the answer was always the same. Without a will, the shop went to Lionel Taylor. And no, it wasn't fair, but it was the law.

Making breakfast, Suzannah heard the back door open

and turned, hoping to see Bert. Not that she wanted him to come back for her, but to visit Jacob, who was already wondering why his friend hadn't called round.

But it wasn't him, it was Girton, bringing in the coal. 'We should order some more, we're getting low now.'

He paused. They were all thinking the same thing. Why get in new coal when they would be out by the end of the week?

'I've decided on something,' Jacob said, his voice resigned. 'We should begin to pack up. You know, get ready to move.'

Suzannah didn't like to tell him that she had already started. That the shed was full of boxes. It wasn't that she had given up, just that the days were passing so fast and the result looked inevitable. Besides the packing, she had been investigating flats to rent, even suggesting that Helen stay with Nan Siddons to save some money.

'If there's no shop,' Girton said suddenly, breaking into her thoughts, 'there's no tailor.'

Suzannah looked over to him. 'We haven't lost yet.'

'But why carry on when we know we're done for? Why should I bother learning tailoring?'

'Just do it!' Suzannah snapped, unusually sharp, then softened her tone. 'Just do it, Girton, please. We can't hang around uselessly. Besides,' she said, thinking of something else, 'Stanley's old landlady came round this morning. Apparently Lionel Taylor took what he wanted, but didn't take all of Stanley's belongings. So she asked if we could sort out the flat as the lease is coming up for renewal.'

'I doubt there'll be anything much left, after that fat slob's been in,' Girton replied sourly. 'But we could ask if we could rent the place for a while.'

'Yeah, I thought about that too,' Suzannah replied, picking up her coat and making for the door. 'I'll be home later. Tell Helen if she wants me I'll be over at Vera Street.'

The landlady was sorry, she told Suzannah, but she had already made other arrangements. Not that she would ever get a tenant like Mr Tobarski again. Such a lovely old gentleman, not a bit like his brother.

'Call me if you want anything, dear,' the woman told Suzannah. 'Not much left to clear out really. Poor Mr Tobarski, dying like that. So sudden and such a shock to everyone.'

Thanking her, Suzannah closed the door and then looked round. As expected, Lionel had picked the flat clean, leaving only a bare bed, an old lamp and an empty wardrobe. And a couple of boxes on the kitchen table. Rummaging through them, Suzannah found batches of faded papers and an old photograph of a young man and his girl. But no will.

'Blimey,' Helen said suddenly, materialising behind her sister and looking at the old photograph. 'Was that Stanley?'

Suzannah nodded. 'I hoped you'd come. Look at all this stuff. Old letters from his mother and father. Some jewellery invoices. And photographs. Stanley was quite a looker when he was young.'

Perching on the table, Helen picked up an old smoking cap and twirled it round her finger.

'I remember Stanley wearing this. When he was smoking that Meerschaum pipe.' She dug further into the box. 'No pipe?'

'At Lionel's pawnshop, I bet,' Suzannah replied. 'Or sold by now. I can't bear to think of him pawing all Stanley's stuff. He hated his brother so much.' She looked around her, pushing aside the box. 'Nothing in there.'

'We'll keep the photographs anyway.'

'Yes,' Suzannah agreed. 'But not the rest. We have our own stuff to move now. We need to cut back.'

A long moment passed. Both of them realised that time was running out for them. And for the shop.

'He's going to win, isn't he?'

'Maybe,' Suzannah replied, knowing full well that Lionel Taylor was already halfway inside the shop door.

'We could kill him.'

'Yeah,' Suzannah agreed, smiling wryly. 'No one ever would suspect us, would they?'

Pulling the second box towards her, she began to empty it. More letters, statements, invoices. But no will. Nothing to say that the Clark family was safe; that Lionel Taylor was never going to get his claws into Hankerton Street.

After another half an hour of fruitless searching, Helen stretched and stood up. 'I have to get back to work now. I was hoping we'd find something. You know, at the eleventh hour.'

'Me too,' Suzannah replied regretfully. 'Me too.'

Brushing the dust off her hands, she got to her feet and moved back into the bedroom. So little left after such a long life ... Suddenly she noticed something under the bed. A chamber pot, and the old stuffed alligator.

Smiling, she leaned down and pulled the curiosity out. She would take it home, couldn't leave it behind. Not when it had been so much a part of her childhood. A memory stirred: the alligator next to the range in the kitchen, Stanley swearing blind that he had known the man who shot it. And everyone had *hated* it, never touched it, Gloria always praying that someone would steal the thing. But who would steal a stuffed alligator?

Still smiling, Suzannah tucked the large, cumbersome animal under her arm and moved to the door. But before she reached it, she felt her fingers break through the dry skin of the reptile's stomach. Surprised, she held it at arm's length and then stared at it closer.

It wasn't ... *It couldn't be* ... Gently, Suzannah's fingers slid into the opening. Even more gently they caught hold of the tiny edge of paper and pulled. It came out an inch, then another. Finally, after a little more patient persuading, Suzannah found herself unfolding a carefully drawn-up document, dated five years earlier.

She had found the last will and testament of Stanley Tobarski.

PART THREE

For the sake of the soul
With the pastor's smile;
And the childhood demons in cupboards,
And ghosts in glory holes.

Anon

I can remember the feeling so vividly, the euphoria. Stanley had made a will, we were safe. The paper said – in black and white, witnessed and signed – that Jacob Clark was to inherit the tailor's shop. Apparently Stanley had drawn up the will and then hidden it in the stuffed alligator, carefully restitching the skin over the slit in the animal's belly. It was so like Stanley, in a way. He knew how to keep a secret, and he'd always lived in fear of his brother.

And so life, which had seemed so bleak, suddenly opened up like the first spring flower after a crushing winter. It took a while for me to come to terms with the loss of the baby, and I missed Bert, but soon he began visiting my father once more and I would watch him. From a distance. When he left he would always look back – but he never winked at me again.

Secure, Girton began his slow haul back to respectability. And I loved him for it. I would see Denny Cathcart around and hear about the old villains down the 'Oller and think – cringing – how close we came to counting my brother amongst them.

I remember being so grateful that no one had discovered my secret, which could so easily have wrecked my life. But the months passed without incident, Helen courting Archie Culshaw, Dad teaching Girton, and me visiting our mother and waiting for the day when Gloria would finally agree to come home. And best of all, Lionel

Taylor was out of our lives for ever. We all relaxed, believing our biggest threat was gone.

How wrong we were.

THIRTY-EIGHT

1933

The unemployment – rising to two and three-quarter million – hadn't touched Eccles Old Road. Men might hang around street corners in Salford and Manchester, but there was no discernible difference to life for the elite. They might see the job queues in the papers or on the Pathé News, they might listen to the radio reports of men desperate for work, but it meant little.

In Hanky Park the unemployment was biting hard. Men who had relied on having a job for life were now facing ruin. Factories had closed, and the lines of desperate men outside the gates grew daily. Many were too ashamed to return home when the bosses had turned them away; some spent their time walking the streets aimlessly; a few took to wearing placards:

**I KNOW TWO TRADES
I FOUGHT FOR THREE YEARS
I HAVE A WIFE AND 2 CHILDREN
I ONLY NEED <u>ONE</u> JOB**

Very few took to drink; it was too expensive to get blind drunk, and besides, the pubs were long past taking tick from the unemployed. Men who had had decent jobs took to doing the dirtiest work to feed their families. Night soil man, sewage worker, rat catcher. Anything was considered, taken up, no grumbles. It was a job. It was a wage.

But some weren't even that lucky and their wives fell

back on the oldest profession – and solution – in the world. On the game, previously respectable women mixed with hardened prostitutes. Some – the very young – were taken under their wing. But the older women would hang around for days, ashamed and rebuffed, desperate for someone to pay them for sex.

There was no money for hotels, even the worst commercial haunts in Hanky Park, so instead the women took their customers to the nearest ginnel, the men walking back out a few minutes later and hurrying off, the women hanging back, then scurrying home, hoping against hope that no one had seen them.

It wasn't that uncommon to hear of both men and women committing suicide. The shame got to both sexes: for men, not being able to provide; for women, the loss of their dignity. Sexually transmitted diseases became rife in some quarters, along with the usual problems of rickets and tuberculosis. Gonorrhea and syphilis, unchecked, led to open sores, blindness, even the eating away of facial features. And for some, madness – a life concluded in the wasteland of the Manchester Asylum or Snowhill.

The Great Depression which had killed off so many jobs and trades was now picking off the workers. Treasured objects and furniture had to be sold to pay the rent man – only the likes of Lionel Taylor thriving, the mounds of pawned items growing daily, his loan business, with its exorbitant rates, keeping his head well above the mire. His head, and his wife's.

But go a little way out of the worst-hit areas, into the likes of Old Eccles Road, and life was still pleasurable. Life for Noel Lyle particularly so. He was – in the loosest of senses – a businessman. In which particular business no one was quite sure, but it was bound to be legal and respectable. After all, Noel Lyle had friends in high places. He was also, to many, *their* friend in high places. His ability to charm was impressive; he could count MPs, doctors and judges in his coterie of friends, and was always ready to give advice. And money – where it could do him most good.

Noel Lyle was fifty plus, rather dandyish, his thick grey hair setting off the merry expression in his eyes. He seemed like a genial family doctor or a trusted, kindly solicitor, his urbane, benign image hiding the instincts of a snake. Life – to Noel Lyle – was lived on three levels. Who you were really; who you pretended to be; and who you could make yourself appear to further your progress.

Simplicity was only for common people.

'Your mother,' Noel said to his son at the breakfast table, 'is going to show us her new outfit.'

Teddy Lyle's expression was amused. At twenty-seven he was as open-hearted as his father was closed; as artless as his father was manipulative.

'What is it this time?'

'Marlene Dietrich,' Noel replied, putting down the morning paper and turning to his son.

He was very fond of Teddy, liked having him around. Which was fortunate, as his son worked for him as an accountant-cum-manager. Of course Teddy didn't do all the accounts. Just the ones Noel allowed him to see. Other accountants worked on other sets of figures. That way, no one had the complete picture of his business interests. It didn't do to be *too* trusting.

'You know what to do when your mother comes down, don't you?' Noel queried.

'I just smile.'

'Absolutely. And if she asks you for your opinion, say that you couldn't improve on perfection.'

'But we say that every time,' Teddy replied, turning to the door as a tall, dark-haired woman walked in, wearing a man's trouser suit.

'Oh, boy—'

Noel kicked his son under the table. 'Splendid, my love. A triumph.'

She turned, her slim figure androgynous in the pale

worsted suit. On the side of her head she had perched a cream beret, her hair shingled, as shiny as a magpie's wing.

'I *had* to have it,' she said, her voice betraying a faint American accent. 'No one around here will have seen anything like it.'

Teddy didn't doubt that for a moment.

'Thing is, sweetness,' Noel went on, ever indulgent of his glamorous wife, 'where can you wear it?'

She had already thought of that. Sliding into the seat next to her husband, she leaned towards him, her carmined lips smiling. 'I have to go to that Van Gogh exhibition in London, Noel. I just *have* to. People expect me to be there. I mean, someone with my abilities, my talent . . .' She paused, shaking her head incredulously. 'I can't be held back, Noel. I really can't. People just don't understand me. They can't fathom what I'm setting out to achieve. My paintings . . .' she paused, to give the word emphasis, 'are my soul.'

'And it shows in every one,' Noel replied, thinking of the cack-handed mock-Cézannes in the drawing room. God, he thought wryly, why did it have to be *modern* art? He might have taken to a faux-Gainsborough.

'My soul,' she repeated, looking over to Teddy to check her son's reaction.

He was watching her with admiration. Another woman as patently daft as his mother would have been a laughing stock, but CC – Catherine Caroline – was so stylish she could carry off her eccentricities as well as her clothes. In her time she had fought for votes for women, had championed free speech, and posed nude for Alfred Munnings – or so the story went. Her theories were unstable, her logic unassailable and her talent minuscule.

Which didn't bother her in the least.

'I realise what I have to do with my life now,' she went on, Noel smiling at her indulgently. 'I have to bring art to the people.'

'I think jobs might be more useful at the moment,' Teddy interrupted deftly.

His mother blinked. 'Work is one thing, but art is what feeds the soul.'

'You can't live by eating a *painting*, Mother. You need bread for that.'

Looking her son up and down, CC was, as always, impressed by her offspring. Not his opinions, but his appearance. Long-limbed, with dark eyes and dark hair like hers. So lucky to have dodged Noel's weedy genes.

'Teddy, you can't go through life being so pedestrian,' she admonished him. 'Beauty is everything. A man cannot exist without beauty—'

'Or food.'

'Beauty is brain food.'

'Bread is belly food.'

She rolled her eyes dramatically and turned to her husband. 'You see what we've done, Noel? We've raised a revolutionary! A man with no love of the arts.'

Teddy sighed. 'I didn't say that. I just think that an art exhibition is no good to a man without a job or enough food to feed his family.'

'You've been listening to all that propaganda about the unemployed, haven't you?'

'I don't have to listen, Mother, I just have to walk five minutes and I'm into Hanky Park.'

'Why ever would you do that?' she countered, genuinely surprised. 'We don't know anybody who lives there.'

'Thank God,' Noel murmured, reaching for his newspaper.

Giving up, Teddy turned his attention back to his boiled egg.

'We give money to charities all the time,' CC went on. 'You really can't say we don't do anything to help the less fortunate.'

'You're a wonder,' Noel murmured soothingly from

behind his paper. 'No one does more charity work than you, darling.'

'But my son—'

'Doesn't appreciate you,' Teddy said, interrupting the flow and changing the subject deftly. 'But I think your outfit's marvellous.'

He knew that he could talk every hour, on the hour, for the rest of his life and nothing he said would ever make the slightest impression on his mother. She was off her trolley, eccentric, extraordinary and completely out of touch with the real world. She probably thought that the Great Depression – as the papers were calling it – was a crevasse in the Grand Canyon.

THIRTY-NINE

Yawning, Girton unlocked the front door of the tailor's shop and turned the sign to OPEN. As quietly as he could, he walked into the kitchen at the back and put the kettle on. The fire he had started earlier was blazing nicely. Spring was dragging her heels, the streets still sprinkled with dawn frost, the windows ice-ribbed.

Rubbing his hands to warm them, Girton moved into the workshop and put on his overall, tying it around his waist before turning to the working dummy. Thoughtfully he considered the jacket he was finishing, then realigned the pocket a fraction of an inch.

He was seduced by perfection. His training, slow and protracted, had begun with his father and ended with Suzannah. His desire to make amends, to earn back his father's respect, had driven every stitch. Nothing had been too much trouble, nothing had been too difficult. Nothing had been good enough.

It had taken three years for Girton to earn his spurs: to have his own pair of scissors hanging next to his father's and sister's on the hook by the window. Three years from the day of Stanley Tobarski's death and the police charging Girton with illegal gambling. His case had been dropped and he had been let off with a warning – but the damage was done.

Everyone in Hanky Park had heard what had happened. People had clicked their tongues and said it had only been a matter of time before Girton Clark went bad. He'd been on the slide for a while, running with Denny Cathcart – there was only one way that went. But they'd been wrong.

219

Girton and Denny Cathcart had never spoken again.

Rain falling on the skylight overhead brought Girton's thoughts back to the present. Glancing up, he could see a pigeon pecking idly at the glass and noticed that the ceiling needed painting. But paint cost money, and even though they had kept the shop afloat, there was no excess cash for repairs. As the kettle began to hum, Girton moved back into the kitchen and made himself some tea. Perhaps a sale might help, he thought, or a letter to every customer offering a discount. Sipping his tea, he glanced over to the mantel, staring at an old photograph of his father and Stanley Tobarski. If he could get just one good customer, Girton thought, just *one*. A couple of suits and a jacket, maybe even a coat.

But who the hell in Hanky Park could afford any of that? They were lucky if they sold a couple of shirts and some collar studs in a week. Even sales of the old staples – the long johns, the button vests – had fallen off. Clothes were now darned endlessly, socks more mend than original, shirts scissor-trimmed at the neck to cut off the fraying.

For one brief moment Girton thought of Denny Cathcart. Of the car he had driven, of the way he had seen Cathcart pay people off from a wedge of money in his back pocket. Suddenly Girton could feel the money in his own hand, tickling his palm with its rich greenness . . .

'Bad morning.'

His sister's voice snapped him out of his reverie. Guilty, he nodded towards Helen. 'Raining.'

'You don't say. And there was I thinking it was pigeon spit.' She studied her brother carefully. 'You look green, Girton. You want to get out more. Get away from the shop for a bit.'

'I'm needed here.'

'Not day and night.'

'We have debts!' Girton replied, nettled.

'Everyone's got debts. I could give you a bit. Not much, but a couple of quid.'

He shook his head, secretly rattled. His little sister,

offering him money, when he used to bring in cash enough to carry the whole lot of them.

'Thanks for the offer, Helen, but we can manage,' he replied stiffly. 'It's just been a slow week.'

'To follow all the other slow weeks?'

'It'll change.'

'Yeah, right,' she said, unconvinced.

Anyway, Helen thought, why worry? Before long she wouldn't be living at the tailor's shop any more. Her thoughts went back to the previous night. It had been their anniversary; she and Archie had been going out for six months. To the day. Not that he had remembered – but that was men for you, wasn't it? And anyway, hadn't he been delighted with his packet of ciggies? Surprised, she had to admit, but delighted . . . Helen sighed contentedly. Archie was *bound* to propose soon, and then she'd have a nice little house of her own. In Lever Street, maybe.

'You're in my way,' Girton said suddenly, edging Helen to one side.

She pulled a face, then leaned against the work table. 'Why don't you look for another job?'

Girton started. 'You what!'

'If money's that tight, you could get something on the side. Moonlighting. You'd like to have a bit of extra cash in your pocket. And it's time you found a new girlfriend, Girton. If you did, we could all go out in a foursome, you and her and me and Archie. Think of it, we could have some fun.'

'Fun costs money.'

'A walk along the canal doesn't cost money!' Helen retorted. 'A cuddle behind the Methodist Chapel doesn't cost money.'

'Lucky Archie,' Girton said drily, changing the subject. 'I'm needed here, Helen. I can't shirk my responsibilities.'

'Suit yourself,' she said, pushing herself away from the table. 'But there's a world out there, Girton. Other places, people.'

'There's a depression on.'

'Yeah, there is,' she agreed, walking to the door, then turning back. 'But I'll tell you one thing. It's more depressing in here than it is out on the street.'

Inhaling deeply on one of Helen's cigarettes, Archie leaned against the wall of the Gaumont cinema, his trilby tipped at a jaunty angle. Checking that no one was watching, he felt his upper lip. Not bad, not bad at all. His moustache was coming on nicely. How dare that bloody Frank Bottomly say it looked like Morse code? Sure, it was a bit patchy, but it would fill out. Eventually . . . Inhaling again, Archie eyed up a girl as she passed, although the woman totally ignored him. But not for long, thought Archie. Oh no, everyone knew that women liked masculine men – and nothing made a man more masculine than a moustache. You only had to think of Errol Flynn, drawing the women like shit drew flies.

Smiling to himself, Archie thought of the previous evening. Their anniversary. Their flaming anniversary. *After six months!* Oh, Helen was all right, a feisty girl and good-looking, but Archie Culshaw wasn't intending to get tied down for a while. After all, he was special. He was training to be a chemist. His mind swam with the kudos of it all. He could imagine himself only too easily – white coat, name tag, black moustache. The women would be *panting* for him.

Helen was a great girl, but not that special. Not the girl of Archie Culshaw's dreams. That girl was someone else entirely . . . Admiringly, he studied his reflection in the glass of the cinema doors. He would just have to be patient, that was all. Wait until he was a qualified chemist – and his moustache had grown in.

JACOB CLARK & Son
Bespoke Tailor

Teddy Lyle paused underneath the sign before entering the shop. He had been visiting Unwin Street, checking on his father's premises, and then gone for a walk round. Having never spent much time in Hanky Park before, Teddy was curious. Especially when he came across the tailor's shop. A shop which had a fine new tailor – or so the rumour went.

Good God, he thought, walking in and looking around. Dust mites floated in a flash of sullen sun, the counter coming suddenly into view: dark wood, the top bare, apart from a ledger which looked fifty years out of date. Curious, his gaze travelled towards the two dummies standing either side of the counter, horsehair-stuffed: two silent, tailored eunuchs. They looked – as did everything else about the shop – old-fashioned. And yet hadn't everyone told him that in his time old man Clark had been the best tailor around? And apparently his son was as good.

Of course his own father hadn't thought so. The Clarks' shop was in Hanky Park, so how could it even rate a mention? But then Noel Lyle was a snob, who wore only the best. His suits came from Manchester. Hand-made.

'So are Girton Clark's—'

'Hand-made for the *best* clientele,' Noel had interrupted him. 'Not for every scrubber down Chapel Lane.'

'Well, I'm going to have a look anyway,' Teddy had replied. 'It would do you good to be seen patronising the locals.'

'You want to watch your mouth, dear boy. If I were you I would wait until I was a success before I criticised others.'

Teddy's attention flicked back to the present. Through a gap in the door he could see into the back of the tailor's shop, to where a young, dark-haired woman was marking up a piece of suiting with white chalk. Her hair was piled haphazardly on top of her head, pins in her mouth, a large white apron over the top of her dress. And she wasn't wearing shoes. She *had* shoes, he could see them cast off behind her, but she was working in her stockinged feet. The detail fascinated him.

Suddenly aware of the stranger's scrutiny, the young woman walked to the door and closed it. Embarrassed, Teddy felt his face flush and then jumped as the door opened again.

But this time it was the tailor.

'Morning, sir,' Girton Clark mumbled as he pulled down his rolled-up sleeves. 'Forgive me for keeping you waiting, I was busy in the back. What can I do for you?'

'I heard you were a good tailor.'

Girton shrugged, unexpectedly needled. His customer was around his own age, but obviously rich. Smart suit, nice hat, expensive shirt. So why was he in Hanky Park – unless he'd come slumming?

'I was taught by a master.'

'Who was that?'

'My father,' Girton answered. 'But he's lost his sight now. No more tailoring for Jacob Clark.' He was wondering why he was talking so openly, volunteering information when he was normally so reticent. 'Anyway, I do the tailoring now. And my sister.'

'Your sister?' Teddy repeated. So that was the young woman in the workshop. 'That's very modern, isn't it?'

'You mean, for Hanky Park?'

Teddy had inadvertently hit a nerve. 'No, not at all. I mean for anywhere. But then things have changed so much since the war, haven't they? Women do any job they like now.'

Still on the defensive, Girton answered: 'She's a good tailor. Cuts a better seam than I do . . . Anyway, how can I help?'

'I need a new suit. A day suit, nothing too fancy, but well made. A dark worsted, suitable for the office.'

Girton could see his prayers materialising before his eyes. *This* was the customer he needed so much. A man with money, who might bring others with money too.

'Well, for a start, I should show you some material,' Girton said, moving behind the counter and passing some swatches over to Teddy. 'If there's anything there you like, we have it in stock. But I can get most things ordered if you have a particular material in mind.'

Fingering the swatches, Teddy was impressed by the quality. There wasn't that much choice, but the limited stock was first rate. Glancing over to the dummies in the window, he pointed to one.

'I like that.'

Girton smiled. 'I made that as a sample. Took the cut from a style very much in vogue in London.' He was beginning to relax. 'People say it's a little too modern for around here, and maybe it is, but quality counts in the end. And style.'

'I couldn't agree more,' Teddy replied, studying the suit on the dummy. 'I've seen something like this on Deansgate.'

Deansgate, Manchester – the compliment caught Girton off guard. 'Probably better placed for selling there.'

'Maybe not. Could you make *me* a suit like that?'

Before Girton could answer, the door to the back opened quietly, Suzannah walking into the shop and putting a ledger under the counter. Seeing the customer, she smiled. Girton noticed Teddy Lyle's interest. So that was it! he thought. This benefactor was more interested in his sister than any suit he could make.

'It would be expensive,' Girton said, immediately adding several pounds for the customer's nerve. 'But I could take your measurements now, sir.'

Smiling once again, Suzannah left the shop and then paused behind the door, listening. Clever Girton, she thought with admiration. He'd made the most of an opportunity. Laughing softly to herself, she moved on into the kitchen.

It was amazing how much extra you could charge for a smile.

FORTY

Rina stared out into the yard. God, what a day, she thought, watching the rain teeming down the window. Bored and disconsolate, she kept staring at the ribs of water; the outside privy and coal shed indistinct, dark forms against the grey afternoon sky.

Life hadn't gone according to plan. Not at all. The years were passing and her bastard husband was fit and well. So much for the age difference. Worse, Rina had found that although men still panted after her, the Moss Side men never followed through. Everyone was too frightened of Lionel Taylor to commit adultery with his wife. So, gradually, she had been caught up in the pawnshop's sticky web – trapped and going nowhere.

Rina sighed, hungry for sex. And not sex with Lionel. Still, she consoled herself, her time hadn't been completely wasted. Little did her husband know that she had been carefully siphoning off cash for herself. And lately Rina had begun another sideline – secretly buying from customers *direct* and then reselling on the market. Oh yes, she thought greedily, *that* was turning out to be a nice little earner.

In the pawnshop beyond she could hear her husband moving around, his voice raised against some poor soul who had come to pawn his wedding band.

'It's bloody brass!' Lionel snapped. 'I can't give you money for brass. What d'you think I am? A bloody bank?'

'Please,' the woman begged him, 'just a bit of cash to see to the rent man.'

Her husband's tone softened. Rina disliked his softness the most; the trick of kindness before the kick in the teeth. 'I could arrange a loan for you . . .'

She could sense the woman stiffen. Everyone in Moss Side knew about Lionel's loans and the interest. But she was obviously desperate.

'I . . . I'll have to think about it.'

'Well, think quickly,' Lionel cautioned her. 'The rent man's back tomorrow and he'll not be put off twice.'

When she heard the outer door close, Rina moved into the shop. Lionel was leaning over the counter, a magnifying glass to one eye, a gold chain in his hand. Over the last few years his hair had thinned so much that his scalp shone underneath, his jowls fleshy. He was – she thought resignedly – a toad in a suit.

'What's for dinner?' he asked his wife, without looking up.

Slowly, Rina continued to scrutinise him. His sex drive repelled her, as did any close contact. His slobbering kisses, his rough pawing when the urge overwhelmed him.

'You deaf or what?'

'Huh?'

He looked over to her. 'I asked what was for dinner.'

'Mince and potatoes.'

'I hate bloody mince! Why d'you make it all the time, when I hate it so much?' he asked, dropping the gold chain on to a jewellery tray and then sliding it back into the display cabinet. 'I swear you do it to best me.'

'It was all I could get,' Rina lied. 'The butcher didn't have anything else. No one's got anything better round here.'

'You're Mrs Lionel Taylor, you can *afford* better,' he replied nastily. 'You go back and tell that toerag you want something good, you hear me?'

'I hear you, Lionel,' she replied evenly. 'But I'm not going back. The mince is made—'

'I don't want bloody mince!' he snapped, jutting his face towards hers.

She stepped back immediately. 'OK, OK, I'll have a word with him.'

'Wiggle your arse,' Lionel told her. 'You could get anything you liked if you made up to him.'

'Perhaps I could get chops if I slept with him.'

She had gone too far and knew it when he caught hold of her arm. His fingers pressed into her skin, making her wince, his lips only an inch from her ear.

'If I ever catch you sleeping around, I'll kill you.'

'Lionel, you know—'

'I don't know *anything*!' he shot back, his grip tightening.

Tomorrow she would have a bruise, like so many other times. But although he didn't know it, every time he hurt her, it cost him. A little more revenge money sliding into Rina's secret hoard.

'Lionel, cut it out! I don't cheat on you.'

'You better not. You'd better not even *think* of messing about with another man.' He let her go, certain he had made his point. 'I've put a roof over your head, fed you and clothed you, so don't you dare abuse my kindness. I own you,' he went on, turning away from his wife. 'Forget it, and you'll rue the bloody day.'

His attention drifted suddenly, his eyes alighting on a small gold signet ring. It reminded him of one his brother used to wear and brought back unpleasant memories.

'Bloody Stanley.'

Rina glanced over to him sullenly. 'What?'

'That signet ring. It made my dear departed brother come to mind.'

Rina could easily believe that Lionel seldom thought about Stanley, but *she* thought about the old man often. Thought about how she had missed her chance there. He had had a tailor's shop. Something her sly husband had kept quiet about – until he was bested. Only *then* did Lionel confide in her. Raging about his loss.

His loss. Damn it, Rina thought for the hundredth time, if only *she'd* known about the shop. Stanley had liked her; how long before she convinced him that he loved her? After all, she'd worked her magic on one brother, why not the other? And Stanley had been a kind man, much nicer than Lionel. With a clean little shop . . . Another thought occurred to Rina in that moment and made her smile. She might be miffed that *she'd* lost out, but she was jubilant that Lionel had failed.

Then Rina remembered that day in Peel Park. She had seen Stanley falling and screamed, then panicked. Dear God, what if Lionel heard about it somehow, found out that she had run to his despised brother for help? He would never have believed there wasn't something going on between them.

So she'd run off. A woman no one knew, no one recognised. A beautiful blonde woman who left without looking back. A woman who ran so hard that she was breathless when she finally hailed a tram back to Moss Side, sitting inside shaking, her teeth clenched. By the time she had returned to the pawnshop it was getting dark. Slipping in at the back door, she had found Lionel playing cards with his cronies and had made some excuse about going to the dentist for a broken tooth. He'd been losing, so he hadn't listened. For once not questioning her, allowing her to slip upstairs . . .

'Yeah, Stanley – the lying rat,' Lionel continued, cutting into his wife's memory. 'I should have had that shop. But no, those bloody Clarks got it. Stole it from me. The miserable little shit said he was a council clerk! And I believed him.' Lionel snorted with irritation. 'I were slow there, and it serves me right. Never had a bit of interest in Stanley. Couldn't stand the sight of him. Never thought he'd got more than a couple of quid in the world. Looks like I were wrong.'

Delighted, Rina studied her husband. I'm glad you didn't know, you pig, she thought. Glad your brother got one over on you.

'What are you moaning about, Lionel? You've got enough.'

'Enough! I've got enough! You've never questioned my money before. Never said I had too much in the past.' Pursing his thick lips, Lionel looked at his wife. 'You know, you're a big disappointment to me, Rina. You should wish me well. Should want me to prosper. But from the look on your face it'd seem like you're pleased I lost that shop.' He leaned forward, fingering a chain around her neck. 'Parasites shouldn't get all moral, my dear. You're wearing other people's misery round your throat. And never questioned it before.' He pulled on the chain, drawing her towards him. 'We both know why you married me, and why you stay. I could knock you black and blue and you'd not leave. You like the ring of the cash till too much.'

'I might surprise you one day,' Rina said, her expression flinty.

'Is that a threat? You should watch what you say, Rina. I don't take lip from a woman. Any woman. You just open your legs when you're asked to and keep your mouth shut when you're told to, and we'll rub along nicely, you and me.' He let her go, pushing her away. 'We're married, you made a contract and you'll stick to it. *Till death us do part*, Rina. Remember that.'

FORTY-ONE

It was very risky, but Rina couldn't stop herself. Waiting until Lionel went on his next trip to London, she caught a tram over to Salford and then walked to Hanky Park. The slums were not unfamiliar to her, the women calling out from their pitch on the corner, the queue of unemployed men hanging around the timber yard gates. She had come from slums and knew the territory well. All slums were pretty much the same, in the north, in Glasgow, in London. They all smelled the same and bled you dry the same.

Hurrying along, Rina checked the piece of paper she was holding and then turned into Hankerton Street, finally arriving opposite the tailor's shop. So *this* was Stanley's place? she thought, putting up her umbrella to protect herself from the rain. Carefully, she studied the shop. A couple of funny old dummies in the window, and the blinds had seen better days, but it wasn't bad. Not bad at all. She felt a sudden flicker of glee. Bugger you, Lionel; I'm glad you missed out here.

Her curiosity drawing her closer, Rina crossed the road and looked in at the window. A memory of Stanley came back to her. A dapper little man, comically kind. Already devoted to her. Before much longer he would have been smitten. Hers for the taking. If only she'd been *his* wife, Rina thought, then she would have been the mistress of this shop. Her gaze moved over the dummies' impassive faces, the ornate Victorian light over the door, the OPEN sign in old-fashioned, ornate script.

She could have been set up nicely here, Rina thought,

irritated beyond measure. And Stanley would have been an easy man to fool. Not like Lionel. Oh no, she could have been Stanley's wife *and* had some fun on the side. Her gaze moved to the buildings which flanked the tailor's shop: a net curtain twitching suddenly as Mrs Bradshaw ducked out of sight in her flat over the tobacconist's.

The rain was falling loudly on the umbrella over Rina's head, her heart banging. The thought of the pawnbroker's was suddenly repellent. She couldn't face walking back into the darkened, cluttered shop, its walls hung high with gloomy objects, shelves creaking under the mess of pawned rubbish. It was foul-smelling; rank with greed and melancholy.

A car door banging shut startled Rina and made her step back, her heel catching on the kerb. Trying to steady herself, she lurched forward, her umbrella rolling across the street as she stumbled against the wall.

'Hey!' a man said, helping her regain her balance. 'Careful! It's slippery out here.'

Embarrassed, Rina watched the man run after her umbrella, returning a moment later and handing it to her with a mock bow.

'It's a little the worse for wear.'

'Aren't we all?' she answered, smiling, impressed by her good-looking rescuer.

The rain had now soaked her hair, making it a darker blonde, raindrops running over the curves of her cheek-bones. Even drenched, she looked perfectly, exquisitely beautiful.

'Thank you for helping me,' she said, holding out her hand. 'I'm Rina.'

'And I'm Girton. Girton Clark. The tailor.'

Now wasn't *that* something? Rina thought to herself, smiling even more brightly. Wasn't that something?

FORTY-TWO

Hurrying into the workshop, Helen looked round, then leaned towards her sister. 'You'll never guess what I saw this morning.'

'A giraffe on the tram?'

'Very funny,' Helen replied, sitting down and reapplying her lipstick. Never more than a foot from a mirror, Girton always said. 'So our brother didn't tell you?'

'Tell me what?'

'Girton never mentioned his maiden in distress?'

Suzannah paused, pins in between her pursed lips. She had been securing the shoulder seam on the dummy's right arm, but was now intrigued. 'What maiden in distress?'

'I was going to the post office at dinner time for Mr Cuthbert and I thought I'd drop in to see you.' She held out the bowl of pins towards her sister. 'I was just coming round the corner when I saw Girton running after an umbrella.'

Suzannah took the pins out of her mouth. 'An umbrella? Girton never bothers with those.'

'It wasn't his! It belonged to some blonde piece. Very good-looking.'

Suzannah put the pins back in her mouth and turned to the dummy again. 'A blonde, hey?'

'A *young* blonde. She slipped and he ran after her umbrella. And then they stood talking for a bit.'

Suzannah paused, her voice muffled. 'So what?'

'So what!' Helen retorted. 'So our brother hasn't had a girlfriend for ages.'

'Meg Riley.'

'What?'

Suzannah took the last pin out of her mouth and fixed it to the suit.

'Meg Riley,' she repeated.

'That was over months ago!' Helen replied dismissively. 'I tried to fix him up with that girl from the office. Said all four of us could go out together.'

'How *is* Archie, by the way?'

Helen beamed. 'Wonderful . . . Anyway, to get back to Girton: when I asked him about the blonde, he got all red in the face.'

'Perhaps he was standing too close to the fire?'

'OK, mock me if you like!' Helen replied, rolling her eyes. 'But I think our brother's finally got interested in someone. I could tell.'

'Oh, you and your romances! You never let up, do you? Look at last year – you were desperate for me to go out with that Tommy Hurd,' Suzannah said, laughing and glancing back to the dummy.

'He was nice!'

'He had buck teeth!'

'Useful to take the tops off beer bottles,' Helen teased her. 'Anyway, I reckon that if Girton's found someone he likes, good for her. I just want to hear all the details, that's all.'

Carefully, Suzannah stored away the information to tell their mother later. Gloria loved to hear the gossip, anything about her family. But that was as close as she ever got – gossip. Despite Suzannah's repeated requests, Gloria wouldn't even think of returning to Hanky Park.

It was her past, she told her daughter. There was no going back.

The baker's shop stood on the corner of Union Street, Oldham. Nothing remarkable, its windows large and well-cleaned, three high steps leading up from the kerb. Inside, Gloria was placing some cakes on a tray and setting them out in the window. She was looking forward to seeing Suzannah later, eager to tell her about what she had done with the new flat. Nervously, she looked at her fellow shop assistants. Did they suspect anything? Notice that there was anything different about the new employee? Did she show her past on her face?

Obviously, up to a point. Gloria knew that the pretty young woman Jacob Clark had loved so much had long gone. But she had finally begun to put on some weight and take care with her appearance again – not that she could ever undo the years she had lived rough.

The thought made her cringe. Despair had dragged her down. Despair and madness. Grief-stricken by the death of her child, she had alternated between sanity and booze-soaked forgetfulness . . . Wiping the counter, Gloria calmed herself. She was clean now, in her right mind, stable. Her time at Snowhill over. But however many times Suzannah might ask, Gloria wasn't going back to Hanky Park; not after what she had done. She didn't deserve forgiveness. It was too much to ask of a deserted husband and children.

'Please,' Gloria had begged her daughter the previous week, 'don't keep asking. And don't *ever* tell anyone that you've found me.'

'I won't, Mum,' Suzannah had agreed reluctantly. 'But you'll *want* to come home one day.'

Gloria had put up her hands. 'No, not one day. Not any day. *Never.*'

She knew that her daughter would never stop hoping, but there was no point. However much she loved Suzannah – the daughter who had never given up on her – she couldn't face returning to the tailor's shop. Wasn't it better for Jacob to believe that his wife had gone for ever? That she might even be dead? The Clark family had survived without her for a long time; what good could come of her return? And in such a state? Jacob would never get his Gloria back, she realised sadly. His children would never get their mother back. This Gloria wasn't any Gloria they had ever known.

Her family was better off without her; without knowing what she'd once been – a woman who for years had wandered about from Manchester to Liverpool, mad as a loon. A woman who had been middle-aged but dressed like a child, with ridiculous ribbons in her hair and around the neck of her dog. A woman who had sung for pennies in pubs, and worse, let men take advantage of her in the ginnels outside. A woman who – for a long time – had no history and no memories to tell. Whom no one took seriously, because she had a coat with the Snowhill laundry marking on the label.

'Miss Siddons? Miss Siddons?'

Gloria turned, remembering suddenly that she had reverted to her maiden name. The bakery owner was looking at her. What had she done wrong? Were they going to fire her?

'If you could get the fresh loaves from the back, Miss Siddons, that would be a great help.'

Relieved, she looked at the woman, nodded, then scurried away.

Suzannah might believe her mother could change and turn back time, but Gloria knew better. You can't unlearn what you know, she thought, resigned. You can't unremember events, or undo actions.

Particularly the ones you'll regret for the rest of your life.

FORTY-THREE

Teddy Lyle arrived home whistling. He had been for another fitting and had seen Suzannah again. This time she had been wearing shoes when she let him into the shop, turning the sign to CLOSED as she locked the door. He had – for an intoxicating moment – thought that *she* would be doing the fitting, but only seconds later Girton emerged, tape measure around his neck, his expression professional.

Oh well, Teddy thought happily, he had another appointment on Friday. Three days wasn't too long to wait.

'What on earth are you grinning at?' his father asked him.

Startled, Teddy turned to see Noel watching him from the drawing room door. 'Oh, hello there, Dad. I was just feeling in a good mood.'

'And I know why.'

'You do?' Teddy asked, his eyebrows raised.

'Of course,' Noel went on, moving over to his son and dropping his voice. 'She's just arrived.'

It couldn't be Suzannah? Could it?

'Who has?'

'Emma O'Donelly.'

Emma O'Donelly, the second daughter of the most respected doctor in Manchester. Emma O'Donelly, Irish descent forgiven because of the family money. Emma O'Donelly, dark as a blackbird and about as unique.

Bugger it, Teddy thought. 'I didn't know she was coming.'

It was Noel's turn to be caught off guard. 'Emma and

237

her parents are here for dinner. God, Teddy, you can't have forgotten. This is important.'

'Why?'

'Emma is a very nice girl, with a moneyed family and good connections.' Noel caught his son's arm, drawing him closer. 'Just the kind of match you need to make. She's pretty without being the type to stray, lively without being too smart, and eager to settle down.'

'Did she tell you all this?'

'Don't be stupid, dear boy,' Noel replied, his tone dropping further. 'Your mother gleaned most of it from Emma's mother. Nora O'Donelly was one of the Bagshotts.'

'Bagshotts or big shots?' Teddy asked deftly.

Noel was all mellow charm. 'You know, if you matched up with Emma you would be made for life. With my contacts, and her parents', you would have a wonderful social life. And our personal businesses could only grow. Maybe even expanding abroad.'

Teddy looked impressed. 'Abroad with the big shots?'

'I suppose you believe in love,' Noel said patiently. 'Well, from my experience love is something poor people have to make up for lack of money.'

'My God, no wonder you're so well off, Dad.'

Noel's silky smile never wavered. He was always surprised by his son's nature – so different from his own – but realised that Teddy was no fool. He might protest about injustice but in the end he would embrace that very injustice himself. He liked comfort too much, did Teddy. Liked to think of himself as a radical, but would always end up sitting on the fence. Out of danger. An observer. Amongst, but separate from, the masses.

'Talk to the girl,' Noel urged him. *Never push*, was his motto. If you pushed, they always went the other way. If you protested, they always resisted. 'You might find you like her as you get to know her more.'

'But she might not like me, Dad,' Teddy replied lightly.

'She's been told to like you.'

238

'And are her hands bandaged to cover the marks of the thumbscrews?'

Noel laughed, looping his arm around his son's shoulder, his grip surprisingly strong. 'Always joking, aren't you, Teddy? Well, I know she'll love your sense of humour. Everyone does. You can't imagine how readily people take to a fool.'

Even though several days had passed, Rina was still thinking about the tailor's shop – and the tailor himself. Girton Clark was a good-looking man, just the type she was attracted to. And she could see that he had been taken with her. Besides, Hanky Park was a long way from Moss Side and there would be a certain thrill about bedding Stanley's successor. Rina let her tongue slide over her bottom lip, plotting. The tailor's shop had slipped out of Lionel's grasp, but it would be fun to best him by getting involved with the Clark family herself.

She relished the idea of gloating behind her husband's fat back. Lionel had been treating her like a rubbing rag for too long, but now she had found herself a diversion. And who knew how far the diversion might take her? All she had to do was to get Girton Clark under her heel. She sighed thoughtfully. As always, Rina had sussed out her target at once. Obviously Girton was very attracted to her; he was also young. That was good, Rina realised. Young men were less likely to be shocked. She could be more direct with a young man. Act more decisively, seduce more quickly.

At that moment she heard the shop door slam shut, Lionel hurrying into the pawnbroker's. For once the darkness caught him off guard and he stumbled into something large and metallic directly in his way. Swearing, he leaned over and clicked on the dim counter light.

'Jesus!' he said out loud, stepping back. A large red macaw was staring at him, its eyes beady and black, its grey claws curled around its gently swinging perch. 'What the . . .? RINA!'

She sidled in, folding her arms as she looked over at him.

'Yeah?'

He waved his arms at the cage. 'What the hell is that?'

'A bird.'

'I can see it's a bloody bird! What's it doing here?'

'Someone pawned it.'

'WE DON'T TAKE LIVESTOCK!'

'You ought to check the clothes more carefully, Lionel. Half of them are crawling with livestock.'

Her tone surprised him. Cocky, pushing her luck.

'Why would you be stupid enough to let someone pawn a bird?'

'SOD OFF!'

Glassy-eyed, Lionel turned to the parrot, Rina struggling to keep her face straight.

'I think he likes you,' she said simply, moving back into the living quarters beyond.

It was worth a row to have the bird swear at her husband, she thought gleefully. Lionel's expression had been classic. And anyway, he was afraid of birds and wouldn't attempt to hurt it. Wouldn't even dare to open the cage. Smiling, she remembered how for the last hour or so she had been talking to the macaw, opening and closing the door which led from the shop to the back. And every time the door had squeaked she'd said:

'PIG! Oink. Oink.'

It was just a matter of time, she thought slyly, before the bird caught on. One morning Lionel would open that door and the macaw would perform. She just hoped she was there to see it.

Stomping into the kitchen behind her, Lionel slumped down at the table. Slowly, Rina dished out some potatoes, meat and gravy, piling up her husband's plate. He would eat whatever she put in front of him. Might create if it was mince, but he'd eat it. Too greedy not to. And as he began to eat, she studied him, careful that he didn't catch her. He hated that, her scrutiny always provoking a violent reaction. But this time he was too busy shovelling food into his mouth to notice. Heaped mouthful after mouthful went in, gravy dribbling from the corners of his fleshy lips, his jowls jiggling as he chewed.

Repulsed, Rina turned away, her own food untouched. Her thoughts wandered back to Girton Clark, helping her to her feet and running after her umbrella. A man around her own age, without flabby skin and veins on his nose. Without age spots on his hands. A man a woman would like to have touch her. *The tailor* . . . It seemed incredible that the whim which had taken her over to Hanky Park had resulted in their chance meeting. Of all people to help her: the tailor from Stanley Tobarski's shop. The very place Lionel had wanted so much.

It was a delicious irony.

'I have to go away tomorrow. Just for a day or so,' Lionel said, laying down his knife and fork.

Rina's heart quickened. 'Away?'

Slowly, he turned his menacing gaze on her. 'You put a foot out of line, girl, and I'll hear of it. I've got enemies round here – but I've a lot of friends too. You remember that.'

'I've never cheated on you, Lionel.'

'Only because you know I'd kill you if you did.'

She looked away, pushing the congealed gravy around with her fork. 'Where are you going?'

'Liverpool.'

'Why?'

'I don't like you nosing into my affairs!' he snapped. 'You're not questioning me as to where I go and why.'

'I was just interested.'

'Aye, well be interested in running this place and you'll keep your interest where it should be,' Lionel replied, turning back to his food.

Rina's thoughts turned back to Girton Clark.

'Do you live around here?' he had asked her.

'Manchester.'

He had looked disappointed. 'Are you visiting someone?'

And she'd lied. 'My aunt.'

'Where does she live?'

'She doesn't. She's dead. I go to visit her grave.' God knows how Rina had thought so quickly, but she had had to, to keep his interest. A dead relative was reason enough to visit Hanky Park.

He'd smiled with relief. Obviously he hadn't wanted to part from her either.

'Perhaps, when you come again, we could meet . . . Sorry, I shouldn't suggest—'

'It's all right,' she had reassured him hurriedly. 'We *could* meet up. Maybe you could run after my umbrella again?'

'So, where is it?'

Rina's mind came back to the present with a thud. There was no young man, no rain, no tailor's shop. Only her husband glaring at her.

'Where's what?'

'The raincoat!'

'There are dozens in the shop . . .'

'I don't want them, I want mine! I need a bloody raincoat for my trip. Looks like the wet's set in.' His eyes narrowed suspiciously. 'You look after this place whilst I'm gone, you hear me?' He reached out, his fleshy hand resting on her knee, his fingers drawing up her skirt. 'I think we'll have an early night, Rina. It'll be good to leave you with a nice memory whilst I'm away.'

FORTY-FOUR

Emma O'Donelly didn't stand a chance. Her mother, redoubtable in a black taffeta evening dress, might kick her under the table repeatedly to make her join in, but it was obvious to everyone that romance wasn't on the cards. Dr O'Donelly had been plied with burgundy by Noel, and CC was berating Mrs O'Donelly about the lack of artistic talent coming out of the Manchester College of Arts, but Teddy and Emma had nothing to say. Either to their parents or to each other.

Instead Teddy was plotting. He realised that all his life he had been prone to infatuation: falling in love was for Teddy as simple as falling downstairs. And usually as painful. He could fall in love with a voice, a face, or even a mannerism – but Suzannah Clark was different. There was no single thing about her that infatuated him. No look, no scent, no expression. She had no power to intrigue him or to fascinate; no subtle creeping into his dreams or hopscotching through his fantasies.

And yet she had put her mark on him. If she had branded him, stamped him, or signed her signature on his arm, Edward Lyle could not have been more her property. The fact was disquieting. He had none of the giddy moments he usually experienced when he was in love. No leaps of the heart. Just a nagging – but deliriously pleasant – sensation that he was done for.

'Do you like the theatre, Teddy?' Emma said, finally goaded into conversation.

He glanced over to his dinner companion, bored. 'Er . . . sometimes.'

'I hear there's a wonderful play on at the Adelphi.'

He missed his cue. His parents didn't. Emma's parents didn't. But Teddy did.

If the truth were known, Emma was delighted. Teddy Lyle was pleasant enough, but not at all the kind of man she hankered after. She thought of Rudolph Valentino and wondered how she could get herself to Italy. To all those dark-eyed, romantic men who loved women. Away from the north-west of England, the smoggy streets, the debilitating rain. A failed romance would be the perfect excuse. She could pretend that Teddy Lyle had broken her heart and that she needed to go abroad for a while. Her parents would ship her off eagerly. *Poor Emma, rejected and disheartened. A spell in Italy might lift her spirits . . .* Only Teddy wasn't playing. Damn it.

'I think you two might like a walk in the garden,' CC said, gesturing to the French doors as if they might try exiting via the roof. 'Such a lovely early summer evening.'

'It's raining, Mother.'

Her tongue clicked. 'Not on the veranda, Teddy.'

Manipulated out of the house, Emma stood under the cover of an awning, Teddy beside her. She was wearing a pale-coloured shift, her arms ghostly white in the damp evening air.

Sighing, she pulled a silk shawl around her shoulders. 'You should play along, you know.'

Teddy jumped. 'What?'

'Look, I don't want you, and you obviously don't want me, but we could turn this whole ghastly episode to our advantage.'

He leaned towards her, relieved. 'This *is* a surprise . . .'

'Parents always think their children are stupid,' Emma replied, gazing out into the garden. 'Look, Teddy, to be honest I just want to get away from here. Go abroad. Italy.'

'Are you in love with someone out there?'

'Not yet,' she said cheerfully. 'What about you? I reckon you've got someone in mind.'

He was surprised by her perception. 'Does it show?'

'Only to anyone with half a brain.' She paused, looking him up and down. 'So who is it?'

'Somebody very unsuitable.'

'Excellent,' Emma replied. 'I hope to break my parents' hearts as well.'

Teddy found himself suddenly confiding. It was easy when the pressure was off. 'She's not *our* type.'

'That's a bonus.'

'My parents won't like her.'

'But you do?' Emma replied, turning her intelligent face up to his. 'What's she like?'

'Striking. Different.'

'How long have you known her?'

'Ten days,' he said, flushing as Emma laughed.

'God! It'll either be the love of the century or a complete disaster. Have you kissed her?'

'Emma!' Teddy replied, shocked. 'You don't hold back, do you?'

'Why should I? So – *have* you kissed her?'

'No. I've not even spoken to her that much.'

'So why are you besotted?'

'I'm not,' Teddy replied. 'It's not like that. It's more like I *have* to be with her. Like I've always known her. Or maybe it's like I *once* knew her, then lost touch. And now she's back in my life – where she should be.' He paused, struggling for words. 'I'm sorry, it sounds so stupid, but I can't explain it any better. It doesn't really make sense.'

'It makes perfect sense,' Emma replied, smiling. 'Some day I want a man to talk about me like that.'

'But what if I'm wrong?' Teddy asked anxiously. 'You see, I don't even know her.'

'*You* might not. But your heart does.'

FORTY-FIVE

'Who?' Girton asked, surprised, as he listened to the caller. 'Oh, hello there! It's good to hear from you.'

On the other end, Rina's voice was silky. 'I probably shouldn't have called you like this, but you *did* ask me to let you know when I was coming to Hanky Park again.'

'I did! I mean, yes, *of course* I wanted you to call.' Girton was falling over his words, a verbal bulldozer. 'When can we meet?'

'Well, the thing is, I'm *not* coming over for a while. But if you liked, we could meet in Moss Side.'

Hanky Park, Moss Side, who cared?

'That's fine,' Girton replied eagerly. 'I can come over. When?'

'Tomorrow?' Rina suggested, then tugged at the metaphorical string she was slowly winding around his neck. 'No! Maybe we shouldn't meet up after all—'

'Don't say that!' Girton replied anxiously. 'I want to see you.'

'Oh, and I want to see you so much,' she replied, her voice throaty.

'So what time shall we meet up, and where?'

'The corner of Manchester Street, Moss Side. At three thirty?'

'Fine. I'll be there,' he assured her. 'Rina?'

'Yes?'

'I can't wait to see you again.'

The next day Rina was looking down Manchester Street impatiently. Girton was late. Naughty boy. Agitated, she tapped her right foot, keen to put her plan into action. After all, the first part had been so easy. Lionel had left for Liverpool and she had waited only minutes before phoning Girton and suggesting that they meet up. It was obvious that there had been someone else in the tailor's shop, but she could tell he was pleased. Excited even.

Her gaze moved up and down the street. No one knew her in this part of Moss Side, and certainly no one would know Girton Clark. No one would think they were anything other than a courting couple. Smiling, she realised that she was amused by the idea: a courting couple. Well, that wasn't *quite* what she wanted, was it? Primarily, she was out for sex: but the more Rina thought about it, the more there was to it. Sex with Girton Clark would mean involvement with the tailor's shop. The very shop Lionel had seen slip through his fingers. Now that *was* a tasty little sauce to add to the dish, wasn't it?

Rina kept looking down the street, her excitement building. God, if Girton would just come. She was tired of waiting for him. Tired of waiting for sex with a good-looking, young man . . . Her thoughts moved on. She hadn't told him she was married. Better not to, she had decided, or he might not want to see her again. Especially when he found out who she was married *to*.

Uncomfortable, Rina remembered Lionel, and *their* first meeting. He had found her working at a London pub, and had fallen so hard, and made himself so desperate, that he would rather have cut off his arm than lose her. And she had been glad of him at the time. Glad to accept his slobbering kisses, his presents – and yet clever enough to hold out for a ring. The sob story about her family had got Rina what she wanted: an escape from London and imminent poverty. Oh yes, *then* she had been glad to get into Lionel's car and be taken up north to another life.

But not so glad *now*. Not so glad years later when Lionel used her as a punchbag, when she found him more repellent every day. When his mouldering shop and his vicious cronies became ever more oppressive. She had grown to loathe each item, every sad or sordid piece of furniture or cloth that had been pawned. Every wedding band, every kettle, every out-of-tune instrument, every pair of summer shoes pawned in the winter for reclamation in spring. If their owner was lucky.

And Lionel had sat amongst it all for years, in the dim counter light, soaked in the miasma of pawned objects, his tab of tickets in his drawer, his cash box under the till, locked, with only him having a key. Never Rina, not even after years of marriage. Because Lionel trusted no one. And besides, he believed that keeping his wife poor kept her at home. Kept her in his bed, under his thumb, under his heel . . . Little did he know about Rina having had his key copied; about her growing stack of cash; her adept pilfering over the years.

'Rina!'

She spun round at the sound of her name; terrified for an instant that it might be Lionel. But it wasn't. It was Girton, running towards her. And then she remembered something, and, in one deft movement, slid off her wedding ring and slipped it into her pocket.

All day Girton had been telling himself he would be calm, wouldn't show his interest too quickly. But when he saw Rina it was impossible. Hope and passion propelled him along, forced him to throw out his arms and pull her to him. For once, he was spontaneous, reckless, dizzy with hope.

'You came—' she said, but her next words were drowned out, Girton kissing her hungrily, holding her to him.

And she responded, her body pressed against his, their mouths feeding off one another, their hands touching, running over each other's bodies as though their fingers could memorise each line and curve. She was so incredible, so sexual, Girton thought, leading her towards a doorway, enthralled by her boldness.

'God . . .' Rina said, finally pulling back and looking up

into his face. 'I don't know what's happening to me! But I want you so much, Girton. I've never felt like this. I can't help myself.' She took his hand, laid it on her breast, kissing him again. 'I can't stop thinking about you. I want you . . .'

Overwhelmed, he was ready to be absorbed by her. For the first time in his life a woman wanted him desperately. And he wanted her: this glorious, amoral angel who had fallen into his life.

'Rina, we can't . . . Someone might see us.'

She laughed, feigning embarrassment. 'It's your fault. You're making me behave so badly.'

And, like a fool, Girton ignored his misgivings, revelling in behaviour which would have made him question any other woman.

Tenderly, Rina touched his arm, leaning her head on his shoulder. 'I had to see you again. I would have *died* without seeing you.' Her voice was low, pulling him in. Part virgin, part whore, she unbalanced Girton masterfully. 'Did you think of me? Even a little?'

'I never *stopped* thinking about you,' he replied truthfully, aching as she stroked the back of his neck with her fingers.

'I want you to think about me all the time,' Rina said slowly, running her tongue along his lips, then sliding it into his mouth.

He moaned, gripping her tightly, besieged with craving. From that moment on, he would have done anything for her. Where Rina had come from, he wasn't interested. What her background was, he didn't care. All he *did* know was that she wanted him.

'Sweetheart,' she said suddenly, pulling back.

'What is it?'

'I want to be with you so much . . .' she said, her voice low, the pupils of her eyes dilated. 'I want you.' Everything was going to plan for her. He was sexually excited, completely in her power. 'Girton, I want you so much—'

'God, Rina, I can't think of anything else. Anyone else,'

he went on, cupping her face in his hands and studying every angle. 'I feel crazy, like another man. Ever since I saw you outside the shop, ever since I—'

'I feel the same!' she said eagerly.

'You do?'

'Of course, don't you realise that?' She smiled, her face flushed with excitement. His eagerness was familiar to her; but this time it was welcome.

'We should find somewhere to talk.'

The hell with talking, Rina thought. Taking his hand, she kissed his palm.

'No, I don't want to be around people. I just want to be with you.'

He could feel the warmth of her breath on his skin. 'But where can we go?'

Laughing, she tugged him along the street. It was still light, on a warm June evening, as she paused and then pulled him behind a row of shops.

Surprised, he hesitated: 'Rina, this isn't right—'

She cut him off. 'I want you. Wherever we are.'

All Rina's years of repressed sexuality suddenly consumed her. She could act like a whore again – because she wanted to, and because no one would know. Drawing Girton with her, both of them looked for a convenient place to be intimate. If Girton had considered their actions for only a moment, he would have paused. But he had been controlled too long. He was hungry for affection. And sex.

'In here,' Rina said hurriedly, moving into a deserted storage shed.

He followed her in. They were suddenly enveloped in the musty darkness, the only light coming through the cracks in the brickwork.

'No! We can't!' he said urgently. 'Not like this. It's so sordid.'

She paused, her voice disembodied in the half-light. 'Girton, don't think about it. We belong to each other, you and I. This is all right, this is how it should be.' Her breath was on his cheek, her hand moving gently against his chest and then sliding downwards to rest against his crotch. 'Don't think,' she urged him. 'Don't think . . .'

'Rina, we can't—'

Her left hand moved around his neck, her fingers lacing through his hair. Gently she tugged, pulling his face towards hers.

'Please, darling, please . . .'

And he gave in. Just as she knew he would.

They had sex as though their lives depended on it. Tenderly she kissed him, lovingly he touched her, and then afterwards they leaned against the wall of the storeroom, both breathing heavily.

'I'm sorry. I shouldn't have done that,' Girton said, ashamed of his loss of control. And terrified that he had somehow driven her away.

'But I wanted you to,' Rina reassured him, reaching for his hand, feigning anxiety. 'Didn't you enjoy it?'

He kissed her forehead. 'Do you need to ask?'

'You must think so badly of me,' Rina said, her voice low, the lies already in place. 'I'm not really like this. God, I feel so ashamed. But I don't care, Girton . . . I don't care.'

Pretending affection, she leant her head against his chest, listening to his breathing. The sex had been a release for her, and better than she had expected. Obviously Girton Clark was no virgin. And his body had been so unlike Lionel's. Firm, without the overhang of belly, his smell sweet, not sour and beer-soaked. And his lips had been soft: warm but dry, gentle against hers. No slobbering, no hands – sweaty and podgy – forcing themselves on, and into, her.

'I want to see you again,' Girton said quietly. 'But not like this. I want to get to know you. *Talk* to you.'

Talk was the last thing on Rina's mind. But she wasn't going to tell him that. Pulling open the door, she looked out. The ginnel was empty. Hurriedly, she beckoned for Girton to follow her.

'Come on, we can walk for a while.'

He fell into step with her, unsettled by her sudden composure. 'I want to know all about you, Rina.'

'You know enough,' she said, linking arms with him. Her blonde hair was partially dishevelled and falling on to her shoulders.

'But I want to know *everything*.'

'No you don't,' she replied, finding the conversation awkward. She hadn't planned further than the seduction and was suddenly irritated.

'What's the matter?'

'Don't spoil it—'

He cut her off. 'Spoil *what*, Rina?'

'Today.' She smiled, composed again and sweet as an angel. He was under her heel, just where she wanted him; all she had to do was to keep him there. 'Sweetheart, I have to go now—'

'What!' he said, aghast.

'I have to go.'

He was distraught, blundering. 'Rina, look, I know I behaved badly. I'm sorry for that. I got carried away. It won't happen again, I promise.' He clutched her hand. 'I rushed you—'

Her hand went up to his mouth, covering his lips for an instant. 'No you didn't.'

'Then why go?'

Oh, he was hers all right. She had played this set of cards very well, lured him in, confused him, and now he was dancing on one leg. And *now* was the time to really throw him off balance.

Sighing, Rina looked down, her voice so quiet that he had to strain to hear her. 'I should never have got in touch with you, Girton, I'm so sorry . . . You see, I'm married.'

He stepped back. 'What?'

'I'm married.'

He paused, shaking his head. 'So you just wanted some fun?'

'It wasn't like that!' she said hurriedly. 'I'm not happily married. My husband's a lot older and doesn't treat me well.' She paused, her voice trembling. 'I couldn't risk telling you sooner ... You might never have agreed to meet up with me. I'm married to Lionel Taylor, Stanley's brother.'

He paled, watching her, wondering what else she hadn't told him. Wondering what other thunderbolt she was about to hit him with. Wondering why – from all the women he could have chosen – he had picked her.

'You're married to Lionel Taylor?'

She hurried on. Look all pathetic now, she told herself; sex and helplessness was a potent mix.

'I met Stanley when he came to visit his brother. He was very kind to me. Knew how his brother treated me.' She paused, her tone plaintive. 'Stanley was my only friend. It was because of him I came to Hanky Park the other day to look at the shop. I was missing him, and thinking about the things he had told me about all of you.'

Girton was staring at her, horrified. 'Your husband tried to throw my family out of the shop!'

She went on, her face flushed with indignation. 'I tried to talk Lionel out of it, but he ignored me! I was hoping against hope that he wouldn't get the shop – and was so pleased when he failed.' She paused, searching Girton's face. Was he buying it? 'Believe me, it was an accident that I fell over in Hankerton Street. And that it was you that picked me up. I wasn't planning anything. Dear God, think about it. Lionel would do for me if he knew I was here now, with you.'

'So why *are* you here?' Girton asked suspiciously.

She relaxed. He was wavering. Soon he would be convinced, captivated.

'I couldn't stop thinking of you after we'd met. And when Lionel went away for a couple of days I took my

253

chance to see you again.' She hurried on, her voice imploring. 'I thought it was a sign that it was all right to see you, because we'd met outside Stanley's shop.' Feigning desperation, she reached for his hand, Girton resisting for only an instant then clasping her fingers tightly. 'I should have told you, I know! I should never have met you again . . . But I had to. I'm not happy, Girton. In fact, I've been wretched for a long time.'

Silent, he stared at her. She was married. To Lionel Taylor. How was that possible? Girton wondered. How could someone so young and beautiful be married to such a pig?

'Why did you marry him?'

'I was on my own in London, no family, and no money. He offered security and I took it.' She looked up into Girton's face, challenging him. 'What else could I do? I had no education, no training. Lionel was my way out. I thought that if I made him a good wife, it might be bearable – but he's not easy to please.' Her voice wavered. 'I've paid for the decision I made. Every day of my life I pay for it.'

Pity welled up in him. 'Does he hit you?'

'Sometimes.'

'Then you have to leave him!'

She shook her head. 'And go where?'

'Somewhere safe.'

'I'm from down south, Girton. I don't *know* anywhere safe in the north. I don't know where to go. And anyway, with what? I've no money.' She could see that he was swallowing every word. 'Lionel has the money *and* the contacts. He knows what goes on, and where. His cronies keep him up to date, and he keeps a very close eye on me. If I left him, he would . . . God, I don't know *what* he'd do!'

Expertly manipulated, Girton was suddenly reckless. 'You could come and stay at the tailor's shop.'

She smiled wistfully. Dear God, he'd really fallen for her. Fast and hard.

'That's not possible, my love.' Her grip on his hand increased. 'If I went with you, Lionel would ruin you *and* your business. Your shop was Stanley's. The shop Lionel wanted. Now imagine – how would he react to me running *there* for help?'

'We could go to the police—'

'He knows the police.' She put her head on one side. 'You don't understand, do you? Everywhere you look, Lionel owns pieces of people. It might be an old coat or an old favour. But he's got control, and he uses it when it suits him. The police? He knows quite a few coppers. They gamble with him. Some even owe him money. How easy it would be for him to put the pressure on.'

'Rina, you can't go on living with him.'

'I have to stay with him.' She paused, then looked into Girton's eyes, her expression tender. 'But I can't give you up. I thought I could walk away – but I can't. I don't think I could go back to Lionel without knowing I had you . . . I want to see you again.'

Touched, he wrapped his arms around her protectively. 'I want that too.'

'But it would be so dangerous,' she said, her head resting against his chest, her eyes cunning. 'Lionel's so jealous, Girton. If he found out about us—'

'I can't let you go back there,' Girton replied anxiously. 'What if he hurt you again?'

'Don't worry, sweetheart. If my husband suspects nothing, he'll get on with his work and leave me alone. He always does – if I don't provoke him in any way.' Rina paused for a long moment, then opted for the martyr role. 'But I've been so selfish! I should *never* have got you involved in all this.'

'I *am* involved.'

'But at first – if I'd told you I was married – would you have got involved then?'

He didn't even pause. 'I couldn't have stopped myself.'

Triumph made Rina light-headed. 'Are you sure? Are

255

you really sure you want to keep seeing me? You have to be careful, Girton, very careful. I might turn out to be bad for you.'

'Maybe I *like* things that are bad for me,' he replied, the intimation of danger inflaming him. Certain of her control, Rina lifted her head, her lips parting as he kissed her.

And in the distance the sun, finally, began to set.

FORTY-SIX

He would be here at any minute, Suzannah thought, excited. Mr Edward Lyle, *Teddy* . . . She let the name slide into her head and linger. Then she flushed. Good God, what was she doing? She was acting like a foolish kid with a crush on the local wealthy heir. Grow up, she told herself. He was bound to be spoken for; a rich young man like him would have potential suitors lined up by the yard.

'Morning,' Teddy said suddenly behind her.

She spun round, flushing as she saw him.

'Morning. If you wouldn't mind waiting for a moment, I'll just go and get your jacket.' When she returned, she helped Teddy into the half-made jacket. 'How does that feel?' she asked, her tone professional although her hands were shaking. 'Not too tight around the top of the sleeve?'

'It feels perfect,' Teddy replied, his arms raised to shoulder level as though he was being held up at gunpoint. 'Perfect.'

Today he was going to do it – ask her out. Surely she wouldn't refuse, would she? Or maybe she would. Maybe she already had someone in her life. Not that Teddy had seen anyone at the tailor's shop. But then a boyfriend wouldn't visit in working hours . . . Oh get on with it, he told himself, just ask her.

'Miss Clark—'

'I believe that Girton has already checked the fit of your trousers, Mr Lyle?'

'Teddy. Call me Teddy.'

She smiled, trying to hide her nervousness. 'Well then, Teddy. Has my brother seen to your trouser fitting?'

'Yes,' he replied, hurrying on. 'D'you like the theatre?'

'You can put your arms down now.' She paused. What had he just said? 'Yes, I like the theatre. Although I don't go very often.'

'There's a play on – something by Noel Coward. My mother says it's very amusing.' He was standing awkwardly, his jacket tacked up with pins and covered with a criss-cross of white chalk marks. 'Would you like to see it with me?'

The surprise made Suzannah clumsy. Driving a pin half an inch into her thumb she winced, but kept smiling.

'I'm very flattered to be asked . . .'

'But it's a no?'

'Mr Lyle—'

'Teddy.'

'*Teddy* . . . It's not that simple.'

'It is. You just say yes.'

She shook her head. She might have been day-dreaming about Teddy Lyle, but there was no point beginning a relationship that couldn't go anywhere. No matter how much she was tempted.

'You know what I mean. You come from a very different background to mine. You're from money. Eccles Old Road, all that. We're not in your class.' She put up her hands to prevent him interrupting. 'I don't really think your parents would approve of me.'

'My parents aren't asking you out.'

Smiling, Suzannah turned back to the work table, wondering what to say next. She could imagine only too easily what Noel Lyle would think of her. Hanky Park slum fodder, no better than the men he had working for him on Unwin Street . . . The old secret nudged at her uncomfortably. Dear God, if he ever found out about her affair with Bert Gallager, if *anyone* ever found out . . . But they wouldn't. She had confided in no one about the baby.

And as for the affair – no one knew about that either. Or did they?

Once or twice Suzannah had wondered about that. Just how lucky had they been? Their meetings; their drives in Pa Gallager's van – surely *someone* had seen them? And hadn't she been worried about the last time they had met in Peel Park? When she thought she had spotted someone she knew? Someone who might possibly have seen her. With Bert . . . The thought made her queasy. Hanky Park was a small place, everyone looked out for each other – and gossiped: rumours ground out relentlessly to season their pedestrian lives.

Unnerved, Suzannah shook her head. No one had gossiped about her – she would have heard. She was safe. No one knew, apart from Bert, and she could trust him. Besides, hadn't he found someone else and looked set to marry? Which was more than Suzannah did.

It wasn't that she hadn't been interested in romance; in fact she had been on plenty of dates. But she couldn't, in all honesty, pretend to be something she wasn't. Unmarried, she had carried a child. The truth – if it ever came out – would ruin her. How could she really act like a pure, untouched virgin? And would any man want her if she told him about her past?

So Suzannah had skirted relationships and resisted temptation. Until Teddy Lyle . . . Fiddling with her pins and tape measure, she kept her face averted. She liked Teddy Lyle, liked him a lot. Thought he was attractive – but more than that, honest, amusing, unaffected. He could so easily have come to the shop and lorded it over them. Could have treated Girton as a minion and her as a lackey. God knows, from all she had heard of Noel Lyle, his father would have done. But instead Teddy had come in for a suit. A good suit. He'd been appreciative of the tailoring – and of the female tailor.

But how far could it go? How far would Noel Lyle *let* it go? Suzannah wasn't about to allow some rich man's son to break her heart. She had seen that happen before: Hanky Park girls duped and then dumped. She wasn't going to let that happen to her.

'I can't hold my breath any longer,' Teddy said finally. 'Just say yes, will you? I mean, what's there to lose? We might have an awful time. You might hate me, might never want to see me again.'

She turned back to him. 'I don't think, so.'

'I don't think so either. Miss Clark—'

'Suzannah.'

'*Suzannah* . . . will you come out with me?'

She was about to say no, but hesitated. Perhaps they *could* just go out for an evening somewhere. Nothing serious, maybe even a friendship. She longed for male company again, missed linking arms with a man as she walked down the street. It was obvious from their disparate backgrounds that it would never come to anything – so why *not* accept?

'Yes,' she said finally, 'I'd love to go out with you.'

Delighted, he clapped his hands and then winced as several tacking pins dug into his shoulders. Hearing the laughter, a curious Helen walked into the workshop to see what was happening.

At once her gaze took in the scene – and Teddy Lyle.

'Oh, sorry, Suzannah, I didn't realise you were still working,' she said, scrutinising the stranger. 'It's past six.'

'Mr Lyle's sitting took rather longer than expected,' Suzannah replied, dodging her sister's gaze.

'So *you're* the famous Mr Edward Lyle,' Helen said, her tone teasing. 'We're honoured to have you grace our humble shop.'

'The pleasure's all mine,' Teddy replied gallantly as Suzannah helped him out of his jacket. Accidentally her fingers brushed against his chest and a frisson went through her. He had asked her out. Teddy Lyle had asked her out . . .

'So when will the suit be ready?' Helen queried. 'Because

frankly, I've never known anything take so long. You'd think we were trying to hold on to you, Mr Lyle.'

Surprised, Suzannah shot a look at her sister. Helen winked mischievously.

'A good suit takes a while,' Teddy replied smoothly. 'You should see how long the tailors take in Deansgate.'

'We don't get to Deansgate that often,' Helen replied, baiting him. 'Personally I prefer Savile Row.'

He laughed, Helen perching on the side of the work table and crossing her legs.

'You must be Suzannah's sister.'

'That's me. Helen.' She dropped her voice, feigning secrecy. 'I'm the black sheep of the family. Forced out of the nest to earn an honest crust at Clegg, Cuthbert and Rathbone.'

He laughed again. 'An honest crust – working for solicitors? Anyway. I thought old Cuthbert was dead.'

'Nah, just sleeping,' Helen replied archly. 'My God, he comes in at nine, then dozes off until eleven. If we're lucky we can get him to see a couple of clients a week.'

'Well, he must be over seventy now. My father used to use your firm – but that's a while back.'

'Why did he move?' Helen asked lightly, imagining the coup if she could get the Lyles reinstated at the firm.

'I don't know why, he just did. But if I remember rightly, they organised my father's purchase of the Unwin Street property. Anyway,' Teddy replied easily, picking up his coat, 'I should be going. It was nice meeting you, Miss Clark.'

'Likewise,' Helen replied, still sitting on the edge of the work table. She could sense an attraction between her sister and Teddy Lyle and was fascinated.

Guiding Teddy out of the workroom and back into the shop, Suzannah moved over to the appointments book. Knowing only too well that Helen was eavesdropping, she kept her voice professional.

'Can you come for a sitting on Friday, Mr Lyle?'

He noticed the change to her tone and was perceptive enough to realise what was going on. Catching her eye, he smiled – but kept his voice steady.

'Around five?'

'That would be perfect,' Suzannah replied, also smiling.

'Fine, Friday then,' Teddy agreed, scribbling something on a piece of paper and pushing it over the counter towards her. It read: *Theatre, next Saturday?*

And underneath she wrote, *YES*.

FORTY-SEVEN

Mercilessly ragged by Helen, Suzannah tried on four different outfits. Or rather her only decent dress with three different scarves and jackets. Nothing looked right; everything was well cut and well made – as befitted a tailor's daughter – but dull. Provincial. Uninspiring. Hardly suitable for a night at the theatre. Uncharacteristically overwrought, Suzannah had wondered repeatedly why she had ever accepted Teddy's invitation. After all, wasn't this débâcle with the outfit just one example of how unsuited they were?

'Relax,' Helen chided her. 'You look great in that. Wear the red jacket.'

'It's the oldest one!'

'He won't notice.'

'Oh, no!' Suzannah replied drily. 'Not when his mother's the north-west's fashion plate.'

'I heard she'd had surgery – to lengthen her legs.'

'I heard it was her tongue,' Suzannah retorted, staring hard at her reflection in the mirror. 'I can't go, I just can't! I haven't got the right outfit and I'll be out of place. I'll let myself down! God, he might even be ashamed of me.'

Surprised, Helen studied her sister. Who was *anyone* to be ashamed of Suzannah Clark?

'Ashamed of you,' she repeated curtly. 'Well if he is, I can tell you – Mr Edward Lyle's no damn good.'

Mr Edward Lyle was – at that very moment – standing outside the Manchester Palace Theatre looking, and feeling, very stupid. How could he tell her? he wondered, embarrassed to the core. How could he have been so dense? There he was, wanting desperately to impress Suzannah Clark on their first date, and he had ruined it before it had even started.

Tapping his foot impatiently, Teddy stared at the tickets again, and then crammed them back in his pocket. He would tell her outright. She might walk off; never talk to him again . . . He would take her for a drink to explain. She might not drink; think he was being a cheapskate . . . God, Teddy thought, mortified. Why had he been such a clown? And then he saw her, walking towards him. Dressed in red, her dark hair tied back from her face. Gorgeous. She was gorgeous. He was lucky to be seen out with her; lucky she had accepted his invitation.

Approaching nervously, Suzannah noticed his scrutiny and flushed. It was the damn dress! It was too old, too out of date. Hurriedly, she touched her hair to calm herself. He was looking so embarrassed. She had embarrassed him, just as she had known she would. Dear God, why had she said she would go out with him? *Why?*

'Suzannah,' he said, smiling, 'it's so good to see you.'

'And you,' she replied, wondering why he wasn't leading her on into the theatre.

'About the show tonight . . .'

This was it, Suzannah thought. He was going to cry off, couldn't face being seen with a Hanky Parker.

'I've been a bit of a chump . . .'

Not as much as I have, Suzannah thought, flushing to her roots. He was going to let her down, leave her standing – outside the Manchester Royal.

'You see,' Teddy went on hurriedly, 'I've got the wrong bloody date! We should have been here *yesterday*. Can you believe it?' He took the tickets out of his pocket and handed them to her, praying she wouldn't throw them back at him. 'I'm so sorry, it's the wrong day.'

Taking the tickets from him, Suzannah studied them closely, and then smiled. Then she burst out laughing, Teddy watching her in amazement for an instant before joining in. He would never know how glad Suzannah was. Both of them had started out on the wrong foot – and because of that the playing field was even.

Delighted by her good humour, Teddy held out his arm. 'As our theatre date has been inadvertently cancelled, would you like to go for a bite to eat instead?' he suggested happily. 'Noel Coward can wait for another day.'

That June passed in a soup of heat and flies. In Hanky Park the carters sweated on the coal faces, the horses flicking their tails to dislodge the marauding insects on their flanks. Steam rose from the canals, Mr Leonard sitting in his front doorway, complaining of gout; Mrs Bradshaw breathing heavily in her widow's weeds.

In Peel Park the overheated tenants of the terraces spilled over the parched grass and lolled around the lakeside. Under the bridge, boys up to no good running errands for Denny Cathcart met with older lads, whilst the gamblers sweltered in their stinking dry patch of the 'Oller.

The heat didn't abate when July came in; in fact it intensified. Lying on her back, Suzannah had thrown off the bed sheet and was listening to the sound of the knocker-upper. All along the street he went, rapping at the bedroom windows with a metal pole, rattling the sleepers to work.

Suzannah doubted that he was needed much in such heat. Who the hell could sleep? Sighing, she rolled over and heard the sound of Mrs Bradshaw calling for her cat, Micky, in the yard next door. On the other side, Mr Leonard was silent. The clock next to her bed read 5.45 a.m. Soon Girton would get up. He was always the first and was already hard at work before anyone else came down. Suzannah knew why. Her brother might not mention the Manchester blonde, but he was smitten. A blind man could have seen that.

She wondered then if it was the same for men as it was

for women. Wondered too what it would be like to exchange confidences with her brother. To ask Girton, do you dream of her? Think of her constantly? Do you do things and make mental notes to tell her later? Does a man long for a woman as much as a woman aches for a man?

Smiling, she thought of her latest outing with Teddy. They had gone to Peel Park and he had decided – on the spur of the moment – to take a boat out on to the lake.

'It's a breeze,' he had told her, untying the rope, 'Anyone can row a boat.'

Trouble was that Teddy wasn't dextrous. In fact, he was borderline clumsy and had no concept of rowing. Something Suzannah didn't realise until she got in the boat. But the sun had been high overhead and she'd been happy, leaning back and day-dreaming. Things were going well. The friendship she had hoped for was terrific. Teddy *was* a good friend – but it was obvious that they both wanted romance as well as friendship.

'Damn thing!' Teddy had said, as the boat crashed awkwardly into another couple. 'Why don't they look where they're going?'

Suzannah had tried hard not to laugh, Teddy pulling on the oars and smiling at her. He had been a little sunburnt, his sleeves rolled up and the water flecking the dark brown of his eyes. And in that instant she had realised how much she loved him.

'You know, you're quite something, Suzannah,' he had said, leaning towards her, over the oars. 'I might be falling in love. Well, actually I *am* falling in love with you.' He had paused, staring into her face. 'You look stunned.'

In truth she had been delighted and anxious at the same moment. 'I'm . . . I'm very fond of you too.'

'Fond?'

But before she could answer, a large duck had landed on the water next to Teddy, splashing him. 'Flaming duck!' he'd said, flinching. 'Talk about spoiling the moment.'

She had pulled a sympathetic face. 'Don't you realise that poor duck is probably on its way home?'

'To its wife and children?'

'And its nest. It might have been working all day to find food for them and it's tired out. So tired its little wings can hardly flap any more . . .'

'You're *such* a soft touch, Suzannah,' Teddy replied, teasing her and stretching out to take her hand. '*I'd* like to work and come home to *you* every day.'

She felt his fingers close over hers and was suddenly fretful. It couldn't go on any longer, she had to stop it. Or tell him. If she really believed they had a future, then she *had* to tell him about the past. It was only fair. He couldn't go on thinking she was something she wasn't.

'Teddy, aren't we rushing things a bit?'

He had shaken his head. 'People only say that when they're not sure about how they feel. Aren't you sure, Suzannah?'

'Your family—'

'Has nothing to do with this.'

'Teddy, don't kid yourself,' she had replied gently.

'All right, we'll face that one head on. You should meet my parents,' he'd said, determined. 'My father would be impressed by you. I know he would. He'll see you're special.'

'Teddy, sweetheart—'

'I won't give up on you, Suzannah,' he had replied emphatically. 'I won't.'

Thrilled by him, and by the rush of love she was experiencing, Suzannah reached out and squeezed his hand; 'Perhaps . . . perhaps we *could* sort this out . . .'

It was the encouragement he had been waiting for. Laughing with relief, he whooped madly with joy, and then moved towards her – the boat tipping upwards suddenly. Also laughing, Suzannah had tried to hold on to him, but despite her efforts Teddy lost his balance and the boat had overturned, throwing both of them into the lake.

Spluttering, Suzannah came to the surface first, Teddy catching hold of her and kissing her in the water, the other rowers staring at them and laughing.

'I want to marry you,' he said, both of them soaked to the skin, treading water in the middle of the Peel Park lake. 'I want to marry you, Suzannah Clark. And I won't take no for an answer.'

Tossing the pillow aside, Suzannah's thoughts came back to the present. However she might day-dream about them living happily ever after, it wasn't going to be easy. She knew only too well that Noel Lyle wouldn't see her as Teddy did, but as some Hanky Parker on the make. A slum girl trying to get out of the terraces and up the social ladder.

Teddy couldn't see that she would look like a scrubber in his parents' eyes, that no amount of coaching, clothing, training or money could ever turn a slum girl into a respectable wife. Even without him knowing her history, she was damned. Teddy's parents and all their acquaintances would say the same: she had no breeding, no money. She wasn't one of them . . .

Suzannah sighed to herself. No good pretending her past had never happened. If she *really* loved Teddy, she had to tell him – and risk losing him. Turning over again, she wiped the sheen of sweat from her forehead, then got up and moved to the window. Her brother was standing outside, smoking a cigarette. Odd, she didn't know Girton had started smoking. And he looked different; unexpectedly handsome in the glowing early daylight. Curious, Suzannah leant out further to watch him as he blew smoke from between his lips, his left hand in his trouser pocket, his collar not yet fastened as he stared, preoccupied, at the brick wall of the yard.

Moving away from the window, Suzannah crossed the landing. Tapping gently on her father's bedroom door, she walked in, her voice low. 'Are you awake?'

He turned over. 'What time is it?'

'Not yet six.'

'Can't you sleep?'

She sat down at the end of the bed. 'It's hot . . .'

Yawning, Jacob sat up in bed, his eyes unfocused. He was almost blind now, and yet, at home, he managed well. There was the occasional trip or breakage, but if the furniture remained in the same place, Jacob coped.

'It's too hot to sleep.'

His head turned in her direction. 'And today's going to be another scorcher. But I don't suppose you came in to talk about the weather?'

She smiled, her voice confiding. 'Dad, you know I've been seeing Teddy Lyle, gone out with him a lot recently? Well . . . he says he loves me.'

'Oh.'

A silence settled between them. Suzannah waited for her father to speak again, but when he didn't she found herself blustering.

'He's asked me to marry him.'

'Goodness,' Jacob replied, obviously stunned.

'He really cares for me, Dad.'

'But that's not what matters, is it, love? He could love you until hell froze over, but he's a Lyle, and I doubt his father will look kindly on this.'

'He won't think I'm good enough for his son, will he?'

'You're good enough for any man. You know you are,' Jacob replied, reaching for his water glass and draining it. He wasn't surprised that Teddy Lyle loved his daughter, but he was anxious that Suzannah shouldn't get hurt. 'Do you want to marry him?'

'Yes,' she said simply, wanting desperately to confide in her father, to explain *why* she was so afraid. Not just because of Noel Lyle, but because of Bert Gallager . . . Yet how could she ask for reassurance when the truth would be catastrophic?

'I just want you to be happy,' Jacob said, his tone wistful. 'You deserve it. And if you want Teddy Lyle, then you go for him, love. If it's meant to be, it'll work itself out – whatever the opposition. If it's not right, it'll fold.' He paused, thinking back. 'When I met your mother, she was the spoilt little princess of Rivaldi Street. A slum kid in ribbons and a white dress her mother had made for her. God bless Betty, she made Gloria believe that she was extraordinary. And I believed it too. Made myself good enough for her. Made something of my life to impress her. I wasn't a carter's kid; I was going to be a tailor. When I first saw your mother I thought she was a world above me. Out of reach. Out of my league . . . But I got her.'

Suzannah nodded. 'I understand, Dad.'

'We were very happy, love. You don't remember much of those years, but we were so bloody happy at the beginning.' He smiled into the distance. 'Before it all went sour. Before things got too much for her. I know that if Arthur had lived we'd still be together now.'

The secret shuddered between them.

'D'you miss her, Dad?'

'Not as she became. Not as she was at the last . . . I miss the kid in the white dress with those damn silly ribbons. The kid I threw soot at. I don't let myself dwell on the bad things that happened to us – I just linger on that moment when I first saw her. When we had it all before us.' He turned back to his daughter. 'If you love Teddy Lyle, fight for him. And when you've got him, hold on. And never, *never* let go.'

FORTY-EIGHT

'A word, Teddy, if you don't mind,' Noel Lyle said, ushering his son into the study. Closing the door behind him, Teddy sat down facing his father. The evening was stuffy, made worse by the pall of cigar smoke. 'So, how are things?'

'Everything's fine. Absolutely fine.'

'How about Emma O'Donelly? She took your rejection hard, you know. Quite threw the poor child. Her parents have had to send her away to Italy to recuperate.'

'I'm sorry,' Teddy lied, imagining Emma in her element. 'We weren't suited.'

'Speaking of *suited*,' Noel said smoothly, 'I've been hearing some strange stories. About you and some lady tailor.' He paused, puffing on his cigar, a present from the local Tory MP. 'Now, I understand that young men like to have a bit of fun – and there are ladies you have a bit of fun with, and others you marry. I just want to ask you to be a little careful not to be seen out with *your* bit of fun.'

'The lady tailor?'

Noel nodded. 'Lady tailor! My God, nothing's been the same since the war. Women take on everything now. Think they're as good as the men.'

'She *is* as good as any male tailor,' Teddy replied, fingering his lapel. 'She made this jacket.'

Slowly Noel looked at the jacket. Slowly he considered the skill – and then he considered something else.

'It's immoral.'

'Oh, I don't know. I like the cut.'

'Don't bugger about with me, Teddy!' his father replied

heatedly. 'I mean it's immoral for a woman to take a man's personal measurements.'

'I agree. But Suzannah doesn't do that. Her brother does. Girton Clark measures the customers and then *together* they make the suits. It's quite respectable.'

'For Hanky Park, maybe. But not for a decent woman in a decent area. She's in trade, for God's sake!'

'*We're* in trade.'

'We *own* the trade.'

'They own the shop.'

'I'm not arguing with you,' Noel said coolly, 'I'm just telling you that I don't want you to be seen out and about with this woman. You're not a boy any longer, Edward. It's time you found yourself the right kind of female. Someone you can settle down with.'

'So you think the lady tailor is just a fling?'

'No one is criticising you for that.'

Teddy's eyebrows rose. 'You condone it? Approve of my having a bit of fun with some Hanky Park woman? You think that's the right thing to do? Use them and then move on?'

'I wouldn't have put it so bluntly.'

'How *would* you have put it, Dad?'

'That it's time for you to settle down and find a wife.'

'And what if I already have done?'

Slowly Noel blinked. 'Are you joking? The tailor girl?'

'She's special.'

'Are you out of your mind! Do you really think I would let that happen? Let you marry some scrubber from Hanky Park? Someone with no breeding, no manners? Someone who could only ever show you up? Someone you couldn't take anywhere?' He puffed on his cigar hard. 'You're mad!'

Teddy paused, then took a deep breath. 'I care for her very much. Her name is Suzannah Clark and she has very good manners. No money, but plenty of skill. No background, but a good heart.'

'Jesus!' Noel snorted. 'Grow up!'

'If you'd just meet her, see what she's like—'

'I'm not meeting some gold-digger,' Noel sneered, then paused, realising that he was breaking his own long-held principle – *never directly oppose*. Taking a breath, he modified his tone. 'Teddy, I know how confusing love can be. You think – when you're young – that you love someone. Whereas it's just infatuation. You'll move on from this lady and look back and see it for what it is.'

'Which is?'

'A romance,' Noel replied, tempted to say *fling*, but resisting.

He had to play this very carefully; back-pedal if he must, but get his son away from any female tailors. Dear God, he thought, agitated, reflecting on the scandal such an alliance would cause. A son of his marrying some slut. The Lyle inheritance going to some Hanky Park bint . . .

'Break it to her gently.'

'Break what? Her heart?'

'Don't be melodramatic, Teddy, that only happens in Russian literature. No one dies of a broken heart in this day and age.'

'Then what *do* I do?' Teddy asked, as though he was prepared to go along with his father's plans.

'We'll introduce you to some young ladies of your own class and you'll find yourself a wife. Someone with breeding and wealth. Someone you could be proud of.'

'So really *you* decide who I marry?'

Noel's expression was flinty. The soft approach hadn't worked. His son was going to oppose him, was he? Well, he would see about that.

'Not one penny will be yours if you continue to make a fool of yourself with this Clark girl.' He paused, staring at his son and trying to intimidate him. Teddy could stand up for himself, but he was no street fighter. 'I don't want to act the heavy father, Edward, but this is for your own good. You can still see the girl, if you really want to, but you have to find a wife elsewhere. It's your responsibility. The debt you owe to your family.'

But Teddy stood his ground. 'So being unhappily married is a debt? Well, you certainly paid yours, Dad.'

Noel blanched, genuinely taken aback. 'How dare you talk to me like that!' he hissed.

At that moment CC came into the study. She was dressed in a long ivory sheath, her hair newly shingled, her expression pained. 'What on earth is the matter?' she drawled. 'I could hear your voice on the stairs, Noel. What's going on in here?'

'Teddy thinks he's in love.'

'Not Emma—'

'Emma O'Donelly is in Italy!' Noel snapped, exasperated, and then modulated his tone as he looked over to his wife. 'Edward is in love with a tailor.'

She paled. 'Oh my God, no! It's against the law!'

'Not a male tailor, a *female*.'

'*Are* there any female tailors?' CC asked her husband curiously. 'I never knew—'

'That doesn't matter!' Noel replied, irritated. 'What *does* matter is that she's not suitable. She's from Hanky Park, for God's sake.'

'Oh, Teddy,' CC replied blithely, turning to her son. 'You *are* a scream.'

Stunned, Noel stared at his wife. Teddy was surprised, but hopeful that he had found an unexpected ally. 'I really care about her, Mother.'

'Well, there's no reason to be unkind, darling. We'll compose a nice little note together and then you can pop a present in with it – that should do the trick.'

Teddy could feel the colour drain from his face. For a long, incredulous moment he stared at his mother, but she wasn't joking. She meant it. Suzannah could be written off, quite literally, with a note and a token gift from the wealthy Edward Lyle.

'I'm *not* finishing with her.'

'Of course you're not,' CC said lightly, sliding her arm through her son's. 'Not today, anyway. But no more drama about this now, you two. It will all work itself out in time.' She gave her husband a conspiratorial look which said, *Let it drop, I can handle our son.* Then she led Teddy towards the door, calling over her shoulder: 'Come on, Noel, let's all go into dinner. We're having lamb.'

Teddy could imagine *exactly* how the animal must have felt.

FORTY-NINE

Lionel had fallen asleep in his chair, a string of dribble coming from the left side of his mouth. Stuffed with meat and potato hash, he had settled by the grate and had soon been snoring. Expressionless, Rina watched him. Watched the rise and fall of his chest, his collar undone, his podgy hands clasped over his belly. Bored, her gaze moved to the clock – 9.45 p.m. – and she thought of what she had been doing at the same time a week ago. When she had been with Girton Clark.

Her heart speeded up. How in God's name could she get to see him again? Touching her throat, Rina remembered the way he had kissed her and felt suddenly greedy for sex. If she could just get away from Lionel . . . But how? She had already thought of a hundred excuses, but knew he wouldn't buy any of them. Hadn't he come back from his trip suspicious, sniffing for the odour of adultery like a pig sniffs for truffles? And watching her, eyeing her up, asking her questions.

But she had stayed calm, even managed to look pleased to see him, to offer her cheek for a kiss. A kiss which had revolted her. She had wanted to push him away instead, and taunt him. Say: *I've been with a young, good-looking man. He made love like an angel. Not like you, puffing and blowing like a bull on top of me* . . . But she'd resisted. Thank God she knew how to avoid getting pregnant. By Girton *or* her husband. Not that Lionel expected any offspring. Hadn't she told him at the start that she couldn't have babies? *I can't give you a family,* she had said, faking sorrow. *It breaks my heart, but I can't* . . .

Rina looked at the clock again, trying to compose herself. Whatever Girton said, she wasn't going to leave Lionel. Not yet, anyway. After all, if she left her husband now, would Girton stand by her? And if he didn't, what was there for her then? Rina inhaled, the thought of grubbing a living again unappetising. Better the devil you know than the devil you don't. So for the moment she had better buckle down to life as it was. *This* was reality. *This* husband, *this* shop – and she had better adjust to it. Anyway, Lionel was a lot older than her; she was bound to outlive him.

She *would* have her day. It just wouldn't be yet . . . But suddenly waiting seemed unbearable to Rina. She might have used the last years constructively – kept a roof over her head and squirrelled money away – but sex with Girton Clark had reminded her of what she was missing. And besides, *his* business was infinitely preferable to Lionel's. In fact, Rina mused, the tailor's shop could be quite stylish, if she was let loose on it. No old dummies and dusty counters for her; she would make it a showplace, certain to draw in a bevy of potential, male, clients.

Rina sighed, shifting her position, her thoughts wandering. She had phoned the shop the previous day, Girton answering. He had sounded desperate, begging to see her. Asking if she was all right, if Lionel was treating her well. So concerned, caring . . . But Rina didn't trust him yet. Not until she was certain he wanted her. *Really* wanted her. Then she might consider her escape. But not now. Now she had to sit by the blackened hearth, beside her husband, looking into the red embers of the pawnbroker's fire.

'What you thinking about?' Lionel said, opening one eye. Rina turned to look at him, holding his gaze. 'Stop bloody staring at me, woman! You know I hate you looking at me like that.'

'I wasn't—'

'You were!' he snapped, leaning forward in his chair, his big red hands on his knees. 'You up to something, girl?'

'No,' she replied sullenly, sensing trouble. He was irritated, looking for a fight, his stomach too full, the beer too strong.

'You *have* been up to something!' he snapped, getting to his feet and weaving over to her chair. In one quick motion he hauled Rina up by her hair, pulling his face towards hers. 'Don't you lie to me.'

She ducked out of his way impatiently. 'I'm not lying, you oaf! You're drunk.'

'Not drunk enough to put up with a bitch like you,' he hurled back. 'Get me another beer.'

Seething, Rina moved to the cellar door, not realising Lionel had followed her until she felt a sharp kick in the middle of her back. Losing her footing, she fell down the stone steps, landing heavily at the bottom. Winded, it took her a moment to regain her breath – and then she looked up. Against the kitchen light she could see her husband silhouetted: huge and ominous.

'What d'you do that for!'

'For looking at me wrong!' he snapped back, coming down the steps towards her.

Reacting quickly, Rina snatched up a beer bottle, scuttled under the cellar steps and listened to her husband's descent. She would let the bastard get down into the basement, then run past him back up the stairs and lock him in. With luck, he was so drunk he'd fall asleep and not remember in the morning how he'd got there.

'Oi, Rina!' he shouted, halfway down the steps. 'Hey, you bitch, come here. I haven't finished with you yet.'

So he wanted to slap her around a bit more, did he? Rina thought, her temper roused, her back aching from the kicking she had already taken. Well, he wasn't going to get the bloody chance. He wasn't *ever* going to lay a finger on her again.

Come on, she willed him, *Come on, you fat pig. Come on!*

His steps were heavy, booze slowing him down as he took the stone stairs one at a time. Underneath Rina crouched, her heart thumping to the sound of his footsteps, her mouth dry.

'I know you're down there!' he called out, taunting her. 'Come here now, Rina – or it'll be the worse for you. You hear me? You hear me, bitch?'

Oh, she heard him all right. Hunched under the stairs, she waited in the shadows, the bottle gripped tightly in her hand. If he struck her again, she'd let him have it ... Slowly Lionel lumbered down the steps. And, holding her breath in the semi-darkness, Rina listened to the sound of the footsteps coming closer and closer into the cellar below.

FIFTY

Dishevelled, Rina ran into the Nag's Head pub, the drinkers all turning to look at her. She was shaking, her lips colourless, the landlord walking over to her anxiously.

'Now then, Mrs Taylor,' he said. 'Whatever's the matter?'

'My husband . . . My husband . . .'

The whole pub was listening avidly, drinkers turning round from the bar, the old men watching from around the smoky fire.

'What about yer husband?'

Rina's eyes were blank. Hurriedly the landlord pulled her a tot of brandy and watched her drink it, the colour coming slowly back into her face as she cupped her trembling hands around the glass.

'Now, tell m'what 'appened.'

'It's my husband . . .'

'Yer said that, Mrs Taylor. What about 'im?'

'He fell. He was coming for me . . .' She stared ahead, her expression unreadable. 'He'd kicked me down the cellar steps and I was hiding from him . . .' She paused, the whole pub listening.

Many knew that Lionel Taylor knocked his wife around – but who was going to argue with the violent pawnbroker? Time and time again the neighbours on either side had heard raised voices, but no one had intervened; and besides, it wasn't an unusual state of affairs in Moss Side.

'Go on, Mrs Taylor.'

'I was hiding from him . . .' She caught hold of the

landlord's arm, her grip tight, her fear convincing. 'I had to . . . He was coming down the steps for me. And . . .'

'And what?'

'He fell.'

A murmur went around the customers, people exchanging glances and staring sympathetically at Rina. Serves the bastard right, someone muttered in the snug, might knock some of the nastiness out of him.

'We'll fetch the doctor,' the landlord said, Rina's grip tightening on his arm.

'I think he's dead.'

' 'E what?'

'I think he might be dead,' Rina repeated, her hand releasing its grip. Slowly she looked at the watching customers, her voice wavering. 'Lionel was so angry. He was coming after me. He'd already pushed me down the stairs. I was so scared of him, I hid under the steps. He was coming for me. I couldn't see him, but I could hear him. He fell down the steps. He lost his footing.' Her voice speeded up, the onlookers hanging on every detail. 'I heard him coming. I heard him fall. I ran over to him. He wasn't breathing.'

It seemed everyone was holding their breath, hardly believing what they were hearing. Hurriedly, the landlord signalled to an off-duty constable at the bar.

'Tom, go and 'ave a look over at the pawnbroker's, will you?'

Muttering discontentedly, the man hurried out, the landlord turning back to Rina. 'Yer might be mistaken, luv, yer hubby might just be knocked out.'

She looked up at him appealingly. 'I tell you, he was coming to get me . . .' She paused, her voice hardly above a whisper. 'He was going to kill me.'

It was just beginning to get dark as Tom Goodman approached the pawnbroker's. The hot day had given way to a clammy, early August night, the darkness coming thick, without moonlight. He was piqued at having been dragged away from his beer. And for what? Some domestic fight which would amount to nothing. Besides, he didn't want to get on the wrong side of Lionel Taylor.

For a moment Tom was tempted to walk on, pretend he'd been in to check. After all, Taylor was probably sitting nursing a headache now, and not in the mood for talking. Especially about his wife come crying to the local pub. Bloody hell, Tom thought nervously, this was a right do and no mistake.

Moving over to the entrance of the pawnbroker's, he tried the door. It was locked. Flicking on his torch, Tom walked round to the ginnel beyond. The night was quiet; only the sound of a tram clattering along a few streets away. Tripping over some rubbish in the alley, Tom cursed, and then trained his light on the back door of the shop.

It was open and there was a light on inside. Well, that was all right then, wasn't it? he told himself. Lionel must have come round and turned on the light as he went into the kitchen. Unless Rina had left the light on when she left . . .

Reluctantly, Tom moved into the kitchen, looking round. There was no sign of a struggle. There was no sign of Lionel.

'Hello there, Mr Taylor?'

Silence.

'Mr Taylor, are you there?'

Again silence.

What a waste of time, Tom thought, as he looked round. The old pawnbroker certainly didn't spend money on his house; the kitchen was out of date and the dark lino on the floor sticky with use. God, it was depressing, Tom thought, moving towards the front of the building and the shop beyond.

'PIG!'

He jumped, dropping the torch, the beam shining upwards and illuminating the macaw.

Its beady eyes fixed on him. 'PIG!' It said again. 'OINK, OINK.'

'Flaming hell!' Tom muttered, picking up his torch and giving the cage a wide berth.

Slowly, he shone the light around the pawnbroker's shop. At once the old soldier's cap came into view, beside the stag's antlers and a set of water-spotted *Family Doctor*'s. Fascinated, he continued to pan the light around, picking out the shapes of old coats and hats, of shop dummies, fire irons, prams, even a mangle propped up against the counter. It was an eerie place, made more so by the stale smell of dust and mould.

Shivering, even though the evening was warm, Tom moved back into the kitchen beyond, the macaw cursing him once more before he closed the door. Obviously Lionel Taylor had recovered and gone out. He might even be in the pub now, giving his wife a right talking-to.

Then another thought struck him. Old Taylor wouldn't go out without locking up the shop. The man was greedy, secretive about his business and his money; he would *never* leave his premises unlocked . . . Uneasily, Tom moved on, and as he entered the hall he saw the cellar door open.

Shining his torch down into the darkness, he called out: 'Mr Taylor, are you all right?'

No reply.

'Mr Taylor, are you down there?'

Now anxious, Tom began to descend the cellar steps. His footfall echoed loudly, the torch beam picking out the crates of beer and stacked tin chests. God only knew what the old pawnbroker had down here, he thought, aiming the torch directly beneath him at the bottom of the stairwell.

And then he saw him. Lionel Taylor, his neck broken, his eyes wide open and staring upwards.

'Christ!' Tom said, panicked. 'Oh, Christ!'

Nervously, he moved towards the body, then forced himself to reach down and feel for a pulse. But as he did so, he inadvertently nudged the corpse, which shifted its weight and fell towards him.

Screaming, Tom Goodman dropped the torch and ran up the cellar steps two at a time, without looking back.

FIFTY-ONE

The news was all over Manchester by morning. Lionel Taylor was dead. Good, many said, serve the old bastard right. Others revelled in the fact that their debts had died with him. And more than a few winked and said – in low voices – that it was lucky his wife had got out when she did. After all, hadn't she said that Lionel wanted to kill her? But she'd escaped and he was dead. Lucky, that. Could so easily have gone the other way . . .

But whatever the gossips said, they all agreed that Rina would be well off now the old man was dead. 'Young, pretty, with money in the bank,' her neighbour said as she walked by. 'You watch, there'll be many a man sniffing around Rina Taylor's doorstep now.'

Rina heard the comment, but ignored it. Instead she walked back into the pawnbroker's and locked the door behind her. The body had been removed and Lionel was now in the local funeral home. Expressionless, Rina closed the door to the cellar and locked it, then moved into the kitchen. Lionel's tobacco and mug were still on the table, alongside his paper, and on the rack above the fireplace his clothes were still drying on the wooden slats.

She knew she would have to tell Girton what had happened – but not yet. Instead she wandered upstairs: the hated marital bed was unmade, Lionel's hair cream still marking the pillow. Calmly, she stared at the stain, and then moved to the wardrobe. Automatically she hurled all of her dead husband's clothes on to the bed. Next she threw his shoes on top and lastly his shaving equipment.

Returning briefly to the kitchen for a couple of sacks, Rina stuffed everything of Lionel Taylor's into the bags and then pulled them downstairs. They were heavy, but she managed to drag them out into the back yard, and left them propped up against the outside privy. The rag and bone man would be along later that week; he could take them.

Exhausted, Rina moved back into the house, pausing at the cellar door and remembering the previous night. Lionel's footsteps coming down the cellar steps towards her, his voice calling:

'Oi, Rina! Hey, you bitch, come here. I haven't finished with you yet.'

'But I've finished with *you*,' she said aloud, moving on into the shop.

The macaw looked over to Rina, but said nothing as she pulled out the cash box from under the counter. Prising open the lock, she counted the money, pleased by the amount, then put half in her pocket.

Finally, she picked up the telephone.

Arriving early for his appointment, Teddy Lyle found Helen leaning against the counter, reading a book. She was obviously pleased to see him, smiling as he walked in.

'Suzannah's been held up. She'll be along soon. I think I'm supposed to keep you amused.'

He returned her smile. 'That should be easy for you.'

'Now there you go again, being unusual.'

His eyebrows rose. 'Hey?'

'Most men don't like funny women,' Helen went on. 'They feel awkward about women making jokes. Always think they're taking the mickey.'

'Aren't you?'

'Of course, but we don't like men to know that.' She smiled. 'So, did you talk to your father about returning to Clegg, Cuthbert and Rathbone?'

Teddy hesitated. 'Well, my father and I aren't exactly talking at the moment.'

'Oh, family strife?'

'Something like that.'

'Let me guess. You won't go into the business?'

'I *am* in the business.'

'You won't use your father's tailor?'

'Very good. But that's not all.'

She put her head on one side. 'You won't eat your greens?'

'Everything but broccoli.'

'But broccoli is the important one,' Helen replied, po-faced. 'You can make a case for dodging cabbage, or even beans, but to refuse broccoli . . . Oh, Mr Lyle, you *have* let your family down. When you think of all the sacrifices they made to get you that broccoli. All the work, the heartache . . .'

'The years of dedication.'

'And the *money*.' She paused, shaking her head. 'Have you no idea, young man, just how much broccoli costs?'

He laughed, then Girton walked in, and at once the light-hearted mood sobered up. Business as usual.

'Good morning, Mr Lyle, have you come for your appointment?'

'I have, and I know that your sister's running a little late,' Teddy replied gallantly. 'But your other sister has been keeping me amused.'

Beside them, the phone rang suddenly. Helen picked it up. 'Jacob Clark, Tailors. Can I help you?'

There was a momentary pause at the other end before a woman spoke: 'Is Mr Clark there?'

Helen frowned. 'Jacob? Or Girton?'

'Girton.'

'Who's calling?'

'My name's Rina.'

Smiling archly, Helen passed the phone over to her brother, mouthing the name as she did so.

Surprised, Girton took the handset, turning away from Teddy and Helen.

'Hello? Is everything all right?'

Much as she liked Teddy Lyle, Helen was more curious about the unexpected phone call. So *this* was the mystery blonde – and judging from the look on her brother's face, all was not well.

Tactfully pretending to be studying some collar studs, Teddy glanced into the display cabinet as Girton continued.

'What! What happened? God, are you all right?'

Helen was aching to know what was going on. All this excitement on a Saturday morning! Thank God she hadn't gone shopping.

'I can't talk, Rina. I'll come over . . . No, of course you can't stay there.'

'How much are these?' Teddy asked suddenly, dragging Helen's attention from her eavesdropping. He'd noted Girton's embarrassment and had decided to help him out.

By contrast, Helen was miffed at having her curiosity thwarted.

'What?'

'The cuff links, how much are they?'

Fiddling with the key to open the cabinet, Helen tried to listen in on her brother's call.

'I can't leave you there.'

'I like the ones on the right,' Teddy said.

'On the right?' Helen repeated, infuriated that she was missing the drama.

'Yes, those. How much are they?'

At that precise moment she wanted to *throw* the bloody cuff links at him. Jesus, couldn't he see that something important was going on with Girton? How typical of men. Always thinking of themselves.

'I won't let you stay there. I'm coming over.'

'And the ones on the left?' Teddy asked, Helen's eyes boring into him.

'The ones on the left?'

'Yes. On the left.'

'We can be together now, Rina . . . I'm coming over.'

'How much are they?'

'Read the damn label!' Helen snapped. Girton glanced over at her and then put the phone down.

'What on earth's got into you, Helen?' he asked, turning to Teddy apologetically. 'How can I help?'

'I thought *you* had to go out, Girton,' she said, her tone curt. 'I can deal with Mr Lyle.'

He wavered. 'Well . . . if you're sure you can cope?'

'Yeah, I'm sure,' Helen replied, adding wickedly, 'I think someone else needs you more than we do.'

The first rain in almost a week was falling on the Moss Side street as Rina waited by the tobacconist's. She was dressed in a plain suit, her hair tied up, but her beauty was heightened, not lessened, by the severity of her outfit. It had been wise of her to choose somewhere away from the pawnbroker's. Not that it mattered who she met now. There was no Lionel to stop her. But she didn't want to invite gossip.

Not yet. Not until she knew exactly where she stood with Girton Clark . . . From having nothing, Rina was suddenly quite well off. It was obvious that Lionel had had a full till in the shop, but what else? He'd been a sly man, and secretive – so what other finances had he hidden away? All Rina knew for certain was that he hadn't made a will. He had meant to, after losing out on his brother's shop, but had never got around to it. Didn't trust the law or anyone connected with it.

A mistrust that would serve her well . . . Rina took a deep breath, trying to stop herself smiling. She was a property owner, a shopkeeper. Rina Taylor, widow, a woman of standing. The thought tickled her. No one could tell her what to do any more. No more sleeping with a pig to keep a roof over her head. She was free.

'Rina.' Girton had appeared, snapping her attention back to the present. 'Thank God you're all right!' He hugged her tightly, and then drew back, stroking her cheek. The affection was genuine, unforced. 'When you told me what happened ... Dear God, that bastard could have killed you.'

'But he didn't,' she replied, smiling bravely at him. 'I'm OK, Girton. Shaken, but OK.'

He looked around the street at the falling rain and then pulled her into the shelter of the tobacconist's doorway. Rina thought for a moment that he was going to kiss her, to act the way men usually did. After all, they were lovers. Adulterous lovers. So what right had she to expect to be treated any differently now?

But she was wrong. Girton had changed; he now had the look of a man who had everything worked out. A confidence, even a commanding air about him. Gently he took her hands in his. The shock of her news had thrown him. She might have been killed. The woman who intoxicated him, who thrilled him. The one woman who had made him feel like he was worth something; who had made him feel important. *She could have been killed ...* But she hadn't been. Rina was alive, and Girton was going to make sure that nothing bad ever happened to her again.

'I've been thinking,' he began. 'We can see each other openly now. We can be a proper couple, make plans for the future. People will talk at first. But once you've left Moss Side, no one will know you in Hanky Park.'

'Leave Moss Side?' Rina queried. 'Why would I do that?'

It was his turn to be wrong-footed. 'You can't stay here.'

'But this is my home.'

'This was *his* home. Not yours.'

'I've lived here for years,' Rina replied, surprised at his presumption. 'I've worked in that pawnbroker's and run that house like a skivvy. My sweat has gone into those walls. My hard work into that shop.'

'And now you can leave it. Leave all the bad memories behind.'

'It's a good business,' she said, her lovely face set. 'Maybe I don't *want* to give it up. The pawnbroker's makes a healthy living. I don't mean the loan side of it. I wouldn't do that. But the rest – that's not to be sneezed at.'

'Look, love,' Girton replied, his tone reasonable, 'you're still in shock; perhaps this isn't the time to reorganise everything. But honestly, Rina, you can't *want* to carry on living there? Not after what happened.'

Something shifted inside her; clicked like a lock into place: a reluctance to be manipulated ever again. She had choices now. She could choose to be with Girton – or to stay in Moss Side. She wasn't a nobody any more. Girton obviously wanted her, but was part of that wanting to do with her change in status? After all, a widow was less provocative than a married lover. And a widow with a business was a catch for any man.

'Rina, why are you looking at me like that?'

She flinched. Hadn't Lionel asked her that only the previous night?

'I was just thinking . . .' she replied, glancing down as though confused. 'Everything's happened so quickly. And now you're saying all these things. I can't make decisions so fast. I just *can't*.'

Gently, he pulled her towards him, not forcing kisses, just holding her in the doorway of the tobacconist's shop. He could feel her shiver and then relax, her breathing becoming more regular, and all the time he was looking over her head and imagining what he would have done if it had been *her* body, not Lionel's, lying on a slab in the morgue.

She was his woman. The only one he wanted. Girton had known that from the moment he had seen her. And now fate had made it possible for them to be together. He nuzzled the top of Rina's head, overwhelmed with love for her. His every thought, every feeling, was centred upon her. She had made him feel needed. With her, he had a role in life: as her lover, her protector. He wasn't lost any more. He had sorted out his professional life and now, finally, Girton Clark had found his love match.

Whilst Rina lived, he would live only for her. Whilst she breathed, he would breathe only for her. And whilst she was his, he would live only for her.

He was – without realising it – obsessed.

PART FOUR

A kind of moon wickedness

Anon

I remember very well the first time I saw Rina Taylor.

All that August morning I had been working, finishing Teddy's suit, and then finally I went into the back for a break. I remember stretching in the doorway of the kitchen, watching Girton as he stood up and smiled at me.

He had brought her to the tailor's shop. And there she was – sitting at the kitchen table, fascinating and pale, holding a bunch of peonies.

I've never liked them since.

Passing the flowers to me, she smiled and, God forgive me, I hated her. I'd like to say different, but I could see under all the ivory prettiness something I had seen before – in the faces of the streetwalkers. Some secret look of sly cunning. Some half-hidden belief that people were merely currency.

I put it down to being over-careful of my brother. Girton, doing so well at last, master of his own kingdom. Stable; the turbulence of his past all gone. I put it down to being over-protective of our mother; so determined to bring Gloria home that I couldn't consider another woman being in the tailor's shop, the place I considered rightfully hers. I put it down to everything and anything but what I knew. The one thing I realised without doubt. The thing that shocked me to the core.

She was going to bring chaos.

FIFTY-TWO

Carefully hanging up his white pharmacist's coat, Archie Culshaw straightened the label on the pocket. He could have sworn that Miss Schofield had given him the eye that morning; as for Mrs Morris, she could hardly stop smiling as he got her prescription ready. Bathed in contentment, Archie took the evening paper out and turned to the entertainment page. He fancied a good Western; thought he might have made a bit of a gunslinger himself – if he'd been around in the Wild West. All the women fell for gunslingers, didn't they? Mind you, being a chemist was bait enough . . .

Unfortunately, Archie's perception was like his moustache – patchy. Convinced that he was physically and mentally irresistible, he never saw the look of ridicule on some women's faces. If they didn't go for him, it was because they were too shy, Archie reasoned. After all, what other explanation could there be?

Not that all females were immune to Archie's charm. There was always Helen, and Sally Rice . . . Archie paused, thinking. Sally was quite a good-looking girl, not overly bright, but very smitten by him. He could tell that by the way she flushed every time she came into the chemist's. And the way she got clumsy around him. Hadn't she knocked a whole card of babies' dummies off the counter only the other day?

One thing Sally's crush had done for Archie was to make him question his whole relationship with Helen. Oh, he was very fond of her; had been for a while. In fact, he had even wondered if his future might not lie with Miss Clark. She admired him, giggled when she was around him – and his new white coat had an almost magical effect. But still, now he was soon to be a qualified chemist, might he be wrong to rush into things?

Archie checked his reflection in the shiny side of the medicine cabinet. He was a looker, all right. How could he *help* attracting the girls? Maybe it was only fair that he didn't get himself tied down too soon. Didn't commit himself to one woman for life when there were so many others waiting in the wings.

Like Sally Rice.

Reapplying her lipstick, Helen sighed, giddy with happiness. Hadn't she and Archie had a whale of a time the previous night? And it was obvious he was crazy in love with her. Couldn't keep his hands off her – although he would have to, until they were married.

Smiling to herself, Helen decided that everything in life was just peachy. Suzannah had Teddy Lyle, Girton had Rina and she had Archie. Heaven knows, there could be a spate of marriages, the whole Clark family settling down at once. *Her and Archie* . . . How he adored her. She was so pretty, he said repeatedly. Much nicer than that ghastly Joan Crawford, or Carole Lombard. Well, he might be pushing it a bit there, but still, Helen thought, it was good to be admired. Just like she admired him. Not only for his looks, but his brain. Oh, people might say Archie Culshaw was a bit of a know-it-all, but he was simply confident. After all, he was training to be a chemist. Helen glowed at the thought. A chemist . . . One day they might have their own pharmacy.

She would wear white for her wedding, Helen decided. Maybe have a little reception at the Swan's Nest. Nothing too fancy, but then again you didn't want to look poverty-stricken. Mrs Archie Culshaw, Helen thought with delight.

It was just a matter of time now until Archie asked her.

And she could see he had something on his mind . . .

As they walked down Park Road, Oldham, Gloria stole a glance at Suzannah. Good-looking girl, she thought proudly, wanting for an instant to tell everyone that this was her daughter. She was so proud of Suzannah. Of the way she had coped in her mother's absence; the way she had kept looking for her; the way she never judged her; the way she kept Gloria's re-emergence a secret. And even when Gloria tried to tell her about the past, Suzannah would wave it aside. It wasn't important, she would say. All that matters now is the future.

At first Gloria hadn't believed her, but as time passed it was obvious that Suzannah was in for the long haul. She hadn't given up on her mother when she was missing, and by God, she wasn't giving up on her now. Gloria smiled to herself, patting her hair in place. How long had it been since she'd visited a salon? She couldn't remember, and if she'd been left to her own devices, she wouldn't ever have gone again. But Suzannah had arranged it, watching as Gloria's brittle, dry hair was trimmed and styled. Just as she had arranged to take her mother shopping.

'You'll look so nice in that blue dress, Mum,' she said, turning to Gloria as they walked along. 'You're still so slim.'

'I can't thank you enough, love,' Gloria replied, 'for taking all this trouble.'

'It's no trouble. I like being with you.'

Overcome, Gloria glanced down at the pavement. She had begun, gradually, to get little snatches of her confidence back. And her curiosity. She would never return to Hanky Park, but now she wanted to know more and more about her family.

'You said Helen thought her boyfriend was about to propose?'

Suzannah nodded. 'She can't wait.'

'What's he like?'

'Archie? He's cocky, vain as she is . . .' Suzannah rolled her eyes. 'And he's still trying to grow that moustache. I keep telling Helen he'll look like Hitler, but she won't have it. She's crazy about him, runs around after him, all silly, at his beck and call. *Helen*, of all people! And he lets her wait on him hand and foot. Still, they seem happy enough.'

'And what about Girton? Is he seeing anyone?'

Although she felt it, Suzannah didn't show any surprise. Only lately had Gloria found the courage to refer to her son by name.

'Yeah, he's seeing someone, Mum.'

'And what does Jacob think of her?'

'Dad likes her,' Suzannah replied, her tone expressionless.

Six months after their first meeting, Jacob *had* become very fond of Rina. Probably because she had been careful to cultivate him, to flatter him, to be the consummate potential daughter-in-law. It fooled Jacob, but didn't convince Suzannah – and although she had nothing firm to base her mistrust upon, she was guarded with Rina. Suspicious of that unslipping sweetness which took in so many.

'In fact, Dad likes her very much.'

'Is it serious between Girton and this woman?'

Suzannah stopped walking. The shop lights were throwing illumination on to the rain-buffeted streets and lighting her mother's face.

'He told me last night that he wants to marry her.'

'Oh . . . What do you think of that?' Gloria asked carefully.

'Rina's a widow. She's free. She makes him happy. She makes him laugh – I never used to hear him laugh much before. He was always so ill at ease. But not since she's been around.' Suzannah paused, anxious to sound out her mother's opinion. 'Rina's done nothing wrong. Behaved like a real lady. Even living next door, at Mrs Bradshaw's flat, so people won't talk about her and Girton.'

'Mrs Bradshaw's!'

'Yeah, it's amazing, but apparently Rina's won her over too. She's been living there since she sold the pawnshop.'

Gloria was getting more curious by the moment. 'Who bought it?'

'Denny Cathcart wanted to, but Rina sold it to some old connection she had down south. Dad was saying that she must have quite a stash put away now, what with inheriting everything from Lionel and the sale of the shop.'

'You don't like her, do you?' Gloria asked suddenly, putting her hand on Suzannah's arm.

'No, I don't,' she admitted. 'And thoughts keep nagging at me, Mum. It's not like they haven't occurred to me before, but now they *keep* nagging.'

'What kind of thoughts?'

'Don't you think it's strange that Rina should end up with Girton? I mean, she knew Stanley—'

'She would. He was her brother-in-law.'

'But he never mentioned her,' Suzannah said evenly. She struggled with the next words. 'It just makes me wonder, that's all. About Rina and Stanley. You know?'

'You think they were having an affair?' Gloria asked, stunned.

'I honestly don't know, Mum,' Suzannah replied, hurrying on. 'I don't think Stanley was like that. But why would he keep it a secret that he knew Rina? Oh, I can see that he would have admired her. Fallen a little in love with her perhaps – but why didn't he ever *mention* her?'

They walked on together a little further in silence, until Gloria spoke again. 'Enough about your brother and sister. What are you going to do?'

'About Teddy?'

Gloria nodded. 'About Teddy.'

Suzannah stopped walking. 'It's so difficult, Mum. I love him. I *really* love him. But . . .'

'But?'

'When you really love someone you can't keep anything from them, can you? I mean, if they love you they have to know everything about you, don't they? Good *or* bad.'

'I can't imagine there's anything bad about you,' Gloria said, momentarily troubled.

For an instant Suzannah was tempted to tell her mother everything. To confess the secret she had kept to herself for so long. But something stopped her; and looking into her mother's anxious face, she understood what. Gloria was recovering, but she wasn't back. She couldn't be what Suzannah needed at that moment: a mother she could turn to and confide in. It would be too much for her, Suzannah realised, and instead of making them closer, might even push them apart.

And that was something she couldn't risk.

'I was just talking rubbish, Mum,' she said, linking arms with Gloria and walking on. 'Just a load of old rubbish.'

FIFTY-THREE

'So pay her off!' CC snapped, walking over to her husband's chair and kicking the front leg petulantly.

'Hey, be careful! That's a valuable antique.'

'Oh, stuff your antiques!' CC shot back. 'It's about time we sorted this ridiculous affair out once and for all. That Clark girl will have to be bought off.'

'Teddy's very smitten with her. And he's in just the frame of mind to make a grand gesture. You know the kind of thing.' Noel paused, his voice assuming a martyred air. 'I'll stand by my love, she's the one for me, and nothing you can ever say will shake me.'

'Then we'll shake *her*, not him.'

'Money?'

'What else?' CC countered. 'Look, she's poor. Times are hard at the moment; don't tell me that tailor's shop is thriving. No one's buying suits when they haven't got a job.'

Impressed, Noel raised his eyebrows. 'Are you getting a social conscience?'

'Of course, my love. I've always had a social conscience – about how we look in society. That's the only social conscience that matters to me.' She smoothed down her tailored suit with a manicured hand. 'Edward is spoilt. He'll have to learn that life isn't always about getting what you want. If he wants to be rich and important, he can't afford to get sentimental.'

Noel watched her, his expression amused. 'We've never been sentimental, have we?'

'We've been very successful instead,' she replied. 'And

Teddy will have to learn that a good marriage is good business.'

'Nothing more?'

'Usually, no.'

'No love?'

'An option.'

'Did you *ever* love me?'

She paused, surprised. 'We are ideally suited.'

'But do you love me?'

'Does it matter, Noel?'

Sighing, he turned back to his desk, averting his face. He was, although loath to admit it, cut to the bone.

But who would have suspected *him* of being emotional? Who would have imagined that Noel Lyle felt pained at the thought of not being loved? Who would have thought he *cared*? But Noel cared very much. The years of their marriage had been comfortable, well padded with amusements and money. He had presumed – when they made love or laughed at something together – that there had been affection. Not passion, but fondness. But apparently he had been wrong, and his ego was now smashed. In the end his wife had turned out to be as good an actor as he was – but smarter. Because he was the one who'd been fooled.

And *this* was the life he wanted for his son? Noel reached for a cigar and lit up, comforted by the luxuriant prop. Another father would have undergone a sea change then; would have sworn to turn his child away from his own disappointment. But Noel was not only clever, he was proud: so proud that he would never admit to failure.

Even if it cost his son his happiness.

'I'll go and see her,' he said at last. 'I'll make the girl see reason.'

CC moved over to her husband and laid her head on his shoulder. 'If anyone can do it, darling, you can.'

'I might ask around too. You know, see if she's any skeletons in her closet.' Noel paused. 'It would be nice to have some extra ammunition – if needed.'

FIFTY-FOUR

She was counting the bricks to calm herself, sitting on the outside privy. The bastard! Helen thought violently. The bastard . . . Her head bowed, uncharacteristic tears came fast as she clenched her fists. God, she was so embarrassed, so bloody embarrassed.

Hearing laughter from inside the tailor's shop, Helen felt her face flushing. They were enjoying themselves! Well, good for them! Lucky someone was having a good time! An image rose up before her eyes – Archie Culshaw in the shop, waiting for her. They had been due to go to the pictures and Helen had *known* that tonight was the night. Tonight he was going to propose.

And he had looked so smart, so handsome in his overcoat, his hat dusted with snow, his moustache almost fully grown. And Helen had known she was looking her best too. Blue always suited her so well . . . Of course Archie had noticed at once. Complimenting her and looking all confused. Like a man with something on his mind.

Helen shuddered with embarrassment, burying her face in her hands. Oh God, she hadn't seen what was coming! Jesus, why *hadn't* she seen it? Instead she had leaned across the counter and flirted with him, then grabbed her coat and followed him out.

'Oh Christ,' she moaned, furious and mortified as she sat there on the privy, the February cold whistling under the door. 'Oh, bugger!'

She had been talking away blithely to Archie and then suddenly realised that he wasn't listening. Instead he had paused by the bus shelter and sat down. Smiling with anticipation, Helen had sat down next to him, just the two of them. Not the best place in the world for a proposal, but it would do.

'Helen,' he had said, his head low, 'I have to talk to you. A *serious* talk.'

She would get the white wedding dress with the nipped-in waist. That would show off her figure best . . .

'Helen, are you listening to me?'

'Sure I am, Archie,' she said, huddling up to him. Surprised, she felt him flinch, but thought it was the cold.

'I have something to say . . .'

'Yeah?' She was holding her breath. They would get the engagement ring on Saturday . . .

'You know when you get all hung up on someone?'

'Oh yeah.'

'So much that you can't imagine life without them?'

Helen was flushing with joy. A spring wedding would be nice . . .

'And you can't stop thinking about them? Even though you know it's wrong?'

'I don't think it's *wrong*, Archie,' she replied, baffled.

'You don't?'

She giggled, silly with anticipation. 'No, it's normal.'

'God!' he had said, impressed. 'You're a hell of a girl.'

'I know!' Helen had replied, facing him eagerly. 'So ask me.'

'You sure?'

'Course I'm sure!'

He had taken a deep breath, then asked, 'So you won't mind too much if we break up?'

'YOU WHAT!' Helen had replied, smacking him full in the teeth. 'YOU BASTARD!'

And now she would die of shame, she thought dully. She would stay out in the bleeding privy and die of humiliation. It was all so unfair. All the nights of planning, of romantic dreams, came back to her with painful clarity. And whilst

305

she had fantasised, Archie bloody Culshaw had been seeing someone else on the quiet.

'Helen!'

She winced as she heard her sister calling for her.

'Helen! Come in, food's ready.'

Sod off! she thought bitterly. She could imagine Suzannah's face when she finally re-entered the house. The sympathy, the pity . . . Helen found the pain of rejection unbearable and her stupidity dumbfounding. She had missed all the signs. All the pointers she could now see so clearly.

'Helen!'

Again her sister called for her, the snow beginning to fall, the cold intense. Slowly Helen got to her feet and unlocked the privy door. The light was on in the kitchen, throwing a dirty ochre shadow on the yard as she walked to the back door.

Suzannah, Girton . . . everyone was going to get married apart from her, she thought self-pityingly. No happy-ever-afters for *her*.

'Come on,' Suzannah said kindly as her sister walked in. 'I've made your favourite. Apple pie.'

At once, Helen erupted: 'I never *really* thought he was going to propose! I mean, who's Archie Culshaw when he's at home? Who'd want that pompous bloody cretin?' she asked, bursting into tears. 'He wasn't even good-looking. And that bloody moustache was *awful*.'

FIFTY-FIVE

This was the perfect time to put pressure on his parents, Teddy thought. The depression had hit some of Noel's businesses hard and he needed his son's support more than ever. Needed to have someone around he could trust. Teddy glanced through his office window, watching his father having a heated discussion with the factory foreman. Noel Lyle might charm everyone within his own social circle but he lacked the common touch. He relied on his son to supply that. Just as he had always done.

Which Teddy might now refuse to do. Might get a little bolshie, a little reluctant to soothe the business path for his father when Noel was making his personal route so rocky . . . Teddy stared down at his father, noticing the bald spot at the top of his crown. He wouldn't like that, had always prided himself on keeping his hair.

'TEDDY!' Noel shouted suddenly, turning to look up at the office window. 'Come down here a moment, will you?'

Pulling on his coat, Teddy walked into the yard, over to the two men. The foreman had the settled look of someone who had heard it all before – and hadn't believed it then.

'My son will explain—'

'You can't ask three men to do the job of five,' the foreman said shortly. 'Not when there's more than enough men wanting work.'

Noel glanced over to his son, his look imploring.

'I understood, Mr Cooper,' Teddy began, 'but do you really need *five* men?'

'Yeah, I really do! This bloody factory will be on its

knees before long if your father doesn't start putting some more money and men into it.'

'Now look here—'

Teddy cut his father off. Turning to the foreman he said: 'Could you manage with four men?'

He shrugged. 'Could try.'

'Edward,' Noel said coldly, 'it is not your place to make these decisions.'

'Well, if it's not my place, *you* make the decisions, Father. You make all the decisions and we'll see how long this factory stays open.'

Stunned, Noel stared at his son, Mr Cooper watching the altercation with amusement. About time the lad flexed his muscles. Edward Lyle was a good sort – or would be if he ducked his father's influence.

'You know nothing about business!'

'Then you must have been a poor teacher,' Teddy replied, his impatience flaring up.

The argument wasn't about the workers, or the factory; it was about the simmering animosity regarding Suzannah. It had gone on for months, Teddy refusing to stop seeing her; Noel at first feigning indifference, then becoming more and more irritated.

But in reality Teddy had the trump card. It was obvious that his parents needed him. Not just for his ability at work, but for that magical union only he could pull off – a good marriage. A consort who could bring more money into the Lyle family. A woman who could shore up the fortune against the depression. Or worse . . . Teddy had heard the murmurs from the local politicians that there might well be another war.

It was nonsense, of course. The upheavals in Europe had little to do with England. And yet the depression was shaking people badly, no one quite so certain of the future any more. Teddy had listened in on a number of conversations between his father and his political friends. America was in dire straits with its own depression, something few had predicted. So what might follow now? Teddy didn't know. He only knew that he wasn't about to help his parents when they were determined to ruin his happiness.

Despite asking them on numerous occasions, they would never agree to meet Suzannah. In fact, they employed the tactic of ignoring her existence, and presented a plethora of young women in the hope that Teddy could be manipulated away from his Hanky Park tart. But they had failed.

Just as Noel was failing now.

'I will *not* argue with you in the factory yard!' Noel replied, his calm evaporating as quickly as the steam from a water cooler. 'We don't need more men.'

'Mr Cooper says we do.'

The foreman nodded. 'Or we can't do the job.'

'Hire one more,' Teddy retorted, then turned back to his father defiantly. 'We've no choice. He has to.'

They stared at each other for a long moment, no longer father and son, but two strong-willed men both determined not to back down. At another time Noel would have admired his son for his stand, but not now. Now he saw it as Edward trying to humiliate him; to use his personal popularity with the workers to score a point.

He also knew his son had won. Smiling, although his eyes were cold, he submitted.

'All right, you can hire another man,' he told the foreman, turning to re-enter the factory.

As he walked, his chest thumped with rage, although his exterior was composed. So Teddy was flexing his muscles, was he? he thought sourly. Showing him how important he was.

Well, his son might have won a point, but he was about to lose the game.

Mr Leonard propped his painful foot up on the old horsehair stool and stared at Mrs Bradshaw. He had never liked her, and she had always loathed him, but they were temporarily bonded. By Rina Taylor.

'I don't believe it.'

Mrs Bradshaw leaned her bulk towards Mr Leonard. Her stays creaked as she moved.

'I tell yer, she's a strange one. All sweetness and light, but there's something underneath it all. I mean, who'd have been the wife of Lionel Taylor? And as for the money – God knows where all that is. She's not paying me a penny above the going rate.'

'Maybe there *is* no money.'

'He were a pawnbroker! They're like bookies, they always have money.' Mrs Bradshaw leaned back in the armchair, her corset creaking again.

Slowly she picked at her front teeth, then sucked a crumb out noisily. Repelled, Mr Leonard watched her. It was a bugger when you couldn't get out and about, he thought. You had to wait until people came to you. But lazy as Mrs Bradshaw was, even *she* could waddle her bulk two doors down the street to gossip. And he had to admit – it was good gossip.

'It's cold in 'ere,' she moaned suddenly, reaching for the scuttle.

'Hey, go easy with that, it's not fer flinging around.'

'Yer'll die in yer bed rather than put a bit of nutty slack on, yer mean old fool.'

'I know what I'm doing.'

'Which is more than Girton Clark does,' Mrs Bradshaw replied, rubbing her hands together to warm them. 'Rumour I 'eard was that 'e and Rina Taylor are getting wed.'

'Yer never 'eard that! Unless it were through the bloody wall.'

She pulled a face at him, but carried on. 'He'll have his hands full.'

'And his pockets. If she's got money.'

'Money from the shop sale, and God knows how much

more that that old bugger left 'er.' Mrs Bradshaw sucked her teeth again. 'If they do wed, they'll not go short.'

'Unless she's plans of her own.'

Mrs Bradshaw froze in her seat. The old bastard had some gossip!

'Yer know something I don't, Mr Leonard?'

'I might.'

'Want to share yer news?'

'I might 'ave a mind to.' He paused. 'But then again, I might 'ave a mind *not* to.'

I might have a mind to kick yer bloody foot off that stool, Mrs Bradshaw thought meanly.

'Aye, come on, tell yer old friend,' she coaxed him. 'What yer know?'

He *had* news of Rina but decided he would keep it to himself a little longer and changed tack.

'Suzannah Clark might wed Edward Lyle.'

'He'll never marry her!' Mrs Bradshaw replied, apoplectic at the thought.

It was at times like these that the world seemed positively cheery, Mr Leonard thought, grinding salt into the wound.

'Maybe there won't be just one wedding, but *two*. Rina and Girton, and Suzannah and Edward Lyle.' He winked, leaning towards his visitor, an unpleasant leer on his face. 'And what about *us*, Mrs Bradshaw?'

Her face was puffy with confusion. 'Yer what?'

'I know yer don't just come by to talk. I've a good idea about life,' he winked, 'and love.'

As fast as her girth would allow, Mrs Bradshaw heaved herself to her feet.

'Yer off yer head, Mr Leonard! There's no woman would look at yer favourably – unless she were using a white stick.'

FIFTY-SIX

It was a cold night, just entering March, and Rina huddled further into her coat. The tram had emptied; now there was only her and the conductor left: a middle-aged man with a TB cough. Idly she glanced out of the window, a billboard advertising Aspro on the approaching corner. It showed a young woman, permed hair, short skirt, newly independent, working at an office typewriter. Underneath it read:

ASPRO – Stops Pain and Nerviness

Rina considered the image, her thoughts scrabbling. Girton had asked her to marry him. Well, why wouldn't he?

'There's no reason to wait any longer,' he had said the previous evening. 'We've waited for six months, Rina. You're a widow, a young widow. People won't think it's strange for you to marry again.'

He was wrong. People would think it *very* strange that the newly widowed Rina was suddenly getting wed to the local tailor. They would put two and two together and then deduce that this was no sudden infatuation. In fact, they would conclude, their romance had probably started long before the late Lionel Taylor had so conveniently broken his disagreeable neck.

But who cared *what* they thought? Rina was on top – and staying there. Having money had propelled her out of her role as slum wife. Even the bank manager said good morning to her and nodded. Rina liked that. She had had to rely on her looks and charm before, but this financial power was infinitely more pleasing. For the first time in Rina's life she didn't have to care if men liked her. Didn't have to rely on them for a meal or a roof over her head.

Just as it had been in Moss Side, when Rina walked around Hanky Park she was never overlooked. She saw the admiring stares from the men, and the jealous ones from the women. The latter didn't envy Rina just for her appearance, but for her status too. She was self-sufficient, and even after the war there were few women who could say that.

So what was to stop her from *staying* that way? Rina thought, as the tram passed a headline on a board which read:

JOHN DILLINGER FLEES FROM
POLICE TRAP IN USA

Her eyes alighted on the word *trap*. She had been trapped for years with Lionel. A shudder ran through her. What was the rush to get trapped again? Girton was a good lover and he adored her. But then she didn't *have* to marry him for sex, did she? Rina pulled out her lipstick and applied it, sneaking a quick glance at the conductor in her mirror as she did so. She would have to think about her relationship with Girton carefully. Not jump to a decision.

She had never known a man like Girton Clark before. Never been treated so well, so kindly. There was nothing on earth he wouldn't do for her. Hadn't he told her that often? Hadn't his every thought been for her good? Even down to her living with the ghastly Mrs Bradshaw after she had sold the pawnbroker's? And selling had been the right thing to do; running the shop alone had been just too much work for her.

'It will look better,' Girton had continued. 'You know how people gossip. I don't want anyone saying anything bad about you. It's only until we're married.'

Couldn't he see that people had been saying bad things about her from the start? Her history was common gossip.

How she'd been married to the sordid old pawnbroker; how she'd inherited his money. And now here she was, about to snaffle one of Hanky Park's most eligible men. It was galling for the locals, to say the least.

Reaching her stop, Rina got off the tram and began to walk. She had only gone a few paces when she heard footsteps running up behind her and turned.

'Well, hello there,' Helen said cheerily. 'Been shopping?'

Well, well, well, Girton's little sister, recently dumped by Archie Culshaw. Rina didn't really want to talk, but then decided it might be a good idea. Since moving to Hankerton Street she had been envious of the close relationship between the two Clark sisters and aware that Suzannah wasn't going to be easy to fool. Perhaps if she cultivated Helen's friendship, she could make herself a useful ally.

Smiling sweetly, she took two sweaters out of a bag and held them up for Helen to see. 'You like them?'

'I love them!' Helen replied honestly, stroking the wool.

'Pick one.'

Helen paused, head on one side. 'I can't be bought with gifts, you know.'

Rina flushed, surprised that the girl had seen through her. 'What?'

'I was joking!' Helen replied, taking the pale blue jumper and holding it up against her. 'How do I look?'

'Expensive.'

'Good,' she said, laughing and linking arms with Rina.

Helen was delighted that they had become friends, because lately Suzannah had been even more preoccupied with Teddy. Obviously her sister had a lot on her mind and for once was withdrawn. Helen missed their talks; but if Rina was going to be around, that would certainly make life easier. And besides, Rina was glamorous. In fact, Helen was sure that her new friend could teach her a thing or two.

'You know, I could help you with your hair,' Rina offered suddenly, picking her moment to perfection. 'I mean, it looks lovely now, but it could look even better.' She entered her role of friend with confidence, even gusto. 'That Archie Culshaw! What a fool he was. Missed his chance there, and no mistake. But don't you worry; no man will be able to resist you when I've worked my magic.' She squeezed Helen's arm. 'I could do your make-up for you too – if you'd like that?'

Helen was touched. 'I'd love it! When?'

'Why not now?' Rina replied, Mrs Bradshaw nodding from the window as her tenant walked in. Together Rina and Helen climbed the stairs and entered the cramped rented room, Helen perching on the end of the bed as Rina put down her shopping.

'I suppose we should have popped into the tailor's shop first. Just to say hello.'

Rina shook her head. 'I don't think it looks too good walking in with all this shopping.'

'But it's your money!'

'It's not fair when other people are struggling,' Rina replied, impressively thoughtful.

'Like us, you mean?'

Feigning embarrassment, Rina looked shocked. 'I didn't mean to insult you.'

'I know you didn't!' Helen replied hurriedly. 'I know you wouldn't say anything deliberately mean.'

Smiling, Rina opened the top drawer of her dressing table and took out a neat bag of make-up. Carefully she emptied it on to the glass top, then reached for her brush and comb. In silence she scrutinised Helen's face in the mirror and then began to restyle her hair. Grateful and flattered, Helen bathed in the attention.

Now was the time for a little confidence, Rina thought slyly, bending down towards the girl.

'Look, keep this to yourself, will you? But I've offered Girton some of my money to spruce up the tailor's shop. You know the kind of thing, Helen. He needs to get a couple of new dummies in the window, and as for that awful lamp over the door . . .'

315

Helen wavered, unwilling to offend her new friend but knowing how much Suzannah loved the heavy glass Victorian lamp with JACOB CLARK, TAILOR written on it.

'We've never had enough cash to replace it.'

'I could help out.'

'Dad wouldn't like that, Rina. It's *your* money; you don't have to give any to us.'

'But I *want* to. If I become a member of the family—'

Excited, Helen spun round to face Rina. 'Girton's asked you to marry him!'

At once, Rina put her forefinger to her lips, her expression conspiratorial. Girton had proposed repeatedly – but not for the last month. And suddenly Rina was worried. Maybe it wasn't wise to spend too long thinking . . .

Not that she was going to tell Helen that.

'Girton *has* asked me to marry him, yes. But it's not right to accept. Not now. Maybe one day.'

'Oh, but why wait? You *have* to accept!' Helen went on, eager to get this attractive addition to the family. 'Girton adores you, Rina. He's obsessed. You'd break his heart if you didn't marry him.'

Rina pretended to be torn. 'It's too soon after Lionel's death.'

'It's six months.'

'That isn't long,' Rina replied. 'We should wait.'

'Maybe it *would* look a bit quick to some people,' Helen said reflectively, then hurried on. 'But I have to say my piece – Girton needs some happiness in his life. You understand all about his childhood; I know he's told you what happened. But *you* can make him forget the bad times. I see the way he looks at you, adores you. You can give him stability, Rina, and happiness. *Please*,' she begged, honestly believing she was doing the right thing. 'For my brother's sake, say yes. Say yes.'

FIFTY-SEVEN

'I love you so much,' Girton said softly, as he held Rina in the crook of his arm. They had gone to the park and were sitting under a tree, Rina leaning against him with her eyes closed. Plotting. 'Have I told you that already today? How much you mean to me?'

She turned away from him suddenly, throwing Girton off guard.

'Rina! What's the matter?'

'You don't love me any more.'

He was so shocked, he laughed. 'You're crazy! I adore you.'

'No you don't. Not any more.' She stood up and started to move off.

Hurriedly he followed her, catching her arm and turning her round to face him. 'Rina, what *is* the matter with you? Have I said something? Hurt you somehow?'

She glanced down, allowing the full power of her beauty to work its magic. 'I thought . . . Oh, never mind . . .'

'Thought what?'

'It doesn't matter.'

'Of course it does! Anything that makes you unhappy matters to me. Tell me what it is.'

She glanced at him, eyes moist with tears. 'You haven't asked me today.'

'Asked you what?'

'To marry you . . . Don't you want to marry me any more?'

He laughed, dizzy with relief as he caught her up in his

317

arms. 'Of course I do! I've asked you over and over again, but before you've always said we had to wait. So I dropped the idea for a bit . . . Oh, Rina, was *that* what you were worried about?' He paused, lifting her chin up and looking into her eyes. 'You're crazy! I love you so much. I adore you and always will. I'll never want another woman, or long for anything if I have you.' His voice softened, low with tenderness. 'My beautiful, caring, wonderful Rina, will you marry me? Well, darling – will you?'

And he thought it was all his own idea.

Listening to the radio, Jacob tapped his fingers to the rhythm of the music. It was so kind of Rina to have bought him a new radio – the old one had been getting steadily worse for years and was difficult to tune. She had noticed. Not only noticed, but done something about it. Only yesterday she had arrived at the shop with a parcel, putting it beside Jacob's armchair and then standing back, smiling.

'Now, listen to that. That's a *good* radio.'

He had blinked with surprise. 'Rina, we can't afford—'

'Oh yes *I* can,' she had remonstrated, touching him kindly on the shoulder. It would be well worth the money for a radio to get the tailor on her side. 'I couldn't see you listening to that tired old thing any more. I know how much you love your music, Mr Clark—'

'Oh, it's Jacob, my dear. Jacob to you,' he had replied, touched by her generosity.

This young woman was a real find, Jacob thought, delighted. His son would be mad not to marry her. Snatch her up. Hadn't she been so considerate? So caring? Buying him the radio, being a good friend to Helen? And as for Girton – he was like another man, laughing and vivacious. In fact, the whole tailor's shop had changed since Rina had been around; had become bright, bursting with life. Oh yes, Jacob had decided, they would all benefit from having this woman in the family.

'Well?' Rina asked, ready to tune the new radio. 'What's it to be, Jacob? Jazz or classical?'

'Whatever you say, my dear. Whatever you say.'

As the town hall clock struck three Suzannah walked up Unwin Street. The council was doing some work on the next street so she had had to take a diversion. Hurriedly she moved along, crossing over so that she wouldn't have to walk directly past the abattoir.

Yet just as she passed, Suzannah caught sight of two men silhouetted in the entrance. From behind them, the noise and clatter of the slaughterhouse drifted into the afternoon air. Suzannah recognised Bert at once – although the other man was unknown to her.

The ex-lovers had remained on speaking terms – mostly for Jacob's sake – but Suzannah still avoided being alone with Bert. He had been badly hurt by her, and even though he had now found someone else, the old injury had left its mark. Hurrying past, Suzannah noticed that Bert was in deep conversation with the stranger; a slight, well-dressed man in his fifties.

Glad that she hadn't been spotted, Suzannah struggled to keep hold of the bundle of tailoring swatches she was carrying. Then just as she came round the corner of Hankerton Street she stopped dead. Outside the tailor's shop there was a man up a ladder, unscrewing the old lamp over the door, another man waiting underneath to take it from him.

'What are you doing?' she asked, hurrying up to them.

'Taking this down,' the man replied, from the top of the ladder.

'Who said?'

'Yer father, Jacob Clark. Yer got a problem, miss, yer take it up with 'im.'

Hurrying inside, Suzannah put the swatches on the counter, nodded to Girton as he served a customer, and then ran into the kitchen. Jacob was sitting by the new radio, trying to tune into a music station.

'Dad—'

'Oh, hello, love,' he said, turning the radio off. 'What's the matter?'

'They're taking the lamp down!' she said, horrified. 'And they said you told them to.'

'I did,' Jacob replied, smiling. 'It was going to be a surprise, but you're back early. We were trying to get the new one up and running before you came home.'

'But I *love* that lamp.'

'It's old-fashioned.'

'You never said that before. And it's got your name on it. It's been there for years, Dad. People know that lamp, it's like a landmark round here. And it brings in trade.'

'Oh, don't take on, sweetheart,' he said, laughing and reaching for her hand as she sat down next to him. 'Times change. We have to move with them. Get more modern.'

She smelt a rat at once. 'Whose idea was it?'

'Girton's.'

'And how does he think we can afford a new lamp with so little trade coming in?'

'Rina helped out.'

The name took a swing at her. 'We can't take her money!'

'She didn't pay for all of it,' Jacob said blithely. 'She just wanted to help. She has some good ideas about the shop too. Some modern—'

'This is *your* shop!'

'Suzannah, calm down. What's got into you?'

'What's got into *you*?' she countered. 'That woman can't come in here and start changing things around. This is your business.'

'It's only a lamp,' Jacob said, amazed. 'And besides, I couldn't refuse. It was a present.'

'For what?'

'I'll let them tell you.'

They didn't have to; Suzannah knew already.

She took a deep breath. 'They're getting married, aren't they?'

'It's good news, isn't it?' Jacob replied, obviously delighted. 'She makes Girton so happy.'

'But he hasn't known her that long.'

'Long enough.'

Suzannah chose her next words carefully. 'Doesn't anything about her worry you?'

'No, I like the girl,' Jacob replied, unperturbed. 'Anyway, she loves my son and he loves her. I want to see them happy. Besides, the place will have a proper tailor's wife again.'

Suzannah winced, thinking of Gloria. For the first time she was almost angry with her mother. *Why* had she insisted on making Suzannah keep her secret? For so long Suzannah had wanted to bring Gloria home. Or even arrange a meeting on neutral territory. But it hadn't happened, Suzannah patiently biding her time. One day, she had told herself repeatedly. One day her mother and father would be reunited. One day the tailor's wife would come home.

But now the tailor's wife would be Girton's wife. Rina; in her mother's role.

'Dad, I think you should talk to Girton a bit more about this. I think he's hurrying into things.'

'Don't throw cold water on it!' Jacob replied, suddenly impatient. 'I approve and Helen's delighted. Perhaps you should be a little more pleased for your brother, Suzannah. Frankly your attitude isn't what I would have expected from you.'

'Really?' Suzannah replied, stung. 'Well, I think my brother needs a certain kind of woman to keep him out of trouble. And I don't believe that's Rina Taylor.'

Slamming his hand down hard on the kitchen table, Jacob's voice rose. 'You can't run everyone's life!'

'No, but I've earned a right to my say!'

At once, Jacob turned away. 'I don't want to talk about

this any more. You're making a happy day miserable.'

'We'll let time decide, Dad,' Suzannah snapped, uncharacteristically sharp. 'In time we'll see just who made this day miserable.'

FIFTY-EIGHT

It was just past eight when Teddy entered the park. As she frequently did, Suzannah was sitting on the third bench, staring at the gravel under her feet. They hadn't made an agreement to meet that night, but he had come along just in case.

Smiling, he walked over to her. 'Is this seat taken?'

Startled, she looked up. Much as she loved him, Teddy was the last person Suzannah wanted to see. Her indecision had been gnawing away at her for weeks. She *had* to tell him the truth – it was the right thing to do. And yet she was so in love she couldn't risk it.

'Teddy, hi . . . how are you doing?'

He sat down, immediately picking up on her mood. 'Bad day?'

'They're getting married.'

'Who are?'

'My brother and the Moss Side Medusa.'

He laughed, and then thought better of it. 'You *are* joking? Your brother and Rina Taylor?'

'My father thinks it's a good idea. He thinks she's wonderful. But I don't trust her. I don't even like her.'

'But you're not marrying her.'

She looked over to him, her head on one side 'So I should just let my brother go ahead and make a terrible mistake?'

'It's his life,' Teddy replied circumspectly. 'Perhaps it's time to think about your own.'

'Meaning?'

'Us.'

Flinching, she glanced away. 'Sweetheart, this isn't the time.'

'When *is?*' Teddy replied. 'You never talk about our future.'

'I *can't* talk about it. I don't know what to do yet.'

'Well I do. It's obvious. In fact, Suzannah, my love, everything's playing into our hands perfectly. Your brother's getting married, so you no longer have to be stuck at the shop, running things, any more. You'll be free – and that means you can marry me.'

She turned to look at him, her expression unreadable.

'It's not that simple, Teddy. It's not just about the shop and my family. Everything's so complicated between us . . . I *can't* think about it now.'

'It's not complicated,' he replied, baffled. 'I don't understand.'

Now was the time. She knew it and there was no escape.

'Couples can't have secrets,' she began slowly. 'They have to be able to trust one another. *We* have to be able to trust one another.' She paused, finding the words drying in her mouth. 'There are so many obvious things to keep us apart. Different backgrounds, lifestyle, your parents – but what if there was more?'

'That's enough to be going on with,' he replied, smiling.

She couldn't bring herself to tell him directly and took a roundabout route. 'You're Edward Lyle. You're expected to marry money – and maybe you should. Maybe you'd be happier.'

'You don't believe that!'

'No, and nor do you. Not now. But in time – would you? Would you look at me with embarrassment when I didn't know which knife and fork to use?'

'It's only bloody cutlery!'

She smiled ruefully, taking his hand. 'Yeah, but it wouldn't only be the cutlery, would it? It might be the wrong word at the wrong time. The wrong dress, the wrong reaction. You'd be watching me day and night.'

'Like you used to watch Girton?'

'Yes,' she admitted, '*just* like I used to watch my brother.'

'But he turned out all right.'

She nodded. 'Until now. But after marrying Rina, who knows? That's not a good match either.'

'I'd bet on it.'

'No, she's no good for him.'

'Not on them! On us.'

Gently she lifted Teddy's hand and laid it against her cheek. 'Teddy, think clearly for once. Think with your head, not that great heart of yours. Am I *really* worth losing a fortune for? Status? Your position in life? Maybe I'm not quite what you think. Maybe you've an idea of me that isn't accurate.'

'I know what you are.'

'Are you sure?'

He didn't even pause. 'Suzannah, I want *you*. That's all. I don't care about the past.'

'But we are who we are *because* of our past. My experiences made me; yours made you. Nothing can change that.' She took a breath and hurried on. 'I have to tell you about something—'

He cut her off, his voice firm. 'I don't want to know.'

'Please—'

'No, Suzannah.'

For a long moment they both stared ahead in silence. The light had gone with the day, the sky deepening to indigo, the few last, late birds making for home. At the park gates, the gas lamps were slowly being lighted, a watchman nodding to them as he passed.

'I can't marry you, Teddy.'

'You will. One day.'

'It'll never happen.'

'You're wrong.'

'You could miss the love of your life, tying yourself to me.'

'I could miss the love of my life *untying* myself *from* you.'

Her fingers curled around his, both of them watching the lamps being lighted around the perimeter of the lake. Suzannah knew then that she should have forced the issue, confessed everything – whether he wanted to hear it or not. But she couldn't. She would, but not that evening, not that moment. She would, but not yet. God forgive her, not yet.

'Teddy?'

'Yes?'

'I'm afraid.'

He was momentarily spooked. 'Of what?'

'Of what's coming. Of what I can't see or understand.' She turned, clinging to him, unexpectedly vulnerable. 'I'm afraid of all the changes.'

'Oh, sweetheart,' he replied, stroking her hair. 'Nothing ever stays the same.'

'Why not? Why can't we stay here, like this, for ever? Why can't the tailor's shop stay like it is, with the old lamp over the door?' She pressed her face against his shoulder. 'When I was little I used to wait for that lamp to be lit. It would shine up into my bedroom and write JACOB CLARK, TAILOR on the wall. It was as though everything was all right with the world as long as someone lit that lamp every night. And now it's gone. And suddenly nothing's ever going to be the same again.'

FIFTY-NINE

Beside himself with excitement, Jacob was moving around too fast and stumbling over pieces of furniture which he usually avoided deftly. They were married! Girton and Rina were married! He loved the idea, relished the thought of being in a real home again. Because now there was another tailor's wife.

Suzannah had been a marvel, but even in such changing times no one *really* accepted a female tailor. And besides, Jacob thought, he didn't want to see his daughter tied to a business for life. It wasn't normal. He wanted to see her married to Edward Lyle – if they could work it out. The shop meant a lot to her, he had always been aware of that, but it wouldn't really matter when she had a home of her own. And the man she loved.

His thoughts moved on, and he smiled to himself, hardly able to believe that his dearest wish had finally been granted. His son was finally going to inherit the tailor's shop. Girton, who had once caused so much anxiety, was taking over his father's mantle. And not alone. With a wife. A wife he clearly adored. A wife who was young, cheerful, enthusiastic. A woman who had all the charm and openness Girton lacked.

Jacob could hardly stop himself smiling. Please God, before long there would be grandchildren. Another genera-tion to carry on the business, to keep the shop going . . . It was perfect, Jacob thought, hugging the thought of the future as another man would hug a child. Everything was going to be perfect for the Clark family. *Finally* their luck had turned.

Suddenly he longed for Gloria. She would have been so thrilled. The first tailor's wife handing over to the second. She would have taught Rina everything she had learned about being a wife, a mother, a shopkeeper's spouse. Jacob frowned. But then Rina already knew about that, didn't she? After all, she'd been married before, had run a home and a shop before. But she hadn't had children. That was new territory. Territory Gloria could help her with.

Jacob stopped short, holding on to the back of a chair. Gloria wasn't around to help anyone. Gloria had been long gone. How strange – but for a moment Jacob had been convinced that he would see her again. Suddenly deflated, he felt his way around the seat and sat down. He would never see Gloria again. She was dead – and he was blind.

'Oh come on,' he said out loud, chivvying himself back into good humour. This wasn't the moment to think of sad times. The newlyweds were coming home soon, and he wanted to surprise them. Wanted to welcome Rina properly and thank her for her kindness to him. And he wanted to reward Girton. His son . . .

Rising, Jacob felt his way to the table where he had placed his present. His fingers ran over the lettering, lingering on the gold words he could feel, but not see.

GIRTON CLARK, TAILOR

He could imagine his son's face when he saw it. Girton's pride and Rina's delight. She hadn't just married into a tailor's business; she had married the principal tailor. Jacob laughed out loud. It was the best present he could have imagined. It would give them a solid foundation on which to start their married life. He was giving them the thing he had treasured for so long. The tailor's shop. And in giving it, Jacob was passing over his power, and his trust, to his son.

328

Footsteps outside made him flustered suddenly. They were back early! Knowing he couldn't get upstairs in time, Jacob snatched up his coat and felt his way into the back. There, he hid himself in the understairs cupboard and waited.

The key turned in the lock.

'Wait a minute!' Girton said. 'I have to carry you over the threshold.'

Jacob could hear Rina laughing. 'Let me down! Let me down!'

There was a scurry of movement, then a long pause. Jacob flushed. They were obviously kissing. To his relief, they soon moved into the kitchen, Rina's voice perfectly audible from his hiding place.

'Oh, what a mess . . .'

'Dad's just knocked over a couple of things,' Girton replied, surprise in his voice. 'But his coat's not here, so he must have gone out.'

'You know, darling,' Rina said sweetly, 'I've been thinking about your lovely father . . .' In his hiding place Jacob blushed with pleasure. 'It's so sad he's blind. And it must be so difficult for him with all these stairs and things.' Pressing his ear close to the cupboard door, Jacob listened. How kind she was, how concerned about him. 'And it's going to be even more difficult for him now. With us living together. Here.'

'I don't follow,' Girton said simply.

'Your father can't stay in his old bedroom.'

'I can't turn him out!'

Jacob could hear the sound of her kissing him. 'I don't mean to turn him out, you goose! I just think that *we* should have the big bedroom. It makes sense: two people need more room than one.'

'And put my father where?' Girton countered. 'He's always been in that room. Since my mother lived here.'

'But she doesn't live here any more, does she?' Rina replied, her tone light. 'And anyway, it's at the top of the house, with all those stairs; your father can't find it easy going up and down all the time.'

'He's not old.'

'No, but he's blind,' she replied, her voice kindly. 'He would be so much better in your old room.'

'We can't move him, Rina. That would be like demoting him, taking over his territory,' Girton replied, obviously uneasy. 'I mean, it's his home, that room. Everything he loves is there. He knows his way around. His memories are there.'

'You really don't care about him at all.'

'What!' Girton replied, shocked. 'How d'you make that out?'

'Because your father would be so much better, so much safer,' she wheedled, 'in your old room. And he would understand. I *know* he would. He isn't a selfish man; he'd see that a wife needed space with her new husband. After all, he's had his time here. And his own wife. Everything changes. Everyone has to move on, move over.'

Jacob's mouth had dried, the shock making him tremble. In the space of minutes Rina had pulled his world out from under his feet. The bedroom which had been his and Gloria's, the room in which each of their children had been born, Rina was now usurping. All Jacob's memories of Gloria were within those four walls: all their whispered lovemaking, their caresses, their shared secrets were held there. Their tragedies ... He had gone blind there. As the years had passed the room had faded, blurred, until every beloved inch of wall and ceiling had disappeared, only remembered and loved in his head.

Agonised, Jacob leaned back against the wall of the cupboard. He could see nothing, only blackness. But suddenly the darkness of his blindness was nothing to this new void. He had presumed that he would be loved and revered amongst his family. In the only place he called home.

How could she take it away from him! Jacob raged

inwardly. His room ... He couldn't give it up. He didn't want to give it up. He didn't want to hand it over to them, along with everything else. The shop, the status, the promise of a future.

Biting down hard on his fist to prevent himself from crying out, Jacob waited in the darkness. His nightmare was suddenly reality: he had become a burden. A blind man made to feel his position. A person of little worth to be shunted around. Endured. And for how long? Decades? Why not? He wasn't old.

But he certainly wasn't going to live as he had once hoped – not now that Rina had arrived. There wouldn't be any idle chats in the workshop, his ideas listened to. No reminiscences about Stanley Tobarski, or summer night conversations on the back steps. Oh, Girton might make a token gesture of resistance, but he would soon give way to his new, adored wife. Why should he want to carry on his father's old ways when Rina had her own, modern ideas?

Jacob's naiveté was suddenly embarrassing. Rina hadn't been making changes out of kindness. She hadn't put her money so generously into the shop out of love for Girton – but as a means of getting power. A power which would only intensify as the days passed. A power Jacob could do nothing to staunch.

On the other side of the door, they were talking again.

'Come to bed,' Rina murmured, her voice low. 'There's no one here.'

Jacob could hear his son laughing. 'All right, just a minute.'

'Let's go up to the top room.'

'Rina! We can't—'

She cut him off.

'Your father's out, he won't know. And anyway, darling, soon it won't be his room any longer.'

SIXTY

It was pouring with rain as Suzannah stood knocking frantically on Bert Gallager's door. She had run all the way from the tailor's shop and was out of breath when Bert finally opened up.

'Come in, I were expecting yer,' he said, stepping back. 'Yer wet through.'

'Is Dad here, Bert?'

He nodded. 'Through there.'

Jacob was sitting in front of the kitchen fire, a battered suitcase beside him, his wet overcoat hanging on the wooden rack above the mantel.

Kneeling down beside him, Suzannah touched his arm. 'Come on, come home with me, Dad.'

'That's not home to me any more!' he said flatly, grasping Suzannah's hand as she took his.

'It *is* your home,' she insisted, glancing over to Bert, who was watching them both. '*You* tell him.'

'I can't say I blame him for leaving that place after what he overheard.'

Sighing, Suzannah turned back to her father. 'Girton told me what happened. Look, we can sort this out. I'll talk to Rina, Dad. Get things straight. You're coming back home with me.'

'I was so stupid!' Jacob said suddenly. 'So bloody stupid.'

'Rina took everyone in.'

'No she didn't! She didn't fool you. But *I* wouldn't listen. *I* knew better. I let her in. Welcomed her. And now she's there for good, with Girton.'

'It's still your home.'

'It'll never be my home again!' Jacob said bleakly. 'They made love in my bed, that's what they did. I bet your brother didn't tell you that, did he? They were in my bed – the bed me and your mother slept in. The bed we used to nurse all you kids in, when you were little, or sick . . . She took him up there and he went with her. I could hear them. In my bed.' Jacob hung his head. 'I couldn't sleep in that bed again. Not for *anything*.'

Imploringly, Suzannah looked over to Bert again. 'Please help me. We have to get him home.'

Shrugging, Bert folded his arms. 'I'm on my own at the moment; there's plenty of room. I think he should stay.'

'Here?'

'Yeah, here. He can live with me from now on,' Bert replied evenly.

Catching her hand, Jacob turned back to Suzannah. 'I want you to get Helen out of that place. Tell her to go over to Nan Siddons . . .' He paused, looking at his daughter urgently. 'But I need you there. I need you to stay at the shop, look out for us. Be my eyes and ears. You're smarter than I am, Suzannah, don't let that woman wreck everything.'

'I wouldn't think of leaving the shop.' Suzannah reassured him. 'And don't worry, Helen will be fine whilst I'm there. Look, Dad, I'll sort this whole mess out—'

'Sort it out! How?' Jacob snapped. 'Rina's married to Girton, she's in the shop now. And I'd be willing to bet she's not leaving for anyone. And to think what I did to you.'

Suzannah frowned, baffled. 'You did nothing to *me*, Dad.'

'I did . . .' He paused, shamefaced. 'I gave the shop over to your brother. I had a sign made – as a present for them. It says GIRTON CLARK, TAILOR . . . I thought it was the right thing to do. He'd proved himself, after all. Kept to the straight and narrow these last years. I thought he was sorted out, reliable. That he deserved it . . .'

'You gave it to Girton? But I love that shop,' Suzannah stammered, getting to her feet and walking to the door. 'You stay here, Dad; but I'm going back. And I'm not leaving the tailor's shop for anyone – no uppity tart's going to run me out.'

SIXTY-ONE

May went out with the Whit Walks, but Rina didn't join in the festivities. The other young women and girls of Hanky Park wore their white dresses and walked alongside the lads, their banners fluttering overhead, the names of the local churches embroidered on them. On the streets, the locals turned out to watch, crowded several deep on some corners, as a band marched from Broad Street down to Ellor Street and then onwards.

From downstairs, Rina could hear the sound of laughing and felt uncomfortably excluded. The Clark sisters sharing a joke about something; close again. How irritating. But still, Rina had got what she wanted from Helen. Oh yes, Helen had been a great help encouraging Girton. But now Rina was married, her sister-in-law had outlived her usefulness and was now little more than a vain nonentity to her.

Blissfully unaware of Rina's contempt, Helen was deep in conversation with her sister.

'I just wanted to know what you thought, Suzannah,' she said, pulling on her white gloves. 'I mean, I know you're smitten with Teddy, but—'

'But what?'

'It's Archie. I've had some good news about him.'

'He's dead?' Suzannah asked teasingly, raising her eyebrows.

'Aw, come on . . . He's broken up with that Sally Rice.' Helen paused, not meeting her sister's gaze. 'And I was thinking – what if he wanted to get back with me?'

'You wouldn't take him back?' Suzannah asked, dumb-founded. 'Would you?'

'Why not? I mean, he wouldn't dare try anything again,' Helen retorted, moving to the stairwell and calling up: 'Rina! Rina! Are you ready?'

There was the sound of the door opening, and Rina's head appeared over the banister. She was still in her nightdress, her hair dishevelled.

'What for?'

'We're off to watch the Whit Walks.'

'Oh no, you two go along,' she said, mock-pleasant. 'I'm not feeling too good. A bit of a headache.'

The sisters exchanged a knowing look: Rina had plenty of headaches. Not that she hadn't been on sparkling form the previous evening. Always a good storyteller, she had told them all about Lionel, and how he had wanted his brother's shop so much. Wasn't it romantic, she said, how she had met Girton outside this very shop? It was meant to be, she went on. It was fate . . . And whilst she listened, Suzannah occasionally caught a flinty expression in Rina's eyes, a look which said, *Lionel didn't get the shop, but I did. He'd be turning in his grave if he could see me now . . .*

'Come on,' Suzannah said, taking her sister's arm. 'I'm not missing the Walks for anyone.'

Hearing the sisters leave, Rina began to brush her hair. The old bedroom furniture had to go; it was ghastly, grim. She would talk to Girton about it later, when they had lunch together. Smiling, she moved to the window and watched the street below, hearing the sound of the band coming closer. It was so nice not to have to work, not to have to live with Mrs Bradshaw any more. To be the real mistress of her own home.

Remembering Lionel, Rina winced. She had never been the true mistress of the pawnbroker's; he had always had the last say on everything. What soap she bought, what blinds. And as for the bills, dear God, every penny had had to be accounted for, otherwise the toad wanted to know why.

But that was the past, Rina reassured herself. Girton would let her have anything she wanted. He was loving, considerate, generous to a fault. She could hardly believe her luck. In fact, Rina thought delightedly, her husband would do anything she asked of him.

She had been worried about the old man, but luckily Jacob had taken umbrage and moved out. Rina wasn't sorry; she didn't want her father-in-law around, didn't want to have to look after a blind man. Besides, they had his room now. And he seemed perfectly content with his old friend Bert Gallager. Probably better off, if the truth be known.

Putting down the hairbrush, Rina moved back to the window. She had hung new curtains and nets – the street agog at the changes – and now fingered them lovingly. There had been only greasy, damp-spotted blinds at the pawnbroker's. Blinds that – however much you scrubbed them with carbolic – always smelt sour. There was going to be *nothing* sour in her life any more, Rina promised herself, thinking of the Clark sisters.

Helen was a walkover, but Suzannah was another matter. Thoughtful, Rina considered her options. Perhaps she could become Suzannah's confidante? Help her with Edward Lyle? Encourage her to get married and move out of the tailor's shop? She knew at once that it wouldn't work. Suzannah didn't trust her and wasn't about to confide in her over the price of eggs, let alone her relationship. So perhaps she should try and win her over as a friend? Persist in being pleasant and hope that she would relent?

But that, Rina thought, disgruntled, might take years. And she didn't want the tall, good-looking Suzannah around for a moment longer than necessary, taking her husband's attention from her, or, worse, interfering in the business.

After all, if Suzannah couldn't run Edward Lyle to ground, there were plenty of other men she could marry. It wasn't difficult, Rina knew only too well, and anything was better than being some spinster oddity. A woman tailor! Dear God – who would *choose* to do that, when all you had to do was get married instead?

Stopping for the third time to get something out of her shoe, Helen pulled a face as someone barged past her. The street was crowded – as were all the streets in Hanky Park that day – people jostling to get nearest to the edge of the kerb to see the procession go by.

'Honest to God!' Helen snapped, readjusting her hat as she was shoved from behind. 'Why don't they just walk over us?'

Spotting an opportunity, Suzannah grabbed her sister's arm and pulled her towards the kerb. They were now in the second row, with a good view of the street.

'So what d'you think about Archie?' Helen asked suddenly.

'You can do better.'

'I might have.'

Suzannah glanced at her sister. 'Someone caught your eye?'

'A new clerk at work. He's not – mind my feet! – too bright, but good-looking,' Helen replied, struggling to see over the heads of the people in front as the procession entered the street. 'But I still like Archie best . . .'

Beside Helen, Suzannah was also straining to see the Whit Walks pass, one hand on her hat, the other on her sister's shoulder as she stood on tiptoe. The sunlight was in her eyes, and it was only when she shaded them that she noticed a woman watching from the other side of the street.

She stared, then smiled delightedly. It was Gloria, dressed in a dark suit, completely unnoticed, unrecognised. After so long her mother had ventured back into the Hanky

Park streets. Finally Gloria Clark, the tailor's wife, was only yards away from the home she had left so long ago. But why now? Suzannah asked herself. Why had her mother come today? And then she realised . . .

Standing behind Helen, Suzannah motioned to her mother frantically. Gloria tried to make out what she was saying, but shrugged, confused. Again Suzannah waved and then, slowly and deliberately, she pointed to her sister standing in front of her and mouthed:

'H-E-L-E-N.'

She could see that Gloria understood by the way her mother looked at her sister. Totally unaware that she was being watched, Helen kept her eyes fixed on the procession, while Gloria stared at the child she hadn't seen for years.

Then, suddenly, someone knocked into Suzannah and she spun round. 'Hey, mind out!' she said, before turning back. But this time, when she searched the crowd, there was no sign of her mother.

Gloria had proved as elusive as ever. She had come. And gone.

The music from the band was getting closer. Rina opened the window and perched on the sill. She knew that the sun would light up her blonde hair and show off her curves to their best advantage; knew that the procession would look up at her when they passed. Smiling to herself, Rina saw the band turn the corner, the procession, carrying their banners, following on. She leaned out a little further, one of the drummers catching her eye.

Without thinking she waved, the action catching the attention of many, who looked up, waving back. In that moment Rina laughed as she shimmered high above their heads like some glowing ship's figurehead.

'Bloody 'ell,' one of the bandsmen said to his companion, 'I wouldn't mind betting that our local tailor's got 'is hands full there – and I don't mean with suiting!'

The other man laughed, looking up at Rina.

'She's a looker, and no mistake.'

'And she knows it,' the other man replied, waving as he passed under Rina's window.

Behind them, at the head of the procession, followed Mrs Bradshaw with Miss Hull. Mrs Bradshaw had seen Rina's performance and was red in the face. Puffing with the effort of moving her bulk – and with indignation – she turned to her companion.

'Yer see that?' she asked, jerking her head up towards Rina's window. 'Trouble – that's what that is. Her showing off like that.'

Miss Hull didn't like to agree with anything Mrs Bradshaw said – but she was about to make an exception. Rina Clark was just too attractive to tolerate.

'She's a tart!'

'It wouldn't surprise me,' Mrs Bradshaw harrumphed, panting madly, 'if we found out she'd been on the game.'

'Aye, never! You think?'

'Looks the type.'

Quickly, they moved on, the military tune stepping up the pace of the procession.

'And no one knows much about her past.'

' 'Cept for her time with the pawnbroker.'

'That . . .' Mrs Bradshaw panted as she waddled along, 'were a right do . . . What were . . . a woman like 'er . . . doing wed to . . . that turd Taylor?'

'Makes you think.'

'True . . . enough.'

'Makes you wonder.'

Mrs Bradshaw was gasping with exertion. 'Yer right there . . . No . . . decent woman . . . would . . . have wed . . . 'im . . . Hey!' she said suddenly, rapping the bandsman in front of her sharply with her parasol. 'Is there a bloody fire or something?'

SIXTY-TWO

'Please, darling,' Teddy said imploringly, 'just meet him. I know you can win my father over. And he *is* making an effort.'

'I know, but can't you come with me?'

'I want to, but he wants to talk to you alone. Said he didn't want me around distracting him,' Teddy replied, raising his eyes heavenwards. 'He won't eat you.'

'All right, I'll go. But I'm not keen,' Suzannah replied. The woman behind was hissing at her. Annoyed, Suzannah turned round. 'The film hasn't started yet!'

'I like to watch the Pathé News.'

'That hasn't started yet either.'

'How would you know? You never stop bloody talking.'

Sighing, Suzannah turned back round in her seat and dropped her voice, leaning her head towards Teddy. 'Where does your father want to meet me?'

'The Midland.'

'Where?'

'Sssh!'

She dropped her voice lower. '*Where?*'

'The Midland Hotel,' Teddy whispered. 'It's in the middle of Manchester. He wants to treat you right.'

Suzannah could feel her mouth drying. The Midland Hotel was for nobs. No one from Hanky Park ever went there – unless it was to work as a waitress. How would she know what to wear? How to act? She would be out of her depth, floundering – which was precisely what Noel Lyle wanted. *Wants to treat you right* – like hell.

341

'I can't go there—'

'Either shut up or get out!' the woman hissed from behind them. Suzannah lapsed into silence.

A moment later she could feel Teddy take her hand and stole a glance at him. Did he *really* believe that his father was going to approve of her? Yes, Suzannah thought, he did. Her gaze fixed blindly on the images in front of her, the Pathé News recounting the latest – that Hitler had been voted head of state as well as Chancellor of Germany.

Her attention drifted. Try as she might, she couldn't get Teddy to understand her situation. God, she thought miserably as she slumped lower in her seat, she *couldn't* meet up with Noel Lyle. She just couldn't face him. Absent-mindedly, her gaze alighted on the screen: Joan Crawford sashaying into view, her dress and make-up perfect. Noel Lyle would never think of *her* like that; more like Gracie Fields. A Lancashire lass, the salt of the earth, quietly despised by his class.

Well, it was obvious she couldn't meet up with him, Suzannah decided, suddenly wanting to leave the cinema. It was all going too far. *She* had let it go too far ... Suddenly the film broke, the tape melting, magnified up on the screen, distorted against the white background. At once loud whistling broke out, the lights coming on, a paper pellet flying past Suzannah's left ear.

'Damn, I was enjoying that—' Teddy stopped short, staring at Suzannah. Her head was bowed, the outcry exploding around her. And she was crying. 'God, sweetheart, what is it?'

'We should stop now.'

'Stop? Stop what?'

'Stop all this.' She glanced at him, then looked away.

The house lights were dimming again, the film reel chugging back on to the screen, the sound track speeded up, abnormally fast. Around them, people were laughing. Suzannah's voice was hardly audible.

'I have to go.'

'Suzannah!'

He ran after her, their figures outlined blackly against the cinema screen as she hurried for the exit.

At the door, he caught her arm. 'Suzannah, what's going on?'

'I can't meet your father.'

'What!' he replied, then dropped his voice. She was nervous, he could see that. 'Look, sweetheart, don't be scared. He'll like you and then it'll work out for us. You have to believe we can do this.'

'But what if we *can't*?' she asked helplessly. 'What if we're just prolonging the agony?'

'We're not! We love each other,' he answered simply. 'Suzannah, just go and meet my father, will you? Don't back down. Show him how wonderful you are. This isn't the time to throw in the towel. What if he's going to agree to our marriage? Give us his blessing?'

'And what if he isn't?'

'Just go and see him,' Teddy urged her. 'We'll decide what happens after that.'

SIXTY-THREE

Nodding to a doctor friend, Noel Lyle sat down at the window of the Midland Hotel's dining room. He was pleased at his choice; he felt at home here. It was his territory, the staff knew him, and it was a certainty that he would see several of his friends. He could only hope that the woman didn't show him up. Arrive in some terrible clothing, or make a scene.

But then again, Noel consoled himself, he would have witnesses. People who would commiserate with him and say, *Yes, I see what kind of woman she is. Absolutely impossible.* He had no worries that people might assume he was out with his mistress. Noel didn't have a mistress. He wanted to live . . . He thought of his wife then, and of their breakfast conversation.

'Don't be too charming, darling,' she had said, already dressed in something she referred to as a kaftan. Very Bloomsbury, apparently. 'You know how stupid women can be; we don't want Miss Clark thinking that she has *you* under her spell as well as poor Teddy.'

'As if.'

'You have to be firm. Should I come with you?'

The thought had rattled inside Noel's head like a stick run along iron railings.

'I can cope, darling.'

'You remember what we agreed?'

'I'm not a child, CC.'

'No, but women can be very manipulative. I know you find that hard to believe, my love . . .' He had stared at her, glassy-eyed. 'But the female of the species can be very tenacious. We have to get Miss Clark's grappling hooks out of our son, and fast.'

'I'll see to it.'

She had nodded, fingering his sleeve. 'Don't waver, Noel.'

'I don't waver, CC.'

'Don't enter into any argument with her. After you've put your case, no other conversation is needed.'

'So if she asks any questions, should I use sign language?'

The sarcasm had gone right over her head. 'No if or buts – just a firm statement of fact.'

'And if that fails?'

'You kill her.'

Noel had blinked, CC bursting out laughing. 'Oh darling, you can be so gullible sometimes! You should have seen your face!'

Uncomfortable, Noel forced his thoughts back to the present. Having signalled for the wine waiter, he hurriedly downed a few good mouthfuls of Chablis and relaxed. Thank God his wife hadn't come along; he couldn't have coped with CC or her bizarre sense of humour.

Scanning the entrance, Noel waited for his guest. He had little idea of how Suzannah Clark looked, but guessed that he would be able to spot a Hanky Park scrubber on sight. So it came as some surprise when the head waiter brought a tall, soberly dressed young woman over to his table.

'Mr Lyle, I believe this is your guest, Miss Clark.'

Suzannah put out her hand automatically, realising with surprise that Teddy's father was familiar to her. She had seen him before. But where?

Smiling, Noel motioned for her to sit down. 'You weren't what I expected.'

Suzannah looked at the array of cutlery and swallowed, her mind going blank with panic. She suspected she wouldn't be able to hold a knife without her grip trembling, let alone remember *which* knife to hold. Pressing her hands together on her lap, she tried to keep her voice steady.

'Teddy said you wanted to meet me.'

Fascinated, Noel studied her. She was good-looking, not a bit common. In fact, CC would have been impressed. It was true that her clothes were plain and of no discernible fashion, but she had a good figure and obvious intelligence. He would – Noel thought, rather disappointed – have liked to have met her in other circumstances, when his charm hadn't been leashed.

'I thought we could have a pleasant lunch . . .' Noel paused as the waiter came over and poured Suzannah some wine. She watched him silently, wondering if she should thank him, her hand shaking as she reached for the glass. Slowly she sipped the wine, and then replaced the glass on the table, using both hands.

She felt gauche and hot. On the next table a middle-aged couple were watching her; the judgemental head waiter was hovering like a summer fly over an outside privy.

'Would you like to see the menu?'

Nodding, she was suddenly confronted with a list of French dishes. At that moment all Suzannah wanted to do was push back her chair and leave. Say, *Keep your meal. I can't speak French and I don't belong here.* But she didn't – because she loved Teddy. And because she knew this was her only chance to win over Noel Lyle.

'What would you like to eat?'

'You choose,' she croaked, clearing her throat and passing the menu back to the waiter.

Noel ordered, reeling off the French dishes. He knew exactly what he was doing; choosing his own patch where he was comfortable and she was at a loss. And yet he did – for one tiny instant – feel almost sorry for her.

The moment didn't last.

'I believe you're a lady tailor,' he said, managing to extract the maximum humour from the words.

346

'Yes, I am . . . My father taught me.'

'How quaint,' Noel replied. A long pause followed.

Slowly, he looked around the dining room, nodding to several other diners. He knew only too well that the suspense would be tying Suzannah's stomach in knots, and so he prolonged it. Suzannah cast around for something to say, something witty, and all the time she was trying to remember just where she had seen Noel Lyle before. Preoccupied, she reached out for her glass and – to her complete mortification – knocked it over, the expensive wine spilling over the crisp white tablecloth.

Without uttering a word, Noel clicked his fingers, a waiter appearing and clearing up the mess.

'I'm so sorry, so sorry, Mr Lyle,' Suzannah blundered, mortified. 'That was clumsy of me.'

He ignored her, just let the waiter change the cloth and then watched as their meal was served. The aroma of roast lamb hit Suzannah with the force of a gale. Nerves made her stomach contract as she reached for the cutlery, then paused. Gingerly, she glanced over to Noel Lyle and waited for him to pick up the right knife and fork.

But he was on to her, and instead said: 'Please, do carry on, my dear. Don't wait for me.'

The cutlery seemed suddenly massive, weighing a ton as Suzannah lifted first one knife and then another. Without looking up, she knew that he was watching her, amused. She had had little chance before they had met, but now she had none. She had knocked over her wine, and now her hands were fiddling with the silverware as though she was about to steal it, not use it.

You should have seen her, my dear, she could imagine Noel Lyle telling everyone later. *Didn't know which knife to use! And her hands were sticky – wet with perspiration. Ghastly woman . . .*

Finally, Noel picked up his own knife and fork and Suzannah copied him. Her head bowed, she cut into the lamb and watched the pink juices run into the gravy.

'Delicious,' Noel said happily. 'When my wife and I were in Cannes earlier this year we had lamb, but it wasn't as good as this. You know Cannes?'

Suzannah shook her head, her mortification complete as she struggled to chew the food. Her mouth was dry, no saliva left, her face burning as the meat balled up in her gullet.

'Of course, you don't travel, do you?' Noel went on. 'Shame, as my family are great travellers. Travel broadens the mind. I mean, who would want to live and die in one city?'

I would, Suzannah thought miserably. At this moment I would swap all of this for the back room at the tailor's shop.

'My son Teddy – of course, you know Teddy well – he loves travel. So naturally he would want to marry a woman who knows about such things. A person of culture, of some learning.' Noel paused, delighting in his cruelty as he watched Suzannah struggle to eat. 'A woman with an understanding of how to run a big home, and a wide circle of influential friends. Someone he could show off, be proud of.'

He was mocking her. Triumphant. Noel Lyle had made up his mind and wasn't open to change, Suzannah realised. Teddy might believe otherwise, but there was no chance for them. Agonised, she wiped her hands on her napkin, her heart hammering. As though she had momentarily stepped out of body, Suzannah saw herself as he must see her. Her clothes simple, her hair hardly styled, her corsage limp and cheap. The women around her were wearing full make-up and hats: but she wasn't. They had silk stockings and leather handbags; her stockings were plain, her bag old-fashioned. And they had earrings, rings, necklaces, brooches; whilst Suzannah had only a simple string of amber beads. Which looked cheap.

Humiliated, she bent her head lower. All she could do was eat the bloody lamb and pray for the meal to be over as quickly as possible.

'This romance with my son,' Noel said smoothly, finishing off his lamb and leaning back in his seat. 'You can't seriously imagine that I will allow it to continue?'

She paused, putting down her knife and fork. 'Why not?'

'Why not!' he repeated, surprised. 'Why, look at yourself.'

At that instant her humiliation turned into anger.

'My dear Miss Clark, you're hardly in my son's league, are you? I mean, that dress, and your *hair*.' Noel smiled, tapping the back of her hand paternally. 'You're very pretty, but out of your depth.'

'Go on, please,' Suzannah said, her tone expressionless. 'I always like to learn from my betters.'

'I understand,' he replied, ducking the barb. 'And that's most commendable of you. You see, I wanted to *show* you how unsuitable you are, Miss Clark. I find it's always better to illustrate a point. You can tell people, but they only believe something when they see it for themselves.'

Her face crimson, Suzannah kept her voice quiet. 'So you brought me here to make me a laughing stock?'

'No need for dramatics, dear,' Noel replied evenly. 'I just wanted you to realise for yourself how hopeless it is for you to continue seeing my son.'

'Even if he loves me?'

'Love is a very over-rated emotion,' Noel replied. 'It's all right for the common herd, it gets many through hard times. But as a concept, it is unreliable. And can be expensive.'

She nodded. 'You're right, Mr Lyle, true love is never cheap.'

He winced, seeing some spark in her. 'Look, Miss Clark, there's no future in your relationship with my son. Edward can't be involved with a woman like you.'

'Like me?'

'With your background. Or lack of it.'

'My background?' Suzannah repeated cautiously. 'I can't help that. I was born in Hanky Park, but my family is respectable—'

'My dear, I think we should leave the whole matter here, don't you? Before it becomes embarrassing.'

Staggered, Suzannah stared at him. 'What are you talking about?'

'I'm talking about good old common sense. Now if you have any – and I think you do – you will finish that delightful wine of yours and leave. I've tried to be pleasant, but I can see you're a stubborn woman.'

Her temper unravelled. 'How dare you talk to me like that! I'm not an idiot, or a child.'

He leaned towards her, all pleasantries suddenly over.

'But obviously you're not as bright as I thought, Miss Clark. A hint is not enough, so I'll elucidate. I don't want a daughter-in-law from Hanky Park – particularly not one with a past.'

And then Suzannah remembered where she had seen Noel Lyle before. Visiting his property on Unwin Street – and talking to Bert Gallager.

She paled, but held his gaze.

'I don't know what you mean.'

'You want me to spell it out?'

'Spell *what* out?'

Noel's eyebrows rose. She was feisty; he had to give her that.

'You know Bert Gallager. Rather too well.'

Her heart was thumping, but she kept her face expressionless.

'Of course I know him. He's an old friend of my father's.'

'*Old* being the operative word,' Noel replied smoothly. 'I mean, for you. Couldn't find a boyfriend of your own age?'

Suzannah was finding breathing difficult, but she wasn't about to give up without a fight.

'My past has nothing to do with you!'

'On the contrary, it has *everything* to do with me,' Noel retorted cuttingly. 'My son is *not* marrying a woman like you. And believe me, I *will* stop it.'

'You wouldn't dare!' She was calling his bluff and he knew it.

Enraged, Noel flared up. 'Don't take me on! Remember, I own property in Unwin Street, including the abattoir. That was how I heard all about you and Bert Gallager. No one told me – directly, I mean, you Hanky Parkers are a very close-knit bunch – but you were seen. People talked when you two were involved. And I overheard.' He paused, looking at her coolly. 'But don't worry, I can keep a secret, Miss Clark, believe me. No one will know about you and your lover – especially not my son – if you walk away now. End the relationship with Teddy, or I will personally see to it that *everyone* knows about you sleeping with your father's closest friend.'

Shaken, Suzannah struggled to reply. 'You're black-mailing me.'

'Indeed I am,' Noel replied, draining his glass.

'You can't do that! I'll talk to Teddy—'

'Now let's just think about this, shall we?' Noel said smoothly, refilling his glass. 'Forget Teddy for a moment. Do you really want your father to hear about your sordid affair? I hear he's not too well, and frankly, he's had a hard life. I would imagine that hearing about your fling would do very little for him—'

'You're despicable!' Suzannah hissed, white-faced, knowing she was beaten.

'Maybe I am. But then again – like you – I would do pretty much anything to protect my family. The solution is simple, Miss Clark. You just tell Teddy that it would never work out for you two. Say anything, but end it. If you don't, I'll ruin your reputation.' He smiled coldly. 'And if you're thinking of telling my son, don't bother. He'd never forgive you for not telling him earlier, and even he did, I know Edward, you would never be the same in his eyes. So

I'm giving you a chance to remain as pure as a virgin – in his memory, at least.'

'You wouldn't—'

'Would you like to risk it, my dear?' Noel asked confidently. 'I don't think so. Walk away now and you'll stay perfect in my son's eyes – and your father's.'

Pushing back her chair, Suzannah laid down her napkin and stood up. 'Just tell me one thing, Mr Lyle.'

'Anything.'

'Have you *never* made a mistake?'

Noel smiled. 'Many. But the difference between you and me, my dear, is that I never got found out.'

'Not yet,' she said, her tone deadly. 'Not yet.'

SIXTY-FOUR

Noel had forgotten all about Suzannah. Instead, his attention was focused on the factory foreman, Mick Cooper, who was making life difficult again. He wanted to talk to Mr Edward, Cooper had said. He could do business with him. Noel had wanted to kick Cooper in the pants at that moment, but had relented. He needed the foreman, he needed the workers – and most of all, he needed his son.

God damn it, Noel thought, irritated, why now? Why this day, when he wanted to lay down the law? When he wanted to get rid of Suzannah Clark once and for all? But now he couldn't follow through with his plan, Noel thought, smouldering. He would have to compromise – and all because of some bloody factory foreman. That was typical of the working class, they buggered everything up.

'Teddy. Can I have a word?'

'Yes, you bloody can!' his son snapped, pounding into his father's office. 'What did you say to Suzannah?'

'Nothing,' Noel lied. 'I'll be honest with you, Teddy, I was against this from the start – as you well know. I didn't want to like Suzannah Clark, but she was admirable in a way. I thought we had a good understanding.'

'You're a liar!'

'TEDDY!'

'She's just rung up and finished with me.'

Noel's moment of triumph was short-lived.

'So what did you say?'

'We talked about so many things ... Oh, Teddy, I'm sorry it ended like this,' Noel said, feigning sympathy. 'She was asking me a lot of questions about you, your lifestyle. What people expected of you – and of the woman you would marry.'

'Go on.'

'I just explained to her what life would be like. What people would expect,' Noel went on, then changed tack. 'What did she tell you?'

'That we had too many differences. And *who* pointed those out?' Teddy asked furiously.

'No one needed to point them out; they were obvious to everyone. Even her,' Noel replied. 'I know how much this hurts—'

'HAH!'

'Don't be bitter with me, Teddy, it wasn't my fault. But you and Miss Clark will get over this. And it's better that she realises now that she would never fit in.'

'Why *should* she fit in?'

'Because privilege brings responsibility, Teddy. You've got a place in the world which Suzannah Clark couldn't live up to. And she realised it. It had been worrying her for a long time.' He paused, his voice softening. 'She told me how much she loved you, but said . . . she was afraid of letting you down.'

'Dear God—'

'Teddy,' Noel said, staring at his son, 'I know you hate me now. Blame me for what's happened, if you must. But I only wanted to protect you. I'm telling you the truth: Suzannah loved you very much, but she was overawed.'

'Never!'

Noel kept his voice sincere. 'She *was*, Teddy. She couldn't tell you. She said she had been trying to explain for a long time, but you wouldn't listen.' He could see that he had struck a nerve and hurried on. 'But she confided in me. It was easy to talk to me, like a father figure. She couldn't face losing you and yet she couldn't take on your lifestyle.'

'She didn't have to live my lifestyle.'

'That was what she said you'd say,' Noel lied smoothly.

'But she wasn't prepared to ruin your chances in life. She told me she couldn't have lived with herself if she'd done that.'

Noel could see his son wavering. He didn't want to believe his father and yet obviously there was more than a little truth in the story he had concocted. In a while Teddy would get accustomed to the end of the affair. Besides, however much he begged, whatever he said, Suzannah Clark wouldn't and couldn't take him back.

Noel sighed. No sudden elopements now, thank God. Teddy wasn't going anywhere. Except to sort out the trouble with Mick Cooper at the factory . . . Smoothing down his hair, Noel walked over to the sofa, lit a cigar and offered his son one.

'No thanks.'

'Sit down, Teddy.' Noel said, his tone kindly, paternal. 'I liked Miss Clark. Honestly, I did. I was prepared to be persuaded that she *might* be the right one for you.'

'I thought so.' Teddy went on, swallowing the lie, 'I really believed that you were trying to get to know her. But you still managed to scare her off.'

'She scared *herself* off,' Noel replied. 'You mustn't blame her, though. I must say that although I don't believe Miss Clark to be the right woman for you, she does have some merit. She's good-looking and intelligent. I can see why you could be fond of her.'

Noel was feeling his age. All this skulduggery was so exhausting. If only there wasn't trouble at the factory, he might well be tempted to tell his son to sod off with his lady love. But to have to make up all these fairy tales was positively wearing.

'Suzannah even asked *me* to end your relationship for her.' His son's head shot up. 'But I told her that she had to do it . . . What did she say to you on the telephone?'

'Hardly anything,' Teddy replied, slumped in his seat. 'I said we could work everything out. But she said there was no point talking about it any more. It was over.' He stared at the carpet. 'I said that if she loved me we could get through anything.'

Noel drew in his breath. 'And what did she say to that?'

'That she loved me . . . but not enough.'

Even now, it's so difficult to think back and remember.

Noel Lyle had played his ace. The one card I didn't expect him to have. No one knew about my past. Or so I had thought. And although I believed I had kept it a secret from everyone, the person who uncovered it – and threatened me with it – was the person who could do me the most harm.

And so I finished with Teddy. I had no choice. I phoned him and lied; told him I didn't love him enough to try and make our romance work out. Of course I could have confessed then, but Teddy would think I had done it because I'd been backed into a corner. And besides, even if I did confess and Teddy forgave me, Noel Lyle would make sure that the secret didn't stop with his son.

As he had made clear, if I didn't walk away he would expose me without a second's thought. He would wreck my reputation. Make me the object of people's gossip and my father's shame. Jacob Clark, who had endured so much, would have to endure more. My father would cease to trust me – and begin to hate his closest friend.

I had no choice. The secret I had hidden for so long would remain just that – hidden. Like so many others I had kept, and continued to keep. So I said goodbye to my beloved Edward Lyle. He wouldn't accept it at first, but I insisted.

And in breaking his heart, I broke mine.

SIXTY-FIVE

Opening the front door to let in some air, Suzannah sat on the bottom step of the stairs, looking out into the steaming street. The cobbles had long since dried from the brief shower; the August sun was lemon-white with heat. Across the street a young lad pushed an old pram, the wheels rattling as he whistled for his dog. Memories came back. Of Girton pushing his baby brother. Of the ominous sound of the coal carter's horses thundering through the narrow back streets.

Wiping her forehead, Suzannah reached for her half-glass of beer. She wasn't a drinker, but on a summer night there was only one way to quench a thirst. Her gaze wandered to the nearby pub, then alighted on the figure on the street corner. For an instant it looked like Teddy. But then the man turned and it was someone else entirely . . . Suzannah took a long draught of her beer. It was almost two months since they had broken up. For the first few weeks her grief had been so absolute that she could hardly bear it. Many times she thought of going to see him and telling him about her past. Explaining why she had made love to Bert Gallager, on that terrible evening after she had found her mother again. How it wasn't sordid, how she wasn't a typical Hanky Park tramp . . .

But she couldn't, because she couldn't tell anyone about Gloria. And so – her hands tied by her mother and by Noel Lyle – Suzannah had felt helpless, raging inwardly. Sleepless nights had merged with hot, suffocating days, when she day-dreamed about a revenge she could never take; and a love she could never reclaim.

Then, slowly, Suzannah began to rally. She wasn't going to let Noel Lyle ruin her life. Even if it killed her, she *had* to move on. Perhaps, in all honesty, it wouldn't have worked out with Teddy. They had been so different; maybe the problems would have been too much to overcome . . . Anyway, that was what she told herself. And day by day, week by week, Suzannah clawed her way back.

'How do?' Bert said suddenly, pausing by her door.

She looked up, shielding her eyes from the sun. The tailor's shop was closed, Girton and Rina gone out for the evening, Helen at the cinema with Archie. Courting again. God help him if he strayed this time.

'Want a beer with me?'

Bert nodded, sitting down beside her as she passed him the drink.

'I'm sorry about yer and Edward Lyle. I've been meaning to say something for a while, but every time yer came round Jacob were about.' He paused, looking at her carefully. 'I should have said something sooner.'

'It's OK, Bert,' Suzannah replied, waving a fly away with her hand. 'I thought I'd call round and see Dad tomorrow. I might have found a new place for him to live.'

'Yer what?' Bert asked, stunned. If Jacob left, Suzannah wouldn't come around any more. And he didn't want that. 'Yer father doesn't have to move out. I like his company. It'd get lonely being there on my own.'

She laughed, nudging him. 'Lonely! You're getting married.'

'I'm not!' he replied heatedly. 'It didn't work out with Milly and me.'

It didn't work out because Bert had heard about Suzannah finishing with Edward Lyle. Almost at once his future with Milly Collins had evaporated. The one and only woman Bert Gallager had ever loved was free again.

Maybe, he thought hopefully, maybe this time it would work out for them.

'A drop more?' Suzannah asked, slipping into Bert's thoughts.

He nodded, watching her top up his glass. Suzannah's attention was suddenly caught by a group of lads quarrelling in the ginnel opposite. The heat was growing, flies circling the privies beyond, the drain at the end of the street blocked.

'I've been thinking about the future,' Suzannah said, suddenly wanting to confide. 'About how things never turn out the way you think. And how you can't change them. Noel Lyle taught me that – you can't always run away from your past.'

He listened, delighted to have her company to himself after so long. It reminded him of the old days.

'I have to make the best of things now,' Suzannah went on, finally putting her thoughts into words. 'Mum's back in my life, and Dad's OK with you. Thanks again, Bert . . . But I've been thinking: maybe I've been too hard on Rina. She's making Girton happy; I should like her for that alone. And life's settled down again. You won't believe it, but Helen's even got back together with Archie. *And* that bloody moustache . . .'

They both laughed.

'I've been looking at my life and wondering what I want to do next. And I think I'd like a little business of my own.'

He turned to look at her. 'You're a tailor!'

'True, but as we both know, people around here won't really accept a female tailor just yet, so I thought I'd do some seamstress work as well. God knows, there are enough women who'd like well-tailored clothes, at a competitive price.'

'Yer could do anything yer wanted,' Bert replied, impressed. 'Nothing and no one can stop yer.'

His encouragement fired her up. 'I might end up with a shop of my own.'

'Or a *string* of shops,' he teased her, seeing the old Suzannah again. 'Yer always had ideas. Wanted to get on.'

'Of course, I'd still work in the tailor's shop for now, until I'd saved up some money to get my own little patch. In the end, who knows *what* I could achieve.' She smiled, holding up her glass for him to toast her. 'Here's to the future, hey? Whatever it brings.'

'Here's to yer,' Bert replied, his voice low, his affection obvious. 'And if yer need me. I'm always there for yer. I—'

'I know,' Suzannah said, cutting him off kindly. 'You don't have to say it, Bert. I know.'

At the very same moment, Edward Lyle was sitting in a company flat overlooking Baker Street, in London. He was homesick, wretched to the bone. His life was empty and he missed Suzannah so much it was a physical ache. He stared out on to the street below. The road was heavy with traffic, the street lamps coming on.

Not the lamps around the Peel Park lake, but row after row of lights stretching towards Euston. An area he didn't know, in a city he didn't like. He sighed. *Have a good time in the capital*, his mother had urged him. *You need to go to exhibitions, plays, museums* . . . She had pressed a dozen telephone numbers on him. *Ring these people, go and visit them. They'll show you around*. But he hadn't called anyone. He had been to work in his father's offices and then returned home, longing – always longing – to pick up the phone and dial the tailor's shop.

But if Suzannah picked up she would probably put the phone down on hearing his voice. Hadn't she made it clear it was over between them? *Don't contact me, it's useless. I'm sorry, so sorry, Teddy, but it wasn't meant to work out for us. Please forgive me for hurting you, but it's over* . . . Should he write a letter? he wondered, tormented with confusion. He dragged his hands through his hair. What if

– at this very moment – Suzannah was catching another man's eye? What if she had turned to someone else?

He couldn't accept her loss. Couldn't believe it. Suzannah Clark had been meant to be with him. Teddy sighed. *Had* she, though? Maybe it was only him that believed that. After all, Suzannah hadn't telephoned or written since they split up. She hadn't had a change of heart. Or mind. She hadn't loved him enough. Hadn't she said that? Hadn't she made it plain? She had loved him.

But not enough.

Fluttering with excitement, Helen entered the chemist's and stood, glowing, looking at Archie. He was behind the counter, in the pharmacy area, in his white coat. Like a doctor. Touching her curls to make sure nothing was out of place, Helen looked at the other customers. A middle-aged woman was talking to the chief chemist and a woman with a snivelling kid was waiting to be served.

The kid sneezed and Helen stepped back. She wanted to say to the woman: *That's my boyfriend over there. He's a pharmacist. All qualified now, and mad about me . . .*

But she couldn't, so she just looked down at the little boy. He looked back at her and poked his tongue out. Helen winced. She might marry Archie, but she was *never* having children.

Which made her think about Rina. No offspring there. Why was that? She knew that her brother longed for kids, but apparently Rina had just told him to be patient. It would happen, she said, in time. Let nature take its course . . . Yet only the other day Helen had walked into the bathroom by mistake when Rina had been in there. The door hadn't been fully locked and she hadn't meant to intrude, but Rina had over-reacted, hurriedly shooing her away. But not before Helen had seen enough: the douche bag on the washstand, only half hidden by a towel. It didn't take a genius to work out that Rina was using contraception. Which would have come as quite a surprise to Girton. But then wasn't that typical of her sister-in-law? Helen mused. Saying one thing and doing another? And beginning to flex her muscles too, her sweetness now tempered with flashes of pure bile.

Still, Helen thought, that was *their* life; she had her own to live. Checking her reflection in the countertop, Helen saw Archie and waved. He raised his eyebrows pompously in return. He was such a prig at times, Helen thought indulgently, but you couldn't have everything. People might think she was crazy to have given him another chance, but what did they know? Besides, the girl who had set her cap at Archie wouldn't be trying anything again. Not after Helen had had a word with her . . . Moustache or no moustache Archie Culshaw was the man for Helen. She wasn't marrying a Hanky Park carter or a bloody miner. Archie was a catch – and Helen Clark wanted to better herself.

Finally it was her turn to be served. Helen passed over her prescription and watched as the chemist handed it to Archie. This was his big moment. Transfixed, she watched her boyfriend weigh out the ingredients, then mix them together into a paste, then carefully cut them. Finally he rolled them into perfect little pink pills.

Rembrandt, Helen decided, couldn't have done it better.

SIXTY-SIX

'Well, I do like to feel comfortable. All tucked in,' Mrs Dunne said as she stood in the workshop. Suzannah Clark had been recommended to her: apparently she was doing some seamstressing on the side. And doing it well too. 'Not too tight around the arms. My husband – *the vicar* – says that it doesn't look nice for a suit to be cut too tight around the arms.'

'I'll let it out a bit,' Suzannah said, unpinning and repinning the sleeve. 'You happy with the cut of the jacket?'

'Oh, yes,' Mrs Dunne replied, staring at herself in the long mirror. 'Most flattering.'

That was Suzannah's real gift. She could – with a bit of judicious tailoring – knock a stone off anyone's appearance. Big thighs? No problem. Big backside? Could be concealed. And if you were flat-chested, you came away from Suzannah Clark looking like Jean Harlow.

It had worked out better than even she had hoped, Suzannah thought, delighted. Over the months her little sideline had grown and now, every afternoon from 4.30 until 6.30, she had the run of the tailor's shop. That way none of her female customers would be surprised by any men walking in.

For two hours a day Suzannah ran a little kingdom of her own, giving her brother money for rent.

'I don't want it,' Girton had said at first.

'Well, I want you to take it,' Suzannah had replied. 'If I was working elsewhere I'd have to pay rent. Come on, take it, and let me feel like a *real* businesswoman!'

Carefully Suzannah turned her attention back to Mrs Dunne. The vicar's wife was pleasant enough – and luckily had a big mouth. If she was happy with her suit, the whole of her husband's Harvest congregation would hear about it. And that meant more trade.

'You think I should have it a little shorter?' Mrs Dunne asked, raising her skirt hem slightly and flushing. 'I mean, I don't want to look cheap, but my husband always says I have good legs.'

'You don't have good legs, Mrs Dunne, you have *great* legs,' Suzannah replied, turning up the hem. 'Always make the most of what you've got.'

Ten minutes later Mrs Dunne left, glowing with confidence and itching to tell her neighbours about her suit. *And so reasonable, the girl's a marvel ...* Smiling with satisfaction, Suzannah hung up the suit, tidied away the offcuts and pocketed the ten shillings Mrs Dunne had paid for her next instalment. Another week should see the suit finished – and then there was that wedding outfit for Mrs Edwards.

Jingling the money in her hand, Suzannah thought of the cash hidden away in the chimney of her bedroom. It was hardly a fortune, admittedly, but week by week she was saving, putting aside what she could. Maybe, in the future, a shop of her own wasn't an impossibility. It was a long way down the line, but so what? It was good to have a purpose in life.

'You're doing well,' Girton said, walking in and sitting down at the bench. 'I'm glad.'

'And you're busy.'

'Not really. Just ticking along.' He stretched his arms and yawned. 'I miss Dad, but apart from that, things are going well for us, aren't they?'

Suzannah nodded. 'We're all doing fine.'

'No dramas, thank God.'

'No. We've had more than enough of those.'

'I was so lucky to meet Rina,' Girton said suddenly,

smiling at the thought of his wife. 'It feels good to have the future all mapped out. To know where you're going. I never realised how miserable I was before. How lonely I was . . .' He trailed off, standing up. 'Can you lock up or d'you want me to?'

'I'll do it,' Suzannah replied, watching her brother thoughtfully as he left the workshop.

Girton was obviously a changed man; it was most unlikely that he would slip back into his old, destructive ways. Instead of ruining him, it seemed that Rina had been the making of her brother.

But then again, Suzannah thought pragmatically, it was early days.

In the back room of the bakery, Gloria was having her lunch. Just a sandwich and a cup of tea, and then later she might exchange a few words with the other shop assistant. But not too many words, and nothing of any importance.

Taking an old photograph out of her purse, Gloria studied it. Jacob had been so different then, and their children so young. Sighing, she put the photograph away and began to eat her sandwich. It had been a while, but she hadn't relapsed; hadn't had another breakdown or begun drinking again.

Why was that? Gloria asked herself, knowing the answer only too well. It was because of her daughter. And with the ever-constant support from Suzannah, she had finally faced up to her past. Gloria paused. Had she really been that drunken tart? Dear God, had that been *her*? Memories of Snowhill came back suddenly: the smell of disinfectant and hot water. The days spent staring up at a ceiling light which was never turned off.

And the ribbons. All those ribbons . . . Gloria put her sandwich down. She had been wearing ribbons when she first met Jacob and he threw the soot at her. Ribbons – even when she was half mad – had been a happy memory, some phantom of her previous life . . . Reaching back into her bag, Gloria brought out the new photographs she had been given: Suzannah, Girton and Helen, all grown up. Strangers – apart from Suzannah. But she had seen Helen at the Whit Walks recently, hadn't she? Pretty and vain, just like she had been once.

They were her children, Gloria thought longingly, and she had missed their growing up. She had missed out on so much. And then there was Jacob, her husband . . . God, she had loved him to distraction. Been so happy with him at the tailor's shop.

Gloria closed her eyes, picturing the interior layout, the workroom, the kitchen, the bedroom at the top of the house where she and Jacob had made love, where she had had her babies. Suddenly she wanted to go back. Say, *Stop it now, stop time, turn it back, let me go back. Let me go home.*

The overwhelming homesickness shook her and she opened her eyes abruptly. She had no right to ask for anything. She had walked away; she had left them all; she had made her choice. And there was no going back. The little flat on Peel Street was now her home, and the bakery was where she worked. She was lucky she had one daughter who accepted and loved her. She had no reason to expect more.

And yet the longing wouldn't fade. Later, when Gloria went home, the feeling even intensified. Impatiently, she tried to busy herself, but it was no good. Every cushion she moved reminded her of the old sofa at Hankerton Street. Every dish she dried recalled the china from the Flat Iron Market. And every window she passed conjured up the image of the tailor's shop. She had to go back. Just once. Just to see the place where she had had so much. And been so happy. She would go and see the tailor's shop. Take one last look.

And never look back again.

SIXTY-SEVEN

December had begun well enough. Cold, but winter was always cold in Salford, the hill snow coming down at the end of November, the windows iced up, the streets treacherous underfoot. Sand and salt were thrown around on the walkways, but in the ginnels and back yards the ice settled, making glass mirrors for the moon to admire herself in.

Over the previous few months, Rina realised, there had been a shift in the household, and she was feeling left out. Helen – who could still be a welcome diversion at times – was now busy with Archie. That was all she talked about, Archie Culshaw, Archie flaming Culshaw. And as for Suzannah, she was humming along. Busier every week, from the look of it. And making a bundle, Rina thought resentfully. After all, no one worked for nothing, did they?

As a manipulator first and foremost, Rina's patience was wearing thin. Much as she might try to become involved with the Clark sisters, they didn't really want to include her. They did so at times – for Girton's sake – but it was obvious that the three of them would never be close. Fine, Rina thought, who needs them anyway? Helen could marry her bloody Culshaw and Suzannah could sew herself into the ground. She didn't need them. She had her husband.

But Rina was getting bored with Girton. Not that he had noticed. He was too in love, and too committed to keeping the business afloat. For a long time the shop had been struggling, but Rina's timely injections of money always came to the rescue – and intensified her control. She might have tired of her lapdog husband, but she didn't have to work, and his devotion was more than a little satisfying to her ego.

So, to stem her ennui, Rina began to change the tailor's shop. The old dummies went first, and in their place came two new mannequins, as hard and perfect as Rina herself. Bit by bit all traces of Jacob, Stanley Tobarski, and the old life of the Clark family were whittled away. Helen and Suzannah noted every change; but Girton didn't see it. Saw only a stunning wife who caressed him out of his worries and offered him money to help.

Go on, take it, darling. What's mine is yours. Go on, I love you, take it . . .

Grateful, Girton willingly agreed to whatever his new wife suggested. Yes, they would paint the shop a bright cream colour.

'But don't you think it'll fade with all the soot and dirt round here?' Suzannah asked. 'You'd have to do it over every year.'

'And you have to move with the times,' her brother replied. 'Honestly, Suzannah, Rina has a much better idea of such things. She *did* come from down south, after all. You could learn things from her. I know she'd be only too willing to help. Ask her about clothes, anything. She really wants to be friends with you. She tells me that all the time.' He dropped his voice. 'She really cares about you. Was so sorry about what happened with you and Edward Lyle.'

Suzannah flinched, embarrassed. 'You talked to her about that!'

'Why not? She's my wife. And she's so sympathetic,' he went on earnestly. 'She was really concerned. If only you'd talk to her. Trust her, let her help.'

And Rina liked to help – but not in the way her husband thought. Her caramel sweetness was fading rapidly, her bitterness showing. Under-occupied, she became provocative, spiteful.

'No man cares how fast a woman can type, only what she's like in his bed,' she had told Helen only the previous day, adding peevishly, 'You don't want to end up on the shelf, do you? I mean, look at your sister – she was left high and dry by Teddy Lyle.'

'Hey, watch it!' Helen had snapped, stung by the unpleasant change in her supposed friend.

Rina hadn't turned out at all as Helen had wanted. The girlie talks had all but ended, their shopping excursions curtailed. All Helen's hopes of having a close relationship with her sister-in-law had evaporated. But instead of being disappointed, she was suddenly wondering if she actually wanted the friendship any more. Just who was this Rina?

'Don't talk about Suzannah like that!'

'Oh, come on,' Rina had mollified her. 'I don't mean any harm. I just wanted to give you some advice. I mean, Suzannah's good-looking, but she really fouled up her big chance.'

'Oh yeah?' Helen had retorted viciously. 'And how would *you* have caught Teddy Lyle? By getting pregnant?'

The words had struck out at Rina and rocked her. For an instant she hadn't reacted and then she leaned towards Helen, her face only inches from her sister-in-law's.

'What's *that* supposed to mean?'

'If you're so bored, Rina, why don't you have a baby? After all, my brother's desperate to start a family. And there's no reason why you couldn't have children. Is there?'

'Don't push your luck,' Rina had replied, the cherub's mask slipping. 'You don't want to mess with me, little girl. You're not up to it.'

'You want to watch who you're bossing around, Rina. You might fool Girton, but I can see through you like a pane of glass,' Helen replied, stalking off.

But when she was out of her sister-in-law's sight she stopped, leaning against the outside wall. She was shaking; dear God, she was shaking. And then she realised something far more disturbing; Rina had actually scared her.

Many others in Hanky Park noticed the shift in atmosphere at the tailor's shop.

'Only one thing comes from having too many women in one house – trouble. That's what it causes, *trouble*.' Mrs Bradshaw looked delighted by the prospect. 'That Rina in the shop, showing off. Flirts with all the men. And I bet she'd leap at the chance of taking their inside leg measurements.'

Miss Hull flushed. 'She's a married woman!'

'She needs a ring through 'er nose, not on 'er bloody finger,' Mrs Bradshaw replied, biting into a custard cream. 'Yer should 'ear the goings-on I 'ave to put up with at night. Laughing and all sorts from their bedroom.'

'Like what?'

Mrs Bradshaw wiped the crumbs away from her mouth. 'Like things decent people don't talk about. But I'll tell yer one thing.' She leaned forward, Miss Hull straining to catch every word. 'That woman's a tart. Jacob knew it – that's why 'e cleared off.'

'*How* did he know it?'

'I 'eard some gossip,' she lied with aplomb. ' 'Eard that she . . . yer know . . .'

'No. What?'

'She flirted with 'im.'

'Never!'

'That's what I 'eard. And as yer know, I'm not one to talk, but 'e did leave in a hurry.' Mrs Bradshaw paused, finishing the custard cream. 'That Rina would go with anyone. Any man, any age. I know the type. And that soppy great husband of hers can't see it. Sick with love, like a lapdog.'

'She might love him.'

'And I might be Shirley Temple,' Mrs Bradshaw replied

shortly. 'Yer watch – there'll be trouble soon. What kind I don't know, but trouble. *Big* trouble.'

'Get the hell away from my house!' Rina snapped, throwing open the back door which led out on to the ginnel. A group of lads were hanging around, playing football, like they always did. But no one had complained before. Surprised at her shouting, they watched her approach. 'Clear off, I don't want kids around.'

'But Mr Clark told us—'

'Look, I'm *Mrs* Clark, and what I say goes.' Rina leaned down and picked up the football. 'Keep away from my wall.'

'Yer gonna make us?' one of the lads asked, standing up to her. He was showing off in front of his friends, cocky with confidence. 'We can play where we like!'

Smiling, Rina moved over to the boy, took his arm, then led him away from the others. Whooping, they watched, calling out encouragement. But so far away, they couldn't hear what Rina said, could only see a sudden change in their friend's demeanour. Red-faced, he was shifting from foot to foot, all cockiness gone.

'I hope we understand each other now,' Rina was saying, so softly that she couldn't be overheard. 'You keep away from my house, you hear? Or I'll have a word with your dad about you playing around with that Miller girl. And she's only fourteen. Shame on you, putting your hand up a little girl's skirt.'

The boy was waxy with unease. 'We weren't doing nowt wrong! Yer wouldn't tell on me!'

'Oh yes I would,' Rina replied, pushing the football into his chest. 'I know what people get up to around here, lad, remember that. I have eyes and ears. I *know* what people are like. What nasty little secrets they have – and want to keep.' She smiled, tracing his cheek with her index finger. 'Do we understand each other now?'

Scuttling off, the lad ran back to his friends. He didn't tell them what Rina Clark had said, but from then on he steered clear of the tailor's shop. And no one ever played football around there again.

Tentatively, Gloria turned into Hankerton Street and stood on the corner. It was raining, and there were few people on the street. Not that anyone would have recognised the old Gloria Clark in this stooped little figure. Slowly she crossed over, checking that the sign on the door of the tailor's shop was turned to CLOSED.

No one around, Gloria thought. Thank God for that. Wiping the rain off the window, she looked in. Everything was the same, and yet different. Old Stanley's mannequins had gone, as had the aspidistra – but the yellow blind was still in place. Hurriedly, she rubbed the window pane again, peering in at her old life. Without even trying, Gloria could see herself as she had once been: pretty, young, children around her, and Girton coming in with the pram.

Shaken by the recollection, Gloria stepped back. She had seen the shop; it was time to go. But she couldn't leave, and again she moved to the window and looked in. Suddenly the interior was transformed by memory: the lamps bright, Stanley Tobarski shaking his coat dry, Jacob laughing at the entrance to the workshop. Inside the kitchen, the fire was lit, and a little girl was doing her homework at the table.

Distracted, Gloria stepped back. The memory shop altered. At once the fire went out, Jacob moved away, and the little girl finished her homework and grew up.

SIXTY-EIGHT

'That sister-in-law of yers is a bitch,' Mrs Mitchell said, buttonholing Suzannah outside the grocer's shop. 'Yer warn 'er off my husband, yer 'ear me? Buying Rina Clark drinks in The Brewer's Arms! What the 'ell is that about?'

Stunned, Suzannah glanced around. She could see that several other women in the queue outside the grocer's were listening avidly. Obviously this ambush had been planned in advance.

'Mrs Mitchell—'

'When I think of yer mother, what the shop were like when she were around. Always decent, she were. Tried her best, did poor Gloria, but couldn't cope. Well, that's one thing – not being able to cope – but being no bloody good is another. And that Rina is a bitch, and little more than a whore—'

'Could we talk about this somewhere else?' Suzannah asked hurriedly.

'Oh, there's nothing I can say that others round 'ere don't know about!' Mrs Mitchell turned to the nearest woman in the queue. 'Am I telling the truth, or not?'

'Yer are that,' Mrs Harrison replied eagerly. 'Rina Clark clipped my lad round the ear the other day for nothing. Just for spite.'

'She wouldn't have done that for nothing!' Suzannah remonstrated, embarrassed. 'I'm sure she didn't mean it—'

But Mrs Mitchell wasn't having any of it. 'Oh, she meant it all right! All that sugar-sweet front were just fer show.

Now she's Mrs Clark, she's sharpening her claws. Yer should have a word with yer brother; tell him to pull her back into line.'

'Mrs Mitchell, I can't interfere in Girton's marriage.'

'Well if yer don't, I reckon there won't be a marriage fer long.'

Annoyed, Suzannah turned on her. 'What's *that* supposed to mean?'

'Yer know as well as I do! She flirts with every man she comes across; bad-mouths every woman; sashaying up and down Hankerton Street like she was on stage. Or maybe she's used to walking the streets—'

'That's enough!' Suzannah said shortly, walking off.

She might have her own doubts about her sister-in-law, but Rina was part of the Clark family now. And they never turned on their own.

Ten minutes later, when Suzannah walked into the kitchen of the tailor's shop, she found Rina sitting at the table, doing her nails. Already unsettled by the fracas at the grocer's, Suzannah looked around the messy kitchen, her impatience obvious.

'Couldn't you have washed up?'

'What?' Rina drawled.

'Or cooked something for tea?' Suzannah paused, looking her sister-in-law up and down. 'Are you going out?'

'Some hope,' Rina replied sullenly. 'Girton's working.'

'He's got a business to run.'

'And how he loves to run it. Just like you, working all the time. You must have a nice little pile stashed away now. Busily making all those dresses for the fat local ladies.' Rina put her head on one side. 'What are you going to do with all your money, Suzannah?'

'Save it,' she replied, moving to the sink and running some cold water.

'We need to update this kitchen. It's hideous.'

'We haven't the money for things like that.'

'*I* have money, so I say what goes. You could contribute, though – if you liked.'

'I pay rent.'

Rina was unimpressed. 'It's not that I don't appreciate what you do around here. But *I'm* the tailor's wife, not you, and I run this place.'

'I have a home here too.'

'And you want to keep it.'

'What's *that* supposed to mean?' Suzannah asked, thrown.

'Just what I say – you want to keep your home here. And so does Helen. Until she marries that ghastly Archie Culshaw.' Rina smiled her belladonna smile. 'And of course you're both welcome to stay – as long as you behave.'

'Behave!' Suzannah repeated, outraged.

'Neither of you treats me right,' Rina went on petulantly. 'You always exclude me—'

'We asked you to the pictures last week.'

'Only because Girton insisted.'

'You're just bored, Rina,' Suzannah said, starting on the pile of dishes. 'Get a hobby.'

'I'm Girton's wife! You don't tell me what to do.' She paused, smiling pitifully as she changed tack. 'I've had a tough life, Suzannah; it's mean of you to make things unpleasant for me here.'

'I'm not arguing with you. You're just in a mood and you want someone to take it out on.'

Incensed, Rina retaliated. 'Don't patronise me! And don't push your luck, Suzannah – or I'll have a word with Girton.'

Putting her hands on her hips, Suzannah turned to face her sister-in-law. 'What kind of word?'

'Your brother loves me. Adores me,' Rina went on, her expression flinty. 'He would do *anything* to make me happy.'

'Well, he's already made sure our father moved out.'

'Your father went off in a huff!' Rina retorted, irritated.

'Anyway, Jacob's happier where he is. Got his own room—'

'He had his own room here,' Suzannah replied coldly. '*You* took that room.'

'Some room! You'd think this place was some kind of palace. It's just a shop with a flat tacked on. Just a slum shop—'

'Well, you'd know all about those.'

The barb found its mark.

Rina's voice hardened. 'Don't cross me, Suzannah.'

'Or what?'

'I could make a nasty enemy.'

'You're making plenty of those yourself, Rina.'

'What's *that* supposed to mean?'

'I've just been hearing all about you – at the grocer's,' Suzannah replied. 'You should stop flirting with other men, and letting them buy you drinks. What would Girton say if he found out?'

'Oh, the hell with Girton!'

'Look, just because you're feeling hard done by, don't make everyone else's life a misery. This is a happy house – and you're not going to change that.'

Seething, Rina thought of the Clark sisters laughing the previous night as Suzannah coloured Helen's hair. They had been in high spirits, Rina hearing them from below and wincing with envy. Everyone was happy but her.

'You can't expect me to live day after day in this bloody shop, with nothing to look forward to. Some life your brother's given me! Hah, some great life!'

'If you don't like it,' Suzannah said, her tone deadly, 'then get out.'

Rina's eyebrows rose.

'I don't think your brother would be too pleased to hear you talk to me like that.' She walked to the door and turned. 'Face it, Suzannah, if it came to a showdown, Girton would take my side.'

It was true. Always adept in the bedroom, Rina had made her husband feel masculine, complete. Opened a whole new world to Girton. But lately Rina had found herself wondering when *he* would try something else. Kiss her differently, in another place. Touch her in a different way. His sexual technique was limited, and although Rina found her husband attractive, she was no longer satisfied. All her attempts at instigating something new failed. She might have hated Lionel's demanding gropings, but Girton's devoted tenderness was proving to be just as tiresome.

But he *was* generous, and had given her everything she wanted. New furniture, of course. New china, naturally. And not that rubbish off the Flat Iron Market either, but good china from Manchester, Deansgate even. As for her clothes, they had to be the best. Nothing off the market for Rina. Nothing from the Salford shops. Hand-made, by her own chosen seamstress. And every time she had got a new outfit, Rina had paraded around Hanky Park, revelling in the attention from the men and the envy from the women.

Yet after a while even that thrill had faded. It was all right to lord it over the locals, Rina decided, but who were *they*? Just slum fodder, no better than Lionel. She wanted more, from more important people. She wanted to be recognised as someone, a beautiful woman with money. Preoccupied, she walked upstairs and flopped on the bed. All her meticulous planning had worked to perfection: she had become the tailor's wife, with an adoring husband in tow.

But it wasn't going to be enough.

Stacking the shelves, Suzannah saw Mrs Mitchell walk past and then heard the shop bell ring. She braced herself for another onslaught, but when she opened the door, she was surprised to see a corpulent, well-dressed man, with a well-fed, smug look: Denny Cathcart.

He was almost preening himself as she moved towards him. 'Hello there, Suzannah,' he said pleasantly. 'Long time no see.'

Her tone was cool. 'You're not welcome here, Mr Cathcart.'

He laughed. 'Now then, Suzannah, you and I were friends once.'

'We were never friends.'

'Your grandmother and I go back a long way.'

'My grandmother is an old lady.'

'And I knew Girton—'

'You nearly ruined my brother,' Suzannah responded, keeping her voice low. 'We both know that. So what d'you want coming here now?'

'A new suit.'

'We're busy.'

'That's not what I heard,' Denny replied. 'I heard that you were struggling a bit. The market's getting most of your trade at the moment. It's always the same when times are hard – people don't want luxuries. Why pay more for a suit when you can get one for next to nothing down Broad Street?'

'Is that where you got yours, Mr Cathcart?'

He raised his eyebrows. 'You've no reason to be rude, Suzannah. I could help you out.'

'We're doing fine. And besides, I've got my own little sideline.'

'I heard. Well, I always said people would never take to a female tailor,' he replied, smiling. 'Anyway, enough chitchat, Suzannah. I'd like a word with your brother.'

'Girton's out.'

'But he'll soon be back,' Rina said, interrupting Suzannah as she stepped into the shop. She was smiling invitingly, her face flushed pink with expectation. 'Can I help?'

It had been a while since she had seen Denny Cathcart. Not since he'd offered to buy the pawnbroker's shop from her when she was first widowed. But she'd got a better offer elsewhere and sent him packing. Him *and* his money.

Seeing Rina, Denny smiled. There was a flash of interest between them; both on the make, both opportunists.

'Oh, Mrs Clark. How nice to see you again,' he said, adding deftly, 'Perhaps – if your husband is out – you and I could talk?'

Suzannah watched the exchange and willed Girton to return early. The one person she had never wanted to see again was now here, and he was talking to Rina. Suzannah thought back to that hot day Stanley Tobarski died. Girton shamed, seen home by the police, and her father's distress – all caused by the bellicose man now standing in their shop.

Come home, Suzannah thought blindly. Please, Girton, come home . . .

'We could talk in the back,' Rina said, showing Denny into the living room off the kitchen. As she passed Suzannah she smiled; a smile of triumph. As though she was on sure ground again. As though she had found her feet.

The thought unsettled Suzannah further, and for the next fifteen minutes she watched the door of the tailor's shop, willing Girton home. Mr Leonard came in and bought a pair of collar studs, and Mrs Guthrie asked the price of some long johns for her husband, but Girton didn't return. Like an automaton, Suzannah served her customers, unable to interrupt the meeting in the front room. And sensing that there was something malignant in the air again.

Then suddenly Rina re-emerged with Denny Cathcart, shaking hands with him before he left. The two women watched him walk to his car, and then Suzannah turned back to Rina.

'What was all that about?'

'It's private.'

'Rina, please don't have anything to do with Denny Cathcart,' Suzannah said, her tone serious. 'I know you and I have our differences, but that man nearly ruined Girton.'

'He's just a businessman.'

'He's not. He's a bastard. He uses people, Rina. He's bad news. Please, don't let him back here. Don't let him back into our lives. He brought disaster before; don't let him do it again.'

But it was too late. Suzannah could see the look in Rina's eyes and realised that Denny Cathcart was everything Rina understood. And admired.

The old ghosts were back.

SIXTY-NINE

Her head thumping with a heavy cold, Helen walked home. She would go to bed and try to sleep it off. So much for kissing Archie, she thought ruefully. A great big sloppy kiss – and now a cold. Some romance. She sneezed twice, then continued walking.

She wasn't looking forward to getting home; the shop half modernised, half old-fashioned. The new dummies shiny and out of place, the cream paint already beginning to peel. And inside would be Rina reading one of her romantic novels, or showing off her latest purchase. A new coat, a new skirt. Nothing for the shop any more. Nothing for Girton. All that had stopped the previous month, Rina's generosity abruptly turned off. Any money she now spent, she spent on herself. But of course Girton didn't mind.

But Helen did; she minded a lot. She minded all the rumours she was hearing; minded the Clark name being a byword for scandal again. It had been bad enough before, but this was worse. This was due to some vicious cow and her sleazy ways. Ways that were becoming common gossip. Sneezing again, Helen blew her nose . . . Rina was going out a lot now. Said it was to visit friends – but *which* friends? Rina had no friends, no family. So was she seeing another man? Helen shuddered, suddenly thinking of her brother, of what a betrayal like that would mean to him. Poor Girton, so in love – with the wrong woman.

Lucky for her she had Archie. Lucky for her she wasn't going to be living at the tailor's shop much longer. Only another year or so, Archie had told her, until they'd saved

382

up enough for a deposit. Then they'd have their own home.

The thought cheered Helen as she opened the gate and walked in. Rina was sitting with her back to the kitchen door, and Helen could hear voices. At first she thought the radio was on, then she realised there was somebody else there. Curious, she peered in. Rina was sitting, laughing, as a young man rubbed her feet.

'What on earth are you doing?' Helen snapped, walking in on them.

If she expected Rina to act guiltily, she was in for a disappointment. 'Oh, hi.' She turned to her companion, the good-looking man smiling lazily. 'This is Adam Firth.'

'And who's he?' Helen countered, looking at Rina's feet. 'The chiropodist?'

Rina laughed. 'I was caught in the rain. Adam's just rubbing some feeling into my poor cold feet.'

And looking up your skirt at the same time, Helen thought bitterly, sneezing twice.

'Looks like you got caught in the rain too,' the young man said, Rina wriggling her toes to draw his attention back to her.

'Where's your husband?' Helen asked pointedly, her nose getting more bunged up by the second.

'In the shop, where else?'

'Does he know you've got company?'

Adam exchanged a knowing look with Rina before she answered. 'What's your problem, Helen? Can't you get anyone to rub your feet?'

'When I'm married I won't let anyone but my husband do that.'

'Lucky Archie,' Rina replied, stretching languorously, the young man watching the material of her blouse pull across her breasts.

Embarrassed, Helen hurried into the workshop, their laughter following her. 'We've got to do something about that bloody woman!'

Suzannah looked up from the sleeve she was pinning on

the work dummy, her voice unnervingly composed. 'What's Rina doing now?'

'Seducing some bloke called Adam. What if . . .' Helen paused, sneezing. 'What if Girton walks in on them?'

'He'll be told that it's innocent, and he'll believe it.'

'She could be having an affair right under his flaming nose.'

'Maybe she already is. I imagine that being the tailor's wife wasn't quite what Rina expected; she feels cheated,' Suzannah replied coldly. 'Rina's used to a lot of attention. Remember when she first came here, when she was trying to win us over, how she used to tell us about working at that pub in London? How the men all fell for her?'

'I remember.'

'Well, there are no men falling over her here.'

'She's got Girton.'

'A husband's not enough,' Suzannah replied shortly. 'She's on the lookout for excitement again. Taking risks. She knows Girton trusts her. And as for us – Rina doesn't give a damn what *we* think.'

They could both hear the laughter from the other room.

Helen's face flushed. 'We have to tell Girton what's going on.'

'He wouldn't believe us.' Suzannah dropped her voice further, leaning towards her sister. 'Look, I don't want to worry you, but Denny Cathcart's been round. He and Rina were like old pals together. Like he was her sort . . . It gave me a bad feeling, Helen. I don't want Cathcart anywhere near us. And I don't want Rina – of all people – bringing him back.' She paused, making up her mind quickly. 'Go and stay with Nan Siddons, will you? At least until you get over your cold. Rina just irritates you; you'll not get better here.'

'And leave you on your own?'

'Oh, I'll be all right. I need some time to think about Rina. About what we're going to do.'

'She conned me, good and proper.'

'But she's not conning anyone any more – apart from Girton,' Suzannah replied. 'And she's making enemies; showing her true colours. The rumours are flying around Hanky Park. No one likes her any more, now they see her for what she is. And I don't like what she's doing to this family.' Suzannah paused, turning back to her sister. 'Go to Nan Siddons's for a few days.'

Helen eyed her sister carefully. 'What are you going to do?'

'I'm going to try and find out about Rina's life before she came here. Before she married Lionel Taylor.' Suzannah stuck a pin deep into the horsehair-stuffed dummy, her expression relentless. 'I'm going to drive her out, Helen. Ruin her – before she ruins all of us.'

His hand over his face, Bert was dreaming, his sleep unexpectedly shattered by the sound of something striking his bedroom window. Surprised, he got up and looked out. Suzannah was waving to him from below.

At once he ran downstairs to let her in. 'What's the matter?'

'I need your help.'

'Anything, just ask,' he said, leading her into the kitchen and poking up the dying fire.

It was bitterly cold in the early hours of the morning, the room stale, smelling of beer and cigarette smoke, a copy of the evening paper on the table. Pushing it aside, Bert laid out two mugs for them and put on the kettle. He was nervous, stupidly so. Obviously Suzannah hadn't come for romantic reasons, but he was so glad to see her he was clumsy with nerves.

'Have some tea, water will boil in a minute.' He looked round. 'Yer cold?'

'I'm OK,' Suzannah replied, huddled into her coat. 'Sorry to come round like this. I couldn't sleep . . . It's about your dad, Bert.'

His eyebrows rose. 'Pa Gallager?'

'Is he . . . Is he . . .'

'Out of jail?' Bert asked, making the tea and then sitting down again. 'Got out of Strangeways last month. Why?'

'I need to talk to him. I'm worried. Denny Cathcart's been round the shop.' She took the mug of tea offered. 'And that's not all . . .'

There was a noise from above, Bert glancing upward. They both waited, but it was nothing. Jacob was obviously still asleep.

'I've been hearing rumours about yer sister-in-law too,' Bert said, embarrassed. 'What about yer brother? What does he say?'

'He's preoccupied. God knows what Rina tells him, but somehow he's accepting all these comings and goings of hers. Girton's spent a lot of money on Rina. He's just told me that he's taken out a loan, trying to keep the shop open.'

'But I thought Rina were helping him out financially?'

'She was – until lately.'

'But it's her shop too!' Bert replied, puzzled. 'She can't just back off.'

'She can, and she has.'

'So where does Pa Gallager come into all of this?'

'Your dad knows everything that's goes on – and *has* gone on for years. He helped me find Mum, and I need his help again. He could find out about Rina's past.'

Bert winced. 'That's a dangerous path to take.'

'And how dangerous is it to let things go on like this?' Suzannah countered, keeping her voice low. The last thing she wanted was for her father to know she was there. 'There must be something I can threaten Rina with.'

'You mean blackmail?'

Suzannah met his gaze levelly. 'I want that woman gone – and I'll do whatever it takes.' Urgently, she caught Bert's hand. 'Ask Pa Gallager to see me, please. Tell him I need help. Because I do, Bert. I really need help.'

SEVENTY

'I can't believe you said that!' Rina hissed, throwing a shoe at her husband. 'You mean bastard.'

He hurried over to her, trying to take her in his arms. 'Rina, darling, I haven't got the money—'

'Get your damn sisters to give you more rent.'

'They give me more than enough,' Girton replied. 'There isn't any more money.'

'There is! You just don't want me to have it.' She flung him off. 'I thought you loved me!'

'I *do* love you,' he said, genuinely distressed. 'I love you more than anything on earth. But I haven't got any more money.'

'Then find some!' Rina countered. 'I gave you all my money for the shop and I never asked for anything back.' She paused, checking to see that Girton had swallowed the lie. 'I gave you everything I had – but you won't even take me on holiday.'

'Rina, we can't,' he said helplessly, putting his arm around her shoulder. 'God, darling, I didn't realise you'd given me all your money.'

'I had debts to pay off,' she lied. 'Lionel left me with debts . . . Not that I told you! I never worried you with *my* problems. But now all I want is a holiday with my husband and I can't have it. And why? Because he obviously doesn't want to spend time with me.'

'That's not true!'

'It must be! All you think about is the business!' she hurled back. 'No man could be *that* worried about a shop.

God knows, it can't be more important than your marriage.'

'*Nothing* is more important than our marriage, Rina, but I have to keep this business going or we'll have nothing to live on.' Girton sat down on the edge of the bed, his head bowed. 'We're not getting the trade the way we used to. People aren't buying suits—'

'They're buying beer and cigarettes. They're gambling,' Rina retaliated. 'Maybe you're in the wrong business.'

'Tailoring *is* my business,' Girton replied. 'I love this work, this shop—'

'More than you love me.'

'Rina, that's not true!' he said, jumping to his feet.

'Then prove it.'

'How? I'll do anything to show you how much I love you. Anything.'

She smiled sweetly, pulling his head towards her own, her lips resting for a long moment against his. 'There are other ways to supplement our income.'

'What?'

'Denny Cathcart knows a lot of people—'

'Denny Cathcart!' Girton snapped, stepping back. 'I don't want anything to do with that man. I've put up with you seeing him, but I'm not getting involved again.'

'He's a businessman,' she cooed. 'He's got contacts.'

'I knew some of them. Once,' Girton replied bitterly.

'Oh, that was the past,' Rina said, flicking her hand. 'You were a kid then. And you didn't have me. Cathcart can't fool us now. Not *both* of us – but he can be useful.'

'I don't want—'

'*You* don't want!' she snapped. 'Well, maybe *I* don't want to be with *you* any more. Maybe this poky hovel isn't quite what I expected. Maybe being a tailor's wife isn't enough. Maybe the *tailor* isn't enough for me.' She moved over to him, running her index finger along his crotch. 'Maybe you're not man enough for me.'

He caught hold of her, kissing her urgently and then

pushing her back on to the bed. She laughed, responding and wrapping her legs around his back.

'Girton, I don't want to leave you—'

'You can't leave me,' he said, bereft at the thought.

'But I want more. I want us to have more. Lots more. And we have to use people to get it, my darling. We have to use people like Denny Cathcart.' She ran her tongue along her husband's lower lip, knowing she almost had him. 'I love you, Girton. Would I do anything to hurt you?'

'No,' he murmured.

'And you trust me?'

'With my life.'

'So trust me now,' she crooned. 'Do what I say and we'll be on Easy Street. No more Hanky Park for us, Girton. We want more. And we're going to get it.'

Resting his head on her breasts, he listened as she talked on. He didn't want more. Didn't want to leave Hanky Park, or the tailor's shop. He wanted to stay as he was at that moment – transfixed in time – in the arms of his wife.

Who was – without him realising it – crushing the very life out of him.

SEVENTY-ONE

Pa Gallager was sitting by the fire in The Golden Fleece, nursing a pint. The cool spring had warmed up, the fire no longer lit in the snug, the front door of the pub open. From his vantage point, he could see everyone entering and leaving the pub, before they saw him.

He was glad to be out of jail and back in Hanky Park. Glad to be back on his old turf. And he wasn't the only one; within days Pa Gallager had been contacted by Denny Cathcart, who needed some muscle, and then by Gerry Fitt. Nothing much changed, Pa Gallager thought ruefully. Only this time Cathcart and Fitt could whistle – he wasn't intending on going back to jail for a while.

Coughing, Pa Gallager finished his pint and ordered another, watching the tall figure of a woman enter the pub. He knew at once it was Suzannah Clark. She might never have visited the Gallager house but he had seen her around, and Bert had talked about her often. Perhaps more often than he should have done.

Slowly, Suzannah looked around, then walked towards him. 'Thanks for coming, Mr Gallager.'

He nodded, putting out his hand. At once Suzannah took it, his palm so calloused that his skin momentarily scratched hers.

'Want a drink?'

'No, I'm fine.'

The years of imprisonment hadn't dented Pa Gallager's reputation as a rough man, his eyes dark and intimidating.

'I wanted to ask you for some information.'

'Oh, aye.'

'I could pay you,' Suzannah said, uncertainly.

'A shirt.'

'What?'

'I need a white cotton shirt.'

She nodded. 'Fine. It's yours.'

'So go on. Bert said yer wanted some help.'

Nodding, Suzannah hurried on. 'My brother's married a woman called Rina. She was the widow of Lionel Taylor. He used to be a pawnbroker over Moss Side.'

'I know. He was a hard case.'

Suzannah dropped her voice further to prevent anyone overhearing them.

'I'd like to know anything you can tell about Rina. Anything you've heard about her.' She paused, watching Pa Gallager down half of his new pint. On the back of his hand was a tattoo of the head of a snake, its tongue extended.

'She were beaten up by Taylor. Not that she didn't give 'im cause, some said. Taylor gave 'er a roof over 'er 'ead when she needed one. There were some gossip after he died, but nothin' firm. Yer know what people are, they talk bloody crap.' He inhaled on his cigarette, the snake tattoo momentarily visible again. 'Lionel Taylor fell down some steps an' broke 'is neck. 'E'd been after Rina, belting 'er around again. Or so she said . . . Anyway, there were a blow on the back of Taylor's 'ead which didn't look like anything 'e got when 'e fell. Or so Tom Goodman told me – 'e were the copper who found Taylor. He said that maybe the blow was what *caused* the old bugger to fall . . .'

'You mean she could have killed him?'

'She could. But it would be a bugger proving it.'

Dropping her voice, Suzannah asked another question: 'What about *before* Rina married?'

'Come up from London way. I 'eard she were working in a pub.' He paused. 'Pulling pints. Or pulling punters. Yer make yer own mind up.'

'Rina was a prostitute?'

'I didn't say that. I said yer make up yer own mind.' He paused again, downed the remainder of his pint. 'What yer want to knew fer?'

'Because she's going to ruin my brother if I don't do something.' Suzannah leaned towards Pa Gallager earnestly. 'Rina's running up debts and bringing all kinds of people to the shop. The wrong sort.'

His expression was unmoving. In most people's eyes *he* was the wrong sort.

'So?'

'I just need to know everything about her. I have to try and break the hold she has over Girton. And I need ammunition for that.'

Pa Gallager stared at her for a long moment.

'All I know, I've told yer.' He looked Suzannah up and down. So this was the woman his son held a torch for. Bert might never have admitted it, but Pa Gallager didn't miss a thing – especially if it concerned his own family. 'I'll 'ave a word with a few mates. See if I can find out anythin' else 'bout this Rina woman.'

'Thanks . . . thanks,' Suzannah stammered, getting to her feet. 'Oh, and I won't forget about your shirt.'

'Eighteen.'

'What?'

'Eighteen-inch collar,' Pa Gallager said firmly. 'Any less'll choke me.'

Unable to resist any longer, Teddy Lyle made the long drive from London to Salford. Ten months had passed, but his love for Suzannah hadn't dimmed one iota. Dating other women had only underlined their shortcomings and her virtues. She was the one he wanted – and he would have to prove it to her. Their differences weren't insurmountable. What the hell did class, money, status matter? He was miserable without her and driven mad by the idea that some other man might triumph where he had failed.

Slowly, Teddy turned the car towards Hankerton Street. He would make for the tailor's shop. No one knew the car to be his; he could park and watch, maybe even catch a glimpse of Suzannah passing. Then he could get out of the car, face her, and say his piece.

Drawing up at the corner, Teddy parked, his gaze settling on the tailor's shop. At once a chill came over him. It was different. The old lamp had gone, new dummies were in the window, the cream paintwork already dingy and flaking in the smog. His glance travelled upwards to a window in an upstairs room; the room he knew to be Suzannah's. To all intents and purposes the building was the same, but there was a grimness to the place which had never been present before. A sad, melancholic air which made the shop oddly forbidding.

For another hour Teddy sat, waiting, hoping. But no one entered or left the tailor's shop. Custom – which had always been erratic – seemed to have dried up. Then, suddenly, a man inside the shop approached the front door. Leaning forward, Teddy stared hard at the figure. It was Girton Clark. But not as he remembered him from ten months earlier. This Girton had aged, looked tired, waxy from worry as he turned the sign to CLOSED and locked the door.

Obviously Girton's new life and new wife didn't seem to be suiting him too well. Teddy frowned. He wanted suddenly to get Suzannah out of the tailor's shop. Get her away and safe. The word troubled him. *Safe* – why would he presume she was in any danger? His gaze moved back to the shop. All his phone calls and letters had been ignored and he felt at a loss to know what to do. Knock at the door? Invite more rejection? Hadn't she made her feelings plain enough? Wouldn't it be better if he just left her alone and got on with his life? Or should he get out of the car now, bang on the door, demand that she heard him?

But he couldn't, hadn't the words. He had said them all before and they had meant nothing. There had to be another way. Something he hadn't thought of yet. Only one thing was clear: he wasn't going to give up. Somehow he would get Suzannah back in his life. Somehow he would win her over. Somehow he would make her love him again.

And this time she would love him enough.

'Jesus, yer've a right mouth on yer,' Harry Nolan said, slipping on to the wall next to Pa Gallager. 'A right mouth, and no mistake.'

'I've no patience either,' Pa Gallager replied, inhaling on his dimp and looking ahead.

The River Thames was muddy, grey-brown under the mouldering sky. In the distance the landmarks shimmered in a picturesque sun. The sudden deep booming of a ship's hooter sounded in the morning air, the Irishman chewing his tobacco fitfully.

'Yer owe me a favour, Harry.'

It was more than one favour; it was several. Over the past twenty years Pa Gallager had kept Harry Nolan out of jail – and off the critical list at the hospital. He didn't do it for affection, but for information. Saving Harry Nolan's skin meant Pa Gallager had a keen pair of eyes and ears in London. Senses which had served him well. And there was another reason Harry Nolan – like a number of others – served Pa Gallager so eagerly. They were terrified of him.

'I know I owe you! I know, I know!' Harry agreed. 'What is it this time?'

'I want some information about a woman called Rina Clark. Used to be Rina Taylor.'

'Means nothing to me.'

'It'll mean something to someone. She's a looker. Blonde, about thirty now, quite tall. Talks with a London accent, well, southern anyway. Used to work in a pub a bit back.' He pulled out the photograph that Suzannah had given him and passed it to Harry.

'Whoa! Now that's a beauty, no mistake. No family?'

'If there were, I'd have looked 'em up first,' Pa Gallager

replied, inhaling on his smoke again. 'She's a rough girl, Harry. Got married to some old bastard who died conveniently. But that's another story. Now she's got herself married to a decent man and she's leading 'im by the nose.'

'So she'd have a past?'

'I bloody well hope so. I need something to shake a scare into her,' Pa Gallager replied. 'She's not going to ruin this family, not if I can help it. They're good people and I like 'em. Know what I mean?'

Harry nodded eagerly. It paid to be liked by Pa Gallager.

'I wouldn't like to see 'em ruined because of some bint. They're old-school Hanky Parkers. And they've had more than their share of bad luck.' He paused, staring at Harry. 'My eldest had a bit of a thing going for someone in the family. But that were a while back ... Anyway, yer ask around and meet me here in a week with news. Same time.'

'Sure, sure,' Harry agreed, already running names through his head; contacts he could ask about Rina Clark. 'Is there a reward?'

Pa Gallager turned his unflinching eyes on the Irishman. 'Yeah.'

'And that would be?'

'M' thanks,' Pa Gallager replied coldly, rising to his feet and walking off.

Back in Salford, Rina was smirking to herself. Just how big a fool was Girton? she thought, applying fresh lipstick. Her husband believed everything she said. It was laughable. Lionel had doubted her every word; now Girton swallowed every lie. Jesus, she laughed to herself, men were cretins. Satisfied with her reflection, Rina picked up her jacket and fastened it snugly around her waist. She had lost all respect for her husband. Girton was just her lapdog now. And so she had nudged and cajoled him into the grip of Denny Cathcart, her intermittent lover, and back into the dodgy goings-on of Hanky Park.

Her husband's increasing degradation satisfied some quirk inside her. She had had no control over Lionel, so having sway over the helpless Girton was irresistible revenge. Good thing she had the remainder of her money tucked away safely, Rina thought, looking round and thinking of the pawnbroker. How the old bastard would hate her for besting him. *She* had got the tailor's shop, whilst *he* was decomposing in his grave. In fact, Rina suddenly realised, she would like to own the tailor's shop outright. She would be generous enough to keep Girton on as tailor, but his bloody sister would have to go.

Rina thought of Suzannah and burned. The thorn in her flesh, the person she couldn't con. Oh, how she'd grown to hate her sister-in-law. She had managed to get rid of Jacob, and Helen had been edged out. But not Suzannah; that bitch was hanging on. Checking her manicure, Rina glanced once more in the mirror and then made for the stairs. As usual, Suzannah was in the workshop.

'Where's Girton?' Rina asked curtly.

'Over at Shude Hill. Gone for some cloth.'

'To hear him tell it, you'd think we didn't need cloth any more. *There are no customers*,' she parroted her husband unpleasantly. '*We have to pull in our belts*. Still, nice to think he's having a day out. Why don't *you* go out more, Suzannah?'

'I go out enough.'

'Still pining after Teddy Lyle?' Rina goaded her. 'You don't want to do that. No one's worth it – and besides, there are plenty of other men.'

'You'd know all about that.'

Stung, Rina perched on the side of the work table. 'Does Girton talk to you about me?'

'No. He's still infatuated. Even though you're ruining him, he can't see it . . . Not at the moment, anyway.'

Rina's eyes flickered. 'Is that a threat?'

'That rather depends,' Suzannah said coolly, 'on whether or not you have something to hide.'

SEVENTY-TWO

'Don't fuck me about!' Pa Gallager snapped. Harry Nolan was hurrying back down the steps of the Thames Embankment, two at a time. 'I thought yer said yer were bringing someone to see me?'

'I was, I was!' Harry replied urgently. 'He took fright, ran off. Just like that.' He didn't like to say that the sight of Pa Gallager had spooked the man. 'I'll go and find him. Give me a little while.'

'I've got to be somewhere else tonight,' Pa Gallager replied sourly. 'If yer wasting m'time—'

'Now, would I do a thing like that? I ask you, would I?' Harry was hopping from one foot to the other nervously. A narrow-framed, angular man, he seemed as small as a child beside the hulking northerner.

'Did he know anything 'bout Rina?'

'Said he might. Said he thought he knew someone that might know something,' Harry blundered on. 'Acted a bit odd. Asked if there was money in it.'

'No money, just goodwill,' Pa Gallager replied, lighting a roll-up. Exhaling impatiently, he then took the Irishman by the collar of his coat. 'Yer show 'im the picture of Rina?'

'Sure I did!' Harry replied, wriggling frantically. 'That's what set him off. He looked at it and told me she looked familiar. Then he said he'd bring this other bloke, Goring, his name was, with him.'

'And what's Goring to Rina Clark?'

'I don't know yet! I've told you all I know, Pa.'

'Where did you find this bloke?'

'The Grapes on the East Docks,' Harry replied, relieved when Pa Gallager let go of him. Hurriedly he smoothed down his shabby coat, and then smiled. 'He was very worked up, must know something.'

'Yeah, well I'd like to know it too,' Pa Gallager countered. 'I want yer to find your little chum again, and then I want 'im to bring me this Goring fella. Tomorrow. No later. Yer know where I'm staying. Yer fix up a meeting in the evening. Yer hear, Harry? Yer bring 'im to me tomorrow or I might forget what a good friend yer are to me.'

Unsettled, Suzannah turned over in bed. She couldn't sleep. On the few occasions she had dozed off, her dreams stalked her. Her mother, dancing, first as the young Gloria, and then as some old madwoman, beating a dog with a steel ribbon. After that, she dreamed of Rina standing at the door of the tailor's shop and turning the sign to CLOSED. And Suzannah locked outside, people laughing and pointing at her: *She thought Teddy Lyle would have her. But he cleared off soon enough . . . I heard she'd been with that Bert Gallager . . . and there were a baby too . . .*

Sweating, Suzannah sat upright in bed, scrambling for the lamp. In the dim light she descended the narrow stairs and made for the kitchen. Her throat was dry, her stomach knotted. Upstairs she could hear the sound of Girton snoring as she reached for the poker and prodded the mean kitchen fire back into life.

'What the hell!'

Dropping the poker, she turned at the words, as a man leapt up, fastening his trousers. Aghast, Suzannah saw her sister-in-law, her skirt pulled high up around her hips, lying back against the old sofa.

'Rina!'

'Keep your voice down!' Rina hissed, adjusting her clothing.

The man was reaching for his jacket and making for the door. 'I thought yer said there were no one home.'

'Oh, Jimmy, come on, it's only my sister-in-law,' Rina said lazily as she moved over to the man. 'She's always poking her nose in where it doesn't belong.'

Partially mollified, he nuzzled Rina's neck. 'I was just enjoying our little celebration,' he said, glancing over her shoulder to where Suzannah was standing. 'Sorry if I . . . you know . . . embarrassed yer.'

'She's married,' Suzannah said dumbly. 'Her husband's upstairs in bed.'

'Yer a naughty girl,' the man said teasingly to Rina, 'I thought yer told me 'e were away.'

'Away with the birdies,' Rina replied, laughing. 'Girton sleeps like the dead.' She tried to pull the man towards her, but he resisted.

'I can't perform for an audience.'

Angrily, Rina turned back to Suzannah, her voice pure bile. 'You going to stand there all night? Want to watch? Maybe see how it's done?'

Disgusted, Suzannah ran out, hurrying back to her room. It was the final straw. Rina had to go. Her heart pounding, Suzannah looked out of the bedroom window. Hankerton Street was empty. No one about. No burly man standing at the corner, bringing her news. She sighed, frustrated. Maybe there was no news. Maybe there was nothing in Rina's past to uncover. Nothing at all.

No, Suzannah told herself, Rina had a past. She *knew* it, could sense it. After all, didn't she know all about secrets? If only she'd heard something from Pa Gallager. The waiting was crucifying. Fighting to calm herself, Suzannah splashed some water on her face and stared at her reflection in the mirror. The Clark family was depending on her. However difficult it was, she had to stay; look out for her brother and the shop. Protect her absent, ailing father's business. Her head thumped with a sickening, dull ache. Be calm, Suzannah told herself, hearing muted sounds from below. Be calm. Soon Pa Gallager would bring news. Soon she would have the information she needed. *Soon* . . .

'Enjoy yourself, Rina,' Suzannah whispered, her tone deadly, 'because your luck is about to run out.'

Throwing aside the shoebox, Girton leaned down and felt under the mattress. The envelope was still there. Panting, he leaned back against the bed and counted the money inside. Not nearly enough. God, he *had* to pay off Denny Cathcart – but how? He thought of Rina then – he would ask her for help.

But he didn't dare. Hadn't she intimated that she was getting tired of him? That he was getting on her nerves? That she could find another man? Girton's palms were clammy suddenly. He knew he was obsessed, but he couldn't help himself. He had to have Rina, and he had to *keep* her. Whatever that took.

And it was taking a lot. Anxiously, Girton tensed as the door of the tailor's shop opened below. He heard an exchange of voices and then relaxed. Only a customer come for some socks. For a moment he wanted to laugh. *Socks*, at a time like this! Who gave a shit about socks when he was about to lose his business?

Stop panicking, Girton told himself. He would sort it out, somehow . . . Again he counted the money in the envelope, as though by magic it had increased. But it hadn't – and he knew there was little money in the till downstairs. Of course, he shouldn't have agreed to Rina's suggestion – gambling had never been his strong suit – but she had been adamant.

'We need more money. Have a go, Girton. If you're man enough, you'll win . . .'

But he hadn't. He'd lost. And to Denny Cathcart, of all people.

A week had passed before Denny sent a runner for the money. *I haven't got it*, Girton told him. And so Denny had come round, all smiles, and told Girton that he would – because they were old friends – wipe the slate clean. If Girton did him a favour. And then another, and another. By the time the month was up, Girton had only paid off the interest on his loan and was well and truly under Cathcart's thumb. No point appealing to his wife; Rina was dismissive.

'Tell Denny you want a little job that pays,' she had said. 'He said the other day he needed a driver to collect something from London.'

'I don't want to get into that kind of thing,' Girton had remonstrated, wiping his forehead and hands, his voice faltering. 'Rina, we have to back off, we're in trouble.'

'*You're* in trouble,' she had replied, 'and *you* can get out of it. You're not dragging me down with you, Girton. If you want me, you have to work to keep me.'

It had taken him a moment to pluck up the courage to speak again.

'Rina, don't you have *any* money put away?'

She had turned, her eyes blazing.

'Jesus!' he'd said, shaken. 'Don't look at me like that.'

'How *should* I look at you, Girton? With respect? Hardly. I don't have to keep you. I did that in the past. And I won't do it again.'

'I know, I know,' he'd persisted, 'but we could lose the shop.'

And then he saw something in her eyes, and recoiled, finally understanding. Rina had him where she wanted him. There wasn't a flicker of love or sympathy; only the cold, flat look of an animal scenting its prey.

SEVENTY-THREE

Fear was not something Pa Gallager had any truck with, but standing at the back entrance of St Mary's Hospital in Whitechapel he was unusually anxious. The alleyway was dark, empty, the only sounds coming from above his head. Slowly he looked up. The ward lights were on, but offered little illumination in the alleyway below. Jesus, hurry up, Pa Gallager thought impatiently. Get a bleeding move on.

'Are you there?' an Irish voice asked suddenly.

'I've been here fer over ten bloody minutes!' Pa Gallager replied shortly, walking in as Harry opened the basement door. Taking a moment for his eyes to adjust to the light, the northerner blinked as he found himself confronted by a series of pipes and a vast, unlit furnace.

'Come with me,' Harry said, urging Pa Gallager to follow. 'I've someone for you to meet.'

They walked for nearly a hundred yards before Harry paused and then opened another door, which led out on to a fire escape. On the steps two figures stood talking, one immediately running off as soon as he caught sight of Pa Gallager. The other would have followed him, except that Harry grabbed his arm. Nervously, the stranger shrank back against the wall, his face concealed in shadow.

'Yer name Goring?'

He nodded.

'I'm Pa Gallager.' He moved towards the man, Harry gripping Goring's arm even tighter. 'Come out into the light and we'll talk.'

Goring shook his head again, shrinking further back.

'Come out. I mean yer no harm. I just want to talk,' Pa Gallager reassured him, lighting two roll-ups and passing one to Harry. 'For Mr Goring.'

Nodding, Harry held out the smoke. Goring hesitated and then took it. Fitfully he inhaled, and then leaned forward, his face finally illuminated.

He was about twenty-five, undernourished, with the slum look of malnutrition. His face was ingrained with dirt, his peg teeth discoloured, yellowed to the roots. Up his arms and around his neck were old, pitted scars; his ribs were visible at the opening of his shirt. But most disturbing were his eyes; flickering from one place to another, never settling. Rat-like, nervous, hunted.

Christ, Pa Gallager thought, shaken. 'Yer know Rina Clark?'

Goring flinched, looking at Harry. 'Tell Mr Gallager,' Harry urged him. 'You know her, you told me you did. Tell Pa Gallager your story.'

Breaking his usual rule, the northerner approached the young man and offered him a half-crown.

At once, Goring's hand shot out, his fingers bone-thin, his nails bitten to the quick.

'*Now* tell me what yer know about Rina Clark.'

Mute, Goring stared at him.

'Yer *do* know her?'

Slowly Goring nodded, pushing the half-crown deep into his pocket, Harry still holding on to his sleeve and fully aware that if he let go of him, the man would run.

'*How* d'you know her?' Pa Gallager asked – then realised why Goring wasn't talking. He was obviously terrified. Clicking his fingers, Pa Gallager put out his hand towards Harry. 'The picture. Give me the picture.'

Pa Gallager held the photograph up to Goring. His eyes glanced at it and then glanced away. Upwards, downwards, as though even looking at the image might harm him.

'Yer did know her . . . Were she a friend? Sweetheart? Relative?'

'You can't tell her! You can't tell her I'm here!'

Suddenly breaking free of Harry, Goring made for the stairs, Pa Gallager running after him. At the top of the next flight the northerner caught hold of him and pushed him up against the wall.

'I'll tell 'er nothing, yer hear me? Nothing. Yer just tell me. I've no argument with yer. I just need to know 'bout Rina, all right? Just tell me about 'er.'

Goring's eyes flickered, spittle at the sides of his mouth. His voice had dropped to a whisper.

'Sister.'

'She's yer sister?'

Goring nodded. 'Don't tell her you've seen me. Don't tell her—'

'She's called Rina Goring?'

'Jane, Jane Goring.' He paused, his eyes moving relentlessly.

'And what about her?'

'There were just her and me . . . the two of us left after our parents died. They said she was to look after me.' His voice rose, almost hysterical, a shake in the back of his throat. 'But she didn't want to. Wanted to be on her own. Used to hit me, cut me, when she was mad . . .' He touched the old scars on his arm. 'She told me I had to do what she said. Told me I was wicked. That they'd put me in prison. A place for scum.' He paused, biting down on his knuckle suddenly, drawing blood.

On the floor below, Pa Gallager could just make out Harry keeping watch. Hurriedly he continued to question the frightened man.

'What did she do to you?'

'Mustn't tell! Mustn't tell—'

'Yer can tell me. Yer can tell me anythin',' Pa Gallager said. 'She changed her name, didn't she? Married a man called Taylor, moved up north. Yer know about any of this?' Goring shook his head. 'So when did yer last see yer sister?'

'I wasn't bad – *she* was bad,' he said, his voice shaking with terror. 'I have to go, I have to go—'

'Jesus, lad, what she do to yer?'

'Can't tell! Can't tell!'

'Yer can tell me,' Pa Gallager urged him. 'She can't hurt yer any more. She'll not hurt yer now. Not when yer a friend of mine. No one can touch yer when yer a friend of mine . . . Tell me, lad, what she do?'

Goring was panting, struggling for breath.

'Mr Hunt – she worked for him and his family. She was the maid and I was the bootboy. Told me she was going to marry Mr Hunt . . . But he had a wife. Jane was always hanging around, acting nice, but then Mrs Hunt got sick, a bad chill. Doctor said she had to be kept warm, in bed. My sister knew that, but . . . I came in that night, I came in . . .'

'And? What did yer see?'

Goring was shaking, his eyes no longer moving, but staring ahead. He was watching, remembering the whole scene as though it was taking place in front of him.

'She'd opened the curtains and the windows . . . It was January, very cold that night. Mrs Hunt was lying there, no covers on her. White, not moving. I went to close the windows, but my sister pulled me away. Slapped me. I told her, I said: "I'll tell, I'll tell," but she promised me we'd have money when Mr Hunt married her. All I had to do was to keep quiet. After all, she said, she hadn't killed the woman, just hadn't helped her. But she'd killed her as sure as she'd stuck a knife in her! Mrs Hunt was dead. She was lying there in the bed, no covers, the windows open, the cold . . .' Suddenly he began to tremble, hardly able to keep himself upright. 'My sister killed her . . . And I didn't want anything to do with it! Didn't want any money, anything my sister promised me. I just wanted to get away from her. So I ran. I knew she'd come after me, but she couldn't find me. She never found me!' Goring shouted, his head rocking frantically from side to side against the wall. 'I never hurt anyone . . .' He stopped, suddenly quiet. 'I had to keep hiding from her. Hiding, to stay safe. My friend sent out word that I were dead. If she'd known I was still alive, she'd have killed me. She'd still kill me if she knows I'm alive.'

A soft whistle from the floor below tipped Pa Gallager off that someone was coming. Letting go of Goring, he slid another coin into the man's hand, touched by his story. Goring was unbalanced; his mind turned by a violent childhood. A boy terrorised by his sister; the one person he should have been able to rely on and trust.

'If yer ever need a friend, yer ask Harry to fetch me,' Pa Gallager said, his tone grave. 'Yer hear me, lad? Any trouble and yer ask Harry to fetch me. Now, be off.'

Goring turned, then turned back. 'Don't tell her you've seen me. Please, don't tell her—'

'She'll hear nothing from me,' Pa Gallager promised him. 'And she'll pay for what she did. Trust me, she'll pay.'

SEVENTY-FOUR

Suzannah had overheard the argument between Girton and her sister-in-law and waited until Rina went out. She could help her brother a little if she gave Girton the money she had managed to save – on condition he didn't tell his wife. Walking upstairs, she felt the heat dragging on her. God, it was so hot. Too hot for June. There would be a storm later; such oppressive, suffocating heat couldn't last.

Quickly she went over to the fireplace and put her hand up the chimney, then took out the cash box. The lock had been forced. And it was empty. Stunned, Suzannah shook it uselessly, then felt up the chimney again. Nothing there. All her savings had gone. Slumping against the wall, she stared ahead blindly. She knew at once who had taken the money.

It took her several seconds to recover. Then, clutching the empty cash box, Suzannah went back downstairs. Rina had proved to be a whore, and now a thief. She had taken Suzannah's money. Money hard earned, money put away for her dream, her future. Incensed, Suzannah walked back into the shop and moved behind the counter. Her face was expressionless, her eyes fixed on the street. Soon Rina would be back – and Suzannah would be waiting for her.

Miles away, in Liverpool, Girton glanced into his rear-view mirror, watching Denny Cathcart talking to a stranger. In the front passenger seat beside Girton sat Adam Firth. A clammy sensation slid over Girton at that moment, his hands gripping the steering wheel as he realised just how far – and how fast – he had fallen. Only months before he had been a respectable tailor; now he was up to his neck in debt and running around with thieves. And worse, if rumour was to be believed.

Shame took a jab at him. Christ, what was he doing? He would have to have a talk with Cathcart, explain that he was going to pay him off, but in his own time and his own way. In the same instant he realised that Cathcart wouldn't buy it. He had Girton where he wanted him: a tame gofer, a cowed puppet. In fact in the very place he had tried to get him years before.

If his father could see him now . . . Girton thought, pulling over to the kerb as he'd been told to. Ordered around, bossed about by the scum of Salford, men his father would have crossed the street to avoid. He had escaped them once, Girton thought, so why had he been sucked in again? Why, after his father and Suzannah had put so much trust in him? Why, when he had been given the shop, was he now endangering it?

Because of his wife . . . Girton pulled his collar away from his throat, fighting a choking sensation. He could feel his breathing speed up unnaturally. Cathcart was tapping him on the shoulder.

'You deaf?'

'What?'

'I said, drive on.'

Slowly Girton started up the engine again. The smell of hot metal and petrol nauseated him, his gaze moving back to the rear-view mirror.

'Get on with it!' Cathcart barked.

To everyone's surprise, Girton didn't move. Just kept staring at the men in the back seat. He knew then that he had a choice to make – to start the engine and go further into the mire. Or climb out before it was too late.

'Girton, move it!'

Turning off the engine, he got out of the car.

At once, Denny Cathcart was after him. 'What the fuck are you playing at, Clark? Get back in that car.'

'No.'

'Now, you listen to me—'

'I don't want to listen to you,' Girton said firmly, the sun beating down on him. 'It's over; I'm not doing anything else for you.'

'You've no choice!' Denny Cathcart replied. 'You owe me money.'

'I'll pay you back. In my own time.'

'The hell you will!'

'I'm not a bloody lapdog!' Girton snapped, moving off, Cathcart hurrying behind him.

'You can't just throw in the towel like that, Clark. You've your family to think of. And your reputation.'

Girton turned to face his pursuer. 'Don't try and pressure me, Cathcart. You can't hurt me any more than I can hurt you. I know a lot about you and how you run your businesses, remember that. If you try and blacken my name, I can just as easily blacken yours.' Surprised at his own recklessness, Girton continued, 'I'm not like you. Never will be.'

'You're right there,' Cathcart replied coldly. 'You're up to your neck in debt and can't even keep a leash on your wife.'

'Leave my wife out of this!'

'You think she'll stand by you when you're all washed up?' Cathcart asked nastily. 'Listen to me, boy, and listen good. You better get back in that car and do as I say, or you'll live to regret it. Money isn't the only thing I can take away from you.'

Turning away, Girton walked off, leaving Cathcart incredulous. It was only when he had gone another couple of streets that he began to realise just what he had done. He had threatened Denny Cathcart . . . The sun beat down remorselessly, relentlessly, whitening the road to the colour of dry bone.

But Girton kept walking.

'Give it back!'

Surprised, Rina turned round. 'What are you talking about?'

Suzannah moved out from behind the counter, facing her sister-in-law. 'I want my money back. Now.'

'What's your money got to do with me?'

'You took it!'

'The hell I did!' Rina remonstrated. 'Why would I steal your money?'

'The only thing you care about any more is money. It's your religion. Pounds, shillings and pence – your Father, Son and Holy Ghost.' She put out her hand. 'Give it back, Rina.'

'I haven't got it!'

'You have! No one else would have taken it.'

Rina's eyes flickered. 'Perhaps you should ask Girton . . .'

'I was wondering how low you'd stoop, and now I know,' Suzannah replied, her tone disgusted. 'My brother would never steal from me.'

'Why not? He's hard up. He was begging me for money only this morning.' Rina swung her full weight behind the lie. 'How dare you accuse me! I tell you, your brother took it.'

In one quick movement Suzannah caught Rina's sleeve. She could see her sister-in-law was surprised, helplessly trying to shake her off.

'Let go of me!'

But Suzannah held on, catching hold of Rina's cuff and looking at it.

'You're missing a button on your blouse.'

'So what?'

Releasing her grip on Rina, Suzannah reached into her pocket and brought out a small pearl button.

'So what? I found this in my fireplace.' Paling, Rina

stepped back. 'You *did* take the money. How dare you deny it.'

Caught out, Rina decided to change tack. 'Girton made me do it.'

'Don't lie to me!'

'He's been gambling,' Rina went on, almost believing the lie herself. She'd been stupid taking Suzannah's money, but she couldn't resist. Not that she was prepared to take the blame. 'Girton's hard up. He's going crazy. Spent all our money—'

'You're unbelievable!' Suzannah retorted. 'But your lies don't work on me. If Girton's gambling, it's because you drove him to it.' She looked Rina square in the face and held her hand out again. 'I want my money back.'

'I can't—'

'*I want my money back!*'

Throwing back her head, Rina's expression was defiant. 'It's too late . . . I've spent it.'

She thought for an instant that Suzannah was going to hit her. But instead her sister-in-law turned away and without another word walked out of the shop.

SEVENTY-FIVE

Unnerved, Rina sat down. Now why had Suzannah backed off? Rina could see that she had been enraged, but hadn't expected her to walk away. So where was her sister-in-law going in such a hurry? Suddenly Rina felt the first intimation of real unease. But then again, she told herself, she could make up some story for Girton. Some lie he would swallow. And if Suzannah told her brother that his wife had accused him of the theft, Rina would deny it.

Stop worrying, she told herself. Girton would be back soon . . . But the time dragged at her heels, and for the third time in a minute, Rina glanced at the clock. Where the hell was he? she thought irritably.

Before he had gone out that morning, he had been so pitiful, almost whining.

'After this, I'm not doing another thing for Denny Cathcart.'

'You have to. You owe him money.'

'I'll pay him off. Legally,' Girton had replied, white to the gills, anxiety sucking all the colour out of him. 'And I don't want you seeing that Adam Firth again.'

She had turned, eyebrows raised. 'Why not, darling? He's got good contacts.'

'I know the kind of contacts Adam Firth and Denny Cathcart have! And they're not the kind we want.'

'Oh, and what *do* we want?' she had retaliated. 'Hanky Park down-and-outs? Old Man Leonard? Or what about the workers in the abattoir on Unwin Street?'

'They're respectable, at least,' Girton had replied, sitting down. He had been overheated; the relentlessly hot June day seeping into his clothes and making his collar prickle against his neck. 'Mixing with these types will be the death of us if we're not careful. I've seen too many men go that way. I nearly did myself. It's dangerous, Rina.'

Yes, she had thought, it was. And wasn't that the thrill of it? The danger. The wondering if Girton would get away with it. If *she* would ... Her eyes moved to the clock again. He was supposed to be collecting Adam Firth – her latest lover – from the train station and taking him to Liverpool for a meeting. Slowly Rina ran her tongue over her bottom lip. Girton didn't know that the meeting was with one of the north-west's most notorious racketeers. She liked the sound of the word. *Racketeer*. It seemed American, glamorous, the kind of man who would appreciate a good-looking woman on his arm.

A woman like her ... Rina had set it all up perfectly. By offering Girton up on a platter, she had ploughed her own furrow in. It was all so thrilling, so stimulating, exciting and dangerous. She thought of how that worried Girton, and despised him for it. But what did it matter what he thought? He did what he was told. Always would.

The door opening alerted her to Girton's return. 'Where the hell have you been?' she demanded. 'Denny Cathcart's been on the phone, going mad. Said you walked out on him.'

'If you know where I've been, why ask?' Girton replied, glancing over his shoulder towards the shop. 'Where's Suzannah?'

'Gone out.'

'So why didn't you open up the shop?'

'I don't want to talk about the shop!' Rina hurled back. 'I want to know what's going on. Denny said you'd threatened him.'

'He threatened me first.'

'For God's sake! This isn't some scrap in the school playground. This is Denny Cathcart and his cronies,' Rina replied, incredulous. 'Girton, have you lost your mind? You can't go around threatening people like that. They're dangerous.'

Irritated, Girton regarded his wife. Behind her, a pile of unwashed plates was stacked up in the sink, flies buzzing around them. All at once the place seemed sordid to him. So unlike it used to be. And hot, suffocatingly hot.

'*Girton!*' she snapped. 'Get on the phone and apologise to Denny Cathcart now.'

'Are you bloody joking!'

She was rocked by his tone. This wasn't the usually compliant Girton.

'Darling,' she said, swiftly changing tack, 'you're not well. You've got overheated, racing around. You look very flushed . . . *I'll* talk to Denny and explain that you didn't mean what you said.'

'I meant every word.'

'Then you are a bloody fool!' she hissed, her voice rising. 'You're not tough enough to take on the likes of Denny Cathcart. You *have* to do what he says.'

'No, I don't,' Girton replied, his tone chilling. He wasn't going to be pushed around any more. 'I've heard enough about Denny Cathcart to last me a lifetime. Besides,' he said, studying his wife suspiciously, 'Cathcart was making a few suggestions about you.'

'You don't want to listen to Denny; he'd say anything to provoke you,' Rina replied, trying to keep her tone steady. 'But you have to listen to *me*, darling. We're in trouble. We have to do what he says.'

'Or?'

'Oh, don't act stupid! If you don't patch things up with Denny, he's capable of anything. He could have you beaten up; teach you a lesson *that* way. Adam Firth's more than a little handy with his fists.' Her voice took on urgency. 'Look, Girton, you *have* to think clearly. After what you said to him, Cathcart will be out to ruin you.'

'He can't.'

'Of course he can! He can call in his debt.'

Girton shook his head. 'I don't have the money.'

'No, you don't, do you? So you know what Cathcart will do? He'll take the shop in payment.' She paused, watching Girton hesitate. Good, she had him worried again. Under her thumb. Controllable.

'The shop?'

'Yes, the shop. He'll take it, Girton. And that would break your heart. Unless . . .' She paused, her tone honeyed. Now was the time to strike. Now was her opportunity to get what she wanted. 'I can help you, Girton. Don't worry, darling, I can help you.' Hopeful, he looked at her. She was glowing in the sunlight, the only bright thing in that dingy room. 'I'll pay off Denny Cathcart – in return for the shop.'

'What?' he asked, dumbfounded. 'But you've no money, Rina. You told me that. How could you pay him off?'

'*How* doesn't matter, darling,' she replied. 'Just be glad I can help. When I pay off your debts, Denny won't be able to touch you.'

Girton was staring at her incredulously. What was she talking about? If she had money, why hadn't she paid off the debts before now? After all, most of them were hers. Anyway, she was his wife. What kind of wife offered to pay off her husband's debts in return for his business?

'Girton, don't worry, my love. You can still be the tailor here, your name will still be over the door. I mean, we'll have to make a few sacrifices. Suzannah will have to find a job somewhere else . . .' Rina paused. Her husband was watching her with outright distaste. 'What's the matter?'

'You planned this!'

She laughed, although the sound was forced. 'Don't be ridiculous, Girton! How did I know you were going to threaten Denny Cathcart?'

'*You* got me involved with Cathcart. When you already knew about my past.'

'It isn't my fault if you're such a weakling,' she snapped,

415

her eyes flinty. 'I just pointed the way; *you* took it.'

'Yes, I did, didn't I?' he replied, his voice hard, his expression murderous. He had been played for a fool and now realised it. 'God, it must have been so easy for you.'

'Don't act like a martyr, Girton. I didn't force you to love me; you did that all by yourself. I didn't ask you to get obsessed.' She smiled. 'You were always so anxious to please. *Yes, Rina, no, Rina . . .* I could have told you to jump off the roof of the timber works and you would have done.' Her face was suddenly distorted, unwholesome. 'I'm making you a good offer. And if you've any sense you'll take it – unless you want to spend the rest of your life looking over your shoulder.'

'You know something?' Girton asked, shaking his head and smiling bitterly. 'I finally see you for what you are.'

'I'm your wife, darling. And I'm being very generous, helping you out of your mess. I just want this lousy little shop in return. I mean, you owe me that much. After all, you've been a failure as a husband. Can't pay the bills. Can't even keep me interested in bed.'

'You bitch!' he hissed, staring at her.

How in God's name had she fooled him for so long? Girton thought, his rancour burning inside him. There had been so many clues, but he had chosen to ignore them. His mantra had been pathetic: he loved her, so she must love him. Yet patently she hadn't loved him at all. She had just used him. And now she had put her cards on the table. Rina wanted the shop. And with it, total control over him. *He could stay on as tailor . . .* Girton's anger made his heart thump. *He could stay on . . .* as though she was doing him a favour! When he had given her a roof over her head. His love. His respectable name.

The name he had disgraced. Again. Once more he had failed his sisters, his father, and himself. In the end the whole Clark family would be ruined because of his stupidity. He thought then of Jacob, forced out by the rapacious Rina. Of Helen, now staying with Nan Siddons.

Of Suzannah. Every one of them ousted by Rina. And what had he done to protect them? Nothing. He had taken his wife's part. Hadn't sided with his family, but with the outsider. Who despised him.

But it wasn't too late.

'Get out!'

Rina winced. 'What?'

'You heard me. Get out of this place. Pack up and go.'

'You can't do that! If you don't let me help, they'll get you.'

Girton stared at her with loathing. 'I'd rather take on twenty Denny Cathcarts than live with you one more day, Rina. You want the shop? Over my dead body. You know what this shop means to me. Means to my family. It's our home.' He looked at his wife with hatred. 'You picked us off, didn't you? One by one. Breaking up the Clark family. Divide and rule. And now you want the tailor's shop. Just how far – and for how long – did you want me to crawl, Rina?'

'Girton, darling,' she said, reaching out for him. 'You don't know what you're saying. I can keep you safe. I can get you out of this mess with Cathcart.'

'You got me *into* this mess.'

'You can't throw me out! Can't leave me to fend for myself.'

'But you've got plenty of money, Rina, you've just told me that.'

She rocked at the bitterness of his tone. 'Girton, sweetheart, you need me.'

'I *don't* need you!' he shouted. 'You've led me by the nose for too long. But not any more. I'm going out, Rina. When I come back, I don't want to see you here – or any of your belongings.'

She was beside herself. How could she have under-estimated him so badly?

The cold draught of failure made her strike out viciously. 'You can't treat me this way. I'm your wife!'

'I loved you,' he said blindly, catching her arm. His fury was terrifying. 'I would have died for you. You were my world – and you knew it. And how did you repay me? You used me, Rina. You set me up to get what you wanted.'

Pleading, she tried to catch hold of him, but he backed off. 'Girton, please listen to me! I was wrong, I admit it. But I can change. I can see the mistakes I made, I can change—'

'I don't want you to change. I don't want *you* any more.'

The words were so unexpected that she flinched. 'You don't want me?'

'I just want you gone.'

Slowly she circled him, her breathing rapid. 'Be very careful, Girton. You're playing a dangerous game. You can't cross Denny Cathcart – or me – without paying for it.' Her hand reached up to his face and stroked his cheek. 'I have powerful friends.'

'Are you threatening me?' Girton asked, his face implacable. 'Well, don't bother. I'm not afraid of you, Rina. Or of Denny Cathcart.'

She flushed. 'You'll regret this!'

'Not as much as I regret letting you in,' he said, his tone damning. 'I regret bringing you into my family and my home. I regret the day I laid eyes on you. But I *won't* regret throwing you out.' He moved to the door of the shop and turned. 'I'll be back this evening, Rina. That'll give you time enough to get yourself and your belongings moved.'

'You love me!' she screamed hysterically. 'Girton, this is me. *You love me.*'

'I'll love you until I die, Rina, but I want you out of my life.' He held her gaze, unflinching. 'When I return I want there to be nothing to remind me of you, or our life here. I don't want to remember that I even had a wife.'

SEVENTY-SIX

Even as that afternoon began to close, the heat didn't diminish. In fact, the whole of Hanky Park was sweating. Washing strung up in yards was chalk dry, dogs scratching furiously with the sudden outbreak of fleas. And as the hooter for the late shift sounded from the timber works, Pa Gallager rolled a cigarette and looked down the park pathway.

A copper passed him, paused, then moved on, Pa Gallager laughing to himself. He wasn't up to anything; there was nothing to steal in a park, unless you counted the stone lions, and they were too bleeding heavy to lift. He sighed to himself, his hard eyes trained on the park gates as he ran his finger around his collar.

The heat was still building; the night would be unbearable.

Seeing Suzannah approach, Pa Gallager watched as she took a seat next to him on the bench. 'Yer got my message then?'

'I did, thanks. Have you got some news?'

'Oh yeah, I've got news. Yer were right 'bout Rina, she's no good. Worse than yer could imagine.' He paused, breathing in the thin air. 'Christ, it's hot.'

Suzannah nodded. '*Too* hot. There's a storm coming.' She changed the subject, urging him on. 'What did you find out?'

'Rina's got a brother.'

'A brother! She said she had no family.'

'She were lying. And not just about that.' He loosened

his collar, blowing air from between his lips. Overhead the sun was melting into the late-afternoon sky. 'Her real name's Goring, Jane Goring. Her parents died when she were young and she were left with a little brother to look after. Only she didn't look after 'im. She damn near broke 'im, from what I could see.'

'You saw him?'

'Yeah, I saw 'im ...' He remembered the marks on Goring's arms, the old scars. 'She terrorised 'im, frightened the kid into doing what she wanted. Used violence to keep 'im in line. And it worked. Until something 'appened that frightened 'im even more than she did.'

'Tell me,' Suzannah said, her voice even. 'What's she done?'

'She's killed.'

Flinching, Suzannah took a breath. 'You mean Lionel Taylor?'

'Nah, this were someone else. A long time ago, in London. When Rina were working fer a family – and sleeping with the head of the household. She wanted to be in charge, so she got rid of the wife.' Pa Gallager shifted his position on the bench. 'But there were a witness, her brother.'

Suzannah sat forward, alerted. 'So we could go to the police?'

'Nah, he'd never give evidence. Rina thinks he's dead – and I want it to stay that way. I won't betray 'im.' He glanced over to Suzannah. 'Yer should have seen 'im. I've seen some sights in my time, but 'e were pathetic. Poor bugger never stood a chance.'

'So how can we prove that Rina killed this woman?'

'We can't,' Pa Gallager said flatly. 'Because Rina didn't lay a finger on 'er. She just neglected 'er. Let 'er die when she could have saved 'er.'

The heat seemed suddenly to sear into Suzannah's scalp, her mouth dry as asphalt. She was finding it difficult to breathe, her gaze fixed on the angry sky. The sun was setting, the light starting to fade, the horizon blood red over the factory chimneys. An image flooded Suzannah's brain. Of a blonde woman at the top of some cellar steps, watching an old man fall. And then another image, of the same woman standing beside a bed ... Rina, a woman who had been left to bring up her own brother and had wrecked his life instead. Rina, the wife who was dragging her husband into the midden. Rina, cunning, promiscuous, dangerous.

'Oh my God!' Suzannah said suddenly.

Pa Gallager flinched. 'What?'

'My brother. I have to get to my brother.' She stood up anxiously. 'I have to warn him.'

Through the stuffy streets she ran, arriving home breathless ten minutes later. Only to find the back door of the tailor's shop locked. Double-locked. Stepping back, Suzannah looked up to the first-floor windows, calling out frantically.

'Girton! Girton!'

There was no reply. Anxious, she ran round to the front again, noticing the CLOSED sign on the door. That wasn't surprising, it was well past six, but where was everyone? Unnerved, Suzannah banged on the shop door again.

'Is there anyone in there? Girton! Open the door!'

'I wouldn't bother. No one's home,' Mrs Bradshaw said, waddling over to Suzannah. 'They're both out.'

'Where did they go?'

'Oh, I don't know that,' Mrs Bradshaw replied, 'but they went out at different times. Yer brother first, then Rina.' She leaned towards her neighbour. 'Bit of a row. Yer brother were shouting about how Rina weren't getting the shop.'

Suzannah couldn't believe her ears. 'What!'

'Girton weren't having any of it. Told yer sister-in-law to clear off. Said 'e were going out and 'e didn't want Rina there when 'e got back.'

'Where did Girton say he was going?'

' 'E were 'eaded in the direction of Peel Park.'

'And Rina?'

Mrs Bradshaw blew out her cheeks. 'Pah! I can't tell yer! She weren't headed after 'er husband, though, I can tell yer that. Set off in a different direction altogether. And with no luggage. Not even a hatbox. Oh no, that Rina's not going to be thrown out by anyone.'

SEVENTY-SEVEN

The first clap of thunder made Girton jump. The sky was orange, angry, the lightning casting weird white flashes, the rain sultry and warm on the skin. It had grown suddenly and unexpectedly dark, Girton realised, wondering exactly how long he had spent sitting on the bench by the lake, thinking. His thoughts had been erratic, unstable. At one moment he had considered running home, begging Rina to stay. The next he had cursed himself for his stupidity.

It had taken him every once of determination *not* to return to the tailor's shop. If he saw his wife, he would relent. So instead he had waited, alone, in Peel Park. Gradually, as the day ended, the heat had built up until it was hardly bearable, the air still. Kids out from school had played round the lake and skimmed pebbles on the water, paddling in their bare feet. But it had been too hot for the birds, the trees still, leaves unmoving, listless.

Then slowly the kids had made for their homes. Only a few people had stayed on. Lovers lying under the shade of the trees, a group of women in summer dresses eating ice-cream cones and laughing. But as the temperature increased even they had left, only Girton remaining beside the silent, unblinking water of the lake.

He would go and see his father, Girton decided, come clean and tell Jacob what he'd done. And then he would set about paying off Denny Cathcart ... but how? he asked himself, taking off his jacket and rolling up his shirtsleeves. Rina had been right about one thing – Cathcart wouldn't wait. And if the money wasn't forthcoming, he'd take the shop.

The thought chilled Girton, even in the heat. Guiltily he remembered the nameplate Jacob had had made, which should by rights have had Suzannah's name on it. God, how *could* he tell them what he'd done? He had jeopardised his family's security for nothing. A mock marriage. A whore's greed. And yet – at that moment – if Rina had walked down the pathway towards him, he would have taken her back.

But she *didn't* walk down the pathway. And he didn't go back.

Time passed. Hour slid into steaming hour. Minutes slipped past, rubbery seconds dissolving the day. And Girton didn't move. And Rina didn't arrive. It was only the increasing darkness which eventually forced him to leave his post: the fading light and the storm crackling over his head, lightning making the pathway a white rope as he ran towards the Teahouse for cover.

He reached it and sheltered under the row of pillars at the front, his shirt soaked with rain, his hair wet. Then, suddenly, there was an ominous sound behind him, the cracking of a twig underfoot. Startled, Girton turned, but before he could react he was struck from behind, a hammer coming down heavily on his skull. Gasping, he fell, the warmth of his blood mingling with the streaming rain as he was struck again. Blind with rain and blood, Girton looked up, but could only make out a blurred outline: a figure standing over him – and the hammer coming down for the final blow.

But before it could be struck, Suzannah arrived at the Teahouse, screaming and running towards her brother's attacker. The rain was still lashing down; the ground wet, slimy underfoot, both of them falling, the hammer slipping from the man's hand. Scrabbling frantically on the ground, they both struggled for it, but it was Suzannah who finally grabbed hold of the weapon. And then – without hesitating for an instant – she turned and struck her brother's attacker violently on the side of his head.

All her strength went into the blow, Girton's assailant grunting at the impact, and falling head first down the Teahouse steps.

SEVENTY-EIGHT

The storm was finally over, and an eerie silence had descended on Salford. In Hankerton Street the people congregated, waiting. Men, women, even children, all standing silently in the street. Listening, and waiting. Waiting for the tailor's wife to come back. To round the corner and see them.

Rina had done herself no favours. The men she had seduced and rejected, the women she had bad-mouthed, the children she had terrorised, all were out to judge her. She had no apologists, no protectors. Her cohorts were nowhere to be seen. Just the people from Hanky Park. Waiting.

Pa Gallager had told them all about her, giving them the sordid history of Rina Clark. She was suspected of two murders and of abusing her own brother. People were shocked, repelled. But then the mood of the crowd shifted to something altogether more sinister when Pa Gallager told them that she had arranged to have Girton killed. Girton Clark, of Hankerton Street, Salford. A respectable tailor, from a respectable family. A young, innocent man, murdered . . . Not everyone had been that close to Girton in life, but they were all united in his death.

And they knew who to blame. An outsider had turned on one of their own – and no one was going to let her get away with it.

In the silent minutes that followed, every muscle was tensed for the footsteps which would bring Rina within reach. White-faced, Suzannah watched the corner of

Hankerton Street. Fists clenched, she listened for an echo of a football. Her eyes were expressionless, her lips bloodless. Behind her stood her family: Jacob, Helen and Nan Siddons. And behind them, the mob.

All waiting.

Suddenly they heard the footsteps they had been expecting. The noise of the storm over, the streets seemed eerily quiet, every sound magnified. Click, click went the high heels. Nearer, nearer came the tailor's wife. A child cried suddenly and was hushed; every pair of eyes turned towards the corner of Hankerton Street.

She came into sight and stopped, momentarily shaken. Sensing the mood of the mob, Rina glanced from one hostile face to another – and then, surprisingly, walked towards them.

At once Suzannah stepped forward to face her. She was wearing a summer dress, blood spattered down the front.

'Where have you been, Rina?'

'The cinema,' she replied. 'Why the welcome party?'

'There's been a murder.'

'What?' Rina replied, feigning shock, although Suzannah had seen it: the momentary sliver of relief in her eyes. 'Who was murdered?'

'You know, Rina.'

'How would I know?' she blustered, aware of the mob moving around her. 'I told you, I've been at the cinema.'

'That was convenient. Giving yourself an alibi.'

'What are you talking about!' she snapped. But her composure was unsteady. 'Why would I need an alibi?'

'So that you couldn't be accused of your husband's murder.'

'Girton's dead?' Rina exclaimed. 'Who killed him?'

'You did,' Suzannah replied, her voice menacing. 'You got Adam Firth to do it.'

'Don't be ridiculous! How could I possibly arrange that?'

'Oh, you have contacts, Rina. All the wrong contacts.

And don't look at me like that – this isn't the first time you've got someone out of your way, is it?'

She was shaken, Suzannah could see it in her eyes.

'You're talking rubbish—'

Leaning towards her, Suzannah dropped her voice to a whisper, so only Rina could hear her.

'I know about Mrs Hunt . . .' Shaken, Rina took a breath. She was cornered and she knew it. Nervously, she waited for Suzannah's next words. 'And I know that you wanted Girton killed because he was throwing you out.'

'You're lying!' Rina shouted, stepping back. 'You're always lying!'

'My brother wanted you gone, Rina. He'd found out what you were, what you'd done. And he hated you.'

'He loved me and I loved him!' Rina shouted, looking round at the mob, panic just under the surface. 'He adored me. Why would I want him dead? What possible reason could I have for wanting my husband *dead*?' She stared into the faces of the crowd, suddenly pleading. The mood was threatening, nasty. 'We were in love. Why would I want him gone?'

'Because he wanted *you* gone,' Suzannah replied. 'Because he did the one thing you never expected – he turned on you. He wouldn't you have the tailor's shop. He wouldn't even let you live with him any more.'

'You're lying!' Rina shouted hysterically. 'You were jealous of us, you always had been. You wanted me out.' Hostile, she moved towards Suzannah, her voice threatening. 'Well, you'll never get me out now. My poor husband's dead and he wouldn't want me to suffer. He would have wanted me to have the shop.'

'Would he?'

'Of course he would!' Rina hurled back. 'You didn't know him like I did. Only this morning he was telling me how he wanted us to have the place to ourselves. You always thought *you* should have the shop – but Girton didn't want that. He said it was his.' Her eyes were dark with spite, spittle at the corners of her mouth. She was in danger and she knew it. 'And now it's *mine*. That's what Girton would have wanted – and if he was here, he would have told you that.' She looked round at the mob, her voice suddenly triumphant. 'Don't listen to this lying bitch. If my husband was here, he would have told you the truth.'

'Are you sure about that?'

To Rina's surprise, Suzannah then stood aside, to reveal a man slowly making his way to the front of the crowd. A man Rina had known only too well, and had thought never to see again.

Girton.

SEVENTY-NINE

For years afterwards Pa Gallager would tell everyone the story. How he had been worried about Suzannah and followed her after their meeting. First to the tailor's shop, then on to Peel Park. He had watched from a distance as she searched for her brother. She had been calling for Girton repeatedly, but the rain had been so heavy her voice had been drowned out. Struggling to keep sight of her, Pa Gallager had kept following, but the storm had set in fast, blurring visibility. Soon afterwards the thunder and lightning had started, so loud that Suzannah hadn't heard Pa Gallager's shouting, and for a few instants he had lost sight of her.

And then he had come to the Teahouse. He saw Girton on the floor – and then watched what followed . . . It was Pa Gallager who, before calling the police, told everyone in Hanky Park what had happened. It was the recognised hard man who made sure Rina got what was coming to her. Street justice, he said simply.

The best there is.

EIGHTY

The tailor's shop was closed, the yellow blind drawn, the street emptied of people. Walking round to the back, Teddy knocked at the kitchen door. No answer. Hurriedly, he knocked again.

'Oh my God,' Helen said simply, stepping back. 'Come in, come in.'

'Someone phoned me in London and told me what happened,' he said anxiously. 'How's Suzannah?'

'She's fine,'

'And Girton?'

'He'll be OK,' Helen replied, putting her head on one side and studying him. 'I'm glad you've come. Really glad.'

Moving to the stairwell, she called up for her sister. 'Someone to see you, Suzannah.' Then she smiled at the unexpected visitor and left the shop.

For what seemed to be agonisingly protracted minutes, Teddy waited. He took off his coat, checked his hair in the mirror, then checked it again. Finally he heard footsteps on the stairs. A moment later Suzannah walked in – and stopped dead.

'Teddy!'

He nodded, awkward. 'I heard about . . . God, are you all right?'

'I'm OK,' she said. 'I'm fine.'

Ever since their break-up, she hadn't allowed herself to even think of Edward Lyle. She had accepted the fact that he would never play a part in her life and that she would probably never see him again. But now here he was – and she realised in that moment that she loved him more than she ever had done. How could she have driven him away? This was Teddy Lyle. This was her man. There was never going to be anyone else she loved as much.

'I've missed you, Suzannah,' he said tentatively. 'I understand that you don't want anything to do with me any more. But I just wanted you to know that if anything had happened to you it would have broken my heart.'

Mute, Suzannah stared at him.

'Perhaps I shouldn't have come—'

'Perhaps I shouldn't have let you go,' she said quietly, studying his face. She wanted him back in her life. Not for a short time, but for a lifetime. And suddenly she realised that she was going to fight for him. That somehow she was going to make him stay. 'I lied to you when I sent you away, Teddy. I told you I didn't love you enough. It wasn't true.' Now she would finally explain. He loved her, Suzannah could see that only too clearly, and she loved him. Taking the biggest gamble of her life, she went on: 'I finished with you because I was a coward.'

'A coward?'

She nodded. 'I didn't dare tell you about my past. I just didn't dare.'

'You tried to once,' Teddy replied. 'I stopped you.'

'Yes, you did. And I let you. I was so scared of losing you. But then I *did* lose you and now I realise how much you mean to me. So I'm going to tell you my secret, Teddy, and after that, whatever you do is your choice.' She took a deep breath and began to tell him all about her affair with Bert.

When she had finished, Teddy was silent for a while, his face unreadable. At last he spoke. 'You should have told me. I wouldn't have held it against you. And no one else would have needed to know.'

'But your father knew.'

He flinched. 'What?'

'When we had lunch that day at the Midland. Your

432

father had found out and threatened to expose me if I didn't end my relationship with you. He'd keep my secret if I did what he said.' Suzannah waited for Teddy's response, but when there wasn't one she continued, her voice shaking, 'There you are, you see. It *was* too much, wasn't it? I said once that I wasn't the woman you thought I was – and that was true. You need a wife who's from your class, someone without anything in her past which could make you hate her.'

'You think I hate you?' he asked, stunned. *'You think I hate you?'*

'I wasn't honest with you—'

'And that's what hurts,' he replied, 'that you didn't believe I loved you enough to be able to take the truth.'

Her heart shifted. She should have trusted him. He would have understood, he wouldn't have rejected her. *But it wasn't too late.* She wasn't going to let Edward Lyle walk out of her life again.

'Forgive me,' she said, her hand going out and clasping his. 'I made a mistake in not telling you, but I didn't make a mistake in loving you. That was the wisest and the best thing I've ever done. Teddy, you mean everything to me. I can't live without you; I can't let you walk away again. Stay with me. Stay now, always. Forgive me, *please.*'

'God, Suzannah.' Tenderly, he touched her cheek. 'I don't have to forgive you. I love you. I love you so much that the usual rules don't apply. I love you more than status, money or other people's opinions. I love you because every day without you is only half lived.' His eyes never left her face. 'Without you, there is nothing. With you, there is the world.'

EIGHTY-ONE

Surprised, Noel Lyle turned to see his son running up the front steps of their house.

'What are you doing here?' he asked. 'You should be in London, working.'

'Oh, sod the bloody work!' Teddy replied sharply. 'Haven't you heard about Girton Clark?'

Noel's face was expressionless, but his heart had speeded up. 'Why should I have heard about anyone from that family?'

'He was nearly murdered. Suzannah prevented it.'

'Suzannah!'

Teddy nodded. 'She knocked his attacker out cold. Fractured his skull. Can you imagine it? Never worried about her own safety, just went to protect her brother.' Teddy waved the evening paper in front of his father. 'God, what a woman. Just proves that she's one of a kind. *My* kind.'

'Just a minute!' Noel said hastily. 'She broke off your romance. She said she didn't want anything to do with you again. You don't want to be humiliated, do you?'

Teddy looked at his father, leading Noel on. 'She might need my support.'

'She's managed well enough without it,' Noel retorted, floundering. 'I'd leave well alone, Edward, you don't want to be drawn into Hanky Park rough-housing.'

'Well, Dad,' Teddy replied simply, shaking his head, 'I'm sorry, but I'm going to marry her.'

Noel gasped, dropping his cigar. 'WHAT!'

434

'And I want to thank you for something.'

'Thank me?' Noel asked, his voice dry with suspicion. 'For what?'

'For making Suzannah end our relationship. Because I know all about it now. And I want to thank you for sending me to London. You thought I'd get over Suzannah there,' Teddy said, deceptively pleasant, 'but I didn't. I didn't meet another woman, or get interested in anything. In fact, for nearly a year I've been so miserable I've put everything into *your* business.'

Noel couldn't deny it. His son had been impressive, his business acumen and appealing manner oiling the wheels nicely. In fact, Noel realised, the tables had turned completely. Now *he* needed his son, more than his son needed him.

'Where's all this leading, Edward?' he asked, horribly aware that his son was more than a match for him.

Smiling, Teddy leaned towards his father. 'I just want to say thanks for giving me the experience I needed. Before I went away, you were right – I couldn't have got a job anywhere. I was just some rich man's kid playing in the family business. But not now. Because now I can survive. And support a wife. The wife *I* choose. Not one you want to pick for me. *Now* I can hold my own anywhere. Anyone would give me a job.'

'Are you threatening to leave the business?' Noel asked, his voice croaking.

'I just want you to know that I can't be pushed around any more,' Teddy replied, adding: 'But I'll make a deal with you. I'll stay and work for you, but only if you welcome Suzannah as my wife and keep quiet about her past. How's that? You betray her – and I'll sink you.'

Noel swallowed. 'That's blackmail.'

'That's right. And *that*,' Teddy replied, 'is what you taught me.'

* * *

Rina crossed her legs, showing off her calves to their best advantage. She had been badly scared back in Hankerton Street, and was sure that if the police hadn't arrived when they did, she might be nursing more than hurt pride. As for Suzannah – how had she found out about Mrs Hunt? But then again, why worry? If they had had proof, they would have told the police. No, she had got away with that one . . . Thoughtful, Rina stared at the tiled floor, fully aware that she was being watched.

Events hadn't turned out at all as she had expected. The weakling Adam Firth was nursing a fractured skull, and still unconscious in hospital. God only knew what he would say when he came around. So Rina had decided to retaliate first and – seizing her chance – had agreed to turn King's Evidence against her accomplices. In return for her own freedom.

She explained that Adam Firth had been her lover and had attempted to murder her husband. Not for love, though: for money. As for Denny Cathcart, he was going to be charged as an accessory to the murder – and plenty more besides. Hadn't he wanted Girton out of the way after Girton had threatened him? Rina took a breath, thinking about the old pawnbroker – and Mrs Hunt again. Relax, she told herself, there wasn't enough evidence to incriminate her. And besides, there were no witnesses left.

With luck, she would get out unscathed and move on. Pa Gallager had made it only too clear what would happen if she didn't . . . Only one thing still irked her: once Cathcart was jailed, Girton's loan would be written off. It was a pity, that. She would have liked to see her dull husband and his bloody sister penniless. Sighing, Rina lit a cigarette and leaned back in her seat. Soon she would be free again. Find another man, another town. There was always a place for a beautiful woman. She would have to change her name, though. But whatever happened, she'd survive. That was her special talent.

Her days up north were over. She would leave Hanky Park with one husband buried and unmourned – and another lucky to be alive.

Her short reign as the tailor's wife was over.

Is that the whole story? Not quite.

My father and sister moved back into the shop, and after a little while life returned to normal. I think we all wondered if it would last, or if some other outside force would threaten us again. But it never did. Instead I married Teddy, and although we bought a house of our own, I continued to work at the tailor's shop.

Our wedding was a grand affair, Noel and CC smiling with all the enthusiasm of people approaching the guillotine. But what did we care? I didn't know for a long time the deal Teddy had struck with his father; but he continued to work for Noel for many years, until he inherited the businesses. As for CC – in time we actually developed a kind of understanding; an admiration of sorts.

Helen married Archie Culshaw, and he kept his moustache; and Bert moved to Derbyshire, married a local woman and had six kids. Well into his seventies, Pa Gallager was still up to his old tricks – some things never change. Of Rina, we heard nothing more.

Piece by piece our lives were restored. Dad returned to his old stool in the workshop, Stanley Tobarski's photograph went back up on the wall, and the modern dummies I gave to the rag-and-bone man.

Finally, there was only one piece missing . . .

I remember how long the tram took to get to Oldham that day. And when it arrived, I had to wait for a while outside the baker's shop until it closed and my mother came out.

She was prepared, because we had been talking about this day for a long time. But she looked far too old for her years, and although she had made an effort with her appearance, there was a fragility about her which was heartbreaking. Together we returned to Hanky Park and walked down Hankerton Street. No one noticed her or pointed her out. No one recognised this Gloria Clark. She had changed: grief, illness, confusion, all blurring her features until her face was a stranger's.

Finally we paused outside the tailor's shop.

'I can't,' she said simply, losing her nerve.

'Yes you can, Mum. You can.'

'I can't,' she repeated. 'Not after what I did to your father, to Girton. To all of you.' She stepped back then, her courage failing her. 'I can't face your father. He loved me so much. Look at me! I can't come back to him like this.'

And that was when I realised that life – however cruel – sometimes delivers strange blessings. Taking my mother's hand, I led her into the tailor's shop. My father was in the workroom when she walked in and called out his name.

And because he couldn't see her, she was unchanged. As much loved; as much wanted. In my father's mind she would always be the same Gloria. Always the beautiful woman he had loved, lost, and found again.

That was the real story of the tailor's wife.

You can buy any of these other bestselling
Headline books from your bookshop
or *direct from the publisher*.

FREE P&P AND UK DELIVERY
(Overseas and Ireland £3.50 per book)